THE COMPLETE STORIES

The

Complete Stories

Zora Neale Hurston

*With an Introduction by Henry Louis Gates, Jr.,
and Sieglinde Lemke*

HARPER**PERENNIAL** MODERN**CLASSICS**

NEW YORK • LONDON • TORONTO • SYDNEY

HARPER**PERENNIAL** ● MODERN**CLASSICS**

Contents

PREVIOUSLY UNPUBLISHED STORIES
(IN ALPHABETICAL ORDER)

Acknowledgments

The editors would like to thank the following scholars for their editorial assistance: Cynthia Bond, Lisa Gates, Michael Roy, Richard Newman, Jennifer James, Mary Anne Boelcskevy, and Michael Vazquez. Joanne Kendall expertly and enthusiastically prepared this manuscript. To Jennifer Burton a note of special thanks for assiduously comparing the galleys with the original manuscripts, and for overseeing the editorial apparatus of this volume.

Introduction

ZORA NEALE HURSTON: ESTABLISHING THE CANON

Hurston's black characters do not suffer from the sort of
alternative black self-hatred/prideful self-love/hate-envy
of white and black that characterizes many other
Harlem Renaissance fictional creations. —MARGARET PERRY

Since 1990, HarperCollins has committed itself to publishing the complete works of the great American novelist and anthropologist, Zora Neale Hurston (1891–1960). Between 1990 and 1994, we have published, in a uniform edition, the seven books that Hurston published during her lifetime, as well as her previously unpublished play, *Mule Bone*, which she coauthored with Langston Hughes. These eight texts, ranging from her pioneering anthropological studies of African-American myth and ritual, *Mules and Men* and *Tell My Horse*, to her canonical novel, *Their Eyes Were Watching God*, demonstrate for a new generation of readers the astonishingly broad range of Hurston's literary talents. Indeed, using any measure, by the time that she published her third novel, *Seraph on the Suwanee*, Zora Neale Hurston had established herself as a major person of letters in American culture. Within African-American culture, she had few peers.

Hurston "disappeared" from the African-American canon between the mid-1940s—when the naturalism of Richard Wright and the naturalist-feminism of Ann Petry dramatically dominated the black literary landscape, in stark contrast to the lyrical modernism epitomized by Hurston's masterpiece, *Their Eyes Were Watching God*—and the mid-1970s, when a nascent black feminist movement led by Alice Walker and Mary Helen Washington seized upon her as *the* canonical black foremother. Hurston's recovery is one of the most curious instances of canon reformation in the recent history of American letters. A fuller account of Hurston's career and its fate appears in the Afterword.

Under the direction of Miss Hurston's heirs, we have decided to publish an additional seven volumes of Hurston's uncollected and unpublished works, including complete editions of her short stories, her essays, and her plays, as well as a fully restored edition of her autobiography, *Dust Tracks on a Road*, which we are publishing jointly with the Library of America. In this way, we hope to establish Hurston's own canon of texts, so that students and scholars can continue the necessary task of evaluating Hurston's place—both for our generation of readers and, ultimately, for generations to come—in the American literary tradition. We have decided to inaugurate this series of Miss Hurston's uncollected and unpublished works with this edition of her collected short fictional and folkloric narratives and character sketches.

As early as 1931, Zora Neale Hurston's capacities as a master of the short story were widely acknowledged. Otelia Cromwell, Lorenzo Dow Turner, and Eva B. Dykes—three of the most sophisticated black literary critics writing at the time—identified Hurston, in their well-regarded anthology, *Readings From Negro Authors*—as one of the best-known black writers of the short story. This, despite the fact that by 1931, Hurston had published only eight short stories and had not yet published her two great novels, *Jonah's Gourd Vine* (1934) and *Their Eyes Were Watching God* (1937). But Cromwell, Turner, and Dykes were correct: Her command of narrative voice and plotting, her concern with the themes of divine and human justice, her delight in the Southern black vernacular voice as a vehicle for narration, and the use of the complex dynamics among a small group of characters set in her native Eatonville as the site for the unfolding of these themes—all of these signal elements that would assume such magnificent full-blown form in her first two novels are present in these early short narratives. Clearly, Hurston used these stories, perhaps unconsciously, the way an artist uses a sketch for a larger work of art.

What strikes the contemporary reader is that Hurston was deeply passionate about the people whose dreams and desires, whose traumas and foibles she describes with such élan, and that she loved the fictional language in which she cloaks their tales; hers is not the urgency of the essayist or the columnist, intent upon reducing human complexity to a sociological or political *point*. Above all else, Hurston is concerned to register a distinct sense of space—an African-American cultural space. The Hurston voice of these stories is never in a hurry or a rush, pausing over— indeed, luxuriating in—the nuances of speech or the timbre of voice that give a storyteller her or his distinctiveness.

For example, in her story "The Bone of Contention," Hurston narrates the tale that she and Langston Hughes would use as the basis of the plot of their play, *Mule Bone*, which was largely written in 1930 but remained unpublished and unperformed until 1991, when a production premiered at Lincoln Center Theater in New York. Unlike so many of her contemporaries, Hurston frequently commented explicitly on the nature of figurative language, as well as on the process of fiction-making. Her remarks about this story are no exception: "The elders neglected his bones," she writes, "but the mule remained with them in song and story as a simile, as a metaphor, to point a moral or adorn a tale." This level of attention both to the nature of narration and to the functions of figurative language underscores Hurston's determination to represent black culture in the art of fictional narrative rather than primarily in sociological or political terms. Even the anthropologically based narratives that we have chosen to reprint here—her well-known "Eatonville Anthology," her tales about the mythical figure High John De Conquer, and her character sketches "Mother Catherine" and "Uncle Monday"—reveal Hurston to be the storyteller first, the anthropologist second. She is far more interested in human motivation and the idiosyncracies of character as manifested in language-use than in what we might broadly think of as "the nature of the Negro" or the struggle for civil rights.

We have selected for publication here nineteen narratives that Hurston published between 1921 and 1951, including three that she excerpted from her novels *Their Eyes Were Watching God* and *Moses: Man of the Mountain*, as well as seven unpublished stories, including "The Woman in Gaul" and "The Seventh Veil," both of which were clearly intended to be part of her unpublished novel, *Herod the Great*, which was severely damaged in a fire. In these stories, Hurston demonstrates an exceptionally broad range of narrative concerns and skills. Some seem to be dress rehearsals for scenes that she would develop in her novels.

For example, in "Drenched in Light," the second short story that Hurston published (1924), Isis Watt, a playful young girl, is continuously reprimanded by her grandmother for sitting at the gate post and waving at people driving by, whistling, playing with the household boys, and of course sitting with her knees separated. Since she is the only girl, Isis has to wash the dishes and do most of the chores. In spite of her repressive grandmother, Isis retains a certain joyful spirit and keeps dreaming of a better world, one in which she wears golden robes and rides white horses.

One afternoon when Grandma takes her nap, Isis and her brother decide that they will give Grandma a shave. Joel lathers her carefully while Isis holds the razor. Just as the two are to commence their ritual of retribution, Grandma awakes and flees the house, screaming.

Isis steals out the gate and follows a marching band on its way to the festivities that were arranged for the benefit of the new hall. She is delighted to dance and is captivated by the band, which she follows in a parade toward a campground picnic. Suddenly, she realizes that her dress is dirty and torn and runs back to the house, takes Grandma's new red tablecloth, and drapes it around herself like a Spanish shawl. At the picnic grove, her appearance and her dancing attract the attention of all the visitors, who begin to surround the little brown girl. When she hears Grandma yell from afar, "Mah Gawd, Mah brand new tablecloth Ah jus' brought f'um O'landah!," sensibly, Isis flees into the woods.

Loathing the beating that she is bound to receive, the little girl wants to drown herself. As she walks into the creek, a car pulls up. A white couple who had watched Isis dance ask her what she is up to. Isis responds that she is going to kill herself because of Grandma. They laugh and ask her to show them the way back to the Park Hotel. Isis sits next to the driver as they drive. When they come to the child's house, they stop reluctantly; they do not like the thought of giving her up. The white woman whispers to Isis that she will help her by confronting her grandmother. Listening to her complaints about the tablecloth and the silver dollar she had spent on it, the woman gives her five dollars and says she wants Isis to go to the hotel with her and dance on the tablecloth. "I can stand a little light today," the woman says. "I want brightness and this Isis is joy itself. Why, she's drenched in light." Grandma consents to this right away, scarcely able to conceal the fact that she is proud of her grandchild. Isis dances in exalted joy over her fate.

The story resembles a fairy tale in its contrasts of the evil grandmother and the sweet, innocent young girl who has to suffer from her tyranny but who ultimately outwits the evil old witch. The girl's bondage has not stopped her from dreaming and being joyful. She is high-spirited, a characteristic that simultaneously causes her trouble but also secures her liberation. The final sentence spoken by the rich white lady echoes a key trope of primitivism. "I want a little of her sunshine to soak my soul. I need it," she says.

Isis is represented as the natural happy-go-lucky black girl—and her capacity to entertain the white woman saves her from being beaten to death by her harsh grandmother. This reversal of roles—evil black woman and "benevolent" white woman—is noteworthy for showing that Hurston was intent upon breaking with the tradition of using black literature primarily as propaganda in the nascent civil rights struggle. In today's terms Hurston was politically incorrect, which would earn her the ire of contemporaries such as Richard Wright, Sterling Brown, and Ralph Ellison, among others.

In "Spunk" (1925), we encounter Elijah, Walter, and Joe, characters who will reappear throughout Hurston's fiction. Elijah Mosley and Walter Thomas are inside the general store watching Spunk Banks striding along the main road with Joe's wife on his arm. They express their admiration for Spunk—a large and burly man who is physically strong and so courageous that he dares to take another man's wife out publicly. Joe—small and timid—enters the store, angry, hands trembling, swearing to take revenge.

Joe confronts Spunk. Spunk retorts that Lena is his wife from now on. When Joe sees in her eyes the love for this other man, he leaves without saying a word. Days later, when Joe—goaded by the other men—tries to stab Spunk from behind with a razor, Spunk shoots him.

The court considers the murder an act of self-defense and finds Spunk innocent. Consequently, Spunk and Lena move into a house together. On their first night, a black cat howls, making such a ruckus that Spunk takes his gun to kill it. But when he looks into its eyes, he thinks he sees Joe's ghost. Walter's comment on this incident—that Joe was actually braver than Spunk—is met with disapproval by the other men. The next time they meet is to discuss the latest news: the sudden death of Spunk Banks who had been caught in a big saw. On his deathbed, Spunk claims that Joe pushed him. In the final scene, Lena is in despair and the village gathers at the funeral where "the men coarsed conjectures between guzzles of whiskey."

"Spunk" is structurally complex. There are many jumps in the story. The reader never knows how much time has passed between paragraphs in the story's four sections. There are also many unresolved, vague, and indeterminate aspects of the plot. We don't know whether the men identify with Spunk or with Joe, who could not prevent this bully from taking his wife. What is also interesting about "Spunk" is the framing of the story: It is told through the eyes of the men in the store. And the perspective shifts from the protagonists, Joe and Spunk, who narrate in direct speech, to the direct speech of Walter and Elijah. The story also uses an omniscient narrator saying things such as "The men gathered the next evening in a different mood, no laughter, no badinage this time." Hence, there are three levels of narration: action (the two protagonists over Lena); judgment (the men watching them and reflecting); and the narrator's comments.

There is a sense of tragedy to this story about love, jealousy, guilt, superstition, and death, themes to which Hurston would return again and again, culminating in her masterpiece, *Their Eyes Were Watching God*. In "Magnolia Flower" (1925), for instance, a river tells a brook the story of Bentley, a strong ex-slave who builds a big house on the banks of the Savannah River and marries a Cherokee woman. They settle down and he hires many black employees who hate him because he is so cruel. He himself hates many things, particularly all that reminds him of his oppressors, whose oppression he has internalized. But Bentley loves his daughter Magnolia, and builds a schoolhouse so that she and the other children of Bentley's village can learn how to read and write. The schoolteacher, a light-skinned young man, soon falls in love with Magnolia and they have several clandestine meetings at the river. When John proposes to her and Magnolia confesses her love to him, he decides to ask Mr. Bentley for her hand in marriage, in spite of Magnolia's warning that her father would never agree to her marrying a man who was so light.

When John confronts Bentley, Bentley is enraged, but John holds his ground. Bentley demands that John be locked up and hanged the next day. He locks Magnolia up in the parlor and wants her to be married to crazy Joe, so they can have very dark children. Yelling and hammering against the door does not help; Magnolia spends the night in desolation. A watch-guard pities her and opens the door so she can escape. Magnolia, however, refuses to leave without her lover. To free him, she has to sneak into

Bentley's bedroom and steal the key out of his trouser pocket. The couple manages to flee that night. When Bentley awakes the next morning and realizes that the two have escaped, he orders the hanging of his wife and the guard for allowing them to flee. Bentley dies from his own rage.

"Magnolia Flower" is about the triumph of love over evil. The couple is determined and courageous and rewarded with freedom. The conflict between father and daughter is more prominent than racial conflicts; Magnolia loves John in spite of his light skin color. The powerless daughter's victory over her cruel father also echoes the plot of "Drenched in Light," but the peculiarity of this story is that it is told by the river. The story opens with the brook disturbing the river and urging him to tell one of the many stories he has witnessed during the ages. This framing adds a matter-of-fact tone to the story; the constant flow of the water coincides with the flow of human tragedy and happiness. The river makes mocking comments about the human notions of wealth and time: " 'No matter, no matter,' scolded the river, 'I have seen millions of lovers, child. I have borne them up and down, listened to those things that are uttered more with breath than with lips, gathered infinite tears. . . .' " This aloofness and irony and the use of personification would become hallmarks of Hurston's penchant for allegorical narrative.

This volume includes seven unpublished stories. In addition to "The Bone of Contention," Hurston's story "Black Death" is one of special interest. Docia Boger, a chambermaid at the Park Hotel, is in love with Beau Diddley. They spend a few happy months together. When she becomes pregnant, he refuses to marry her. Beau gets angry at her for attempting to make him settle down and mentions that he is married already. When Docia confronts him with the fact that he had said he was not, he responds that he did not feel obliged to be honest to a girl like her. Docia's heart is broken. She has lost faith in the person she loved. She also pities herself for being a fallen woman.

Docia's mother wants to take revenge for her daughter's misery and goes to see Old Man Morgan, the Hoodoo doctor. Dr. Morgan does not allow her to tell her story but asks her how she wants to kill Beau Diddley. Mrs. Boger decides to shoot him. She looks into a mirror, waits until she sees Beau's image, then fires at him. The mirror collapses, grows misty, and then clears.

The next day, the news spreads that Beau dropped dead while making love to a chambermaid: While bragging about his conquest of Docia, he suddenly clutched his heart and died. The verdict was death by natural causes. Mrs. Boger and Docia move to Jacksonville, where Docia marries happily.

Although this is another story with a happy ending that once again celebrates the triumph of the powerless over evil oppressors, this time success is dependent on outside forces. This story is about the power of hoodoo, superstition, and conjure. Although there are only black protagonists, the narrative frame explicitly refers to the blacks' magic and the whites' ignorance: "The Negroes in Eatonville know a number of things that the hustling, bustling white man never dreams of. He is a materialist with little ears for overtones." Moreover, "White folks are very stupid about some things. They can think mightily but cannot feel."

This stark contrast between cerebral white folks and the black villagers who *knew* can be extended to the received oppositions between reason and emotion. But Hurston suggests that whites are not knowing because they don't believe in a knowledge that goes beyond pure reason. The message of this story is not that blacks have feeling, but that they have another kind of knowledge, which is usually dismissed as superstition. This story is also about black justice outside of the white man's law.

In "The Gilded Six-Bits" (1933), Hurston continues this theme. Every Saturday, Miss May would put special care into cleaning the house and preparing a delicious dinner while waiting for her husband, Joe, to come home from work. Always while getting dressed, she would hear the sound of nine silver dollars hitting the wooden floor. This was the opening to a ritual that began with her demanding: "Who dat chunkin' money in mah do'way?" Then Miss May would track Joe down behind the jasmine tree and chase him around the house. When she caught him in the kitchen, they would start a mock battle. Their shouting, laughing, twisting, and turning would end in Miss May's reaching into Joe's pockets to get the candy kisses he has put there for her. Exhausted from their play-fighting, Joe would take a bath and then they would eat dinner.

One day, Miss May cooks a glorious dinner of ham hocks, new potatoes, stringbeans, and potato pudding. Joe suggests that they go to the ice-cream parlor that has just opened. He wants the new owner, Otis D. Slemmons, to meet his beautiful wife. Although Joe has neither a big belly nor gold jewelry, like Slemmons has, he has a wife he loves more than anything. And Miss May loves him more than anything in this world. When Joe expresses his feelings of inferiority in talking about all those prestigious things Otis brags about—white women lovers and wealth—Miss May responds, "Dat stray nigger jes' tell y'all anything and y'all b'lieve it."

Miss May manages to console her husband, and their happy marriage continues with its weekly mock battles. But apparently she is just as impressed as Joe by that shining gold chain Otis would not allow anybody to touch because one day Joe comes home to find his wife and Otis in bed. To Joe, a world has broken apart. And from that day on, the romance and the ritual are over. Their love has lost its mystique.

They do not break up, but regret on her part and dismay on his predominate; their life becomes a practical arrangement: "No laughter, no banter." They are polite but aloof and do not touch one another for three months. Then Joe complains about a backache and Miss May rubs his back and they make love once again. Soon after, Miss May finds out that Otis's gold chain was only a gilded half-dollar coin.

Months later, after Miss May delivers a son, a strong boy who looks just like Joe, the couple return to their old routine. Joe buys candies with the gilded coin and Miss May, who has awaited him, cries, "Joe Banks, Ah hear you chinkin' money in mah do'way. You wait Ah got mah strength back and Ah'm gointer fix you for dat."

This fetching story is the magic that is produced by two people, a play they have written and performed themselves for themselves. What Hurston called elsewhere a fundamental characteristic of Negro expression—the tendency to dramatize and the art of lovemaking—makes up the allure of this narrative. A love that seems to be stronger than money, however, is broken because Miss May seeks the gleaming gold chain of a "rich" man, thereby jeopardizing a sweet and pristine relationship. The tragic moment of Joe walking in on an act of adultery—the moment when "the great belt on the wheel of time slipped and eternity stood still"—is the culmination point of the story. Due to the happy ending—the fact that their love could be retrieved and reactivated—the story teaches us about the importance of an emotional attachment over material wealth, about a justice that transcends grief, and about the power of reconciliation.

"High John De Conquer" was published in 1943. Originally, High John De Conquer was not a natural person; he was the "wish to find something worthy of laughter and song." He had come walking on the waves of sound from Africa. And when he became a real man, he worked on the plantations where everybody knew him for his laughter and his drumming. Whenever the work was most dreadful and cruel, High John De Conquer helped the slaves to endure. John, the personification of hope, was superior to everything and everybody, including Old Massa. Moreover, he made a "way-out-of-no-way" because he was "winning with the soul of a black man whole and free." One day, John decided to leave the plantation and find a "particular piece of singing." After initial reluctance, because of the slaves' fear of being caught, they decided to join him and all mounted on the back of a big crow. They flew to several places and had many adventures. They stopped off in Hell, where John not only married the Devil's daughter but also roasted the Devil himself, becoming the High Chief Devil. The group was delighted over John's power, but since they were trying to find their song, they decided to move on to Heaven. When they reached that splendid place and met the Old Maker, He made them a tune without words and put it in their mouths.

All of a sudden Heaven turned dark and they heard a voice shouting: "Get up from there and get on back to the field." It was Old Massa calling them back to finish chopping cotton. This made them feel bad but then they heard John's voice saying, "Don't pay what he say no mind. You know where you got something finer than this plantation and anything it's got on it, put away. Ain't that funny? Us got all that and he don't know nothing at all about it. Do't tell him nothing. Nobody don't have to know where us gets our pleasure from." These words were so consoling that they felt neither the heat nor the burden of working. The song they had sought returned to them in their memories.

This story is about a famous black mythological figure and represents the power of the seemingly powerless. The capacity to be ironic and to laugh makes the workers superior to their apparently better-off master. John is the figure of courage and faith. He embodies joy over misery and he is the hero who shows that all that counts is in the soul and in the imagination. Those who are deprived of material wealth discover that their principal asset is spiritual wealth, rhythm, and laughter.

This reemerging theme in Hurston's fiction reaches its fullest form in the character of Tea Cake in her novel *Their Eyes Were Watching God*. In fact, it seems that Hurston draws on this folk hero as a basis for a certain philosophy of life. An anti-materialist and carefree attitude, she suggests, offers political and economic power. This view, implying that blacks had not succumbed to a culture of poverty, is at the core of the accusations against Hurston that she was not politically correct (see the Afterword).

Instead of criticizing discrimination directly, as Richard Wright did, for example, Hurston constructed a myth—she invented an enabling fiction—that would depend upon a reversal of the roles between blacks and whites. Instead of lamenting, she urged a pride in cultural features that were, according to her, characteristic of being a Negro. The joy of life, rhythm, and singing were key to "the Negro" Hurston had in mind. "High John de Conquer" is about the power of imagination, creativity, and memory.

Furthermore, "High John de Conquer" returns to Hurston's

great theme of justice. Those who are physically and economically humiliated are spiritually exalted. Hence, it fits into the general theme of her short stories: the focus on the nature of justice, either attained by hoodoo, as in Docia's case, or by a desire for love, as in Magnolia's case, or due to personal abilities, such as Isis's joyous, beautiful, and sunny self or Laura's integrity and loyalty. The concern for justice beyond race, class, or gender seems to be at the center of so very much of Hurston's fiction and her fascination with myth.

Hurston published her last original short story, "The Conscience of the Court," in the *Saturday Evening Post* in 1950. This story, like "Black Death," is concerned with the quality of justice. Laura Lee Kimble, the black maid of Mrs. Celestine Clairborne, has been charged with felonious aggravated assault. In the courtroom Clement Beasley, who appears to be in pain from severe fractures, testifies that he had lent $600 to Mrs. Clairborne. He reports that one day he came to the house to collect the money, but Mrs. Clairborne had left. When he saw the maid packing away the silver, he decided to protect his loan by taking at least the furniture. On entering the house, he was attacked by the maid and beaten almost to death, Beasley complains.

Laura Lee, who has no defender, is called into the witness stand to give her testimony. Calling herself an unlearned and ignorant woman, she starts out defending her employer, saying that she would never try to escape the obligation of repaying a loan and that her furniture was worth far more than $600. In her version of the story, Mr. Beasley had come to the house when Mrs. Clairborne was away at Miami Beach and she promised to give him her address so he could get in touch with her. When Mr. Beasley returned the next day with a truck, determined to take the furniture, Laura stood in his way to stop him from taking her employer's property. When he tried to enter forcefully and hit Laura, she attacked him so hard that he was unable to stand up.

Laura leaves the question of whether or not she is guilty to the jury. On the one hand, she feels that it was right to protect Mrs. Clairborne's property; on the other hand, Laura thinks of her husband who had always complained about her excessive devotion to other people. Laura then talks about her relationship to Mrs. Clairborne, whom she has cared for ever since she was born. Laura's love for her was so strong that she decided to marry a man who worked for the Clairbornes. And when they had to move, Laura and her own husband, Tom, followed them in spite of his objections. When Tom died, Mrs. Clairborne paid for the transportation of his coffin to his home town, which is why she had to borrow money from Beasley.

The note for the loan, which Beasley had withheld, is finally submitted to the jury. It reveals that the due date of the loan was three months away. The judge accuses Mr. Beasley of attempted burglary and of insulting the court for appealing to it to justify an attempted theft. After the judge has given a long speech on the American constitution and civilization, he expresses his respect for the defendant. The story ends with the jury congratulating Laura Lee for her integrity.

This story is about altruism, about a woman who loved so much that she almost went to prison because of her devotion to her employer. It is also about an idea of justice and the fact that the court was on the side of a simple black woman. Good is being rewarded—even in a black skin—and those who mean well will be rewarded in the end. In most of Hurston's stories, the good guys win and the bad guys fail. Actually, morality is the issue in most of her stories, which usually end happily for the disenfranchised and powerless. The moral values that Hurston cherishes are loyalty, justice, and love. Structurally, most of her narratives are framed tales, with a story within a story, as in *Their Eyes Were Watching God*. And direct speech is prominent—as if it would bring alive, in the guise of the language of fiction, the empirical reality of what troubles, and indeed defines and delights, a culture, while the narrative frame raises the broader ethical issues, especially the complex reaction between divine or supernatural and legal retribution—an African-American version of the tension between Themis (Divine Justice) and Dike (Human Justice).

*   *   *

The stories gathered here allow us to examine the evolution of Hurston's skills at fiction-making, from her earliest experiments at the height of the Harlem Renaissance to the eve of the Korean War and the civil rights movement half a century later. Taken together, they attest to Hurston's sustained concern with the structures of myth and allegory as vehicles for the representation of the conflicts and dilemmas that African-Americans share with all other human beings. Above all else, Hurston's great themes—obsessions, really—are love, betrayal, and death, the great themes of modernism, which she elaborated upon so eloquently for the African-American tradition.

Henry Louis Gates, Jr.
Sieglinde Lemke

John Redding
Goes to Sea

The Villagers said that John Redding was a queer child. His mother thought he was too. She would shake her head sadly, and observe to John's father: "Alf, it's too bad our boy's got a spell on 'im."

The father always met this lament with indifference, if not impatience.

"Aw, woman, stop dat talk 'bout conjure. Tain't so nohow. Ah doan want Jawn tuh git dat foolishness in *him*."

"Cose you allus tries tuh know mo' than me, but Ah ain't so ign'rant. Ah knows a heap mahself. Many and many's the people been drove outa their senses by conjuration, or rid tuh deat' by witches."

"Ah keep on telling yuh, woman, tain's so. B'lieve it all you wants tuh, but dontcha tell mah son none of it."

Perhaps ten-year-old John *was* puzzling to the simple folk there in the Florida woods for he was an imaginative child and fond of day-dreams. The St. John River flowed a scarce three hundred feet from his back door. On its banks at this point grow numerous palms, luxuriant magnolias and bay trees with a dense undergrowth of ferns, cat-tails and rope-grass. On the bosom of the stream float millions of delicately colored hyacinths. The little brown boy loved to wander down to the water's edge, and, casting in dry twigs, watch them sail away down stream to Jacksonville, the sea, the wide world and John Redding wanted to follow them.

Sometimes in his dreams he was a prince, riding away in a gorgeous carriage. Often he was a knight bestride a fiery charger prancing down the white shell road that led to distant lands. At other times he was a steamboat captain piloting his craft down the St. John River to where the sky seemed to touch the water. No matter what he dreamed or who he fancied himself to be, he always ended by riding away to the horizon; for in his childish ignorance he thought this to be farthest land.

But these twigs, which John called his ships, did not always sail away. Sometimes they would be swept in among the weeds growing in the shallow water, and be held there. One day his father came upon him scolding the weeds for stopping his sea-going vessels.

"Let go mah ships! You ole mean weeds you!" John screamed and stamped impotently. "They wants tuh go 'way. You let 'em go on!"

Alfred laid his hand on his son's head lovingly. "What's mattah, son?"

"Mah ships, pa," the child answered weeping. "Ah throwed 'em in to go way off an' them ole weeds won't let 'em."

"Well, well, doan cry. Ah thought youse uh grown up man. Men doan cry lak babies. You mustn't take it too hard 'bout yo' ships. You gotta git uster things gittin' tied up. They's lotser folks that 'ud go on off too ef somethin' didn' ketch 'em an' hol' 'em!"

Alfred Redding's brown face grew wistful for a moment, and the child noticing it, asked quickly: "Do weeds tangle up folks too, pa?"

"Now, no, chile, doan be takin' too much stock of what ah say. Ah talks in parables sometimes. Come on, les go on tuh supper."

Alf took his son's hand, and started slowly toward the house. Soon John broke the silence.

"Pa, when ah gets as big as you Ah'm goin' farther than them ships. Ah'm goin' to where the sky touches the ground."

"Well, son, when Ah wuz a boy Ah said Ah wuz goin' too, but heah Ah am. Ah hopes you have bettah luck than me."

"Pa, Ah betcha Ah seen somethin' in th' woodlot you ain't seen!"

"Whut?"

"See dat tallest pine tree ovah dere how it looks like a skull wid a crown on?"

"Yes, indeed!" said the father looking toward the tree designated. "It do look lak a skull since you call mah 'tention to it. You 'magine lotser things nobody else evah did, son!"

"Sometimes, Pa dat ole tree waves at me just aftah th' sun goes down, an' makes me sad an' skeered, too."

"Ah specks youse skeered of de dahk, thas all, sonny. When you gits biggah you won't think of sich."

Hand in hand the two trudged across the plowed land and up to the house, the child dreaming of the days when he should wander to far countries, and the man of the days when he might have—and thus they entered the kitchen.

Matty Redding, John's mother, was setting the table for supper. She was a small wiry woman with large eyes that might have been beautiful when she was young, but too much weeping had left them watery and weak.

"Matty," Alf began as he took his place at the table, "dontcha know our boy is different from any othah chile roun' heah. He 'lows he's goin' to sea when he gits grown, an' Ah reckon Ah'll let 'im."

The woman turned from the stove, skillet in hand. "Alf, you ain't gone crazy, is you? John kain't help wantin' tuh stray off, cause he's got a spell on 'im; but *you* oughter be shamed to be encouragin' him."

"Ain't Ah done tol' you forty times not tuh tahk dat low-life mess in front of mah boy?"

"Well, ef tain't no conjure in de world, how come Mitch Potts been layin' on his back six mont's an' de doctah kain't do 'im no good? Answer me dat. The very night John wuz bawn, Granny seed ole Witch Judy Davis creepin outer dis yahd. You know she had swore tuh fix me fuh marryin' you, 'way from her darter Edna. She put travel dust down fuh mah chile, dat's whut she done, tuh make him walk 'way fum me. An' evuh sence he's been able tuh crawl, he's been tryin tuh go."

"Matty, a man doan need no travel dust tuh make 'im wanter hit de road. It jes' comes natcheral fuh er man tuh travel. Dey all wants tuh go at some time or other but they kain't all get away. Ah wants mah John tuh go an' see cause Ah wanted to go mah self. When he comes back Ah kin see them furrin places wid his eyes. He kain't help wantin' tuh go cause he's a man chile!"

Mrs. Redding promptly went off into a fit of weeping but the man and boy ate supper unmoved. Twelve years of married life had taught Alfred that far from being miserable when she wept, his wife was enjoying a bit of self-pity.

Thus John Redding grew to manhood, playing, studying and dreaming. He attended the village school as did most of the youth about him, but he also went to high school at the county seat where none of the villagers went. His father shared his dreams and ambitions, but his mother could not understand why he should wish to go strange places where neither she nor his father had been. No one of their community had ever been farther away than Jacksonville. Few indeed had ever been there. Their own gardens, general store, and occasional trips to the county seat— seven miles away—sufficed for all their needs. Life was simple indeed with these folk.

John was the subject of much discussion among the country folk. Why didn't he teach school instead of thinking about strange places and people? Did he think himself better than any of the "gals" there about that he would not go a-courting any of them? He muss be "fixed" as his mother claimed, else where did his queer notions come from? Well, he was always queer, and one could not expect the man to be different from the child. They never failed to stop work at the approach of Alfred in order to be at the fence and inquire after John's health and ask when he expected to leave.

"Oh," Alfred would answer. "Jes' as soon as his mah gits reconciled to th' notion. He's a mighty dutiful boy, mah John is. He doan wanna hurt her feelings."

The boy had on several occasions attempted to reconcile his mother to the notion, but found it a difficult task. Matty always took refuge in self-pity and tears. Her son's desires were incomprehensible to her, that was all. She did not want to hurt him. It was love, mother love, that made her cling so desperately to John.

"Lawd knows," she would sigh, "Ah nevah wuz happy an' nevah specks tuh be."

"An' from yo' actions," put in Alfred hotly, "you's determined *not* to be."

"Thas right, Alfred, go on an' 'buse me. You allus does. Ah knows Ah'm ign'rant an' all dat, but dis is mah son. Ah bred an' born 'im. He kain't help from wantin' to go rovin' cause travel dust been put down fuh him. But mebbe we kin cure 'im by disincouragin' the idee."

"Well, Ah wants mah son tuh go; an' he wants tuh go too. He's a man now, Matty. An' we mus' let John hoe his own row. If it's travelin' twon't be foh long. He'll come back to us bettah than when he went off. What do you say, son?"

"Mamma," John began slowly, "it hurts me to see you so troubled over my going away; but I feel that I must go. I'm stagnating here. This indolent atmosphere will stifle every bit of ambition that's in me. Let me go mamma, please. What is there here for me? Why, sometimes I get to feeling just like a lump of dirt turned over by the plow—just where it falls there's where it lies—no thought or movement or nothing. I wanter make myself something—not just stay where I was born."

"Naw, John, it's bettah for you to stay heah and take over the school. Why don't you marry and settle down?"

"I don't *want* to, mamma. I want to go away."

"Well," said Mrs. Redding, pursing her mouth tightly, "you ainta goin' wid *mah* consent!"

"I'm sorry mamma, that you won't consent. I am going nevertheless."

"John, John, mah baby! You wouldn't kill yo' po' ole mamma, would you? Come, kiss me, son."

The boy flung his arms about his mother and held her closely while she sobbed on his breast. To all of her pleas, however, he answered that he must go.

"I'll stay at home this year, mamma, then I'll go for a while, but it won't be long. I'll come back and make you and papa oh so happy. Do you agree, mamma dear?"

"Ah reckon tain' nothin' tall fuh me to do else."

Things went on very well around the Redding home for some time. During the day John helped his father about the farm and read a great deal at night.

Then the unexpected happened. John married Stella Kanty, a neighbor's daughter. The courtship was brief but ardent—on John's part at least. He danced with Stella at a candy-pulling, walked with her home and in three weeks had declared himself. Mrs. Redding declared that she was happier than she had ever been in her life. She therefore indulged in a whole afternoon of weeping. John's change was occasioned possibly by the fact that Stella was really beautiful; he was young and red-blooded, and the time was spring.

Spring-time in Florida is not a matter of peeping violets or bursting buds merely. It is a riot of color in nature—glistening green leaves, pink, blue, purple, yellow blossoms that fairly stagger the visitor from the north. The miles of hyacinths lie like an undulating carpet on the surface of the river and divide reluctantly when the slow-moving alligators push their way log-like across. The nights are white nights for the moon shines with dazzling splendor, or in the absence of that goddess, the soft darkness creeps down laden with innumerable scents. The heavy fragrance of magnolias mingled with the delicate sweetness of jasmine and wild roses.

If time and propinquity conquered John, what then? These forces have overcome older men.

The raptures of the first few weeks over, John began to saunter out to the gate to gaze wistfully down the white dusty road; or to wander again to the river as he had done in childhood. To be sure he did not send forth twig-ships any longer, but his thoughts would in spite of himself, stray down river to Jacksonville, the sea, the wide world—and poor home-tied John Redding wanted to follow them.

He grew silent and pensive. Matty accounted for this by her ever-ready explanation of "conjuration." Alfred said nothing but smoked and puttered about the barn more than ever. Stella accused her husband of indifference and made his life miserable with tears, accusations and pouting. At last John decided to bring matters to a head and broached the subject to his wife.

"Stella, dear, I want to go roving about the world for a spell. Would you stay here with papa and mamma and wait for me to come back?"

"John, is you crazy sho' nuff? If you don't want me, say so an' I kin go home to mah folks."

"Stella, darling, I do want you, but I want to go away too. I can have both if you'll let me. We'll be *so* happy when I return . . ."

"Naw, John, you kain't rush me off one side like that. You didn't hafta marry me. There's a plenty othahs that would have been glad enuff tuh get me; you know Ah wan't educated befo' han'."

"Don't make me too conscious of my weakness, Stella. I know I should never have married with my inclinations, but it's done now, no use to talk about what is past. I love you and want to keep you, but I can't stifle that longing for the open road, rolling seas, for peoples and countries I have never seen. I'm suffering too, Stella, I'm paying for my rashness in marrying before I was ready. I'm not trying to shirk my duty—you'll be well taken care of in the meanwhile."

"John, folks allus said youse queer and tol' me not to marry yuh, but Ah jes' loved yuh so Ah couldn't help it, an' now to think you wants tuh sneak off an' leave me."

"But I'm coming back, darling . . . listen Stella."

But the girl would not. Matty came in and Stella fell into her arms weeping. John's mother immediately took up arms against him. The two women carried on such an effective war against him for the next few days that finally Alfred was forced to take his son's part.

"Matty, let dat boy alone, Ah tell you! Ef he wuz uh homebuddy he'd be drove 'way by you all's racket."

"Well, Alf, dat's all we po' wimmen kin do. We wants our husbands an' our sons. John's got uh wife now, an' he ain't got no business to be talkin' 'bout goin' nowheres. I lowed dat marrin' Stella would settle him."

"Yas, dat's all you wimmen study 'bout—settlin' some man. You takes all de get-up out of 'em. Jes' let uh fellah mak uh motion lak gettin' somewhere, an' some 'oman'll begin tuh hollah, 'Stop theah! where's you goin'? Don't fuhgit you b'longs tuh me.' "

"My Gawd! Alf! Whut you reckon Stella's gwine do? Let John walk off an' leave huh?"

"Naw, git outer huh foolishness an' go 'long wid him. He'd take huh."

"Stella ain't got no call tuh go crazy 'cause John is. She ain't no woman tuh be floppin' roun' from place tuh place lak some uh dese reps follerin' uh section gang."

The man turned abruptly from his wife and stood in the kitchen door. A blue haze hung over the river and Alfred's attention seemed fixed upon this. In reality his thoughts were turned inward. He was thinking of the numerous occasions upon which he and his son had sat on the fallen log at the edge of the water and talked of John's proposed travels. He had encouraged his son, given him every advantage his own poor circumstances would permit. And now John was home-tied.

The young man suddenly turned the corner of the house and approached his father.

"Hello, papa."

" 'Lo, son."

"Where's mamma and Stella?"

The older man merely jerked his thumb toward the interior of the house and once more gazed pensively toward the river. John entered the kitchen and kissed his mother fondly.

"Great news, mamma.' "

"What now?"

"Got a chance to join the Navy, mamma, and go all around the world. Ain't that grand?"

"John, you shorely ain't gointer leave me an' Stella, is yuh?"

"Yes, I think I am. I know how both of you feel, but I know how *I* feel, also. You preach to me the gospel of self-sacrifice for the happiness of others, but you are unwilling to practice any of it yourself. Stella can stay here—I am going to support her and spend all the time I can with her. I am going—that's settled, but I want to go with your good will. I want to do something worthy of a strong man. I have done nothing so far but look to you and papa for everything. Let me learn to strive and think—in short, be a man."

"Naw, John, Ah'll nevah give mah consent. I know yous hard-headed jes' lak yo' paw; but if you leave dis place ovah mah head, Ah nevah wants you tuh come back heah no mo. Ef Ah wuz laid on de coolin' board, Ah doan want yuh standin' ovah me, young man. Doan even come neah mah grave, you ongrateful wretch!"

Mrs. Redding arose and flung out of the room. For once, she was too incensed to cry. John stood in his tracks, gone cold and numb at his mother's pronouncement. Alfred, too, was moved. Mrs. Redding banged the bed-room door violently and startled John slightly. Alfred took his son's arm, saying softly: "Come, son, let's go down to the river."

At the water's edge they halted for a short space before seating themselves on the log. The sun was setting in a purple cloud. Hundreds of mosquito hawks darted here and there, catching gnats and being themselves caught by the lightning-swift bullhats. John abstractly snapped in two the stalk of a slender young bamboo. Taking no note of what he was doing, he broke it into short lengths and tossed them singly into the stream. The old man watched him silently for a while, but finally he said: "Oh, yes, my boy, some ships get tangled in the weeds."

"Yes, papa, they certainly do. I guess I'm beaten—might as well surrender."

"Nevah say die. Yuh nevah kin tell what will happen."

"What *can* happen? I have courage enough to make things

happen; but what can I do against mamma! What man wants to go on a long journey with his mother's curses ringing in his ears? She doesn't understand. I'll wait another year, but I am going because I must."

Alfred threw an arm about his son's neck and drew him nearer but quickly removed it. Both men instantly drew apart, ashamed for having been so demonstrative. The father looked off to the woodlot and asked with a reminiscent smile: "Son, do you remember showin' me the tree dat looked lak a skeleton head?"

"Yes, I do. It's there still. I look at it sometimes when things have become too painful for me at the house, and I run down here to cool off and think. And every time I look at it, papa, it laughs at me like it had some grim joke up its sleeve."

"Yuh wuz always imagin' things, John; things that nobody else evah thought on!"

"You know, papa, sometimes—I reckon my longing to get away makes me feel this way. . . . I feel that I am just earth, *soil* lying helpless to move myself, but *thinking*. I seem to hear herds of big beasts like horses and cows thundering over me, and rains beating down; and winds sweeping furiously over—all acting upon me, but me, well, just soil, *feeling* but not able to take part in it all. Then a soft wind like love passes over and warms me, and a summer rain comes down like understanding and softens me, and I push a blade of grass or a flower, or maybe a pine tree— that's the ground thinking. Plants are ground thoughts, because the soil can't move itself. Whenever I see little whirls of dust sailing down the road I always step aside—I don't want to stop 'em 'cause they're on their shining way—moving! Oh, yes, I'm a dreamer. . . . I have such wonderfully complete dreams, papa. They never come true. But even as my dreams fade I have others."

"Yas, son, Ah have them same feelings exactly, but Ah can't find no words lak you do. It seems lak you an' me see wid de same eyes, hear wid de same ears an' even feel de same inside. Only thing you kin talk it an' Ah can't. But anyhow you speaks for me, so whut's the difference?"

The men arose without more conversation. Possibly they feared to trust themselves to speech. As they walked leisurely toward the house Alfred remarked the freshness of the breeze.

'It's about time the rains set in," added his son. "The year is wearin' on."

After a gloomy supper John strolled out into the spacious front yard and seated himself beneath a China-berry tree. The breeze had grown a trifle stronger since sunset and continued from the south-east. Matty and Stella sat on the deep front porch, but Alfred joined John under the tree. The family was divided into two armed camps and the hostilities had reached that stage where no quarter could be asked or given.

About nine o'clock an automobile came flying down the dusty white road and halted at the gate. A white man slammed the gate and hurried up the walk toward the house, but stopped abruptly before the men beneath the China-berry. It was Mr. Hill, the builder of the new bridge that was to span the river.

"Howdy John, Howdy Alf. I'm mighty glad I found you. I am in trouble."

"Well now, Mist' Hill," answered Alfred slowly but pleasantly. "We'se glad you foun' us too. What trouble could *you* be having now?"

"It's the bridge. The weather bureau says that the rains will be upon me in forty-eight hours. If it catches the bridge as it is now, I'm afraid all my work of the past five months will be swept away, to say nothing of a quarter of a million dollars' worth of labor and material. I've got all my men at work now and I thought to get as many extra hands as I could to help out tonight and tomorrow. We can make her weather tight in that time if I can get about twenty more."

"I'll go, Mister Hill," said John with a great deal of energy. "I don't want papa out on that bridge—too dangerous."

"Good for you, John!" cried the white man. "Now if I had a few more men of your brawn and brain, I could build an entirely new bridge in forty-eight hours. Come on and jump into the car. I am taking the men on down as I find them."

"Wait a minute. I must put on my blue jeans. I won't be long."

John arose and strode to the house. He knew that his mother and wife had overheard everything, but he paused for a moment to speak to them.

"Mamma, I am going to work all night on the bridge."

There was no answer. He turned to his wife.

"Stella, don't be lonesome. I will be home at day-break."

His wife was as silent as his mother. John stood for a moment on the steps, then resolutely strode past the women and into the house. A few minutes later he emerged clad in his blue overalls and brogans. This time he said nothing to the silent figures rocking back and forth on the porch. But when he was a few feet from the steps he called back: "Bye, mamma; bye, Stella," and hurried on down the walk to where his father sat.

"So long, papa. I'll be home around seven."

Alfred roused himself and stood. Placing both hands upon his son's broad shoulders he said softly: "Be keerful, son, don't fall or nothin'."

"I will, papa. Don't *you* get into a quarrel on my account."

John hurried on to the waiting car and was whirled away.

Alfred sat for a long time beneath the tree where his son had left him and smoked on. The women soon went indoors. On the night breeze were borne numerous scents: of jassamine, of roses, of damp earth of the river, of the pine forest near by. A solitary whip-poor-will sent forth his plaintive call from the nearby shrubbery. A giant owl roared and boomed from the wood lot. The calf confined in the barn would bleat and be answered by his mother's sympathetic "moo" from the pen. Away down in Lake Howell Creek the basso profundo of the alligators boomed and died, boomed and died.

Around ten o'clock the breeze freshened, growing stiffer until midnight when it became a gale. Alfred fastened the doors and bolted the wooden shutters at the windows. The three persons sat about a round deal table in the kitchen upon which stood a bulky kerosene lamp, flickering and sputtering in the wind that came in through the numerous cracks in the walls. The wind rushed down the chimney blowing puffs of ashes about the room. It banged the cooking utensils on the walls. The drinking gourd hanging outside by the door played a weird tattoo, hollow and unearthly, against the thin wooden wall.

The man and the women sat silently. Even if there had been no storm they would not have talked. They could not go to bed because the women were afraid to retire during a storm and the man wished to stay awake and think with his son. Thus they sat: the women hot with resentment toward the man and terrified by the storm; the man hardly mindful of the tempest but eating his heart out in pity for his boy. Time wore heavily on.

And now a new element of terror was added. A screech-owl alighted on the roof and shivered forth his doleful cry. Possibly he had been blown out of his nest by the wind. Matty started up at the sound but fell back in her chair, pale and trembling: "My Gawd!" she gasped, "dat's a sho' sign uh death."

Stella hurriedly thrust her hand into the salt-jar and threw some into the chimney of the lamp. The color of the flame changed from yellow to blue-green but this burning of salt did not have the desired effect—to drive away the bird from the roof. Matty slipped out of her blue calico wrapper and turned it wrong side out before replacing it. Even Alfred turned one sock.

"Alf," said Matty, "what do you reckon's gonna happen from this?"

"How do Ah know, Matty?"

"Ah wisht John hadn't went way from heah tuh night."

"Humh."

Outside the tempest raged. The palms rattled dryly and the giant pines groaned and sighed in the grip of the wind. Flying leaves and pine-mast filled the air. Now and then a brilliant flash of lightning disclosed a bird being blown here and there with the wind. The prodigious roar of the thunder seemed to rock the earth. Black clouds hung so low that the tops of the pines were among them moving slowly before the wind and made the darkness awful. The screech-owl continued his tremulous cry.

After three o'clock the wind ceased and the rain commenced.

Huge drops clattered down upon the shingle roof like buckshot and ran from the eaves in torrents. It entered the house through the cracks in the walls and under the doors. It was a deluge in volume and force but subsided before morning.

The sun came up brightly on the havoc of the wind and rain calling forth millions of feathered creatures. The white sand everywhere was full of tiny cups dug out by the force of the falling raindrops. The rims of the little depressions crunched noisily underfoot.

At daybreak Mr. Redding set out for the bridge. He was uneasy. On arriving he found that the river had risen twelve feet during the cloudburst and was still rising. The slow St. John was swollen far beyond its banks and rushing on to sea like a mountain stream, sweeping away houses, great blocks of earth, cattle, trees—in short anything that came within its grasp. Even the steel framework of the new bridge was gone!

The siren of the fibre factory was tied down for half an hour, announcing the disaster to the country side. When Alfred arrived therefore he found nearly all the men of the district there.

The river, red and swollen, was full of floating debris. Huge trees were swept along as relentlessly as chicken coops and fence rails. Some steel piles were all that was left of the bridge.

Alfred went down to a group of men who were fishing members of the ill-fated construction gang out of the water. Many were able to swim ashore unassisted. Wagons backed up and were hurriedly driven away loaded with wet shivering men. Two men had been killed outright, others seriously wounded. Three men had been drowned. At last all had been accounted for except John Redding. His father ran here and there asking for him, or calling him. No one knew where he was. No one remembered seeing him since daybreak.

Dozens of women had arrived at the scene of the disaster by this time. Matty and Stella, wrapped in woolen shawls, were among them. They rushed to Alfred in alarm and asked where was John.

"Ah doan know," answered Alfred impatiently, "that's what Ah'm trying to fin' out now."

"Do you reckon he's run away?" asked Stella thoughtlessly.

Matty bristled instantly.

"Naw," she answered sternly, "he ain't no sneak."

The father turned to Fred Mimms, one of the survivors and asked him where John was and how had the bridge been destroyed.

"Yuh see," said Mimms, "when dat turrible win' come up we wuz out 'bout de middle of de river. Some of us wuz on de bridge, some on de derrick. De win' blowed so hahd we could skeercely stan' and Mist' Hill tol' us tuh set down fuh a spell. He's 'fraid some of us mought go overboard. Den all of a sudden de lights went out—guess de wires wuz blowed down. We wuz all skeered tuh move for slippin' overboard. Den dat rain commenced—an' Ah nevah seed such a down-pour since de flood. We set dere and someone begins tuh pray. Lawd how we did pray tuh be spared! Den somebody raised a song an' we sung, you hear me, we sung from de bottom of our hearts till daybreak. When the first light come we couldn't see nothin' but fog everywhere. You couldn't tell which wuz water an' which wuz lan'. But when de sun come up de fog begin to liff, an' we could see de water. Dat fog wuz so thick an' heavy dat it wuz huggin' dat river lak a windin' sheet. And when it rose we saw dat de river had rose way up durin' the rain. My Gawd, Alf! it wuz runnin' high—so high it nearly teched de span of de bridge—an' red as blood! So much clay, you know from lan' she done overflowed. Comin' down stream, as fas' as 'press train wuz three big pine trees. De first one wuzn't fohty feet from us and there wasn't no chance to do nothin' but pray. De fust one struck us and shook de whole works an' befo' it could stop shakin' the other two hit us an' down we went. Ah thought Ah'd never see home again."

"But, Mimms, where's John?"

'Ah ain't seen him, Alf, since de logs struck us. Mebbe he's swum ashore, mebbe dey picked him up. What's dat floatin' way out dere in de water?"

Alfred shaded his eyes with his gnarled brown hand and gazed out into the stream. Sure enough there was a man floating on a piece of timber. He lay prone upon his back. His arms were outstretched, and the water washed over his brogans but his feet were lifted out of the water whenever the timber was buoyed up by the stream. His blue overalls were nearly torn from his body. A heavy piece of steel or timber had struck him in falling for his left side was laid open by the thrust. A great jagged hole wherein the double fists of a man might be thrust, could plainly be seen from the shore. The man was John Redding.

Everyone seemed to see him at once. Stella fell to the wet earth in a faint. Matty clung to her husband's arm, weeping hysterically. Alfred stood very erect with his wife clinging tearfully to him, but he said nothing. A single tear hung on his lashes for a time then trickled slowly down his wrinkled brown cheek.

"Alf! Alf!" screamed Matty, "dere's our son. Ah knowed when Ah heard dat owl las' night. . . ."

"Ah see 'im, Matty," returned her husband softly.

"Why is yuh standin' heah? Go git mah boy."

The men were manning a boat to rescue the remains of John Redding when Alfred spoke again.

"Mah po' boy, his dreams never come true."

"Alf," complained Matty, "why doantcher hurry an' git my boy—doantcher see he's floatin' on off?"

Her husband paid her no attention but addressed himself to the rescue-party.

"You all stop! Leave my boy go on. Doan stop 'im. Doan' bring im back for dat ole tree to grin at. Leave him g'wan. He wants tuh go. Ah'm happy 'cause dis mawnin' mah boy is goin' tuh sea, *he's goin' tuh sea.*"

Out on the bosom of the river, bobbing up and down as if waving good bye, piloting his little craft on the shining river road, John Redding floated away toward Jacksonville, the sea, the wide world—at last.

Drenched
in Light

"You Isie Watts! Git 'own offen dat gate post an' rake up dis yahd!"

The little brown figure perched upon the gate post looked yearningly up the gleaming shell road that led to Orlando, and down the road that led to Sanford and shrugged her thin shoulders. This heaped kindling on Grandma Potts' already burning ire.

"Lawd a-mussy!" she screamed, enraged—"Heah Joel, gimme dat wash stick. Ah'll show dat limb of Satan she kain't shake huhseff at *me*. If she ain't down by de time Ah gets dere, Ah'll break huh down in de lines" (loins).

"Aw Gran'ma, Ah see Mist' George and Jim Robinson comin' and Ah wanted to wave at 'em," the child said petulantly.

"You jes wave dat rake at dis heah yahd, madame, else Ah'll take you down a button hole lower. You'se too 'oomanish jumpin' up in everybody's face dat pass."

This struck the child in a very sore spot for nothing pleased her so much as to sit atop of the gate post and hail the passing vehicles on their way South to Orlando, or North to Sanford. That white shell road was her great attraction. She raced up and down the stretch of it that lay before her gate like a round eyed puppy hailing gleefully all travelers. Everybody in the country, white and colored, knew little Isis Watts, the joyful. The Robinson brothers, white cattlemen, were particularly fond of her and always extended a stirrup for her to climb up behind one of them for a short ride, or let her try to crack the long bull whips and yee whoo at the cows.

Grandma Potts went inside and Isis literally waved the rake at the "chaws" of ribbon cane that lay so bountifully about the yard in company with the knots and peelings, with a thick sprinkling of peanut hulls.

The herd of cattle in their envelope of gray dust came alongside and Isis dashed out to the nearest stirrup and was lifted up.

"Hello theah Snidlits, I was wonderin' wheah you was," said Jim Robinson as she snuggled down behind him in the saddle. They were almost out of the danger zone when Grandma emerged.

"You Isie-s!" she bawled.

The child slid down on the opposite side from the house and executed a flank movement through the corn patch that brought her into the yard from behind the privy.

"You lil' hasion you! Wheah you been?"

"Out in de back yahd," Isis lied and did a cart wheel and a few fancy steps on her way to the front again.

"If you doan git tuh dat yahd, Ah make a mommuk of you!" Isis observed that Grandma was cutting a fancy assortment of switches from peach, guana and cherry trees.

She finished the yard by raking everything under the edge of the porch and began a romp with the dogs, those lean, floppy eared 'coon hounds that all country folks keep. But Grandma vetoed this also.

"Isie, you set 'own on dat porch! Uh great big 'leben yeah ole gal racin' an' rompin' lak dat—set 'own!"

Isis impatiently flung herself upon the steps.

"Git up offa dem steps, you aggavatin' limb, 'fore Ah git dem hick'ries tuh you, an' set yo' seff on a cheah."

Isis petulantly arose and sat down as violently as possible in a chair, but slid down until she all but sat upon her shoulder blades.

"Now look atcher," Grandma screamed. "Put yo' knees together, an' git up offen yo' backbone! Lawd, you know dis hellion is gwine make me stomp huh insides out."

Isis sat bolt upright as if she wore a ramrod down her back and began to whistle. Now there are certain things that Grandma Potts felt no one of this female persuasion should do—one was to sit with the knees separated, "settin' brazen" she called it; another was whistling, another playing with boys, neither must a lady cross her legs.

Up she jumped from her seat to get the switches.

"So youse whistlin' in mah face, huh!" She glared till her eyes were beady and Isis bolted for safety. But the noon hour brought John Watts, the widowed father, and this excused the child from sitting for criticism.

Being the only girl in the family, of course she must wash the dishes, which she did in intervals between frolics with the dogs. She even gave Jake, the puppy, a swim in the dishpan by holding him suspended above the water that reeked of "pot likker"—just high enough so that his feet would be immersed. The deluded puppy swam and swam without ever crossing the pan, much to his annoyance. Hearing Grandma she hurriedly dropped him on the floor, which he tracked up with feet wet with dishwater.

Grandma took her patching and settled down in the front room to sew. She did this every afternoon, and invariably slept in the big red rocker with her head lolled back over the back, the sewing falling from her hand.

Isis had crawled under the center table with its red plush cover with little round balls for fringe. She was lying on her back imagining herself various personages. She wore trailing robes, golden slippers with blue bottoms. She rode white horses with flaring pink nostrils to the horizon, for she still believed that to be land's end. She was picturing herself gazing over the edge of the world into the abyss when the spool of cotton fell from Grandma's lap and rolled away under the whatnot.

Isis drew back from her contemplation of the nothingness at the horizon and glanced up at the sleeping woman. Her head had fallen far back. She breathed with a regular "snark" intake and soft "poosah" exhaust. But Isis was a visual minded child. She heard the snores only subconsciously but she saw straggling beard on Grandma's chin, trembling a little with every "snark" and "poosah." They were long gray hairs curled here and there against the dark brown skin. Isis was moved with pity for her mother's mother.

"Poah Gran-ma needs a shave," she murmured, and set about it. Just then Joel, next older than Isis, entered with a can of bait.

"Come on Isie, les' we all go fishin'. The perch is bitin' fine in Blue Sink."

"Sh-sh—" cautioned his sister, "Ah got to shave Gran'ma."

"Who say so?" Joel asked, surprised.

"Nobody doan hafta tell me. Look at her chin. No ladies don't weah no whiskers if they kin help it. But Gran'ma gittin' ole an' she doan know how to shave like me."

The conference adjourned to the back porch lest Grandma wake.

"Aw, Isie, you doan know nothin' 'bout shavin' a-tall—but a *man* lak *me*—"

"Ah do so know."

"You don't not. Ah'm goin' shave her mahseff."

"Naw, you won't neither, Smarty. Ah saw her first an' thought it all up first," Isis declared, and ran to the calico covered box on the wall above the wash basin and seized her father's razor. Joel was quick and seized the mug and brush.

"Now!" Isis cried defiantly, "Ah got the razor."

"Goody, goody, goody, pussy cat, Ah got th' brush an' you can't shave 'thout lather—see! Ah know mo' than you," Joel retorted.

"Aw, who don't know dat?" Isis pretended to scorn. But seeing her progress blocked for lack of lather she compromised.

"Ah know! Les' we all shave her. You lather an' Ah shave."

This was agreeable to Joel. He made mountains of lather and anointed his own chin, and the chin of Isis and the dogs, splashed the walls and at last was persuaded to lather Grandma's chin. Not that he was loath but he wanted his new plaything to last as long as possible.

Isis stood on one side of the chair with the razor clutched cleaver fashion. The niceties of razor-handling had passed over her head. The thing with her was to *hold* the razor—sufficient in itself.

Joel splashed on the lather in great gobs and Grandma awoke.

For one bewildered moment she stared at the grinning boy with the brush and mug but sensing another presence, she turned to behold the business face of Isis and the razor-clutching hand. Her jaw dropped and Grandma, forgetting years and rheumatism, bolted from the chair and fled the house, screaming.

"She's gone to tell papa, Isis. You didn't have no business wid his razor and he's gonna lick yo hide," Joel cried, running to replace mug and brush.

"You too, chuckle-head, you, too," retorted Isis. "You was playin' wid his brush and put it all over the dogs—Ah seen you put it on Ned an' Beulah." Isis shaved some slivers from the door jamb with the razor and replaced it in the box. Joel took his bait and pole and hurried to Blue Sink. Isis crawled under the house to brood over the whipping she knew would come. She had meant well.

But sounding brass and tinkling cymbal drew her forth. The local lodge of the Grand United Order of Odd Fellows led by a braying, thudding band, was marching in full regalia down the road. She had forgotten the barbecue and log-rolling to be held today for the benefit of the new hall.

Music to Isis meant motion. In a minute razor and whipping forgotten, she was doing a fair imitation of the Spanish dancer she had seen in a medicine show some time before. Isis' feet were gifted—she could dance most anything she saw.

Up, up went her spirits, her brown little feet doing all sorts of intricate things and her body in rhythm, hand curving above her head. But the music was growing faint. Grandma nowhere in sight. She stole out of the gate, running and dancing after the band.

Then she stopped. She couldn't dance at the carnival. Her dress was torn and dirty. She picked a long stemmed daisy and thrust it behind her ear. But the dress, no better. Oh, an idea! In the battered round topped trunk in the bedroom!

She raced back to the house, then, happier, raced down the white dusty road to the picnic grove, gorgeously clad. People laughed good naturedly at her, the band played and Isis danced because she couldn't help it. A crowd of children gathered admiringly about her as she wheeled lightly about, hand on hip, flower between her teeth with the red and white fringe of the table-cloth—Grandma's new red table-cloth that she wore in lieu of a Spanish shawl—trailing in the dust. It was too ample for her meager form, but she wore it like a gypsy. Her brown feet twinkled in and out of the fringe. Some grown people joined the children about her. The Grand Exalted Ruler rose to speak; the band was hushed, but Isis danced on, the crowd clapping their hands for her. No one listened to the Exalted one, for little by little the multitude had surrounded the brown dancer.

An automobile drove up to the Crown and halted. Two white men and a lady got out and pushed into the crowd, suppressing mirth discreetly behind gloved hands. Isis looked up and waved them a magnificent hail and went on dancing until—

Grandma had returned to the house and missed Isis and straightway sought her at the festivities expecting to find her in her soiled dress, shoeless, gaping at the crowd, but what she saw drove her frantic. Here was her granddaughter dancing before a gaping crowd in her brand new red table-cloth, and reeking of lemon extract, for Isis had added the final touch to her costume. She *must* have perfume.

Isis saw Grandma and bolted. She heard her cry: "Mah Gawd, mah brand new table-cloth Ah jus' bought f'um O'landah!" as she fled through the crowd and on into the woods.

II

She followed the little creek until she came to the ford in a rutty wagon road that led to Apopka and laid down on the cool grass at the roadside. The April sun was quite hot.

Misery, misery and woe settled down upon her and the child wept. She knew another whipping was in store for her.

"Oh, Ah wish Ah could die, then Gran'ma an' papa would be sorry they beat me so much. Ah b'leeve Ah'll run away an' never go home no mo'. Ah'm goin' drown mahseff in th' creek!" Her woe grew attractive.

Isis got up and waded into the water. She routed out a tiny 'gator and a huge bull frog. She splashed and sang, enjoying herself immensely. The purr of a motor struck her ear and she saw a large, powerful car jolting along the rutty road toward her. It stopped at the water's edge.

"Well, I declare, it's our little gypsy," exclaimed the man at the wheel. "What are you doing here, now?"

"Ah'm killin' mahseff," Isis declared dramatically, "cause Gran'ma beats me too much."

There was a hearty burst of laughter from the machine.

"You'll last sometime the way you are going about it. Is this the way to Maitland? We want to go to the Park Hotel."

Isis saw no longer any reason to die. She came up out of the water, holding up the dripping fringe of the table-cloth.

"Naw, indeedy. You go to Maitlan' by the shell road—it goes by mah house—an' turn off at Lake Sebelia to the clay road that takes you right to the do'."

"Well," went on the driver, smiling furtively, "could you quit dying long enough to go with us?"

"Yessuh," she said thoughtfully, "Ah wanta go wid you."

The door of the car swung open. She was invited to a seat beside the driver. She had often dreamed of riding in one of these heavenly chariots but never thought she would, actually.

"Jump in then, Madame Tragedy, and show us. We lost ourselves after we left your barbecue."

During the drive Isis explained to the kind lady who smelt faintly of violets and to the indifferent men that she was really a princess. She told them about her trips to the horizon, about the trailing gowns, the gold shoes with blue bottoms—she insisted on the blue bottoms—the white charger, the time when she was

Hercules and had slain numerous dragons and sundry giants. At last.the car approached her gate over which stood the umbrella China-berry tree. The car was abreast of the gate and had all but passed when Grandma spied her glorious tablecloth lying back against the upholstery of the Packard.

"You Isie-e!" she bawled. "You lil' wretch you! Come heah *dis instunt.*"

"That's me," the child confessed, mortified, to the lady on the rear seat.

"Oh, Sewell, stop the car. This is where the child lives. I hate to give her up though."

"Do you wanta keep me?" Isis brightened.

"Oh, I wish I could, you shining little morsel. Wait, I'll try to save you a whipping this time."

She dismounted with the gaudy lemon flavored culprit and advanced to the gate where Grandma stood glowering, switches in hand.

"You're gointuh ketchit f'um yo' haid to yo' heels m'lady. Jes' come in heah."

"Why, good afternoon," she accosted the furious grandparent. "You're not going to whip this poor little thing, are you?" the lady asked in conciliatory tones.

"Yes, Ma'am. She's de wustest lil' link that ever drawed bref. Jes' look at mah new table-cloth, dat ain't never been washed. She done traipsed all over de woods, uh dancin' an' uh prancin' in it. She done took a razor to me t'day an' Lawd knows whut mo'."

Isis clung to the white hand fearfully.

"Ah wuzn't gointer hurt Gran'ma, miss—Ah wuz jus' gointer shave her whiskers fuh huh 'cause she's old an' can't."

The white hand closed tightly over the little brown one that was quite soiled. She could understand a voluntary act of love even though it miscarried.

"Now, Mrs. er—er—I didn't get the name—how much did your table-cloth cost?"

"One whole big silvah dollar down at O'landah—ain't had it a week yit."

"Now here's five dollars to get another one. The little thing loves laughter. I want her to go on to the hotel and dance in that table-cloth for me. I can stand a little light today—"

"Oh, yessum, yessum," Grandma cut in. "Everything's alright, sho' she kin go, yessum."

The lady went on: "I want brightness and this Isis is joy itself, why she's drenched in light!"

Isis for the first time in her life, felt herself appreciated and danced up and down in an ecstasy of joy for a minute.

"Now, behave yo'seff, Isie, ovah at de hotel wid de white folks," Grandma cautioned, pride in her voice, though she strove to hide it. "Lawd, ma'am, dat gal keeps me so frackshus, Ah doan know mah haid f'um mah feet. Ah orter comb huh haid, too, befo' she go wid you all."

"No, no, don't bother. I like her as she is. I don't think she'd like it either, being combed and scrubbed. Come on, Isis."

Feeling that Grandma had been somewhat squelched did not detract from Isis' spirit at all. She pranced over to the waiting motor and this time seated herself on the rear seat between the sweet, smiling lady and the rather aloof man in gray.

"Ah'm gointer stay wid you all," she said with a great deal of warmth, and snuggled up to her benefactress. "Want me tuh sing a song fuh you?"

"There, Helen, you've been adopted," said the man with a short, harsh laugh.

"Oh, I hope so, Harry." She put her arm about the red draped figure at her side and drew it close until she felt the warm puffs of the child's breath against her side. She looked hungrily ahead of her and spoke into space rather than to anyone in the car. "I want a little of her sunshine to soak into my soul. I need it."

Spunk

A giant of a brown skinned man sauntered up the one street of the Village and out into the palmetto thickets with a small pretty woman clinging lovingly to his arm.

"Looka theah, folkses!" cried Elijah Mosley, slapping his leg gleefully. "Theah they go, big as life an' brassy as tacks."

All the loungers in the store tried to walk to the door with an air of nonchalance but with small success.

"Now pee-eople!" Walter Thomas gasped. "Will you look at 'em!"

"But that's one thing Ah likes about Spunk Banks—he ain't skeered of nothin' on God's green foot-stool—*nothin'!* He rides that log down at saw-mill jus' like he struts round wid another man's wife—jus' don't give a kitty. When Tes' Miller got cut to giblets on that circle-saw, Spunk steps right up and starts ridin'. The rest of us was skeered to go near it."

A round-shouldered figure in overalls much too large, came nervously in the door and the talking ceased. The men looked at each other and winked.

"Gimme some soda-water. Sass'prilla Ah reckon," the new-comer ordered, and stood far down the counter near the open pickled pig-feet tub to drink it.

Elijah nudged Walter and turned with mock gravity to the new-comer.

"Say Joe, how's everything up yo' way? How's yo' wife?"

Joe started and all but dropped the bottle he held in his hands. He swallowed several times painfully and his lips trembled.

"Aw 'Lige, you oughtn't to do nothin' like that," Walter grumbled. Elijah ignored him.

"She jus' passed heah a few minutes ago goin' thata way," with a wave of his hand in the direction of the woods.

Now Joe knew his wife had passed that way. He knew that the men lounging in the general store had seen her, moreover, he knew that the men knew *he* knew. He stood there silent for a long moment staring blankly, with his Adam's apple twitching nervously up and down his throat. One could actually *see* the pain he was suffering, his eyes, his face, his hands and even the dejected slump of his shoulders. He set the bottle down upon the counter. He didn't bang it, just eased it out of his hand silently and fiddled with his suspender buckle.

"Well, Ah'm goin' after her today. Ah'm goin' an' fetch her back. Spunk's done gone too fur."

He reached deep down into his trouser pocket and drew out a hollow ground razor, large and shiny, and passed his moistened thumb back and forth over the edge.

"Talkin' like a man, Joe. Course that's *yo'* fambly affairs, but Ah like to see grit in anybody."

Joe Kanty laid down a nickel and stumbled out into the street.

Dusk crept in from the woods. Ike Clarke lit the swinging oil lamp that was almost immediately surrounded by candle-flies. The men laughed boisterously behind Joe's back as they watched him shamble woodward.

"You oughtn't to said whut you did to him, 'Lige,—look how it worked him up," Walter chided.

"And Ah hope it did work him up. Tain't even decent for a man to take and take like he do."

"Spunk will sho' kill him."

"Aw, Ah doan't know. You never kin tell. He might turn him up an' spank him fur gettin' in the way, but Spunk wouldn't shoot no unarmed man. Dat razor he carried outa heah ain't gonna run Spunk down an' cut him, an' Joe ain't got the nerve to go up to

Spunk with it knowing he totes that Army 45. He makes that break outa heah to bluff us. He's gonna hide that razor behind the first likely palmetto root an' sneak back home to bed. Don't tell me nothin' 'bout that rabbit-foot colored man. Didn't he meet Spunk an' Lena face to face one day las' week an' mumble sumthin' to Spunk 'bout lettin' his wife alone?''

"What did Spunk say?" Walter broke in—"Ah like him fine but tain't right the way he carries on wid Lena Kanty, jus' cause Joe's timid 'bout fightin.' ''

"You wrong theah, Walter. 'Tain't cause Joe's timid at all, it's cause Spunk wants Lena. If Joe was a passel of wile cats Spunk would tackle the job just the same. He'd go after *anything* he wanted the same way. As Ah wuz sayin' a minute ago, he tole Joe right to his face that Lena was his. 'Call her,' he says to Joe. 'Call her and see if she'll come. A woman knows her boss an' she answers when he calls.' 'Lena, ain't I yo' husband?' Joe sorter whines out. Lena looked at him real disgusted but she don't answer and she don't move outa her tracks. Then Spunk reaches out an' takes hold of her arm an' says: 'Lena, youse mine. From now on Ah works for you an' fights for you an' Ah never wants you to look to nobody for a crumb of bread, a stitch of close or a shingle to go over yo' head, but *me* long as Ah live. Ah'll git the lumber foh owah house tomorrow. Go home an' git yo' things together!' 'Thass mah house,' Lena speaks up. 'Papa gimme that.' 'Well,' says Spunk, 'doan give up whut's yours, but when youse inside don't forget youse mine, an' let no other man git outa his place wid you!' Lena looked up at him with her eyes so full of love that they wuz runnin' over an' Spunk seen it an' Joe seen it too, and his lips started to tremblin' and his Adam's apple was galloping up and down his neck like a race horse. Ah bet he's wore out half a dozen Adam's apples since Spunk's been on the job with Lena. That's all he'll do. He'll be back heah after while swallowin' an' workin' his lips like he wants to say somethin' an' can't."

"But didn't he do *nothin'* to stop 'em?"

"Nope, not a frazzlin' thing—jus' stood there. Spunk took Lena's arm and walked off jus' like nothin' ain't happened and he stood there gazin' after them till they was outa sight. Now you know a woman don't want no man like that. I'm jus' waitin' to see whut he's goin' to say when he gits back.''

II

But Joe Kanty never came back, never. The men in the store heard the sharp report of a pistol somewhere distant in the palmetto thicket and soon Spunk came walking leisurely, with his big black Stetson set at the same rakish angle and Lena clinging to his arm, came walking right into the general store. Lena wept in a frightened manner.

"Well," Spunk announced calmly, "Joe come out there wid a meatax an' made me kill him."

He sent Lena home and led the men back to Joe—Joe crumple and limp with his right hand still clutching his razor.

"See mah back? Mah close cut clear through. He sneaked up an' tried to kill me from the back, but Ah got him, an' got him good, first shot," Spunk said.

The men glared at Elijah, accusingly.

"Take him up an' plant him in 'Stoney lonesome,' " Spunk said in a careless voice. "Ah didn't wanna shoot him but he made me do it. He's a dirty coward, jumpin' on a man from behind."

Spunk turned on his heel and sauntered away to where he knew his love wept in fear for him and no man stopped him. At the general store later on, they all talked of locking him up until the sheriff should come from Orlando, but no one did anything but talk.

A clear case of self-defense, the trial was a short one, and Spunk walked out of the court house to freedom again. He could work again, ride the dangerous log-carriage that fed the singing, snarling, biting, circle-saw; he could stroll the soft dark lanes with his guitar. He was free to roam the woods again; he was free to return to Lena. He did all of these things.

III

"Whut you reckon, Walt?" Elijah asked one night later. "Spunk's gittin' ready to marry Lena!"

"Naw! Why Joe ain't had time to git cold yit. Nohow Ah didn't figger Spunk was the marryin' kind."

"Well, he is," rejoined Elijah. "He done moved most of Lena's things—and her along wid 'em—over to the Bradley house. He's buying it. Jus' like Ah told yo' all right in heah the night Joe wuz kilt. Spunk's crazy 'bout Lena. He don't want folks to keep on talkin' 'bout her—thass reason he's rushin' so. Funny thing 'bout that bob-cat, wan't it?"

"Whut bob-cat, 'Lige? Ah ain't heered 'bout none."

"Ain't cher? Well, night befo' las' was the fust night Spunk an' Lena moved together an' jus' as they was goin' to bed, a big black bob-cat, black all over, you hear me, *black*, walked round and round that house and howled like forty, an' when Spunk got his gun an' went to the winder to shoot it, he says it stood right still an' looked him in the eye, an' howled right at him. The thing got Spunk so nervoused up he couldn't shoot. But Spunk says twan't no bob-cat nohow. He says it was Joe done sneaked back from Hell!"

"Humph!" sniffed Walter, "he oughter be nervous after what he done. Ah reckon Joe come back to dare him to marry Lena, or to come out an' fight. Ah bet he'll be back time and agin, too. Know what Ah think? Joe wuz a braver man than Spunk."

There was a general shout of derision from the group.

"Thass a fact," went on Walter. "Lookit whut he done; took a razor an' went out to fight a man he knowed toted a gun an' wuz a crack shot, too; 'nother thing Joe wuz skeered of Spunk, skeered plumb stiff! But he went jes' the same. It took him a long time to get his nerve up. 'Tain't nothin' for Spunk to fight when he ain't skeered of nothin'. Now, Joe's done come back to have it out wid the man that's got all he ever had. Y'all know Joe ain't never had nothin' nor wanted nothin' besides Lena. It musta been a h'ant cause ain' nobody never seen no black bob-cat."

" 'Nother thing," cut in one of the men, "Spunk wuz cussin' a blue streak today 'cause he 'lowed dat saw wuz wobblin'—almos' got 'im once. The machinist come, looked it over an' said it wuz alright. Spunk musta been leanin' t'wards it some. Den he claimed somebody pushed 'im but 'twant nobody close to 'im. Ah wuz glad when knockin' off time come. I'm skeered of dat man when he gits hot. He'd beat you full of button holes as quick as he's look atcher.''

IV

The men gathered the next evening in a different mood, no laughter. No badinage this time.

''Look 'Lige, you goin' to set up wid Spunk?''

''Naw, Ah reckon not, Walter. Tell yuh the truth, Ah'm a lil bit skittish. Spunk died too wicket—died cussin' he did. You know he thought he wuz done outa life.''

''Good Lawd, who'd he think done it?''

''Joe.''

''Joe Kanty? How come?''

''Walter, Ah b'leeve Ah will walk up thata way an' set. Lena would like it Ah reckon.''

''But whut did he say, 'Lige?''

Elijah did not answer until they had left the lighted store and were strolling down the dark street.

''Ah wuz loadin' a wagon wid scantlin' right near the saw when Spunk fell on the carriage but 'fore Ah could git to him the saw got him in the body—awful sight. Me an' Skint Miller got him off but it was too late. Anybody could see that. The fust thing he said wuz: 'He pushed me, 'Lige—the dirty hound pushed me in the back!'— He was spittin' blood at ev'ry breath. We laid him on the sawdust pile with his face to the East so's he could die easy. He helt mah han' till the last, Walter, and said: 'It was Joe, 'Lige—the dirty sneak shoved me . . . he didn't dare come to mah face . . . but Ah'll git the son-of-a-wood louse soon's I get there an' make hell too hot for him. . . . Ah felt him shove me . . . !' Thass how he died.''

''If spirits kin fight, there's a powerful tussle goin' on somewhere ovah Jordan 'cause Ah b'leeve Joe's ready for Spunk an' ain't skeered anymore—yas, Ah b'leeve Joe pushed 'im mahself.''

They had arrived at the house. Lena's lamentations were deep and loud. She had filled the room with magnolia blossoms that gave off a heavy sweet odor. The keepers of the wake tipped about whispering in frightened tones. Everyone in the Village was there, even old Jeff Kanty, Joe's father, who a few hours before would have been afraid to come within ten feet of him, stood leering triumphantly down upon the fallen giant as if his fingers had been the teeth of steel that laid him low.

The cooling board consisted of three sixteen-inch boards on saw horses, a dingy sheet was his shroud.

The women ate heartily of the funeral baked meats and wondered who would be Lena's next. The men whispered coarse conjectures between guzzles of whiskey.

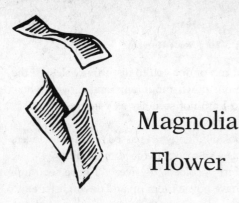

Magnolia
Flower

The brook laughed and sang. When it encountered hard places in its bed, it hurled its water in sparkling dance figures up into the moonlight.

It sang louder, louder; danced faster, faster, with a coquettish splash! at the vegetation on its banks.

At last it danced boisterously into the bosom of the St. John's, upsetting the whispering hyacinths who shivered and blushed, drunk with the delight of moon kisses.

The Mighty One turned peevishly in his bed and washed the feet of the Palmetto palms so violently that they awoke and began again the gossip they had left off when the Wind went to bed. A palm cannot speak without wind. The river had startled it also, for the winds sleep on the bosom of waters.

The palms murmured noisily of seasons and centuries, mating and birth and the transplanting of life. Nature knows nothing of death.

The river spoke to the brook.

"Why, O Young Water, do you hurry and hurl yourself so riotously about with your chatter and song? You disturb my sleep."

"Because, O Venerable One," replied the brook, "I am young. The flowers bloom, the trees and wind say beautiful things to me: there are lovers beneath the orange trees on my banks,—but most of all because the moon shines upon me with a full face."

"That is not sufficient reason for you to disturb my sleep," the river retorted. "I have cut down mountains and moved whole valleys into the sea, and I am not so noisy as *you* are."

The river slapped its banks angrily.

"But," added the brook diffidently, "I passed numbers of lovers as I came on. There was also a sweet-voiced night-bird."

"No matter, no matter!" scolded the river. "I have seen millions of lovers, child. I have borne them up and down, listened to those things that are uttered more with the breath than with the lips, gathered infinite tears, and some lovers have even flung themselves upon the soft couch I keep in my bosom, and slept."

"Tell me about some of them!" eagerly begged the brook.

"Oh, well," the river muttered, "I am wide awake now, and I suppose brooks must be humored."

THE RIVER'S STORY

"Long ago, as men count years, men who were pale of skin held a dark race of men in a bondage. The dark ones cried out in sorrow and travail,—not here in my country, but farther north. Many rivers carried their tears to the sea and the tide would bring some of them to me. The Wind brought cries without end.

"But there were some among the slaves who did not weep, but fled in the night to safety,—some to the far north, some to the far south, for here the red man, the panther, and the bear alone were to be feared. One of them from the banks of the Savannah came here. He was large and black and strong. His heart was strong and thudded with an iron sound in his breast. The forest made way for him, the beasts were afraid of him, and he built a house. He gathered stones and bits of metal, yellow and white—such as men love and for which they die—and grew wealthy. How? I do not know. Rivers take no notice of such things. We sweep men, stones, metal—all, ALL to the sea. All are as grass; all must to the sea in the end.

"He married Swift Deer, a Cherokee Maiden, and five years— as men love to clip Time into bits—passed.

"They had now a daughter, Magnolia Flower they called her, for she came at the time of their opening.

"When they had been married five years, she was four years old.

"Then the tide brought trouble rumors to me of hate, strife and destruction,—war, war, war.

"The blood of those born in the North flowed to sea, mingled with that of the southern-born. Bitter Waters, Troubled Winds. Rains that washed the dust from Heaven but could not beat back the wails of anguish, the thirst for blood and glory; the prayers for that which God gives not into the hands of man—Vengeance,— fires of hate to sear and scorch the ground: wells of acid tears to blight the leaf.

"Then all men walked free in the land, and Wind and Water again grew sweet.

"The man-made time notches flew by, and Magnolia Flower was in full-bloom. Her large eyes burned so brightly in her dark-brown face that the Negroes trembled when she looked angrily upon them. 'She curses with her eyes,' they said. 'Some evil surely will follow.'

"Black men came and went now as they pleased and the father had many to serve him, for now he had built a house such as white men owned when he was in bondage.

"His heart, of the ex-slave Bentley, was iron to all but Magnolia Flower. Swift Deer was no longer swift. Too many kicks and blows, too many grim chokings had slowed her feet and heart.

"He had done violence to workmen. There was little law in this jungle, and that was his,—'Do as I bid you or suffer my punishment.'

"He was hated, but feared more.

"He hated anything that bore the slightest resemblance to his former oppressors. His servants must be black, very black or Cherokee.

"The flower was seventeen and beautiful. Bentley thought often of a mate for her now, but one that would not offend him either in spirit or flesh. He must be full of humility, and black.

"One day, as the sun gave me a good-night kiss and the stars began their revels, I bore a young Negro yet not a Negro, for his skin was the color of freshly barked cypress, golden with the curly black hair of the white man.

"There were many Negroes in Bentley's Village and he wished to build a school that would teach them useful things.

"Bentley hated him at once; but ordered a school-house to be built, for he wished Magnolia to read and write.

"But before two weeks had passed, the teacher had taught the Flower to read strange marvels with her dark eyes, and she had taught the teacher to sing with his eyes, his hands, his whole body in her presence or whenever he thought of her,—not in her father's house, but beneath that clump of palms, those three that bathe their toes eternally and talk.

"They busied themselves with dreams of creation, while Bentley swore the foundation of the school-room into place.

" 'Nothing remains for me to do, now that I have your consent, but to ask your father for your sweet self. I know I am poor, but I have a great Vision, a high purpose, and he shall not be ashamed of me!'

"She clung fearfully to him.

" 'No, don't, John, don't. He'll say 'Naw!' and cuss. He—he don't like you at all. Youse too white.'

" 'I'll get him out of that, just trust me, precious. Then I can just *own* you—just let me talk to him!'

"She wept and pleaded with him—told him of Bentley's terrible anger and his violence, begged him to take her away and send her father word; but he refused to hear her, and walked up to her house and seated himself upon the broad verandah to wait for the father of Magnolia Flower.

"She flew to Swift Deer and begged her to persuade her lover not to brave Bentley's anger. The older woman crept out and tearfully implored him to go. He stayed.

"At dusk Bentley came swearing in. It had been a hot day; the men had cut several poor pieces of timber and seemed all bent on driving him to the crazy-house, he complained.

"Swift Deer slunk into the house at his approach, dragging her daughter after her.

"What followed was too violent for words to tell,—strength against strength, steel against steel. Threats bellowed from Bentley's bull throat seemed no more than little puffs of air to the lover. Of course, he would leave Bentley's house; but he would stay in the vicinity until he was told to leave by the Flower,—his Flower of sweetness and purity—and he would marry her unless hell froze over.

" 'Better eat up dem words an' git out whilst ah letcher,' the old man growled.

"Bentley drew up his lips in a great roll glare.

" 'No!' John shouted, giving him glare for his rage boiling and tumbling out from behind these ramparts, as it were. His eye reddened, a vessel in the center of his forehead stood out, gorged with blood, and his great hands twitched. For good or evil, Bentley was a strong man, mind and body.

"Swift Deer could no longer restrain her daughter. Magnolia Flower burst triumphantly upon the verandah.

" 'Well, papa, you don't say that I haven't picked a man. No one else in forty miles round would stand up to you like John!'

" 'Ham! Jim! Israel!' Bentley howled, on the verge of apoplexy. The men appeared. 'Take dis here yaller skunk an' lock him in dat back-room. I'm a gonna hang 'im high as Hamon come sun up, law uh no law.'

"A short struggle, and John was tied hand and foot.

" 'Stop!' cried Magnolia Flower, fighting, clawing, biting, kicking like a brown fiend for her lover. One brawny worker held her until John was helplessly bound.

"But when she looked at all three of the men with her eye of fire, they shook in superstitious fear.

" 'Oh, Moh Gawd!' breathed Ham, terrified. 'She's cussing us, she's cussing us all wid her eyes. Sump'm sho gwine happen.'

"Her eye was indeed something to affright the timid and even give the strong heart pause. A woman robbed of her love is more terrible than an army with banners.

" 'Oh, I wish I could!' she uttered in a voice flat with intensity. 'You'd all drop dead on the spot.'

"Swift Deer had crept out and stood beside the child. She screamed and clasped her hands over her daughter's lips.

" 'Say not such words, Magnolia,' " she pleaded. 'Take them back into your bosom unsaid.'

" 'Leave her be,' Bentley laughed acidly. 'Ah got a dose uh mah medicine ready for her too. Befo' ah hangs dis yaller pole-cat ahm gwinter marry her to crazy Joe, an' John kin look on; den ah'll hang *him*, and she kin look on. Magnolia and Joe oughter have fine black chillen. Ha! Ha!'

"The girl never uttered a sound. She smiled with her lips but her eyes burned every bit of courage to cinders in those who saw her.

"John was locked in the stout back-room. The windows were guarded and Ham sat with a loaded gun at the door.

"Magnolia was locked in the parlor where she ran up and down, tearing her heavy black hair. She beat helplessly upon the doors, she hammered the windows, making little mewing noises in her throat like a cat deprived of her litter.

"The house grew grimly still. Bentley had forced his wife to accompany him to their bedroom. She lay fearfully awake but he slept peacefully, if noisily.

" 'Magnolia Flower!' Ham called softly as he turned the key stealthily in the lock of her prison. 'Come on out. Ah caint stan' dis here weekedness uh yo pappy!'

" 'No thank you, Ham. I'll stay right here and make him kill me long with John, if you don't let him out too.'

" 'Lawd a mussy knows ah wisht ah could, but de ole man's got de key in his britches.'

" 'I'm going and get it, Ham,' she announced as she stepped over the threshold to freedom.

" 'Lawd! He'll kill me sho's you born.'

"Her feet were already on the stairs.

" 'I'll have that key or die. Ham, you put some victuals in that rowboat.'

"Half for love, half for fear, Ham obeyed.

"No one but Magnolia Flower would have entered Bentley's bed-room as she did, under the circumstances but to her the circumstances were her reasons for going. The big horse pistol under his pillow, the rack of guns in the hall, and her father's giant hands—none of these stopped her. She knew three lives,—her own, her lover's, and Ham's—hung on her success; but she went and returned with that key.

"One minute more and they flew down the path to the three leaning palms into the boat away northward.

"The morning came. Bentley ate hugely. The new rope hung ominously from the arm of the giant oak in the yard. Preacher Ike had eaten his breakfast with Bentley and the idiot, Crazy Joe, had forced himself into a pair of clean hickory pants.

"Bentley turned the key and flung open the door, stood still a moment in a grey rage and stalked to the back-room door, feeling for the key meanwhile.

"When he had fully convinced himself that the key was gone, he did not bother to open the door.

" 'Ham, it 'pears dat Magnolia an' dat yaller dog aint heah dis mawnin', so you an' Swift Deer will hafta do, being ez y'all let 'em git away.' He said this calmly and stalked toward the gun rack; but his anger was too large to be contained in one human heart. His arteries corded his face, his eyes popped, and he fell senseless as he stretched his hand for the gun. Rage had burst his heart at being outwitted by a girl.

"This all happened more than forty years ago, as men reckon time. Soon Swift Deer died, and the house built by strong Bentley fell to decay. White men came and built a town and Magnolia Flower and her eyes passed from the hearts of people who had known her."

The brook had listened, tensely thrilled to its very bottom at times. The river flowed calmly on, shimmering under the moon as it moved ceaselessly to the sea.

An old couple picked their way down to the water's edge. He

had once been tall—he still bore himself well. The little old woman clung lovingly to his arm.

"It's been forty-seven years, John," she said sweetly, her voice full of fear. "Do you think we can find the place?"

"Why yes, Magnolia, my Flower, unless they have cut down our trees; but if they are standing, we'll know 'em—couldn't help it."

"Yes, sweetheart, there they are. Hurry and let's sit on the roots like we used to and trail our fingers in the water. Love is wonderful, isn't it, dear?"

They hugged the trunks of the three clustering palms lovingly; then hugged each other and sat down shyly upon the heaped up roots.

"You never have regretted, Magnolia?"

"Of course not! But, John, listen, did you ever hear a river make such a sound? Why it seems almost as if it were talking—that murmuring noise, you know."

"Maybe, it's welcoming us back. I always felt that it loved you and me, somehow."

Muttsy

The piano in Ma Turner's back parlor stuttered and wailed. The pianist kept time with his heel and informed an imaginary deserter that "she might leave and go to Halimufack, but his slow-drag would bring her back," mournfully with a memory of tom-toms running rhythm through the plaint.

Fewclothes burst through the portieres, a brown chrysalis from a dingy red cocoon, and touched the player on the shoulder.

"Say, Muttsy," he stage whispered. "Ma's got a new lil' biddy in there—just come. And say—her foot would make all of dese Harlem babies a Sunday face."

"Whut she look like?" Muttsy drawled, trying to maintain his characteristic pose of indifference to the female.

"Brown skin, patent leather grass on her knob, kinder tallish. She's a lil' skinny," he added apologetically, "but ah'm willing to buy corn for that lil' chicken."

Muttsy lifted his six feet from the piano bench as slowly as his curiosity would let him and sauntered to the portieres for a peep:

The sight was as pleasing as Fewclothes had stated—only more so. He went on in the room which Ma always kept empty. It was her receiving room—her "front."

From Ma's manner it was evident that she was very glad to see the girl. She could see that the girl was not overjoyed in her presence, but attributed that to southern greenness.

"Who you say sentcher heah, dearie?" Ma asked, her face

trying to beam, but looking harder and more forbidding.

"Uh-a-a man down at the boat landing where I got off—North River. I jus' come in on the boat."

Ma's husband from his corner spoke up.

"Musta been Bluefront."

"Yeah, musta been him," Muttsy agreed.

"Oh, it's all right, honey, we New Yorkers likes to know who we'se takin' in, dearie. We has to be keerful. Whut did you say yo' name was?"

"Pinkie, yes, mam, Pinkie Jones."

Ma stared hard at the little old battered reticule that the girl carried for luggage—not many clothes if that was all—she reflected. But Pinkie had everything she needed in her face—many many trunks full. Several of them for Ma. She noticed the cold-reddened knuckles of her bare hands too.

"Come on upstairs to yo' room—thass all right 'bout the price—we'll come to some 'greement tomorrow. Jes' go up and take off yo things."

Pinkie put back the little rusty leather purse of another generation and followed Ma. She didn't like Ma—her smile resembled the smile of the Wolf in Red Riding Hood. Anyway back in Eatonville, Florida, "ladies," especially old ones, didn't put powder and paint on the face.

"Forty-dollars-Kate sure landed a pippin' dis time," said Muttsy, sotto voce, to Fewclothes back at the piano. "If she ain't, then there ain't a hound dawk in Georgy. Ah'm goin' home an' dress."

No one else in the crowded back parlor let alone the house knew of Pinkie's coming. They danced on, played on, sang their "blues" and lived on hotly their intense lives. The two men who had seen her—no one counted ole man Turner—went on playing too, but kept an ear cocked for her coming.

She followed Ma downstairs and seated herself in the parlor with the old man. He sat in a big rocker before a copper-lined gas stove, indolence in every gesture.

"Ah'm Ma's husband," he announced by way of making conversation.

"Now you jus' shut up!" Ma commanded severely. "You gointer git yo' teeth knocked down yo' throat yit for runnin' yo' tongue. Lemme talk to dis gal—dis is *mah* house. You sets on the stool un do nothin' too much tuh have anything tuh talk over!"

"Oh, Lawd," groaned the old man feeling a knee that always pained him at the mention of work. "Oh, Lawd, will you sen' yo' fiery chariot an' take me 'way from heah?"

"Aw shet up!" the woman spit out. "Lawd don't wantcher—devil wouldn't have yuh." She peered into the girl's face and leaned back satisfied.

"Well, girlie, you kin be a lotta help tuh me 'round dis house if you takes un intrus' in things—oh Lawd!" She leaped up from her seat. "That's mah bread ah smell burnin! . . ."

No sooner had Ma's feet cleared the room than the old man came to life again. He peered furtively after the broad back of his wife.

"Know who she is," he asked Pinkie in an awed whisper. She shook her head. "You don't? Dat's Forty-dollars-Kate!"

"Forty-dollars-Kate?" Pinkie repeated open eyed. "Naw, I don't know nothin' 'bout her."

"Sh-h," cautioned the old man. "Course you don't. I fuhgits you aint nothin' tall but a young 'un. Twenty-five years ago they all called her dat 'cause she *wuz* 'Forty-dollars-Kate.' She sho' wuz some p'utty 'oman—great big robus' lookin' gal. Men wuz glad 'nough to spend forty dollars on her if dey had it. She didn't lose no time wid dem dat didn't have it."

He grinned ingratiatingly at Pinkie and leaned nearer.

"But you'se better lookin' than she ever wuz, you might—taint no tellin' whut you might do ef you git some sense. I'm a gointer teach you, hear?"

"Yessuh," the girl managed to answer with an almost paralyzed tongue.

"Thass a good girl. You jus' lissen to me an' you'll pull thew alright."

He glanced at the girl sitting timidly upon the edge of the chair and scolded.

"Don't set dataway," he ejaculated. "Yo' back bone ain't no ram rod. Kinda scooch down on the for'ard edge uh de chear lak dis." (He demonstrated by "scooching" forward so far that he was almost sitting on his shoulder-blades.) The girl slumped a trifle.

"Is you got a job yit?"

"Nawsuh," she answered slowly, "but I reckon I'll have one soon. Ain't been in town a day yet."

"You looks kinda young—kinda little biddy. Is you been to school much?"

"Yessuh, went thew eight reader. I'm goin' again when I get a chance."

"Dat so? Well ah reckon ah kin talk some Latin tuh yuh den." He cleared his throat loudly. "Whut's you entitlum?"

"I don't know," said the girl in confusion.

"Well, den, whut's you entrimmins," he queried with a bit of braggadocio in his voice.

"I don't know," from the girl, after a long awkward pause.

"You chillun don't learn nothin' in school dese days. Is you got to 'goes into' yit?"

"You mean long division?"

"Ain't askin' 'bout de longness of it, dat don't make no difference," he retorted. "Sence you goin' stay heah ah'll edgecate yuh—do yuh know how to eat a fish—uh nice brown fried fish?"

"Yessuh," she answered quickly, looking about for the fish.

"How?"

"Why, you jus' eat it with corn bread," she said, a bit disappointed at the non-appearance of the fish.

"Well, ah'll tell yuh," he patronized. "You starts at de tail and liffs de meat off de bones sorter gentle and eats him clear tuh de head on dat side; den you turn 'im ovah an' commence at de tail agin and eat right up tuh de head; den you push *dem* bones way tuh one side an' takes another fish an' so on 'till de end—well, 'till der ain't no mo'!"

He mentally digested the fish and went on. "See," he pointed accusingly at her feet, "you don't even know how tuh warm yoself! You settin' dere wid yo' feet ev'y which a way. Dat ain't de way tuh git wahm. Now look at *mah* feet. Dass right put bofe big toes right togethah—now shove 'em close up tuh de fiah; now lean back so! Dass de way. Ah knows uh heap uh things tuh teach yuh sense you gointer live heah—ah learns all of 'em while de ole lady is paddlin' roun' out dere in de yard."

Ma appeared at the door and the old man withdrew so far into his rags that he all but disappeared. They went to supper where there was fried fish but forgot all rules for eating it and just ate heartily. She helped with the dishes and returned to the parlor. A little later some more men and women knocked and were admitted after the same furtive peering out through the nearest crack of the door. Ma carried them all back to the kitchen and Pinkie heard the clink of glasses and much loud laughter.

Women came in by ones and twos, some in shabby coats turned up about the ears, and with various cheap but showy hats crushed down over unkempt hair. More men, more women, more trips to the kitchen with loud laughter.

Pinkie grew uneasy. Both men and women stared at her. She kept strictly to her place. Ma came in and tried to make her join the others.

"Come on in, honey, a lil' toddy ain't gointer hurt nobody. Evebody knows *me*, ah wouldn't touch a hair on yo' head. Come on in, dearie, all th' men wants tuh meetcher."

Pinkie smelt the liquor on Ma's breath and felt contaminated at her touch. She wished herself back home again even with the ill treatment and squalor. She thought of the three dollars she had secreted in her shoe—she had been warned against pickpockets—and flight but where? Nowhere. For there was no home to which *she* could return, nor any place else she knew of. But when she got a job, she'd scrape herself clear of people who took toddies.

A very black man sat on the piano stool playing as only a Negro can with hands, stamping with his feet and the rest of his body keeping time.

Ahm gointer make me a graveyard of mah own
Ahm gointer make me a graveyard of mah own
Carried me down on de smoky Road—

Pinkie, weary of Ma's maudlin coaxing caught these lines as she was being pulled and coaxed into the kitchen. Everyone in there was shaking shimmies to music, rolling eyes heavenward as they picked imaginary grapes out of the air, or drinking. "Folkes," shouted Ma, "look a heah! Shut up dis racket! Ah wantcher tuh meet Pinkie Jones. She's de bes' frien' ah got." Ma flopped into a chair and began to cry into her whiskey glass.

"Mah comperments!" The men almost shouted. The women were less, much less enthusiastic.

"Dass de las' run uh shad," laughed a woman called Ada, pointing to Pinkie's slenderness.

"Jes' lak a bar uh soap aftah uh hard week's wash," Bertha chimed in and laughed uproariously. The men didn't help.

"Oh, Miss Pinkie," said Bluefront, removing his Stetson for the first time, "Ma'am, also Ma'am, ef you wuz tuh see me settin' straddle of uh Mud-cat leadin' a minner whut ud you think?"

"I-er, oh, I don't know, suh. I didn't know you-er anybody could ride uh fish."

"Stick uh roun' me, baby, an' you'll wear diamon's." Bluefront swaggered. "Look heah, lil' Pigmeat, youse *some* sharp! If you didn't had but one eye ah'd think you wuz a needle—thass how sharp you looks to me. Say, mah right foot is itchin'. Do dat mean ah'm gointer walk on some strange ground wid you?"

"Naw, indeedy," cut in Fewclothes. "It jes' means you feet needs to walk in some strange water—wid a lil' red seal lye thowed in."

But he was not to have a monopoly. Fewclothes and Shorty joined the chase and poor Pinkie found it impossible to retreat to her place beside the old man. She hung her head, embarrassed that she did not understand their mode of speech; she felt the unfriendly eyes of the women, and she loathed the smell of liquor that filled the house now. The piano still rumbled and wailed that same song—

> *Carried me down on de Smoky Road*
> *Brought me back on de coolin' board*
> *Ahm gointer make me a graveyard of mah own.*

A surge of cold, fresh air from the outside stirred the smoke and liquor fumes and Pinkie knew that the front door was open. She turned her eyes that way and thought of flight to the clean outside. The door stood wide open and a tall figure in an overcoat with a fur collar stood there.

"Good Gawd, Muttsy! Shet 'at do'," cried Shorty. "Dass a pure razor blowing out dere tonight. Ah didn't know you wuz outa here nohow."

> *Carried me down on de Smoky Road*
> *Brought me back on de coolin' board*
> *Ahm gointer make me a graveyard of mah own,*

sang Muttsy, looking as if he sought someone and banged the door shut on the last words. He strode on in without removing hat or coat.

Pinkie saw in this short space that all the men deferred to him, that all the women sought his notice. She tried timidly to squeeze between two of the men and return to the quiet place beside old man Turner, thinking that Muttsy would hold the attention of her captors until she had escaped. But Muttsy spied her through the men about her and joined them. By this time her exasperation and embarrassment had her on the point of tears.

"Well, whadda yuh know about dis!" he exclaimed, "A real lil' pullet."

"Look out dere, Muttsy," drawled Dramsleg with objection, catching Pinkie by the arm and trying to draw her toward him. "Lemme tell dis lil' Pink Mama how crazy ah is 'bout her mahself. Ah ain't got no lady atall an'—"

"Aw, shut up Drams," Muttsy said sternly, "put yo' pocketbook where yo' mouf is, an' somebody will lissen. Ah'm a heavy-sugar papa. Ah eats fried chicken when the rest of you niggers is drinking rain water.''

He thrust some of the others aside and stood squarely before her. With her downcast eyes, she saw his well polished shoes, creased trousers, gloved hands and at last timidly raised her eyes to his face.

"Look a heah!'' he frowned, "you roughnecks done got dis baby ready tuh cry.''

He put his forefinger under her chin and made her look at him. And for some reason he removed his hat.

"Come on in the sittin' room an' le's talk. Come on befo' some uh dese niggers sprinkle some salt on yuh and eat yuh clean up lak uh radish.'' Dramsleg looked after Muttsy and the girl as they swam through the smoke into the front room. He beckoned to Bluefront.

"Hey, Bluefront! Ain't you mah fren'?''

"Yep,'' answered Bluefront.

"Well, then why cain't you help me? Muttsy done done me dirt wid the lil' pig-meat—throw a louse on 'im.''

Pinkie's hair was slipping down. She felt it, but her selfconsciousness prevented her catching it and down it fell in a heavy roll that spread out and covered her nearly to the waist. She followed Muttsy into the front room and again sat shrinking in the corner. She did not wish to talk to Muttsy nor anyone else in that house, but there were fewer people in this room.

"Phew!'' cried Bluefront, "dat baby sho got some righteous moss on her keg—dass reg'lar 'nearrow mah Gawd tuh thee' stuff.'' He made a lengthy gesture with his arms as if combing out long, silky hair.

"Shux,'' sneered Ada in a moist, alcoholic voice. "Dat ain't nothin.' Mah haih useter be so's ah could set on it.''

There was general laughter from the men.

"Yas, ah know it's de truth!'' shouted Shorty. "It's jes' ez close tuh yo' head *now* ez ninety-nine is tuh uh hund'ed.''

"Ah'll call Muttsy tuh you,'' Ada threatened.

"Oh, 'oman, Muttsy ain't got you tuh study 'bout no mo' cause he's parkin' his heart wid dat lil' chicken wid white-folks' haih. Why, dat lil' chicken's foot would make you a Sunday face."

General laughter again. Ada dashed the whiskey glass upon the floor with the determined stalk of an angry tiger and arose and started forward.

"Muttsy Owens, uh nobody else ain't to gointer make no fool outer *me*. Dat lil' kack girl ain't gointer put *me* on de bricks—not much."

Perhaps Muttsy heard her, perhaps he saw her out of the corner of his eye and read her mood. But knowing the woman as he did he might have known what she would do under such circumstances. At any rate he got to his feet as she entered the room where he sat with Pinkie.

"Ah know you ain't lost yo' head sho' 'nuff, 'oman. 'Deed, Gawd knows you bettah go 'way f'um me." He said this in a low, steady voice. The music stopped, the talking stopped and even the drinkers paused. Nothing happened, for Ada looked straight into Muttsy's eyes and went on outside.

"Miss Pinkie, Ah votes you g'wan tuh bed," Muttsy said suddenly to the girl.

"Yes-suh."

"An' don't you worry 'bout no job. Ah knows where you kin git a good one. Ah'll go see em first an' tell yuh tomorrow night."

She went off to bed upstairs. The rich baritone of the piano-player came up to her as did laughter and shouting. But she was tired and slept soundly.

Ma shuffled in after eight the next morning. "Darlin', ain't you got 'nuff sleep yit?"

Pinkie opened her eyes a trifle. "Ain't you the puttiest lil' trick! An' Muttsy done gone crazy 'bout yuh! Chile, he's lousy wid money an' diamon's an' everything— Yuh better grab him quick. Some folks has all de luck. Heah ah is—got uh man dat hates work lak de devil hates holy water. Ah gotta make dis house pay!"

Pinkie's eyes opened wide. "What does Mr. Muttsy do?"

"Mah Gawd, chile! He's de bes' gambler in three states, cards, craps un hawses. He could be a boss stevedore if he so wanted. The big boss down on de dock would give him a fat job—just begs him to take it cause he can manage the men. He's the biggest hero they got since Harry Wills left the waterfront. But he won't take it cause he makes so much wid the games.''

"He's awful good-lookin,'' Pinkie agreed, ''an' he been mighty nice tuh me—but I like men to work. I wish he would. Gamblin' ain't nice.''

"Yeah, 'tis, ef you makes money lak Muttsy. Maybe yo ain't noticed dat diamon' set in his tooth. He picks women up when he wants tuh an' puts 'em down when he choose.''

Pinkie turned her face to the wall and shuddered. Ma paid no attention.

"You doan hafta git up till you git good an' ready, Muttsy says. Ah mean you kin stay roun' the house 'till you come to, sorter.''

Another day passed. Its darkness woke up the land east of Lenox—all that land between the railroad tracks and the river. It was very ugly by day, and night kindly hid some of its sordid homeliness. Yes, nighttime gave it life.

The same women, or others just like them, came to Ma Turner's. The same men, or men just like them, came also and treated them to liquor or mistreated them with fists or cruel jibes. Ma got half drunk as usual and cried over everyone who would let her.

Muttsy came alone and went straight to Pinkie where she sat trying to shrink into the wall. She had feared that he would not come.

"Howdy do, Miss Pinkie.''

"How'do do, Mistah Owens,'' she actually achieved a smile. "Did you see bout m'job?''

"Well, yeah—but the lady says she won't needya fuh uh week yet. Doan' worry. Ma ain't gointer push yuh foh room rent. Mah wrist ain't got no cramps.''

Pinkie half sobbed: "Ah wantsa job now!''

"Didn't ah say dass alright? Well, Muttsy doan lie. Shux! Ah might jes' es well tell yuh—ahm crazy 'bout yuh—money no objeck.''

It was the girl herself who first mentioned "bed" this night. He suffered her to go without protest.

The next night she did not come into the sitting room. She went to bed as soon as the dinner things had been cleared. Ma begged and cried, but Pinkie pretended illness and kept to her bed. This she repeated the next night and the next. Every night Muttsy came and every night he added to his sartorial splendor; but each night he went away, disappointed, more evidently crestfallen than before.

But the insistence for escape from her strange surroundings grew on the girl. When Ma was busy elsewhere, she would take out the three one dollar bills from her shoe and reconsider her limitations. If that job would only come on! She felt shut in, imprisoned, walled in with these women who talked of nothing but men and the numbers and drink, and men who talked of nothing but the numbers and drink and women. And desperation took her.

One night she was still waiting for the job—Ma's alcoholic tears prevailed. Pinkie took a drink. She drank the stuff mixed with sugar and water and crept to bed even as the dizziness came on. She would not wake tonight. Tomorrow, maybe, the job would come and freedom.

The piano thumped but Pinkie did not hear; the shouts, laughter and cries did not reach her that night. Downstairs Muttsy pushed Ma into a corner.

"Looky heah, Ma. Dat girl done played me long enough. Ah pays her room rent, ah pays her boahd an' all ah gets is uh hunk of ice. Now you said you wuz gointer fix things—you tole me so las' night an' heah she done gone tuh bed on me agin.''

"Deed, ah caint do nothin' wid huh. She's thinkin' sho' nuff you goin' git her uh job and she fret so cause tain't come, dat she drunk uh toddy un hits knocked her down jes lak uh log.''

"Ada an' all uh them laffin—they say ah done crapped.'' He felt injured. "Caint ah go talk to her?''

"Lawdy, Muttsy, dat gal dead drunk an' sleepin' lak she's buried."

"Well, caint ah go up an'—an' speak tuh her jus' the same." A yellow backed bill from Muttsy's roll found itself in Ma's hand and put her in such good humor that she let old man Turner talk all he wanted for the rest of the night.

"Yas, Muttsy, gwan in. Youse *mah* frien'."

Muttsy hurried up to the room indicated. He felt shaky inside there with Pinkie, somehow, but he approached the bed and stood for awhile looking down upon her. Her hair in confusion about her face and swinging off the bedside; the brown arms revealed and the soft lips. He blew out the match he had struck and kissed her full in the mouth, kissed her several times and passed his hand over her neck and throat and then hungrily down upon her breast. But here he drew back.

"Naw," he said sternly to himself, "ah ain't goin' ter play her wid no loaded dice." Then quickly he covered her with the blanket to her chin, kissed her again upon the lips and tipped down into the darkness of the vestibule.

"Ah reckon ah bettah git married." He soliloquized. "B'lieve me, ah will, an' go uptown wid dicties."

He lit a cigar and stood there on the steps puffing and thinking for some time. His name was called inside the sitting room several times but he pretended not to hear. At last he stole back into the room where slept the girl who unwittingly and unwillingly was making him do queer things. He tipped up to the bed again and knelt there holding her hands so fiercely that she groaned without waking. He watched her and he wanted her so that he wished to crush her in his love; crush and crush and hurt her against himself, but somehow he resisted the impulse and merely kissed her lips again, kissed her hands back and front, removed the largest diamond ring from his hand and slipped it on her engagement finger. It was much too large so he closed her hand and tucked it securely beneath the covers.

"She's *mine!*" he said triumphantly. "All mine!"

He switched off the light and softly closed the door as he went out again to the steps. He had gone up to the bed room from the sitting room boldly, caring not who knew that Muttsy Owens took what he wanted. He was stealing forth afraid that someone might *suspect* that he had been there. There is no secret love in those barrens; it is a thing to be approached boisterously and without delay or dalliance. One loves when one wills, and ceases when it palls. There is nothing sacred or hidden—all subject to coarse jokes. So Muttsy re-entered the sitting room from the steps as if he had been into the street.

"Where you been Muttsy?" whined Ada with an awkward attempt at coyness.

"What *you* wanta know for?" he asked roughly.

"Now, Muttsy you know you ain't treatin' me right, honey. How come you runnin' de hawg ovah me lak you do?"

"Git outa mah face 'oman. Keep yo' han's offa me." He clapped on his hat and strode from the house.

Pinkie awoke with a gripping stomach and thumping head.

Ma bustled in. "How yuh feelin' darlin'? Youse jes lak a li'l doll baby."

"I got a headache, terrible from that ole whiskey. Thass mah first und las' drink long as I live." She felt the ring.

"Whut's this?" she asked and drew her hand out to the light.

"Dat's Muttsy' ring. Ah seen him wid it fuh two years. How'd y'all make out? He sho is one thur'bred."

"Muttsy? When? I didn't see no Muttsy."

"Dearie, you doan' hafta tell yo' bizniss ef you doan wanta. Ahm a hush-mouf. Thass all right, keep yo' bizniss to yo' self." Ma bleared her eyes wisely. "But ah know Muttsy wuz up heah tuh see yuh las' night. Doan' mine *me* honey, gwan wid 'im. He'll treat yuh right. Ah *knows* he's crazy 'bout yuh. An' all de women is crazy 'bout *him*. Lawd! lookit dat ring!" Ma regarded it greedily for a long time, but she turned and walked toward the door at last. "Git up darlin'. Ah got fried chicking fuh breckfus' un mush melon."

She went on to the kitchen. Ma's revelation sunk deeper, then there was the ring. Pinkie hurled the ring across the room and leaped out of bed.

"He ain't goin' to make *me* none of his women—I'll die first! I'm goin' outa this house if I starve, lemme starve!"

She got up and plunged her face into the cold water on the washstand in the corner and hurled herself into the shabby clothes, thrust the three dollars which she had never had occasion to spend, under the pillow where Ma would be sure to find them and slipped noiselessly out of the house and fled down Fifth Avenue toward the Park that marked the beginning of the Barrens. She did not know where she was going, and cared little so long as she removed herself as far as possible from the house where the great evil threatened her.

At ten o'clock that same morning, Muttsy Owens dressed his flashiest best, drove up to Ma's door in a cab, the most luxurious that could be hired. He had gone so far as to stick two one hundred dollar notes to the inside of the windshield. Ma was overcome.

"Muttsy, dearie, what you doin' heah so soon? Pinkie sho has got you goin'. Un in a swell cab too—gee!"

"Ahm gointer git mah'ried tuh de doll baby, thass how come. An' ahm gointer treat her white too."

"Umhumh! Thass how come de ring! You oughtn't never fuhgit me, Muttsy, fuh puttin' y'all together. But ah never thought you'd mah'ry *nobody*—you allus said you wouldn't."

"An' ah wouldn't neither ef ah hadn't of seen *her*. Where she is?"

"In de room dressin'. She never tole me nothin' 'bout dis."

"She doan' know. She wuz sleep when ah made up mah mind an' slipped on de ring. But ah never miss no girl ah wants, you knows me."

"Everybody in this man's town knows you gets whut you wants."

"Naw, ah come tuh take her to brek'fus 'fo we goes tuh de cote-house."

"An' y'all stay heah and eat wid me. You go call her whilst ah set de grub on table."

Muttsy, with a lordly stride, went up to Pinkie's door and

rapped and waited and rapped and waited three times. Growing impatient or thinking her still asleep, he flung open the door and entered.

The first thing that struck him was the empty bed; the next was the glitter of his diamond ring upon the floor. He stumbled out to Ma. She was gone, no doubt of that.

"She looked awful funny when ah tole her you wuz in heah, but ah thought she wuz puttin' on airs," Ma declared finally.

"She thinks ah played her wid a marked deck, but ah didn't. Ef ah could see her she'd love me. Ah know she would. 'Cause ah'd make her," Muttsy lamented.

"I don't know, Muttsy. She ain't no New Yorker, and she thinks gamblin' is awful."

"Zat all she got against me? Ah'll fix that up in a minute. You help me find her and ah'll do anything she says jus' so she marries me." He laughed ruefully. "Looks like ah crapped this time, don't it, ma?"

The next day Muttsy was foreman of two hundred stevedores. How he did make them work. But oh how cheerfully they did their best for him. The company begrudged not one cent of his pay. He searched diligently, paid money to other searchers, went every night to Ma's to see if by chance the girl had returned or if any clues had turned up.

Two weeks passed this way. Black empty days for Muttsy.

Then he found her. He was coming home from work. When crossing Seventh Avenue at 135th Street they almost collided. He seized her and began pleading before she even had time to recognize him.

He turned and followed her; took the employment office slip from her hand and destroyed it, took her arm and held it. He must have been very convincing for at 125th Street they entered a taxi that headed uptown again. Muttsy was smiling amiably upon the whole round world.

A month later, as Muttsy stood on the dock hustling his men to greater endeavor, Bluefront flashed past with his truck. "Say, Muttsy, you don't know what you missin' since you quit de game.

Ah cleaned out de whole bunch las' night.'' He flashed a roll and laughed. ''It don't seem like a month ago you wuz king uh de bones in Harlem.'' He vanished down the gangplank into the ship's hold.

As he raced back up the gangplank with his loaded truck Muttsy answered him. ''And now, I'm King of the Boneheads—which being interpreted means stevedores. Come on over behind dis crate wid yo' roll. Mah wrist ain't got no cramp 'cause ah'm married. You'se gettin' too sassy.''

''Thought you wuzn't gointer shoot no mo'!'' Bluefront temporized.

''Aw Hell! Come on back heah,'' he said impatiently. ''Ah'll shoot you any way you wants to—hard or soft roll—you'se trying to stall. You know ah don't crap neither. Come on, mah Pinkie needs a fur coat and you stevedores is got to buy it.''

He was on his knees with Bluefront. There was a quick movement of Muttsy's wrist, and the cubes flew out on a piece of burlap spread for the purpose—a perfect seven.

''Hot dog!'' he exulted. ''Look at dem babies gallop!'' His wrist quivered again. ''Nine for point!'' he gloated. ''Hah!'' There was another quick shake and nine turned up again. ''Shove in, Bluefront, shove in dat roll, dese babies is crying fuh it.''

Bluefront laid down two dollars grudgingly. ''You said you wuzn't gointer roll no mo' dice after you got married,'' he grumbled.

But Muttsy had tasted blood. His flexible wrist was already in the midst of the next play.

''Come on, Bluefront, stop bellyachin'. Ah shoots huy for de roll!'' He reached for his own pocket and laid down a roll of yellow bills beside Bluefront's. His hand quivered and the cubes skipped out again. ''Nine!'' He snapped his fingers like a trap-drum and gathered in the money.

''Doxology, Bluefront. Git back in de line wid yo' truck an' send de others roun' heah one by one. What man can't keep one li'l wife an' two li'l bones? Hurry 'em up, Blue!''

'Possum or Pig?

Before freedom there was a house slave very much in the confidence of the Master. But young pigs began to disappear, and for good reasons the faithful house slave fell under suspicion.

One night, after his duties at the "big house" were over, he was sitting before his cabin fire. From a pot was seeping the odor of young pig. There was a knock at the door.

"Who dat?" he asked cautiously.

"It's me, John," came the Master's voice.

"Lawd, now, Massa, whut you want way down heah?"

"I'm cold, John. I want to come in."

"Now, Massa, ah jes' lef' a lovely hot fire at de big house. You aughter gwan up dere an' git warm."

"I want to come in, John."

"Massa, whut you wanta come in po' niggah's house an' you got dat fine big house up yander?"

"John, if you don't open this door, I'll have you whipped tomorrow."

John went to the door grumbling about rich white folks hanging around po' niggahs' cabins.

The white man sat down before the blazing fire. The pot boiled and breathed of delicious things within.

After a while he said, "I'm hungry, John. What have you got in that pot?"

"Lawd, now, Massa, whut you wanter eat mah po' vittles fuh

and Mistis got roas' chicken an' ham an' chine-bone pie an' everything up to de house? White folks got de funniest ways."

"What's in that pot, John?"

"It's one lil' measly possum, Massa, ah'm bilin' tuh keep fuh a
cold snack."

"I want some of it."

"Naw, Massa, you don't want none uh dat dirty lil' possum."

"Yes I do, and if you don't give me some, I'll have you
whipped."

John slowly arose and got a plate, knife and fork and opened the
pot.

"Well," he said resignedly before dipping in. "Ah put dis heah
critter in heah a possum,—if it comes out a pig, 'tain't mah fault."

Stepped on a tin, mah story ends.

The Eatonville Anthology

THE PLEADING WOMAN

Mrs. Tony Roberts is the pleading woman. She just loves to ask for things. Her husband gives her all he can rake and scrape, which is considerably more than most wives get for their housekeeping, but she goes from door to door begging for things.

She starts at the store. "Mist' Clarke," she sing-songs in a high keening voice, "gimme lil' piece uh meat tuh boil a pot uh greens wid. Lawd knows me an' mah chillen is SO hongry! Hits uh SHAME! Tony don't fee-ee-eee-ed me!"

Mr. Clarke knows that she has money and that her larder is well stocked, for Tony Roberts is the best provider on his list. But her keening annoys him and he arises heavily. The pleader at this shows all the joy of a starving man being seated at a feast.

"Thass right Mist' Clarke. De Lawd loveth de cheerful giver. Gimme jes' a lil' piece 'bout dis big (indicating the width of her hand) an' de Lawd'll bless yuh."

She follows this angel-on-earth to his meat tub and superintends the cutting, crying out in pain when he refuses to move the knife over just a teeny bit mo'.

Finally, meat in hand, she departs, remarking on the meanness of some people who give a piece of salt meat only two-fingers wide when they were plainly asked for a hand-wide piece. Clarke puts it down to Tony's account and resumes his reading.

With the slab of salt pork as a foundation, she visits various homes until she has collected all she wants for the day. At the Piersons, for instance: "Sister Pierson, plee-ee-ease gimme uh han'ful uh collard greens fuh me an' mah po' chillen! 'Deed, me an' mah chillen is SO hongry. Tony doan' fee-ee-eed me!"

Mrs. Pierson picks a bunch of greens for her, but she springs away from them as if they were poison. "Lawd a mussy, Mis' Pierson, you ain't gonna gimme dat lil' eye-full uh greens' fuh me an' mah chillen, is you? Don't be so graspin'; Gawd won't bless yuh. Gimme uh han'full mo'. Lawd, some folks is got everything, an' theys jes' as gripin' an stingy!"

Mrs. Pierson raises the ante, and the pleading woman moves on to the next place, and on and on. The next day, it commences all over.

II

TURPENTINE LOVE

Jim Merchant is always in good humor—even with his wife. He says he fell in love with her at first sight. That was some years ago. She has had all her teeth pulled out, but they still get along splendidly.

He says the first time he called on her he found out that she was subject to fits. This didn't cool his love, however. She had several in his presence.

One Sunday, while he was there, she had one, and her mother tried to give her a dose of turpentine to stop it. Accidently, she spilled it in her eye and it cured her. She never had another fit, so they got married and have kept each other in good humor ever since.

III

Becky Moore has eleven children of assorted colors and sizes. She has never been married, but that is not her fault. She has never stopped any of the fathers of her children from proposing, so if she has no father for her children it's not her fault. The men round about are entirely to blame.

The other mothers of the town are afraid that it is catching. They won't let their children play with hers.

IV
TIPPY

Sykes Jones' family all shoot craps. The most interesting member of the family—also fond of bones, but of another kind—is Tippy, the Jones' dog.

He is so thin, that it amazes one that he lives at all. He sneaks into village kitchens if the housewives are careless about the doors and steals meats, even off the stoves. He also sucks eggs.

For these offenses he has been sentenced to death dozens of times, and the sentences executed upon him, only they didn't work. He has been fed bluestone, strychnine, nux vomica, even an entire Peruna bottle beaten up. It didn't fatten him, but it didn't kill him. So Eatonville has resigned itself to the plague of Tippy, reflecting that it has erred in certain matters and is being chastened.

In spite of all the attempts upon his life, Tippy is still willing to be friendly with anyone who will let him.

V
THE WAY OF A MAN WITH A TRAIN

Old Man Anderson lived seven or eight miles out in the country from Eatonville. Over by Lake Apopka. He raised feed-corn and cassava and went to market with it two or three times a year. He bought all of his victuals wholesale so he wouldn't have to come to town for several months more.

He was different from us citybred folks. He had never seen a train. Everybody laughed at him for even the smallest child in Eatonville had either been to Maitland or Orlando and watched a train go by. On Sunday afternoons all of the young people of the village would go over to Maitland, a mile away, to see Number 35 whizz southward on its way to Tampa and wave at the passengers. So we looked down on him a little. Even we children felt superior in the presence of a person so lacking in worldly knowledge.

The grown-ups kept telling him he ought to go see a train. He always said he didn't have time to wait so long. Only two trains a day passed through Maitland. But patronage and ridicule finally had its effect and Old Man Anderson drove in one morning early. Number 78 went north to Jacksonville at 10:20. He drove his light wagon over in the woods beside the railroad below Maitland, and sat down to wait. He began to fear that his horse would get frightened and run away with the wagon. So he took him out and led him deeper into the grove and tied him securely. Then he returned to his wagon and waited some more. Then he remembered that some of the train-wise villagers had said the engine belched fire and smoke. He had better move his wagon out of danger. It might catch afire. He climbed down from the seat and placed himself between the shafts to draw it away. Just then 78 came thundering over the trestle spouting smoke, and suddenly began blowing for Maitland. Old Man Anderson became so frightened he ran away with the wagon through the woods and tore it up worse than the horse ever could have done. He doesn't know yet what a train looks like, and says he doesn't care.

VI

COON TAYLOR

Coon Taylor never did any real stealing. Of course, if he saw a chicken or a watermelon or muskmelon or anything like that that he wanted he'd take it. The people used to get mad but they never could catch him. He took so many melons from Joe Clarke that he set up in the melon patch one night with his shotgun loaded with rock salt. He was going to fix Coon. But he was tired. It is hard work being a mayor, postmaster, storekeeper and everything. He dropped asleep sitting on a stump in the middle of the patch. So he didn't see Coon when he came. Coon didn't see him either, that is, not at first. He knew the stump was there, however. He had opened many of Clarke's juicy Florida Favorite on it. He selected his fruit, walked over to the stump and burst the melon on it. That is, he thought it was the stump until it fell over with a yell. Then he knew it was no stump and departed hastily from those parts. He had cleared the fence when Clarke came to, as it were. So the charge of rock-salt was wasted on the desert air.

During the sugar-cane season, he found he couldn't resist Clarke's soft green cane, but Clarke did not go to sleep this time. So after he had cut six or eight stalks by the moonlight, Clarke rose up out of the cane strippings with his shotgun and made Coon sit right down and chew up the last one of them on the spot. And the next day he made Coon leave his town for three months.

VII

VILLAGE FICTION

Joe Lindsay is said by Lum Boger to be the largest manufacturer of prevarications in Eatonville; Brazzle (late owner of the world's leanest and meanest mule) contends that his business is the largest in the state and his wife holds that he is the biggest liar in the world.

Exhibit A—He claims that while he was in Orlando one day he saw a doctor cut open a woman, remove everything—liver, lights and heart included—clean each of them separately; the doctor then washed out the empty woman, dried her out neatly with a towel and replaced the organs so expertly that she was up and about her work in a couple of weeks.

VIII

Sewell is a man who lives all to himself. He moves a great deal. So often, that 'Lige Moseley says his chickens are so used to moving that every time he comes out into his backyard the chickens lie down and cross their legs, ready to be tied up again.

He is baldheaded; but he says he doesn't mind that, because he wants as little as possible between him and God.

IX

Mrs. Clarke is Joe Clarke's wife. She is a soft-looking, middle-aged woman, whose bust and stomach are always holding a get-together.

She waits on the store sometimes and cries every time he yells at her which he does every time she makes a mistake, which is quite often. She calls her husband "Jody." They say he used to beat her in the store when he was a young man, but he is not so impatient now. He can wait until he goes home.

She shouts in Church every Sunday and shakes the hand of fellowship with everybody in the Church with her eyes closed, but somehow always misses her husband.

X

Mrs. McDuffy goes to Church every Sunday and always shouts and tells her "determination." Her husband always sits in the back row and beats her as soon as they get home. He says there's no sense in her shouting, as big a devil as she is. She just does it to slur him. Elijah Moseley asked her why she didn't stop shouting, seeing she always got a beating about it. She says she can't "squinch the sperrit." Then Elijah asked Mr. McDuffy to stop beating her, seeing that she was going to shout anyway. He answered that she just did it for spite and that his fist was just as hard as her head. He could last just as long as she. So the village let the matter rest.

XI

DOUBLE-SHUFFLE

Back in the good old days before the World War, things were very simple in Eatonville. People didn't fox-trot. When the town wanted to put on its Sunday clothes and wash behind the ears, it put on a "breakdown." The daring younger set would two-step and waltz, but the good church members and the elders stuck to the grand march. By rural canons dancing is wicked, but one is not held to have danced until the feet have been crossed. Feet don't get crossed when one grand marches.

At elaborate affairs the organ from the Methodist church was moved up to the hall and Lizzimore, the blind man, presided. When informal gatherings were held, he merely played his guitar assisted by any volunteer with mouth organs or accordions.

Among white people the march is as mild as if it had been passed on by Volstead. But it still has a kick in Eatonville. Everybody happy, shining eyes, gleaming teeth. Feet dragged 'shhlap, shhlap! to beat out the time. No orchestra needed. Round and round! Back again, parse-me-la! shlap! shlap! Strut! Strut! Seaboard! Shlap! Shlap! Tiddy bumm! Mr. Clarke in the lead with Mrs. Moseley.

It's too much for some of the young folks. Double shuffling commences. Buck and wing. Lizzimore about to break his guitar. Accordion doing contortions. People fall back against the walls, and let the soloist have it, shouting as they clap the old, old double shuffle songs.

> Me an' mah honey got two mo' days,
> Two mo' days tuh do de buck.

Sweating bodies, laughing mouths, grotesque faces, feet drumming fiercely. Deacons clapping as hard as the rest.

> Great big nigger, black as tar
> Trying tuh git tuh hebben on uh 'lectric car.
>
> Some love cabbage, some love kale
> But I love a gal wid a short skirt tail.
>
> Long tall angel—steppin' down,
> Long white robe an' starry crown.

Ah would not marry uh black gal (bumm bumm!)
Tell yuh de reason why
Every time she comb her hair
She make de goo-goo eye.

Would not marry a yaller gal (bumm bumm!)
Tell yuh de reason why
Her neck so long an' stringy
Ahm 'fraid she'd never die.

"Would not marry uh preacher
Tell yuh de reason why
Every time he comes tuh town
He makes de chicken fly.

When the buck dance was over, the boys would give the floor to the girls and they would parse-me-la with a sly eye out of the corner to see if anybody was looking who might "have them up in church" on conference night. Then there would be more dancing. Then Mr. Clarke would call for everybody's best attention and announce that *'freshments was served! Every gent'man would please take his lady by the arm and scorch her right up to de table fur a treat!*

Then the men would stick their arms out with a flourish and ask their ladies: "You lak chicken? Well, then, take a wing." And the ladies would take the proffered "wings" and parade up to the long table and be served. Of course most of them had brought baskets in which were heaps of jointed and fried chicken, two or three kinds of pies, cakes, potato pone and chicken purlo. The hall would separate into happy groups about the baskets until time for more dancing.

But the boys and girls got scattered about during the war, and now they dance the fox-trot by a brand new piano. They do waltz and two-step still, but no one now considers it good form to lock his chin over his partner's shoulder and stick out behind. One night just for fun and to humor the old folks, they danced, that is, they grand marched, but everyone picked up their feet. *Bah!!*

XII

THE HEAD OF THE NAIL

Daisy Taylor was the town vamp. Not that she was pretty. But sirens were all but non-existent in the town. Perhaps she was forced to it by circumstances. She was quite dark, with little brushy patches of hair squatting over her head. These were held down by shingle-nails often. No one knows whether she did this for artistic effect or for lack of hair-pins, but there they were shining in the little patches of hair when she got all dressed for the afternoon and came up to Clarke's store to see if there was any mail for her.

It was seldom that anyone wrote to Daisy, but she knew that the men of the town would be assembled there by five o'clock, and some one could usually be induced to buy her some soda-water or peanuts.

Daisy flirted with married men. There were only two single men in town. Lum Boger, who was engaged to the assistant school-teacher, and Hiram Lester, who had been off to school at Tuskegee and wouldn't look at a person like Daisy. In addition to other drawbacks, she was pigeon-toed and her petticoat was always showing so perhaps he was justified. There was nothing else to do except flirt with married men.

This went on for a long time. First one wife then another complained of her, or drove her from the preserves by threat.

But the affair with Crooms was the most prolonged and serious. He was even known to have bought her a pair of shoes.

Mrs. Laura Crooms was a meek little woman who took all of her troubles crying, and talked a great deal of leaving things in the hands of God.

The affair came to a head one night in orange picking time. Crooms was over at Oneido picking oranges. Many fruit pickers move from one town to the other during the season.

The *town* was collected at the store-postoffice as is customary on Saturday nights. The *town* has had its bath and with its week's pay in pocket fares forth to be merry. The men tell stories and treat the ladies to soda-water, peanuts and peppermint candy.

Daisy was trying to get treats, but the porch was cold to her that night.

"Ah don't keer if you don't treat me. What's a dirty lil nickel?" She flung this at Walter Thomas. "The everloving Mister Crooms will gimme anything atall Ah wants."

"You better shet up yo' mouf talking 'bout Albert Crooms. Heah his wife comes right now."

Daisy went akimbo. "Who? Me! Ah don't keer whut Laura Crooms think. If she ain't a heavy hip-ted Mama enough to keep him, she don't need to come crying to me."

She stood making goo-goo eyes as Mrs. Crooms walked upon the porch. Daisy laughed loud, made several references to Albert Crooms, and when she saw the mail-bag come in from Maitland she said, "Ah better go in an' see if Ah ain't got a letter from Oneido."

The more Daisy played the game of getting Mrs. Crooms' goat, the better she liked it. She ran in and out of the store laughing until she could scarcely stand. Some of the people present began to talk to Mrs. Crooms—to egg her on to halt Daisy's boasting, but she was for leaving it all in the hands of God. Walter Thomas kept on after Mrs. Crooms until she stiffened and resolved to fight. Daisy was inside when she came to this resolve and never dreamed anything of the kind could happen. She had gotten hold of an envelope and came laughing and shouting, "Oh, Ah can't stand to see Oneido lose!"

There was a box of ax-handles on display on the porch, propped up against the door jamb. As Daisy stepped upon the porch, Mrs. Crooms leaned the heavy end of one of those handles heavily upon her head. She staggered from the porch to the ground and the timid Laura, fearful of a counter-attack, struck again and Daisy toppled into the town ditch. There was not enough water in there to do more than muss her up. Every time she tried to rise, down would come that ax-handle again. Laura was fighting a scared fight. With Daisy thoroughly licked, she retired to the store porch and left her fallen enemy in the ditch. None of the men helped

Daisy—even to get out of the ditch. But Elijah Moseley, who was some distance down the street when the trouble began, arrived as the victor was withdrawing. He rushed up and picked Daisy out of the mud and began feeling her head.

"Is she hurt much?" Joe Clarke asked from the doorway.

"I don't know," Elijah answered, "I was just looking to see if Laura had been lucky enough to hit one of those nails on the head and drive it in."

Before a week was up, Daisy moved to Orlando. There in a wider sphere, perhaps, her talents as a vamp were appreciated.

XIII
PANTS AND CAL'LINE

Sister Cal'line Potts was a silent woman. Did all of her laughing down inside, but did the thing that kept the town in an uproar of laughter. It was the general opinion of the village that Cal'line would do anything she had a mind to. And she had a mind to do several things.

Mitchell Potts, her husband, had a weakness for women. No one ever believed that she was jealous. She did things to the women, surely. But most any townsman would have said that she did them because she liked the novel situation and the queer things she could bring out of it.

Once he took up with Delphine—called Mis' Pheeny by the town. She lived on the outskirts on the edge of the piney woods. The town winked and talked. People don't make secrets of such things in villages. Cal'line went about her business with her thin black lips pursed tight as ever, and her shiny black eyes unchanged.

"Dat devil of a Cal'line's got somethin' up her sleeve!" The town smiled in anticipation.

"Delphine is too big a cigar for her to smoke. She ain't crazy," said some as the weeks went on and nothing happened. Even Pheeny herself would give an extra flirt to her over-starched petticoats as she rustled into church past her of Sundays.

Mitch Potts said furthermore, that he was tired of Cal'line's foolishness. She had to stay where he put her. His African soup-bone (arm) was too strong to let a woman run over him. 'Nough was 'nough. And he did some fancy cussing, and he was the fanciest cusser in the county.

So the town waited and the longer it waited, the odds changed slowly from the wife to the husband.

One Saturday, Mitch knocked off work at two o'clock and went over to Maitland. He came back with a rectangular box under his arm and kept straight on out to the barn and put it away. He ducked around the corner of the house quickly, but even so, his wife glimpsed the package. Very much like a shoe-box. So!

He put on the kettle and took a bath. She stood in her bare feet at the ironing board and kept on ironing. He dressed. It was about five o'clock but still very light. He fiddled around outside. She kept on with her ironing. As soon as the sun got red, he sauntered out to the barn, got the parcel and walked away down the road, past the store and out into the piney woods. As soon as he left the house, Cal'line slipped on her shoes without taking time to don stockings, put on one of her husband's old Stetsons, worn and floppy, slung the axe over her shoulder and followed in his wake. He was hailed cheerily as he passed the sitters on the store porch and answered smiling sheepishly and passed on. Two minutes later passed his wife, silently, unsmilingly, and set the porch to giggling and betting.

An hour passed perhaps. It was dark. Clarke had long ago lighted the swinging kerosene lamp inside.

XIV

Once 'way back yonder before the stars fell all the animals used to talk just like people. In them days dogs and rabbits was the best of friends—even tho' both of them was stuck on the same gal—which was Miss Nancy Coon. She had the sweetest smile and the prettiest striped and bushy tail to be found anywhere.

They both run their legs nigh off trying to win her for themselves—fetching nice ripe persimmons and such. But she never give one or the other no satisfaction.

Finally one night Mr. Dog popped the question right out. "Miss Coon," he says, "Ma'am, also Ma'am which would you ruther be—a lark flyin' or a dove a settin'?"

Course Miss Nancy she blushed and laughed a little and hid her face behind her bushy tail for a spell. Then she said sorter shy like, "I does love yo' sweet voice, brother dawg—but—but I ain't jes' exactly set in my mind yit."

Her and Mr. Dog set on a spell, when up comes hopping Mr. Rabbit wid his tail fresh washed and his whiskers shining. He got right down to business and asked Miss Coon to marry him, too.

"Oh, Miss Nancy," he says, "Ma'am, also Ma'am, if you'd see me settin' straddle of a mud-cat leadin' a minnow, what would you think? Ma'am also Ma'am?" Which is a out and out proposal as everybody knows.

"Youse awful nice, Brother Rabbit and a beautiful dancer, but you cannot sing like Brother Dog. Both you uns come back next week to gimme time for to decide."

They both left arm-in-arm. Finally Mr. Rabbit says to Mr. Dog. "Taint no use in me going back—she ain't gwinter have me. So I mought as well give up. She loves singing, and I ain't got nothing but a squeak."

"Oh, don't talk that a' way," says Mr. Dog, tho' he is glad Mr. Rabbit can't sing none.

"Thass all right, Brer Dog. But if I had a sweet voice like you got, I'd have it worked on and make it sweeter."

"How! How! How!" Mr. Dog cried, jumping up and down.

"Lemme fix it for you, like I do for Sister Lark and Sister Mocking-bird."

"When? Where?" asked Mr. Dog, all excited. He was figuring that if he could sing just a little better Miss Coon would be bound to have him.

"Just you meet me t'morrer in de huckleberry patch," says the rabbit and off they both goes to bed.

The dog is there on time next day and after a while the rabbit comes loping up.

"Mawnin', Brer Dawg," he says kinder chippy like. "Ready to git yo' voice sweetened?"

"Sholy, sholy, Brer Rabbit. Let's we all hurry about it. I wants tuh serenade Miss Nancy from de piney woods tuh night."

"Well, den, open yo' mouf and poke out yo' tongue," says the rabbit.

No sooner did Mr. Dog poke out his tongue than Mr. Rabbit split it with a knife and ran for all he was worth to a hollow stump and hid himself.

The dog has been mad at the rabbit ever since.

Anybody who don't believe it happened, just look at the dog's tongue and he can see for himself where the rabbit slit it right u the middle.

Stepped on a tin, mah story ends.

Sweat

It was eleven o'clock of a Spring night in Florida. It was Sunday. Any other night, Delia Jones would have been in bed for two hours by this time. But she was a washwoman, and Monday morning meant a great deal to her. So she collected the soiled clothes on Saturday when she returned the clean things. Sunday night after church, she sorted them and put the white things to soak. It saved her almost a half day's start. A great hamper in the bedroom held the clothes that she brought home. It was so much neater than a number of bundles lying around.

She squatted in the kitchen floor beside the great pile of clothes, sorting them into small heaps according to color, and humming a song in a mournful key, but wondering through it all where Sykes, her husband, had gone with her horse and buckboard.

Just then something long, round, limp and black fell upon her shoulders and slithered to the floor beside her. A great terror took hold of her. It softened her knees and dried her mouth so that it was a full minute before she could cry out or move. Then she saw that it was the big bull whip her husband liked to carry when he drove.

She lifted her eyes to the door and saw him standing there bent over with laughter at her fright. She screamed at him.

"Sykes, what you throw dat whip on me like dat? You know it would skeer me—looks just like a snake, an' you knows how skeered Ah is of snakes."

"Course Ah knowed it! That's how come Ah done it." He slapped his leg with his hand and almost rolled on the ground in his mirth. "If you such a big fool dat you got to have a fit over a earth worm or a string, Ah don't keer how bad Ah skeer you."

"You aint got no business doing it. Gawd knows it's a sin. Some day Ah'm gointuh drop dead from some of yo' foolishness. 'Nother thing, where you been wid mah rig? Ah feeds dat pony. He aint fuh you to be drivin' wid no bull whip."

"You sho is one aggravatin' nigger woman!" he declared and stepped into the room. She resumed her work and did not answer him at once. "Ah done tole you time and again to keep them white folks' clothes outa dis house."

He picked up the whip and glared down at her. Delia went on with her work. She went out into the yard and returned with a galvanized tub and sat it on the washbench. She saw that Sykes had kicked all of the clothes together again, and now stood in her way truculently, his whole manner hoping, *praying*, for an argument. But she walked calmly around him and commenced to re-sort the things.

"Next time, Ah'm gointer kick 'em outdoors," he threatened as he struck a match along the leg of his corduroy breeches.

Delia never looked up from her work, and her thin, stooped shoulders sagged further.

"Ah aint for no fuss t'night, Sykes. Ah just come from taking sacrament at the church house."

He snorted scornfully. "Yeah, you just come from de church house on a Sunday night, but heah you is gone to work on them clothes. You ain't nothing but a hypocrite. One of them amen-corner Christians—sing, whoop, and shout, then come home and wash white folks clothes on the Sabbath."

He stepped roughly upon the whitest pile of things, kicking them helter-skelter as he crossed the room. His wife gave a little scream of dismay, and quickly gathered them together again.

"Sykes, you quit grindin' dirt into these clothes! How can Ah git through by Sat'day if Ah don't start on Sunday?"

"Ah don't keer if you never git through. Anyhow, Ah done

promised Gawd and a couple of other men, Ah aint gointer have
it in mah house. Don't gimme no lip neither, else Ah'll throw 'em
out and put mah fist up side yo' head to boot.''

Delia's habitual meekness seemed to slip from her shoulders
like a blown scarf. She was on her feet; her poor little body, her
bare knuckly hands bravely defying the strapping hulk before her.

"Looka heah, Sykes, you done gone too fur. Ah been married
to you fur fifteen years, and Ah been takin' in washin' fur fifteen
years. Sweat, sweat, sweat! Work and sweat, cry and sweat, pray
and sweat!''

"What's that got to do with me?'' he asked brutally.

"What's it got to do with you, Sykes? Mah tub of suds is filled
yo' belly with vittles more times than yo' hands is filled it. Mah
sweat is done paid for this house and Ah reckon Ah kin keep on
sweatin' in it.''

She seized the iron skillet from the stove and struck a defensive
pose, which act surprised him greatly, coming from her. It cowed
him and he did not strike her as he usually did.

"Naw you won't,'' she panted, "that ole snaggle-toothed black
woman you runnin' with aint comin' heah to pile up on *mah*
sweat and blood. You aint paid for nothin' on this place, and Ah'm
gointer stay right heah till Ah'm toted out foot foremost.''

"Well, you better quit gittin' me riled up, else they'll be totin'
you out sooner than you expect. Ah'm so tired of you Ah don't
know whut to do. Gawd! how Ah hates skinny wimmen!''

A little awed by this new Delia, he sidled out of the door and
slammed the back gate after him. He did not say where he had
gone, but she knew too well. She knew very well that he would not
return until nearly daybreak also. Her work over, she went on to
bed but not to sleep at once. Things had come to a pretty pass!

She lay awake, gazing upon the debris that cluttered their mat-
rimonial trail. Not an image left standing along the way. Anything
like flowers had long ago been drowned in the salty stream that
had been pressed from her heart. Her tears, her sweat, her blood.
She had brought love to the union and he had brought a longing
after the flesh. Two months after the wedding, he had given her

the first brutal beating. She had the memory of his numerous trips to Orlando with all of his wages when he had returned to her penniless, even before the first year had passed. She was young and soft then, but now she thought of her knotty, muscled limbs, her harsh knuckly hands, and drew herself up into an unhappy little ball in the middle of the big feather bed. Too late now to hope for love, even if it were not Bertha it would be someone else. This case differed from the others only in that she was bolder than the others. Too late for everything except her little home. She had built it for her old days, and planted one by one the trees and flowers there. It was lovely to her, lovely.

Somehow, before sleep came, she found herself saying aloud: "Oh well, whatever goes over the Devil's back, is got to come under his belly. Sometime or ruther, Sykes, like everybody else, is gointer reap his sowing." After that she was able to build a spiritual earthworks against her husband. His shells could no longer reach her. *Amen*. She went to sleep and slept until he announced his presence in bed by kicking her feet and rudely snatching the cover away.

"Gimme some kivah heah, an' git yo' damn foots over on yo' own side! Ah oughter mash you in yo' mouf fuh drawing dat skillet on me."

Delia went clear to the rail without answering him. A triumphant indifference to all that he was or did.

The week was as full of work for Delia as all other weeks, and Saturday found her behind her little pony, collecting and delivering clothes.

It was a hot, hot day near the end of July. The village men on Joe Clarke's porch even chewed cane listlessly. They did not hurl the cane-knots as usual. They let them dribble over the edge of the porch. Even conversation had collapsed under the heat.

"Heah come Delia Jones," Jim Merchant said, as the shaggy pony came 'round the bend of the road toward them. The rusty buckboard was heaped with baskets of crisp, clean laundry.

"Yep," Joe Lindsay agreed. "Hot or col', rain or shine, jes ez reg'lar ez de weeks roll roun' Delia carries 'em an' fetches 'em on Sat'day.''

"She better if she wanter eat," said Moss. "Sykes Jones aint wuth de shot an' powder hit would tek tuh kill 'em. Not to *huh* he aint.''

"He sho' aint," Walter Thomas chimed in. "It's too bad, too, cause she wuz a right pritty li'l trick when he got huh. Ah'd uh mah'ied huh mahseff if he hadnter beat me to it.''

Delia nodded briefly at the men as she drove past.

"Too much knockin' will ruin *any* 'oman. He done beat huh 'nough tuh kill three women, let 'lone change they looks," said Elijah Moseley. "How Sykes kin stommuck dat big black greasy Mogul he's layin' roun' wid, gits me. Ah swear dat eight-rock couldn't kiss a sardine can Ah done thowed out de back do' 'way las' yeah.''

"Aw, she's fat, thass how come. He's allus been crazy 'bout fat women," put in Merchant. "He'd a' been tied up wid one long time ago if he could a' found one tuh have him. Did Ah tell yuh 'bout him come sidlin' roun' *mah* wife—bringin' her a basket uh pee-cans outa his yard fuh a present? Yessir, mah wife! She tol' him tuh take 'em right straight back home, cause Delia works so hard ovah dat washtub she reckon everything on de place taste lak sweat an' soapsuds. Ah jus' wisht Ah'd a' caught 'im 'roun' dere! Ah'd a' made his hips ketch on fiah down dat shell road.''

"Ah know he done it, too. Ah sees 'im grinnin' at every 'oman dat passes," Walter Thomas said. "But even so, he useter eat some mighty big hunks uh humble pie tuh git dat lil' 'oman he got. She wuz ez pritty ez a speckled pup! Dat wuz fifteen yeahs ago. He useter be so skeered uh losin' huh, she could make him do some parts of a husband's duty. Dey never wuz de same in de mind.''

"There oughter be a law about him," said Lindsay. "He aint fit tuh carry guts tuh a bear.''

Clarke spoke for the first time. "Taint no law on earth dat kin make a man be decent if it aint in 'im. There's plenty men dat takes a wife lak dey do a joint uh sugar-cane. It's round, juicy an' sweet when dey gits it. But dey squeeze an' grind, squeeze an' grind an' wring tell dey wring every drop uh pleasure dat's in 'em out. When dey's satisfied dat dey is wrung dry, dey treats 'em jes lak dey do a cane-chew. Dey thows 'em away. Dey knows whut dey is doin' while dey is at it, an' hates theirselves fuh it but they keeps on hangin' after huh tell she's empty. Den dey hates huh fuh bein' a cane-chew an' in de way.''

"We oughter take Sykes an' dat stray 'oman uh his'n down in Lake Howell swamp an' lay on de rawhide till they cain't say 'Lawd a' mussy.' He allus wuz uh ovahbearin' niggah, but since dat white 'oman from up north done teached 'im how to run a automobile, he done got too biggety to live—an' we oughter kill 'im,'' Old Man Anderson advised.

A grunt of approval went around the porch. But the heat was melting their civic virtue and Elijah Moseley began to bait Joe Clarke.

"Come on, Joe, git a melon outa dere an' slice it up for yo' customers. We'se all sufferin' wid de heat. De bear's done got *me!*''

"Thass right, Joe, a watermelon is jes' whut Ah needs tuh cure de eppizudicks.'' Walter Thomas joined forces with Moseley. "Come on dere, Joe. We all is steady customers an' you aint set us up in a long time. Ah chooses dat long, bowlegged Floridy favorite.''

"A god, an' be dough. You all gimme twenty cents and slice away,'' Clarke retorted. "Ah needs a col' slice m'self. Heah, everybody chip in. Ah'll lend y'all mah meat knife.''

The money was quickly subscribed and the huge melon brought forth. At that moment, Sykes and Bertha arrived. A determined silence fell on the porch and the melon was put away again.

Merchant snapped down the blade of his jack-knife and moved toward the store door.

"Come on in, Joe, an' gimme a slab uh sow belly an' uh pound uh coffee—almost fuhgot 'twas Sat'day. Got to git on home.'' Most of the men left also.

Just then Delia drove past on her way home, as Sykes was ordering magnificently for Bertha. It pleased him for Delia to see.

"Git whutsoever yo' heart desires, Honey. Wait a minute, Joe. Give huh two botles uh strawberry soda-water, uh quart uh parched ground-peas, an a block uh chewin' gum."

With all this they left the store, with Sykes reminding Bertha that this was his town and she could have it if she wanted it.

The men returned soon after they left, and held their watermelon feast.

"Where did Sykes Jones git dat 'oman from nohow?" Lindsay asked.

"Ovah Apopka. Guess dey musta been cleanin' out de town when she lef'. She don't look lak a thing but a hunk uh liver wid hair on it."

"Well, she sho' kin squall," Dave Carter contributed. "When she gits ready tuh laff, she jes' opens huh mouf an' latches it back tuh de las' notch. No ole grandpa alligator down in Lake Bell aint got nothin' on huh."

Bertha had been in town three months now. Sykes was still paying her room rent at Della Lewis'—the only house in town that would have taken her in. Sykes took her frequently to Winter Park to "stomps." He still assured her that he was the swellest man in the state.

"Sho' you kin have dat lil' ole house soon's Ah kin git dat 'oman outa dere. Everything b'longs tuh me an' you sho' kin have it. Ah sho' 'bominates uh skinny 'oman. Lawdy, you sho' is got one portly shape on you! You kin git *anything* you wants. Dis is *mah* town an' you sho' kin have it."

Delia's work-worn knees crawled over the earth in Gethsemane and up the rocks of Calvary many, many times during these months. She avoided the villagers and meeting places in her efforts to be blind and deaf. But Bertha nullified this to a degree, by coming to Delia's house to call Sykes out to her at the gate.

Delia and Sykes fought all the time now with no peaceful interludes. They slept and ate in silence. Two or three times Delia had attempted a timid friendliness, but she was repulsed each time. It was plain that the breaches must remain agape.

* * *

The sun had burned July to August. The heat streamed down like a million hot arrows, smiting all things living upon the earth. Grass withered, leaves browned, snakes went blind in shedding and men and dogs went mad. Dog days!

Delia came home one day and found Sykes there before her. She wondered, but started to go on into the house without speaking, even though he was standing in the kitchen door and she must either stoop under his arm or ask him to move. He made no room for her. She noticed a soap box beside the steps, but paid no particular attention to it, knowing that he must have brought it there. As she was stooping to pass under his outstretched arm, he suddenly pushed her backward, laughingly.

"Look in de box dere Delia, Ah done brung yuh somethin'!"

She nearly fell upon the box in her stumbling, and when she saw what it held, she all but fainted outright.

"Sykes! Sykes, mah Gawd! You take dat rattlesnake 'way from heah! You *gottuh*. Oh, Jesus, have mussy!"

"Ah aint gut tuh do nuthin' uh de kin'—fact is Ah aint got tuh do nothin' but die. Taint no use uh you puttin' on airs makin' out lak you skeered uh dat snake—he's gointer stay right heah tell he die. He wouldn't bite me cause Ah knows how tuh handle 'im. Nohow he wouldn't risk breakin' out his fangs 'gin *yo'* skinny laigs."

"Naw, now Sykes, don't keep dat thing 'roun' heah tuh skeer me tuh death. You knows Ah'm even feared uh earth worms. Thass de biggest snake Ah evah did see. Kill 'im Sykes, please."

"Doan ast me tuh do nothin' fuh yuh. Goin' 'roun' tryin' tuh be so damn astorperious. Naw, Ah aint gonna kill it. Ah think uh damn sight mo' uh him dan you! Dat's a nice snake an' anybody doan lak 'im kin jes' hit de grit."

The village soon heard that Sykes had the snake, and came to see and ask questions.

"How de hen-fire did you ketch dat six-foot rattler, Sykes?" Thomas asked.

"He's full uh frogs so he caint hardly move, thass how Ah eased

up on 'm. But Ah'm a snake charmer an' knows how tuh handle
'em. Shux, dat aint nothin'. Ah could ketch one eve'y day if Ah so
wanted tuh.''

''Whut he needs is a heavy hick'ry club leaned real heavy on his
head. Dat's de bes 'way tuh charm a rattlesnake.''

''Naw, Walt, y'all jes' don't understand dese diamon' backs lak
Ah do,'' said Sykes in a superior tone of voice.

The village agreed with Walter, but the snake stayed on. His box
remained by the kitchen door with its screen wire covering. Two
or three days later it had digested its meal of frogs and literally
came to life. It rattled at every movement in the kitchen or the
yard. One day as Delia came down the kitchen steps she saw his
chalky-white fangs curved like scimitars hung in the wire meshes.
This time she did not run away with averted eyes as usual. She
stood for a long time in the doorway in a red fury that grew
bloodier for every second that she regarded the creature that was
her torment.

That night she broached the subject as soon as Sykes sat down
to the table.

''Sykes, Ah wants you tuh take dat snake 'way fum heah. You
done starved me an' Ah put up widcher, you done beat me an Ah
took dat, but you done kilt all mah insides bringin' dat varmint
heah.''

Sykes poured out a saucer full of coffee and drank it deliberately
before he answered her.

''A whole lot Ah keer 'bout how you feels inside uh out. Dat
snake aint goin' no damn wheah till Ah gits ready fuh 'im tuh go.
So fur as beatin' is concerned, yuh aint took near all dat you
gointer take ef yuh stay 'roun' *me.*''

Delia pushed back her plate and got up from the table. ''Ah
hates you, Sykes,'' she said calmly. ''Ah hates you tuh de same
degree dat Ah useter love yuh. Ah done took an' took till mah belly
is full up tuh mah neck. Dat's de reason Ah got mah letter fum de
church an' moved mah membership tuh Woodbridge—so Ah
don't haftuh take no sacrament wid yuh. Ah don't wantuh see yuh
'roun' me a-tall. Lay 'roun' wid dat 'oman all yuh wants tuh, but

gwan 'way fum me an' mah house. Ah hates yuh lak uh suck-egg dog.''

Sykes almost let the huge wad of corn bread and collard greens he was chewing fall out of his mouth in amazement. He had a hard time whipping himself up to the proper fury to try to answer Delia.

"Well, Ah'm glad you does hate me. Ah'm sho' tiahed uh you hangin' ontuh me. Ah don't want yuh. Look at yuh stringey ole neck! Yo' rawbony laigs an' arms is enough tuh cut uh man tuh death. You looks jes' lak de devvul's doll-baby tuh *me*. You cain't hate me no worse dan Ah hates you. Ah been hatin' *you* fuh years.''

"Yo' ole black hide don't look lak nothin' tuh me, but uh passel uh wrinkled up rubber, wid yo' big ole yeahs flappin' on each side lak uh paih uh buzzard wings. Don't think Ah'm gointuh be run 'way fum mah house neither. Ah'm goin' tuh de white folks bout *you*, mah young man, de very nex' time you lay yo' han's on me. Mah cup is done run ovah.'' Delia said this with no signs of fear and Sykes departed from the house, threatening her, but made not the slightest move to carry out any of them.

That night he did not return at all, and the next day being Sunday, Delia was glad that she did not have to quarrel before she hitched up her pony and drove the four miles to Woodbridge.

She stayed to the night service—"love feast"—which was very warm and full of spirit. In the emotional winds her domestic trials were borne far and wide so that she sang as she drove homeward,

> Jurden water, black an' col'
> Chills de body, not de soul
> An' Ah wantah cross Jurden in uh calm time.

She came from the barn to the kitchen door and stopped.

"Whut's de mattah, ol' satan, you aint kickin' up yo' racket?'' She addressed the snake's box. Complete silence. She went on into the house with a new hope in its birth struggles. Perhaps her threat to go to the white folks had frightened Sykes! Perhaps he was sorry! Fifteen years of misery and suppression had brought

Delia to the place where she would hope *anything* that looked towards a way over or through her wall of inhibitions.

She felt in the match safe behind the stove at once for a match. There was only one there.

"Dat niggah wouldn't fetch nothin' heah tuh save his rotten neck, but he kin run thew whut Ah brings quick enough. Now he done toted off nigh on tuh haff uh box uh matches. He done had dat 'oman heah in mah house, too."

Nobody but a woman could tell how she knew this even before she struck the match. But she did and it put her into a new fury.

Presently she brought in the tubs to put the white things to soak. This time she decided she need not bring the hamper out of the bedroom; she would go in there and do the sorting. She picked up the pot-bellied lamp and went in. The room was small and the hamper stood hard by the foot of the white iron bed. She could sit and reach through the bedposts—resting as she worked.

"Ah wantah cross Jurden in uh calm time." She was singing again. The mood of the "love feast" had returned. She threw back the lid of the basket almost gaily. Then, moved by both horror and terror, she sprung back toward the door. *There lay the snake in the basket!* He moved sluggishly at first, but even as she turned round and round, jumped up and down in an insanity of fear, he began to stir vigorously. She saw him pouring his awful beauty from the basket upon the bed, then she seized the lamp and ran as fast as she could to the kitchen. The wind from the open door blew out the light and the darkness added to her terror. She sped to the darkness of the yard, slamming the door after her before she thought to set down the lamp. She did not feel safe even on the ground, so she climbed up in the hay barn.

There for an hour or more she lay sprawled upon the hay a gibbering wreck.

Finally she grew quiet, and after that, coherent thought. With this, stalked through her a cold, bloody rage. Hours of this. A period of introspection, a space of retrospection, then a mixture of both. Out of this an awful calm.

"Well, Ah done de bes' Ah could. If things aint right, Gawd knows taint mah fault."

She went to sleep—a twitchy sleep—and woke up to a faint gray sky. There was a loud hollow sound below. She peered out. Sykes was at the wood-pile, demolishing a wire-covered box.

He hurried to the kitchen door, but hung outside there some minutes before he entered, and stood some minutes more inside before he closed it after him.

The gray in the sky was spreading. Delia descended without fear now, and crouched beneath the low bedroom window. The drawn shade shut out the dawn, shut in the night. But the thin walls held back no sound.

"Dat ol' scratch is woke up now!" She mused at the tremendous whirr inside, which every woodsman knows, is one of the sound illusions. The rattler is a ventriloquist. His whirr sounds to the right, to the left, straight ahead, behind, close under foot—everywhere but where it is. Woe to him who guesses wrong unless he is prepared to hold up his end of the argument! Sometimes he strikes without rattling at all.

Inside, Skyes heard nothing until he knocked a pot lid off the stove while trying to reach the match safe in the dark. He had emptied his pockets at Bertha's.

The snake seemed to wake up under the stove and Skyes made a quick leap into the bedroom. In spite of the gin he had had, his head was clearing now.

"Mah Gawd!" he chattered, "ef Ah could on'y strack uh light!"

The rattling ceased for a moment as he stood paralyzed. He waited. It seemed that the snake waited also.

"Oh fuh de light! Ah thought he'd be too sick"—Skyes was muttering to himself when the whirr began again, closer, right underfoot this time. Long before this, Skyes' ability to think had been flattened down to primitive instinct and he leaped—onto the bed.

Outside Delia heard a cry that might have come from a maddened chimpanzee, a stricken gorilla. All the terror, all the horror, all the rage that man possibly could express, without a recognizable human sound.

A tremendous stir inside there, another series of animal screams, the intermittent whirr of the reptile. The shade torn violently down from the window, letting in the red dawn, a huge brown hand seizing the window stick, great dull blows upon the wooden floor punctuating the gibberish of sound long after the rattle of the snake had abruptly subsided. All this Delia could see and hear from her place beneath the window, and it made her ill. She crept over to the four-o'clocks and stretched herself on the cool earth to recover.

She lay there. "Delia, Delia!" She could hear Skyes calling in a most despairing tone as one who expected no answer. The sun crept on up, and he called. Delia could not move—her legs were gone flabby. She never moved, he called, and the sun kept rising.

"Mah Gawd!" she heard him moan. "Mah Gawd fum Heben!" She heard him stumbling about and got up from her flower-bed. The sun was growing warm. As she approached the door she heard him call out hopefully, "Delia, is dat you Ah heah?"

She saw him on his hands and knees as soon as she reached the door. He crept an inch or two toward her—all that he was able, and she saw his horribly swollen neck and his one open eye shining with hope. A surge of pity too strong to support bore her away from that eye that must, could not, fail to see the tubs. He would see the lamp. Orlando with its doctors was too far. She could scarcely reach the Chinaberry tree, where she waited in the growing heat while inside she knew the cold river was creeping up and up to extinguish that eye which must know by now that she knew.

The Gilded
Six-Bits

It was a Negro yard around a Negro house in a Negro settlement that looked to the payroll of the G. and G. Fertilizer works for its support.

But there was something happy about the place. The front yard was parted in the middle by a sidewalk from gate to door-step, a sidewalk edged on either side by quart bottles driven neck down into the ground on a slant. A mess of homey flowers planted without a plan but blooming cheerily from their helter-skelter places. The fence and house were whitewashed. The porch and steps scrubbed white.

The front door stood open to the sunshine so that the floor of the front room could finish drying after its weekly scouring. It was Saturday. Everything clean from the front gate to the privy house. Yard raked so that the strokes of the rake would make a pattern. Fresh newspaper cut in fancy edge on the kitchen shelves.

Missie May was bathing herself in the galvanized washtub in the bedroom. Her dark-brown skin glistened under the soapsuds that skittered down from her wash rag. Her stiff young breasts thrust forward aggressively like broad-based cones with the tips lacquered in black.

She heard men's voices in the distance and glanced at the dollar clock on the dresser.

"Humph! Ah'm way behind time t'day! Joe gointer be heah 'fore Ah git mah clothes on if Ah don't make haste."

She grabbed the clean meal sack at hand and dried herself hurriedly and began to dress. But before she could tie her slippers, there came the ring of singing metal on wood. Nine times.

Missie May grinned with delight. She had not seen the big tall man come stealing in the gate and creep up the walk grinning happily at the joyful mischief he was about to commit. But she knew that it was her husband throwing silver dollars in the door for her to pick up and pile beside her plate at dinner. It was this way every Saturday afternoon. The nine dollars hurled into the open door, he scurried to a hiding place behind the cape jasmine bush and waited.

Missie May promptly appeared at the door in mock alarm.

"Who dat chunkin' money in mah do'way?" she demanded. No answer from the yard. She leaped off the porch and began to search the shrubbery. She peeped under the porch and hung over the gate to look up and down the road. While she did this, the man behind the jasmine darted to the china berry tree. She spied him and gave chase.

"Nobody ain't gointer be chunkin' money at me and Ah not do 'em nothin'," she shouted in mock anger. He ran around the house with Missie May at his heels. She overtook him at the kitchen door. He ran inside but could not close it after him before she crowded in and locked with him in a rough and tumble. For several minutes the two were a furious mass of male and female energy. Shouting, laughing, twisting, turning, tussling, tickling each other in the ribs; Missie May clutching onto Joe and Joe trying, but not too hard, to get away.

"Missie May, take yo' hand out mah pocket!" Joe shouted out between laughs.

"Ah ain't, Joe, not lessen you gwine gimme whateve' it is good you got in yo' pocket. Turn it go, Joe, do Ah'll tear yo' clothes."

"Go on tear 'em. You de one dat pushes de needles round heah. Move yo' hand Missie May."

"Lemme git dat paper sack out yo' pocket. Ah bet it's candy kisses."

"Tain't. Move yo' hand. Woman ain't got no business in a man's clothes nohow. Go way."

Missie May gouged way down and gave an upward jerk and triumphed.

"Unhhunh! Ah got it. It 'tis so candy kisses. Ah knowed you had somethin' for me in yo' clothes. Now Ah got to see whut's in every pocket you got."

Joe smiled indulgently and let his wife go through all of his pockets and take out the things that he had hidden there for her to find. She bore off the chewing gum, the cake of sweet soap, the pocket handkerchief as if she had wrested them from him, as if they had not been bought for the sake of this friendly battle.

"Whew! dat play-fight done got me all warmed up," Joe exclaimed. "Got me some water in de kittle?"

"Yo' water is on de fire and yo' clean things is cross de bed. Hurry up and wash yo'self and git changed so we kin eat. Ah'm hongry." As Missie said this, she bore the steaming kettle into the bedroom.

"You ain't hongry, sugar," Joe contradicted her. "Youse jes' a little empty. Ah'm de one whut's hongry. Ah could eat up camp meetin', back off 'ssociation, and drink Jurdan dry. Have it on de table when Ah git out de tub."

"Don't you mess wid mah business, man. You git in yo' clothes. Ah'm a real wife, not no dress and breath. Ah might not look lak one, but if you burn me, you won't git a thing but wife ashes."

Joe splashed in the bedroom and Missie May fanned around in the kitchen. A fresh red and white checked cloth on the table. Big pitcher of buttermilk beaded with pale drops of butter from the churn. Hot fried mullet, crackling bread, ham hock atop a mound of string beans and new potatoes, and perched on the window-sill a pone of spicy potato pudding.

Very little talk during the meal but that little consisted of banter that pretended to deny affection but in reality flaunted it. Like when Missie May reached for a second helping of the tater pone. Joe snatched it out of her reach.

After Missie May had made two or three unsuccessful grabs at the pan, she begged, "Aw, Joe gimme some mo' dat tater pone."

"Nope, sweetenin' is for us men-folks. Y'all pritty lil frail eels don't need nothin' lak dis. You too sweet already."

"Please, Joe."

"Naw, naw. Ah don't want you to git no sweeter than whut you is already. We goin' down de road a lil piece t'night so you go put on yo' Sunday-go-to-meetin' things."

Missie May looked at her husband to see if he was playing some prank. "Sho nuff, Joe?"

"Yeah. We goin' to de ice cream parlor."

"Where de ice cream parlor at, Joe?"

"A new man done come heah from Chicago and he done got a place and took and opened it up for a ice cream parlor, and bein' as it's real swell, Ah wants you to be one de first ladies to walk in dere and have some set down."

"Do Jesus, Ah ain't knowed nothin' 'bout it. Who de man done it?"

"Mister Otis D. Slemmons, of spots and places—Memphis, Chicago, Jacksonville, Philadelphia and so on."

"Dat heavy-set man wid his mouth full of gold teethes?"

"Yeah. Where did you see 'im at?"

"Ah went down to de sto' tuh git a box of lye and Ah seen 'im standin' on de corner talkin' to some of de mens, and Ah come on back and went to scrubbin' de floor, and he passed and tipped his hat whilst Ah was scourin' de steps. Ah thought Ah never seen *him* befo'."

Joe smiled pleasantly. "Yeah, he's up to date. He got de finest clothes Ah ever seen on a colored man's back."

"Aw, he don't look no better in his clothes than you do in yourn. He got a puzzlegut on 'im and he so chuckle-headed, he got a pone behind his neck."

Joe looked down at his own abdomen and said wistfully, "Wisht Ah had a build on me lak he got. He ain't puzzle-gutted, honey. He jes' got a corperation. Dat make 'm look lak a rich white man. All rich mens is got some belly on 'em."

"Ah seen de pitchers of Henry Ford and he's a spare-built man and Rockefeller look lak he ain't got but one gut. But Ford and Rockefeller and dis Slemmons and all de rest kin be as many-gutted as dey please, Ah'm satisfied wid you jes lak you is, baby. God took pattern after a pine tree and built you noble. Youse a pritty man, and if Ah knowed any way to make you mo' pritty still Ah'd take and do it.''

Joe reached over gently and toyed with Missie May's ear. "You jes' say dat cause you love me, but Ah know Ah can't hold no light to Otis D. Slemmons. Ah ain't never been nowhere and Ah ain't got nothin' but you.''

Missie May got on his lap and kissed him and he kissed back in kind. Then he went on. "All de womens is crazy 'bout 'im everywhere he go.''

"How you know dat, Joe?''

"He tole us so hisself.''

"Dat don't make it so. His mouf is cut cross-ways, ain't it? Well, he kin lie jes' lak anybody else.''

"Good Lawd, Missie! You womens sho is hard to sense into things. He's got a five-dollar gold piece for a stick-pin and he got a ten-dollar gold piece on his watch chain and his mouf is jes' crammed full of gold teethes. Sho wisht it wuz mine. And whut make it so cool, he got money 'cumulated. And womens give it all to 'im.''

"Ah don't see whut de womens see on 'im. Ah wouldn't give 'im a wink if de sheriff wuz after 'im.''

"Well, he tole us how de white womens in Chicago give 'im all dat gold money. So he don't 'low nobody to touch it at all. Not even put dey finger on it. Dey tole 'im not to. You kin make 'miration at it, but don't tetch it.''

"Whyn't he stay up dere where dey so crazy 'bout 'im?''

"Ah reckon dey done made 'im vast-rich and he wants to travel some. He say dey wouldn't leave 'im hit a lick of work. He got mo' lady people crazy 'bout him than he kin shake a stick at.''

"Joe, Ah hates to see you so dumb. Dat stray nigger jes' tell y'all anything and y'all b'lieve it.''

"Go 'head on now, honey and put on yo' clothes. He talkin'

'bout his pritty womens—Ah want 'im to see *mine*."

Missie May went off to dress and Joe spent the time trying to make his stomach punch out like Slemmons' middle. He tried the rolling swagger of the stranger, but found that his tall bone-and-muscle stride fitted ill with it. He just had time to drop back into his seat before Missie May came in dressed to go.

On the way home that night Joe was exultant. "Didn't Ah say ole Otis was swell? Can't he talk Chicago talk? Wuzn't dat funny whut he said when great big fat ole Ida Armstrong come in? He asted me, 'Who is dat broad wid de forte shake?' Dat's a new word. Us always thought forty was a set of figgers but he showed us where it means a whole heap of things. Sometimes he don't say forty, he jes' say thirty-eight and two and dat mean de same thing. Know whut he tole me when Ah wuz payin' for our ice cream? He say, 'Ah have to hand it to you, Joe. Dat wife of yours is jes' thirty-eight and two. Yessuh, she's forte!' Ain't he killin'?"

"He'll do in case of a rush. But he sho is got uh heap uh gold on 'im. Dat's de first time Ah ever seed gold money. It lookted good on him sho nuff, but it'd look a whole heap better on you."

"Who, me? Missie May youse crazy! Where would a po' man lak me git gold money from?"

Missie May was silent for a minute, then she said, "Us might find some goin' long de road some time. Us could."

"Who would be losin' gold money round heah? We ain't even seen none dese white folks wearin' no gold money on dey watch chain. You must be figgerin' Mister Packard or Mister Cadillac goin' pass through heah."

"You don't know whut been lost 'round heah. Maybe somebody way back in memorial times lost they gold money and went on off and it ain't never been found. And then if we wuz to find it, you could wear some 'thout havin' no gang of womens lak dat Slemmons say he got."

Joe laughed and hugged her. "Don't be so wishful 'bout me. Ah'm satisfied de way Ah is. So long as Ah be yo' husband, Ah don't keer 'bout nothin' else. Ah'd ruther all de other womens in de world to be dead than for you to have de toothache. Less we go to bed and git our night rest.''

It was Saturday night once more before Joe could parade his wife in Slemmons' ice cream parlor again. He worked the night shift and Saturday was his only night off. Every other evening around six o'clock he left home, and dying dawn saw him hustling home around the lake where the challenging sun flung a flaming sword from east to west across the trembling water.

That was the best part of life—going home to Missie May. Their white-washed house, the mock battle on Saturday, the dinner and ice cream parlor afterwards, church on Sunday nights when Missie out-dressed any woman in town—all, everything was right.

One night around eleven the acid ran out at the G. and G. The foreman knocked off the crew and let the steam die down. As Joe rounded the lake on his way home, a lean moon rode the lake in a silver boat. If anybody had asked Joe about the moon on the lake, he would have said he hadn't paid it any attention. But he saw it with his feelings. It made him yearn painfully for Missie. Creation obsessed him. He thought about children. They had been married more than a year now. They had money put away. They ought to be making little feet for shoes. A little boy child would be about right.

He saw a dim light in the bedroom and decided to come in through the kitchen door. He could wash the fertilizer dust off himself before presenting himself to Missie May. It would be nice for her not to know that he was there until he slipped into his place in bed and hugged her back. She always liked that.

He eased the kitchen door open slowly and silently, but when he went to set his dinner bucket on the table he bumped it into a pile of dishes, and something crashed to the floor. He heard his wife gasp in fright and hurried to reassure her.

"Iss me, honey. Don't git skeered."

There was a quick, large movement in the bedroom. A rustle, a thud, and a stealthy silence. The light went out.

What? Robbers? Murderers? Some varmint attacking his helpless wife, perhaps. He struck a match, threw himself on guard and stepped over the door-sill into the bedroom.

The great belt on the wheel of Time slipped and eternity stood still. By the match light he could see the man's legs fighting with his breeches in his frantic desire to get them on. He had both chance and time to kill the intruder in his helpless condition—half in and half out of his pants—but he was too weak to take action. The shapeless enemies of humanity that live in the hours of Time had waylaid Joe. He was assaulted in his weakness. Like Samson awakening after his haircut. So he just opened his mouth and laughed.

The match went out and he struck another and lit the lamp. A howling wind raced across his heart, but underneath its fury he heard his wife sobbing and Slemmons pleading for his life. Offering to buy it with all that he had. "Please, suh, don't kill me. Sixty-two dollars at de sto'. Gold money."

Joe just stood. Slemmons looked at the window, but it was screened. Joe stood out like a rough-backed mountain between him and the door. Barring him from escape, from sunrise, from life.

He considered a surprise attack upon the big clown that stood there laughing like a chessy cat. But before his fist could travel an inch, Joe's own rushed out to crush him like a battering ram. Then Joe stood over him.

"Git into yo' damn rags, Slemmons, and dat quick."

Slemmons scrambled to his feet and into his vest and coat. As he grabbed his hat, Joe's fury overrode his intentions and he grabbed at Slemmons with his left hand and struck at him with his right. The right landed. The left grazed the front of his vest. Slemmons was knocked a somersault into the kitchen and fled through the open door. Joe found himself alone with Missie May, with the golden watch charm clutched in his left fist. A short bit of broken chain dangled between his fingers.

Missie May was sobbing. Wails of weeping without words. Joe stood, and after awhile he found out that he had something in his hand. And then he stood and felt without thinking and without seeing with his natural eyes. Missie May kept on crying and Joe kept on feeling so much and not knowing what to do with all his feelings, he put Slemmons' watch charm in his pants pocket and took a good laugh and went to bed.

"Missie May, whut you cryin' for?"

"Cause Ah love you so hard and Ah know you don't love *me* no mo'."

Joe sank his face into the pillow for a spell then he said huskily, "You don't know de feelings of dat yet, Missie May."

"Oh Joe, honey, he said he wuz gointer give me dat gold money and he jes' kept on after me——"

Joe was very still and silent for a long time. Then he said, "Well, don't cry no mo', Missie May. Ah got yo' gold piece for you."

The hours went past on their rusty ankles. Joe still and quiet on one bed-rail and Missie May wrung dry of sobs on the other. Finally the sun's tide crept upon the shore of night and drowned all its hours. Missie May with her face stiff and streaked towards the window saw the dawn come into her yard. It was day. Nothing more. Joe wouldn't be coming home as usual. No need to fling open the front door and sweep off the porch, making it nice for Joe. Never no more breakfast to cook; no more washing and starching of Joe's jumper-jackets and pants. No more nothing. So why get up?

With this strange man in her bed, she felt embarrassed to get up and dress. She decided to wait till he had dressed and gone. Then she would get up, dress quickly and be gone forever beyond reach of Joe's looks and laughs. But he never moved. Red light turned to yellow, then white.

From beyond the no-man's land between them came a voice. A strange voice that yesterday had been Joe's.

"Missie May, ain't you gonna fix me no breakfus'?"

She sprang out of bed. "Yeah, Joe. Ah didn't reckon you wuz hongry."

No need to die today. Joe needed her for a few more minutes anyhow.

Soon there was a roaring fire in the cook stove. Water bucket full and two chickens killed. Joe loved fried chicken and rice. She didn't deserve a thing and good Joe was letting her cook him some breakfast. She rushed hot biscuits to the table as Joe took his seat.

He ate with his eyes in his plate. No laughter, no banter.

"Missie May, you ain't eatin' yo' breakfus'."

"Ah don't choose none, Ah thank yuh."

His coffee cup was empty. She sprang to refill it. When she turned from the stove and bent to set the cup beside Joe's plate, she saw the yellow coin on the table between them.

She slumped into her seat and wept into her arms.

Presently Joe said calmly, "Missie May, you cry too much. Don't look back lak Lot's wife and turn to salt."

The sun, the hero of every day, the impersonal old man that beams as brightly on death as on birth, came up every morning and raced across the blue dome and dipped into the sea of fire every evening. Water ran down hill and birds nested.

Missie knew why she didn't leave Joe. She couldn't. She loved him too much, but she could not understand why Joe didn't leave her. He was polite, even kind at times, but aloof.

There were no more Saturday romps. No ringing silver dollars to stack beside her plate. No pockets to rifle. In fact the yellow coin in his trousers was like a monster hiding in the cave of his pockets to destroy her.

She often wondered if he still had it, but nothing could have induced her to ask nor yet to explore his pockets to see for herself. Its shadow was in the house whether or no.

One night Joe came home around midnight and complained of pains in the back. He asked Missie to rub him down with liniment. It had been three months since Missie had touched his body and it all seemed strange. But she rubbed him. Grateful for the chance. Before morning, youth triumphed and Missie exulted. But the next day, as she joyfully made up their bed, beneath her pillow she found the piece of money with the bit of chain attached.

Alone to herself, she looked at the thing with loathing, but look she must. She took it into her hands with trembling and saw first thing that it was no gold piece. It was a gilded half dollar. Then she knew why Slemmons had forbidden anyone to touch his gold. He trusted village eyes at a distance not to recognize his stick-pin as a gilded quarter, and his watch charm as a four-bit piece.

She was glad at first that Joe had left it there. Perhaps he was through with her punishment. They were man and wife again. Then another thought came clawing at her. He had come home to buy from her as if she were any woman in the long house. Fifty cents for her love. As if to say that he could pay as well as Slemmons. She slid the coin into his Sunday pants pocket and dressed herself and left his house.

Half way between her house and the quarters she met her husband's mother, and after a short talk she turned and went back home. Never would she admit defeat to that woman who prayed for it nightly. If she had not the substance of marriage she had the outside show. Joe must leave *her*. She let him see she didn't want his old gold four-bits too.

She saw no more of the coin for some time though she knew that Joe could not help finding it in his pocket. But his health kept poor, and he came home at least every ten days to be rubbed.

The sun swept around the horizon, trailing its robes of weeks and days. One morning as Joe came in from work, he found Missie May chopping wood. Without a word he took the ax and chopped a huge pile before he stopped.

"You ain't got no business choppin' wood, and you know it."

"How come? Ah been choppin' it for de last longest."

"Ah ain't blind. You makin' feet for shoes."

"Won't you be glad to have a lil baby chile, Joe?"

"You know dat 'thout astin' me."

"Iss gointer be a boy chile and de very spit of you."

"You reckon, Missie May?"

"Who else could it look lak?"

Joe said nothing, but he thrust his hand deep into his pocket and fingered something there.

It was almost six months later Missie May took to bed and Joe went and got his mother to come wait on the house.

Missie May was delivered of a fine boy. Her travail was over when Joe came in from work one morning. His mother and the old women were drinking great bowls of coffee around the fire in the kitchen.

The minute Joe came into the room his mother called him aside.

"How did Missie May make out?" he asked quickly.

"Who, dat gal? She strong as a ox. She gointer have plenty mo'. We done fixed her wid de sugar and lard to sweeten her for de nex' one."

Joe stood silent awhile.

"You ain't ast 'bout de baby, Joe. You oughter be mighty proud cause he sho is de spittin' image of yuh, son. Dat's yourn all right, if you never git another one, dat un is yourn. And you know Ah'm mighty proud too, son, cause Ah never thought well of you marryin' Missie May cause her ma used tuh fan her foot round right smart and Ah been mighty skeered dat Missie May wuz gointer git misput on her road."

Joe said nothing. He fooled around the house till late in the day then just before he went to work, he went and stood at the foot of the bed and asked his wife how she felt. He did this every day during the week.

On Saturday he went to Orlando to make his market. It had been a long time since he had done that.

Meat and lard, meal and flour, soap and starch. Cans of corn and tomatoes. All the staples. He fooled around town for awhile and bought bananas and apples. Way after while he went around to the candy store.

"Hello, Joe," the clerk greeted him. "Ain't seen you in a long time."

"Nope, Ah ain't been heah. Been round in spots and places."

"Want some of them molasses kisses you always buy?"

"Yessuh." He threw the gilded half dollar on the counter. "Will dat spend?"

"Whut is it, Joe? Well, I'll be doggone! A gold-plated four-bit piece. Where'd you git it, Joe?"

"Offen a stray nigger dat come through Eatonville. He had it on his watch chain for a charm—goin' round making out iss gold money. Ha ha! He had a quarter on his tie pin and it wuz all golded up too. Tryin' to fool people. Makin' out he so rich and everything. Ha! Ha! Tryin' to tole off folkses wives from home."

"How did you git it, Joe? Did he fool you, too?"

"Who, me? Naw suh! He ain't fooled me none. Know whut Ah done? He come round me wid his smart talk. Ah hauled off and knocked 'im down and took his old four-bits way from 'im. Gointer buy my wife some good ole lasses kisses wid it. Gimme fifty cents worth of dem candy kisses."

"Fifty cents buys a mighty lot of candy kisses, Joe. Why don't you split it up and take some chocolate bars, too. They eat good, too."

"Yessuh, dey do, but Ah wants all dat in kisses. Ah got a lil boy chile home now. Tain't a week old yet, but he kin suck a sugar tit and maybe eat one them kisses hisself."

Joe got his candy and left the store. The clerk turned to the next customer. "Wisht I could be like these darkies. Laughin' all the time. Nothin' worries 'em."

Back in Eatonville, Joe reached his own front door. There was the ring of singing metal on wood. Fifteen times. Missie May couldn't run to the door, but she crept there as quickly as she could.

"Joe Banks, Ah hear you chunkin' money in mah do'way. You wait till Ah got mah strength back and Ah'm gointer fix you for dat."

Mother
Catherine

One must go straight out St. Claude below the Industrial Canal and turn south on Flood Street and go almost to the Florida Walk. Looking to the right one sees a large enclosure walled round with a high board fence. A half-dozen flags fly bravely from eminences. A Greek cross tops the chapel. A large American flag flies from the huge tent.

A marsh lies between Flood Street and that flag-flying enclosure, and one must walk. As one approaches, the personality of the place comes out to meet one. No ordinary person created this thing.

At the gate there is a rusty wire sticking out through a hole. That is the bell. But a painted notice on the gate itself reads: "Mother Seal is a holy spirit and must not be disturbed."

One does not go straight into the tent, into the presence of Mother Catherine (Mother Seal). One is conducted into the chapel to pray until the spirit tells her to send for you. A place of barbaric splendor, of banners, of embroideries, of images bought and images created by Mother Catherine herself; of an altar glittering with polished brass and kerosene lamps. There are 356 lamps in this building, but not all are upon the main altar.

The walls and ceilings are decorated throughout in red, white and blue. The ceiling and floor in the room of the Sacred Heart are striped in three colors and the walls are panelled. The panels contain a snake design. This is not due to Hoodoo influence but to

African background. I note that the African loves to depict the grace of reptiles.

On a placard: *Speak so you can speak again.*

It would take a volume to describe in detail all of the things in and about this chapel under its Greek cross. But we are summoned by a white-robed saint to the presence.

Mother Catherine holds court in the huge tent. On a raised platform is her bed, a piano, instruments for a ten-piece orchestra, a huge coffee urn, a wood stove, a heater, chairs and rockers and tables. Backless benches fill the tent.

Catherine of Russia could not have been more impressive upon her throne than was this black Catherine sitting upon an ordinary chair at the edge of the platform within the entrance to the tent. Her face and manner are impressive. There is nothing cheap and theatrical about her. She does things and arranges her dwelling as no occidental would. But it is not for effect. It is for feeling. She might have been the matriarchal ruler of some nomad tribe as she sat there with the blue band about her head like a coronet; a white robe and a gorgeous red cape falling away from her broad shoulders, and the box of shaker salt in her hand like a rod of office. I know this reads incongruous, but it did not look so. It seemed perfectly natural for me to go to my knees upon the gravel floor, and when she signalled to me to extend my right hand, palm up for the dab of blessed salt, I hurried to obey because she made me feel that way.

She laid her hand upon my head.

"Daughter, why have you come here?"

"Mother, I come seeking knowledge."

"Thank God. Do y'all hear her? She come here lookin for wisdom. Eat de salt, daughter, and get yo mind with God and me. You shall know what you come to find out. I feel you. I felt you while you was sittin in de chapel. Bring her a veil."

The veil was brought and with a fervent prayer placed upon my head. I did not tell Mother then that I wanted to write about her. That came much later, after many visits. When I did speak of it she was very gracious and let me photograph her and everything behind the walls of her Manger.

I spent two weeks with her, and attended nightly and Sunday services continuously at her tent. Nothing was usual about these meetings. She invariably feeds the gathering. Good, substantial food too. At the Sunday service the big coffee urn was humming, and at a certain point she blessed bread and broke it, and sprinkled on a bit of salt. This she gave to everyone present. To the adults she also gave a cup of coffee. Every cup was personally drawn, sweetened and tasted by her and handed to the communicants as they passed before the platform. At one point she would command everyone to file past the painted barrel and take a glass of water. These things had no inner meaning to an agnostic, but it did drive the dull monotony of the usual Christian service away. It was something, too, to watch the faith it aroused in her followers.

All during her sermons two parrots were crying from their cages. A white cockatoo would scream when the shouting grew loud. Three canary birds were singing and chirping happily all through the service. Four mongrel dogs strolled about. A donkey, a mother goat with her kid, numbers of hens, a sheep—all wandered in and out of the service without seeming out of place. A Methodist or Baptist church—or one of any denomination whatever—would have been demoralised by any one of these animals. Two dogs fought for a place beside the heater. Three children under three years of age played on the platform in the rear without distracting the speaker or the audience. The blue and red robed saint stood immobile in her place directly behind the speaker and the world moved on.

Unlike most religious dictators Mother Catherine does not crush the individual. She encourages originality. There is an air of gaiety about the enclosure. All of the animals are treated with tenderness.

No money is ever solicited within the enclosure of the Manger. If you feel to give, you may. Mother wears a pouch suspended from her girdle. You may approach the platform at any time and drop your contribution in. But you will be just as welcome if you have nothing. All of the persons who live at the Manger are there at Mother Catherine's expense. She encourages music and sees that her juveniles get off to school on time.

There is a catholic flavor about the place, but it is certainly not catholic. She has taken from all the religions she knows anything about any feature that pleases her.

Hear Mother Seal: "Good evening, Veils and Banners!

"God tells me to tell you *(invariable opening)* that He holds the world in the middle of His hand.

"There is no hell beneath this earth. God wouldn't build a hell to burn His breath.

"There is no heaven beyond dat blue globe. There is a between-world between this brown earth and the blue above. So says the beautiful spirit.

"When we die, where does the breath go? Into trees and grass and animals. Your flesh goes back to mortal earth to fertilise it. So says the beautiful spirit.

"Our brains is trying to make something out of us. Everybody can be something good.

"It is right that a woman should lead. A womb was what God made in the beginning, and out of that womb was born Time, and all that fills up space. So says the beautiful spirit.

"Some are weak to do wisdom things, but strong to do wicked things.

"He could have been born in the biggest White House in the world. But the reason He didn't is that He knowed a falling race was coming what couldn't get to no great White House, so He got born so my people could all reach.

"God is just as satisfied with the damnation of men as He is with their salvation. So says the beautiful spirit.

"It is not for people to know the whence.

"Don't teach what the apostles and the prophets say. Go to the tree and get the pure sap and find out whether they were right.

"No man has seen spirit—men can see what spirit does, but no man can see spirit."

As she was ready to grant blessings an evil thought reached her and she sat suddenly on a chair and covered her face with her hands, explaining why she did so. When it passed she rose, "Now I will teach you again."

Here the food was offered up but not distributed until the call came from the spirit.

St. Prompt Succor brought the basin and towel at a signal. She washed her hands and face.

It is evident that Mother Seal takes her stand as an equal with Christ.

No nailing or building is done on Friday. A carpenter may saw or measure, but no nailing or joining.

She heals by the laying on of hands, by suggestion and copious doses of castor oil and Epsom salts. She heals in the tent and at great distances. She has blessed water in the barrel for her followers, but she feels her divinity to such an extent that she blesses the water in the hydrants at the homes of her followers without moving out of her tent.

No one may cross his legs within the Manger. That is an insult to the spirit.

Mother Catherine's conception of the divinity of Christ is that Joseph was his foster father as all men are foster fathers, in that all children are of God and all fathers are merely the means.

All of her followers wear her insignia. The women wear a veil of unbleached muslin; the men, an arm-band. All bear the crescent and M.C.S. (Mother Catherine's Saints). They must be worn everywhere.

In late February and early March it rained heavily and many feared a flood. Mother Seal exhorted all of her followers to pin their faith in her. All they need do is believe in her and come to her and eat the blessed fish she cooked for them and there would be no flood. "God," she said, "put oars in the fishes' hands. Eat this fish and you needn't fear the flood no more than a fish would."

All sympathetic magic. Chicken, beef, lamb are animals of pleasing blood. They are used abundantly as food and often in healing. A freshly killed chicken was split open and bound to a sore leg.

All of her followers, white and colored, are her children. She has as many of one race as the other.

"I got all kinds of children, but I am they mother. Some of 'em are saints; some of 'em are conzempts (convicts) and jailbirds; some of 'em kills babies in their bodies; some of 'em walks the streets at night—but they's all my children. God got all kinds, how come I cain't love all of mine? So says the beautiful spirit.

"Now y'all go home in faith. I'm going to appear to you all in three days. Don't doubt me. Go home in faith and pray."

There is a period in the service given over to experiences.

One woman had a vision. She saw a flash of lightning on the wall. It wrote, "Go to Mother Seal." She came with pus on the kidneys and was healed.

A girl of fourteen had a vision of a field of spinach that turned to lilies with one large lily in the middle. The field was her church and the large lily was Mother Catherine.

Most of the testimony has to do with acknowledging that they have been healed by Mother's power, or relating how the wishes they made on Mother came true.

Mother Catherine's religion is matriarchal. Only God and the Mother count. Childbirth is the most important element in the creed. Her compound is called the Manger, and is dedicated to the birth of children in or out of wedlock.

Over and over she lauds the bringing forth. *There is no sinful birth.* And the woman who avoids it by abortion is called a "damnable extrate."

Mother Catherine was not converted by anyone. Like Christ, Mohammed, Buddha, the call just came. No one stands between her and God.

After the call she consecrated her body by refraining from the sex relation, and by fasting and prayer.

She was married at the time. Her husband prayed two weeks before he was converted to her faith. Whereupon she baptised him in a tub in the backyard. They lived together six months as a holy man and woman before the call of the flesh made him elope with one of her followers.

She held her meetings first on Jackson Avenue, but the crowds that swarmed about her made the authorities harry her. So some of her wealthy followers bought the tract of land below the Industrial Canal where the Manger now is.

God sent her into the Manger over a twelve-foot board fence—not through a gate. She must set no time for her going but when the spirit gave the word. After her descent through the roof of the chapel she has never left the grounds but once, and that was not intentional. She was learning to drive a car within the enclosure. It got out of control and tore a hole through the fence before it stopped. She called to her followers to "Come git me!" (She must not set her foot on the unhallowed ground outside the Manger.) They came and reverently lifted her and bore her back inside. The spot in the yard upon which she was set down became sacred, for a voice spoke as her feet touched the ground and said, "Put down here the Pool of Gethsemane so that the believers may have holy water to drink." The well is under construction at this writing.

Uncle Monday

People talk a whole lot about Uncle Monday, but they take good pains not to let him hear none of it. Uncle Monday is an out-and-out conjure doctor. That in itself is enough to make the people handle him carefully, but there is something about him that goes past hoodoo. Nobody knows anything about him, and that's a serious matter in a village of less than three hundred souls, especially when a person has lived there for forty years and more.

Nobody knows where he came from nor who his folks might be. Nobody knows for certain just when he did come to town. He was just there one morning when the town awoke. Joe Lindsay was the first to see him. He had some turtle lines set down on Lake Belle. It is a hard lake to fish because it is entirely surrounded by a sooky marsh that is full of leeches and moccasins. There is plenty of deep water once you pole a boat out beyond the line of cypress pines, but there are so many alligators out there that most people don't think the trout are worth the risk. But Joe had baited some turtle lines and thrown them as far as he could without wading into the marsh. So next morning he went as early as he could see light to look after his lines. There was a turtle head on every line, and he pulled them up cursing the 'gators for robbing his hooks. He says he started on back home, but when he was a few yards from where his lines had been set something made him look back,

and he nearly fell dead. For there was an old man walking out of
the lake between two cypress knees. The water there was too deep
for any wading, and besides, he says the man was not wading, he
was walking vigorously as if he were on dry land.

Lindsay says he was too scared to stand there and let the man
catch up with him, and he was too scared to move his feet; so he
just stood there and saw the man cross the marshy strip and come
down the path behind him. He says he felt the hair rise on his head
as the man got closer to him, and somehow he thought about an
alligator slipping up on him. But he says that alligators were in the
front of his mind that morning because first, he had heard bull
'gators fighting and bellowing all night long down in this lake, and
then his turtle lines had been robbed. Besides, everybody knows
that the father of all 'gators lives in Belle Lake.

The old man was coming straight on, taking short quick steps
as if his legs were not long enough for his body, and working his
arms in unison. Lindsay says it was all he could do to stand his
ground and not let the man see how scared he was, but he
managed to stand still anyway. The man came up to him and
passed him without looking at him seemingly. After he had
passed, Lindsay noticed that his clothes were perfectly dry, so he
decided that his own eyes had fooled him. The old man must have
come up to the cypress knees in a boat and then crossed the marsh
by stepping from root to root. But when he went to look, he found
no convenient roots for anybody to step on. Moreover, there was
no boat on the lake either.

The old man looked queer to everybody, but still no one would
believe Lindsay's story. They said that he had seen no more than
several others—that is, that the old man had been seen coming
from the direction of the lake. That was the first that the village
saw of him, way back in the late 'eighties, and so far, nobody
knows any more about his past than that. And that worries the
town.

Another thing that struck everybody unpleasantly was the fact
that he never asked a name nor a direction. Just seemed to know

who everybody was, and called each and every one by their right name. Knew where everybody lived too. Didn't earn a living by any of the village methods. He didn't garden, hunt, fish, nor work for the white folks. Stayed so close in the little shack that he had built for himself that sometimes three weeks would pass before the town saw him from one appearance to another.

Joe Clarke was the one who found out his name was Monday. No other name. So the town soon was calling him Uncle Monday. Nobody can say exactly how it came to be known that he was a hoodoo man. But it turned out that that was what he was. People said he was a good one too. As much as they feared him, he had plenty of trade. Didn't take him long to take all the important cases away from Ant Judy, who had had a monopoly for years.

He looked very old when he came to the town. Very old, but firm and strong. Never complained of illness.

But once, Emma Lou Pittman went over to his shack early in the morning to see him on business, and ran back with a fearsome tale. She said that she noticed a heavy trail up to his door and across the steps, as if a heavy, bloody body had been dragged inside. The door was cracked a little and she could hear a great growling and snapping of mighty jaws. It wasn't exactly a growling either, it was more a subdued howl in a bass tone. She shoved the door a little and peeped inside to see if some varmint was in there attacking Uncle Monday. She figured he might have gone to sleep with the door ajar and a catamount, or a panther, or a bob-cat might have gotten in. He lived near enough to Blue Sink Lake for a 'gator to have come in the house, but she didn't remember ever hearing of them tracking anything but dogs.

But no; no varmint was inside there. The noise she heard was being made by Uncle Monday. He was lying on a pallet of pine-straw in such agony that his eyes were glazed over. His right arm was horribly mangled. In fact, it was all but torn away from right below the elbow. The side of his face was terribly torn too. She called him, but he didn't seem to hear her. So she hurried back for some men to come and do something for him. The men came as fast as their legs would bring them, but the house was locked from the outside and there was no answer to their knocking. Mrs. Pittman would have been made out an awful liar if it were not for the trail of blood. So they concluded that Uncle Monday had gotten hurt somehow and had dragged himself home, or had been dragged by a friend. But who could the friend have been?

Nobody saw Uncle Monday for a month after that. Every day or so, someone would drop by to see if hide or hair could be found of him. A full month passed before there was any news. The town had about decided that he had gone away as mysteriously as he had come.

But one evening around dusk-dark Sam Merchant and Jim Gooden were on their way home from a squirrel hunt around Lake Belle. They swore that, as they rounded the lake and approached the footpath that leads towards the village, they saw what they thought was the great 'gator that lives in the lake crawl out of the marsh. Merchant wanted to take a shot at him for his hide and teeth, but Gooden reminded him that they were loaded with bird shot, which would not even penetrate a 'gator's hide, let alone kill it. They say the thing they took for the 'gator then struggled awhile, pulling off something that looked like a long black glove. Then he scraped a hole in the soft ground with his paws and carefully buried the glove which had come from his right paw. Then without looking either right or left, he stood upright and walked on towards the village. Everybody saw Uncle Monday come thru the town, but still Merchant's tale was hard to swallow. But, by degrees, people came to believe that Uncle Monday could shed any injured member of his body and grow a new one in its place. At any rate, when he reappeared his right hand and arm bore no scars.

The village is even sceptical about his dying. Once Joe Clarke said to Uncle Monday, "I'god, Uncle Monday, aint you skeered to stay way off by yo'self, old as you is?"

Uncle Monday asked, "Why would I be skeered?"

"Well, you liable to take sick in de night sometime, and you'd be dead befo' anybody would know you was even sick."

Uncle Monday got up off the nail keg and said in a voice so low that only the men right close to him could hear what he said, "I have been dead for many a year. I have come back from where you are going." Then he walked away with his quick short steps, and his arms bent at the elbow, keeping time with his feet.

It is believed that he has the singing stone, which is the greatest charm, the most powerful "hand" in the world. It is a diamond and comes from the mouth of a serpent (which is thought of as something different from an ordinary snake) and is the diamond of diamonds. It not only lights your home without the help of any other light, but it also warns its owner of approach.

The serpents who produce these stones live in the deep waters of Lake Maitland. There is a small island in this lake and a rare plant grows there, which is the only food of this serpent. She only comes to nourish herself in the height of a violent thunderstorm, when she is fairly certain that no human will be present.

It is impossible to kill or capture her unless nine healthy people have gone before to prepare the way with THE OLD ONES, and then more will die in the attempt to conquer her. But it is not necessary to kill or take her to get the stone. She has two. One is embedded in her head, and the other she carries in her mouth. The first one cannot be had without killing the serpent, but the second one may be won from her by trickery.

Since she carries this stone in her mouth, she cannot eat until she has put it down. It is her pilot, that warns her of danger. So when she comes upon the island to feed, she always vomits the stone and covers it with earth before she goes to the other side of the island to dine.

To get this diamond, dress yourself all over in black velvet. Your assistant must be dressed in the same way. Have a velvet-covered bowl along. Be on the island before the storm reaches its height, but leave your helper in the boat and warn him to be ready to pick you up and flee at a moment's notice.

Climb a tall tree and wait for the coming of the snake. When she comes out of the water, she will look all about her on the ground to see if anyone is about. When she is satisfied that she is alone, she will vomit the stone, cover it with dirt and proceed to her feeding ground. Then, as soon as you feel certain that she is busy eating, climb down the tree as swiftly as possible, cover the mound hiding the stone with the velvet-lined bowl and flee for your life to the boat. The boatman must fly from the island with all possible speed. For as soon as you approach the stone it will ring like chiming bells, and the serpent will hear it. Then she will run to defend it. She will return to the spot, but the velvet-lined bowl will make it invisible to her. In her wrath she will knock down grown trees and lash the island like a hurricane. Wait till a calm fair day to return for the stone. She never comes up from the bottom of the lake in fair weather. Furthermore, a serpent who has lost her mouth-stone cannot come to feed alone after that. She must bring her mate. The mouth-stone is their guardian, and when they lose it they remain in constant danger unless accompanied by one who has the singing stone.

They say that Uncle Monday has a singing stone, and that is why he knows everything without being told.

Whether he has the stone or not, nobody thinks of doubting his power as a hoodoo man. He is feared, but sought when life becomes too powerful for the powerless. Mary Ella Shaw backed out on Joe-Nathan Moss the day before the wedding was to have come off. Joe-Nathan had even furnished the house and bought rations. His people, her people, everybody tried to make her marry the boy. He loved her so, and besides he had put out so much of his little cash to fix for the marriage. But Mary Ella just wouldn't. She had seen Caddie Brewton, and she was one of the kind who couldn't keep her heart still after her eye had wandered.

So Joe-Nathan's mama went to see Uncle Monday. He said, "Since she is the kind of woman that lets her mind follow her eye, we'll have to let the snake-bite cure itself. You go on home. Never no man will keep her. She kin grab the world full of men, but she'll never keep one any longer than from one full moon to the other."

Fifteen years have passed. Mary Ella has been married four times. She was a very pretty girl, and men just kept coming, but not one man has ever stayed with her longer than the twenty-eight days. Besides her four husbands, no telling how many men she has shacked up with for a few weeks at a time. She has eight children by as many different men, but still no husband.

John Wesley Hogan was another driver of sharp bargains in love. By his own testimony and experience, all women from eight to eighty were his meat, but the woman who was sharp enough to make him marry her wasn't born and her mama was dead. They couldn't frame him and they couldn't scare him.

Mrs. Bradley came to him nevertheless about her Dinkie. She called him out from his work-place and said, "John Wesley, you know I'm a widder-woman and I aint got no husband to go to de front for me, so I reckon I got to do de talkin' for me and my chile. I come in de humblest way I know how to ast you to go 'head and marry my chile befo' her name is painted on de signposts of scorn."

If it had not made John Wesley so mad, it would have been funny to him. So he asked her scornfully, " 'Oman, whut you take me for? You better git outa my face wid dat mess! How you reckon *I* know who Dinkie been foolin roun wid? Don't try to come dat mess over *me*. I been all over de North. I aint none of yo' fool. You must think I'm Big Boy. They kilt Big Boy shootin after Fat Sam so there aint no mo' fools in de world. Ha, ha! All de wimmen *I* done seen! I'll tell you like de monkey tole de elephant—don't bull me, big boy! If you want Dinkie to git married off so bad, go grab one of dese country clowns. I aint yo' man. Taint no use you goin runnin to de high-sheriff neither. I got witness to prove Dinkie knowed more'n I do."

Mrs. Bradley didn't bother with the sheriff. All he could do was to make John Wesley marry Dinkie; but by the time the interview was over that wasn't what the stricken mother wanted. So she waited till dark, and went on over to Uncle Monday.

Everybody says you don't have to explain things to Uncle Monday. Just go there, and you will find that he is ready for you when you arrive. So he set Mrs. Bradley down at a table, facing a huge mirror hung against the wall. She says he had a loaded pistol and a huge dirk lying on the table before her. She looked at both of the weapons, but she could not decide which one she wanted to use. Without a word, he handed her a gourd full of water and she took a swallow. As soon as the water passed over her tongue she seized the gun. He pointed towards the looking-glass. Slowly the form of John Wesley formed in the glass and finally stood as vivid as life before her. She took careful aim and fired. She was amazed that the mirror did not shatter. But there was a loud report, a cloud of bluish smoke and the figure vanished.

On the way home, Brazzle told her that John Wesley had dropped dead, and Mr. Watson had promised to drive over to Orlando in the morning to get a coffin for him.

ANT JUDY BICKERSTAFF

Uncle Monday wasn't the only hoodoo doctor around there. There was Ant Judy Bickerstaff. She was there before the coming of Uncle Monday. Of course it didn't take long for professional jealousy to arise. Uncle Monday didn't seem to mind Ant Judy, but she resented him, and she couldn't hide her feelings.

This was natural when you consider that before his coming she used to make all the "hands" around there, but he soon drew off the greater part of the trade.

Year after year this feeling kept up. Every now and then some little incident would accentuate the rivalry. Monday was sitting on top of the heap, but Judy was not without her triumphs.

Finally she began to say that she could reverse anything that he put down. She said she could not only reverse it, she could throw it back on *him*, let alone his client. Nobody talked to him about her boasts. People never talked to him except on business anyway. Perhaps Judy felt safe in her boasting for this reason.

Then one day she took it in her head to go fishing. Her children and grandchildren tried to discourage her. They argued with her about her great age and her stiff joints. But she had her grandson to fix her a trout pole and a bait pole and set out for Blue Sink, a lake said to be bottomless by the villagers. Furthermore, she didn't set out till near sundown. She didn't want any company. It was no use talking, she felt that she just must go fishing in Blue Sink.

She didn't come home when dark came, and her family worried a little. But they reasoned she had probably stopped at one of her friends' houses to rest and gossip, so they didn't go to hunt her right away. But when the night wore on and she didn't return, the children were sent out to locate her.

She was not in the village. A party was organised to search Blue Sink for her. It was after nine o'clock at night when the party found her. She was in the lake. Lying in shallow water and keeping her old head above the water by supporting it on her elbow. Her son Ned said that he saw a huge alligator dive away as he shined the torch upon his mother's head.

They bore Ant Judy home and did everything they could for her. Her legs were limp and useless and she never spoke a word, not a coherent word, for three days. It was more than a week before she could tell how she came to be in the lake.

She said that she hadn't really wanted to go fishing. The family and the village could witness that she never had fooled round the lakes. But that afternoon she *had* to go. She couldn't say why, but she knew she must go. She baited her hooks and stood waiting for a bite. She was afraid to sit down on the damp ground on account of her rheumatism. She got no bites. When she saw the sun setting she wanted to come home, but somehow she just couldn't leave the spot. She was afraid, terribly afraid down there on the lake, but she couldn't leave.

When the sun was finally gone and it got dark, she says she felt a threatening, powerful evil all around her. She was fixed to the spot. A small but powerful whirlwind arose right under her feet. Something terrific struck her and she fell into the water. She tried to climb out, but found that she could not use her legs. She thought of 'gators and otters, and leeches and gar-fish, and began to scream, thinking maybe somebody would hear her and come to her aid.

Suddenly a bar of red light fell across the lake from one side to the other. It looked like a fiery sword. Then she saw Uncle Monday walking across the lake to her along this flaming path. On either side of the red road swam thousands of alligators, like an army behind its general.

The light itself was awful. It was red, but she never had seen any red like it before. It jumped and moved all the time, but always it pointed straight across the lake to where she lay helpless in the water. The lake is nearly a mile wide, but Ant Judy says Uncle Monday crossed it in less than a minute and stood over her. She closed her eyes from fright, but she saw him right on thru her lids.

After a brief second she screamed again. Then he growled and leaped at her. "Shut up!" he snarled. "Part your lips just one more time and it will be your last breath! Your bragging tongue has brought you here and you are going to stay here until you acknowledge my power. So you can throw back my work, eh? I put you in this lake; show your power and get out. You will not die, and you will not leave this spot until you give consent in your heart that I am your master. Help will come the minute you knuckle under."

She fought against him. She felt that once she was before her own altar she could show him something. He glowered down upon her for a spell and then turned and went back across the lake the way he had come. The light vanished behind his feet. Then a huge alligator slid up beside her where she lay trembling and all her strength went out of her. She lost all confidence in her powers. She began to feel if only she might either die or escape from the horror, she would never touch another charm again. If only she could escape the maw of the monster beside her! Any other death but that. She wished that Uncle Monday would come back so that she might plead with him for deliverance. She opened her mouth to call, but found that speech had left her. But she saw a light approaching by land. It was the rescue party.

Ant Judy never did regain the full use of her legs, but she got to the place where she could hobble about the house and yard. After relating her adventure on Lake Blue Sink she never called the name of Uncle Monday again.

The rest of the village, always careful in that respect, grew almost as careful as she. But sometimes when they would hear the great bull 'gator, that everybody knows lives in Lake Belle, bellowing on cloudy nights, some will point the thumb in the general direction of Uncle Monday's house and whisper, "The Old Boy is visiting the home folks tonight."

The Fire
and the Cloud

Moses sat upon his new made grave on Mount Nebo. His back stooped wearily, but his strong gaze leaped the Jordan and travelled over the land of Canaan.

A lizard popped out of a hole under a rock directly before Moses.

"Good morning, O brother-of-insufficient walking legs. I find you at waking where I left you at sun-rest." So the reptile greeted Moses.

With his eyes still in Canaan, Moses answered. "Ah yes, little kin who-uses-all-his-legs-for-walking, the labor has been long. This is the thirtieth day that I have sojourned upon this mountain." He waved at the mound of stone. "Behold, friend, it is finished."

From the top of a low bush near the left foot of Moses the lizard studied the work. "It is good. But you have been a long time in the building of your nest. Your female must be near death from retaining her eggs."

"No fecund female awaits this labor."

"A male alone!"

"A male alone."

"Perhaps you are a widower also. It is very sad, but you must know that fat lizards have may sudden-striking enemies." A tear dewed the leaf beneath him.

"I am alone, O lizard, because I am alone."

The lizard felt that Moses' answer lacked reason and he would have taught him how to make answer as do the great ones in the council of lizards, but when he lifted his head to speak, he beheld the head of Moses enveloped in a dense white cloud. "The gods have borne away the head of the rock-lifter," he thought aloud, and scurried to his hole in quivering awe. He slept and memory fled away. So soon he emerged and looked into the benign eyes of the nation-maker from the same bush.

"The lizard says that the present hour is much hotter than the tender ones of morning," he began abruptly.

"The lizard is wise," Moses answered casually.

"The words of lizards are full of truth," the reptile went on cunningly. "But even so, O friend-who-digs-his-hole-above-ground, the greatest among us has no rod that can summon fly-swarms at will." The lizard said this and looked at Moses under-eyed.

"That is true," Moses agreed with his thoughts at a distance.

"All your works accumulate praise. Twenty and nine days you have been with me upon this mountain, and each day you have called forth a swarm of flies at the hour when I am most hungry."

"Pardon me, friend," Moses said humbly. "The thirtieth day shall be as the twenty-nine." He lifted his rod ever so slightly and flies swarmed over the bush upon which the lizard rested. "Sup."

The lizard ate. The last fly of the swarm was just enough. Every day it had been so. He looked at Moses in admiration.

"Whence do you come, O Master?"

Moses pointed to the plain of Moab where the tents of Israel crowded the horizon.

"How do you say that you are alone if of your kind such hosts of multitudes be at hand?"

"I am that I am and so I am alone. I am Moses, The-drawn-out. It is given me to call God by his power-compelling names. I bear his rod. The blind and the mute have companionship, but I am a leader."

"I see that your leadership has galled your shoulders. Why then did you go before?"

"I went because I was sent. In my agony I cried into nothingness and enquired 'Why am I called?' There was no answer. Only the voice that again said 'Go!' "

"How long O mighty Moses, have you led?"

"Forty years and more. From the mountain of God I returned to Egypt, and with my stretched-out arm I confounded the Pharaoh, and led my people forth with a mighty hand. From the Nile, where we were bondsmen, to beyond the Jordan, where they shall rule."

"Ah Moses, because you have so exalted your kind and kindred, their love for you must exceed this great mountain in thickness and the height would not be less."

"Lizard, love is not created by service to mankind. But if the good be deemed sufficiently great, man sometimes erects little mountains of stone to the doer called monuments. They do this so that in the enjoyment of the benefit they forget not the benefactor. The heart of man is an ever empty abyss into which the whole world shall fall and be swallowed up."

"Do none of the hosts love their deliverer?"

"Who shall know? However, Joshua is strong in soul and body. He shall follow me. He gives thought to me. If I do not return to my tent before another day begins, he will ascend this mountain in search of me."

"Your labors have brought little joy."

"Lizard, forty years ago I led a horde of slaves out of Egyptian bondage and held them in the wilderness until I grew men. Look now upon the plain of Moab. A great people! They shall rule over nations and dwell in cities they have not builded. Yet they have rebelled against me ever. A stiff-necked race of people. They murmur against me anew because I have held them before the Jordan for forty days. Their taste would humble them before the armies of Canaan. They must wait yet another thirty days. I have not striven with God, with the wilderness, with rebellion and my own soul for forty years to bring them to a new bondage in the land beyond the Jordan. They shall wait for strength."

"How then, Moses will you hold your horde of murmurers on

the brink of the Jordan when their eyes already feast on the good land?''

"If a leader dies in Israel, the hosts mourn thirty days."

Again the head of Moses disappeared in cloud and a sleep fell upon the lizard. But the cloud-splitting eye of Moses carried to the silver gilt hills of Canaan lying half in the late light, and half in shadows of the setting sun, and his soul wandered beyond the Jordan for the space of half an hour. When it returned to him upon Nebo he gazed down upon the tented nation beneath him, and the nation-maker sorrowing, wept over Israel. But Israel, unknowing, sang and danced, hammered its swords, milked its cows, got born and died.

"Ah Moses," the lizard observed on waking. "You shall yet rejoice. Soon your hosts will triumph beyond the Jordan, and you shall be called king of kings."

"I have already known the palaces of the Pharaohs, lizard, but I was not happy in the midst of them."

"You were an alien in the Egyptian palaces, but the mansions in Canaan shall be of your kindred."

"When the Israelites shall erect palaces, God shall raise up abundant palace-dwellers to fill them. I have taught them statutes and judgments fit for the guidance of kings and shepherds alike."

"But will they remember your laws?"

"If I tarry within this that I have erected on Nebo, then shall they remember my laws in Canaan. People value monuments above men, and signs above works."

The lizard travelled around the tomb and studied its contours.

"But Moses, your splendid new dwelling has no hole by which you may enter. A queer dwelling. A hole above ground—no entrance."

"This is no dwelling, lizard. It is a place of burial."

"I am no longer young, Moses, perhaps, I nodded. What buried you there?"

"No, you did not witness it, but here is interred the voice of Sinai, the stretched-out arm of Moses, the lawgiver, the nation-maker."

"Those are your words, but I behold you sitting as you sat at sunrise."

"Those are your thoughts, but you see the old man of the wilderness sitting upon the tomb of Moses."

Whereupon Moses arose and took one long look at the tented nation in the valley, and his face shone as it had done at Sinai when even Aaron had feared to look upon it. He took one dragging look beyond the Jordan, then wrapped his mantle closely about him.

"Sun is set," he said in low rumbles. "I depart."

He laid his rod upon the new-made tomb, set his face sternly towards the wilderness and walked away, leaning lightly on a new-cut staff.

"But wait, O Moses!" the lizard squeaked after him. "You have left your rod behind."

"Oh, Joshua will pick it up," he called back and strode on.

Cock Robin
Beale Street

Uncle July was mad clear through. A'nt Dooby could tell by the way he threw down the load of kindling in the corner behind the kitchen stove. Anyhow, if he wasn't really mad, he was letting on like it. It was an off day with her and she didn't feel like no fussing, so she started in right away to head him off.

"July, don't you come in here starting none of your foolishness wid me this day and year of our Lawd! I done told you now!"

"Who's starting any fussing? I know 'tain't none of me, I ain't broke a breath wid you, 'oman. You better go 'head and leave me be."

A'nt Dooby braced herself for the storm. She plunked her fat fists on her abundant hips and glared him round the room. July could see names like "mule" "fool" "sea-buzzard" "ground-hog" and things like that swimming around in her eyes. So he sat down, pulled off one shoe, looked at it hard, then pulled off the other one, wiggled his toes and lit his pipe.

"Hit's a sin before de living jestice!" July exploded. "Dese white folks ought to talk whut dey know, and testify to whut see."

"Whut's de matter now?" Dooby asked, full of suspicion.

"Going 'round letting on dat Cock Robin was a bird! Jest heard Miz Pendleton reading out of some kind of a book how Cock Robin was a real-true bird wid feathers on him and got kilt wid a arrow. Hit's a sin and a shame! 'Tain't a word of it so! I knowed

Cock Robin well—was right dere when he got kilt wid a forty-four, and was at de funeral.''

A'nt Dooby was unimpressed.

"I ain't knowed nothing 'bout no Cock Robin gitting kilt and you must a' sneaked off to de funeral and never told me nothing 'tall about it.''

"Oh, dat was back dere in Memphis. I used to git around right smart before I was saved. Long before I and you made a wed. And den it wasn't exactly no funeral neither. Dere was some talk about funeralizing him, but it didn't amount to nothing.

"Cock Robin was a high-flier if ever I seed one. Sung solo in de choir, and got round right smart wid de lady-people. Comed to Memphis from off somewhere like a whole heap of us done. Big doings in Memphis in dem days.

"Well, late one evening just 'fore sundown everybody was down 'round Beale Street sort of catching de cool breezes off de gutter wid de Grease Spot doing a heap of business, de pool-room was full, and somebody was jooking on de piano in de Shimmy Shack, dat was a high class hotel run by Sister Buzzard, slap on Beale.

"Quite a few folks was scattered around de place upstairs and down, when all of a suddent we heard three pistol shots down 'round de front. Everybody run to de windows and looked down on de street. Dere was Cock Robin laying on de sidewalk in front of de hotel wid three bullet holes in him.

"Brother Owl, he was around so he naturally took charge and went to asking folks, 'Who kilt Cock Robin?' Not expecting to git much of a answer.

" 'I kilt Cock Robin,' Bull Sparrow says, pushing up front in de crowd. 'Who is it wants to know?' He had his gun wide open in his hand.

" 'Not dat we cares, Brother Sparrow,' Brother Owl sort of simmerized. 'Us just asked for a little information to find out how come.'

" 'Well, it's like dis,' Bull Sparrow told him, and sort of reared back on his dew-claws. 'You all knows dat I am a sparrow, and all my folks was sparrows from way back.'

" 'Dat sho is de truth,' they told him, 'De spitting image of your paw.'

" 'And furthermore, you all know dat sparrows don't never lay nothing but plain white eggs. My great-great-great grandma, she laid white eggs. My mama laid white eggs.'

" 'Dat sho is de truth!' Sister Buzzard put in. 'Your maw and your paw did they nesting right here in my Shimmy Shack.'

" 'Well, now when me and my wife first started to nesting, she never laid nothing but plain white eggs. But things done changed, ever since dat Cock Robin been 'round here. Now, every time I go off on a worm hunt, when I get back, I find another blue egg in my nest.'

" 'Dere now!' Brother Crow hollered and jumped clear up in de air. 'You done got *me* to scratching where I don't itch. Seem like to me, I seen a bluish egg or two 'round my nest, too.'

" 'Tain't no ifs and ands about it,' Brother Bull snorted, 'Cock Robin was in de egg business. Whilst I sympathizes wid Brother Sparrow, I'm glad we don't have no egg-laying 'round our place.'

" 'You mean Cock Robin been laying eggs?' Brother Fly asked.

" 'Aw, naw! You know no rooster don't lay no eggs. Us leaves things like dat to de hen-folks.' Brother Owl hooted. 'But he was too mixified just de same.'

" 'You done right, Brother Sparrow.' Everybody told him. 'Kilt him in de first degree and finished de job off well.'

" 'All we got to do now is to funeralize him,' Brother Owl said, and got him a high chair to sit on. 'He was sort of unfinancial, so we got to do 'round to fix things up.'

"Wid that, he took and signed different ones to do and to fix until he had a burial robe and everything fixed up down to de chief mourner, which was Sister Dove. She was a widow 'oman and used to mourning, and she really could mourn. Den he took up de hall he was going to be funeralized from.

"Right dere was where he throwed de fat in de fire 'cause Brother Cock Robin belonged to every fraternal and benevolent society round dere. De Night-Stepping Owls allowed dat he was a brother in good standing, and naturally dey would parade him to de graveyard. De Never-Been-Caught Fishes, De Ever-Blooming Blackbirds, De Muckty-Duckty Beetle-Bugs, De High-Roosting Crows, and Fun-Feeling Flies all hollered dat dey put on de best funerals in town. Dey argued, and went home and got into regalia to show Brother Owl how dey paraded, and brought along de bands and put de thing on. Brother Owl couldn't say for not knowing which one of dem was de best. Brother Bull, he stood dere by Brother Owl and said, 'I don't care who gits de deceased. I aim to march in front.'

" 'How come, Brother Bull?' Dey all wanted to know. 'You don't belong to none of de orders.'

" 'Matters a difference about dat,' he told 'em. 'You know dat bull goes in front of everything. *I aims to march in front.* I got my parading stick all ready and my strutting hat.'

"Brother Owl scratched his head all over two or three more times and den he said, 'Everybody parades de best. So as not to have no hard feeling, who ever pays de funeral expenses can have de body. Dat's fair.'

"De unfairness of de thing took everybody by surprise, so nobody couldn't say a word for a long time. Finally, Sister Blackbird up and told him, 'Brother Owl, if you was talking about money all dis time, how come you never told nobody? Here you done got us all dressed up to funeralize our dear deceased, and now you come talking about money. My people! My people!'

" 'Yeah, and had us gitting up bands to march by and everything,' Sparrow told him. Everybody was good and mad at Brother Owl.

"Brother Crow snapped his fingers and said, 'Folkses and feathers, I clean forgot! Sister Speckled-Hen is having a big fish fry and barbecue down on Front Street and Beale dis evening. She told me to tell everybody, but all dis mess 'bout Cock Robin put it clean out of my head.' He rolled his eyes at Brother Owl. Everybody begin to get more lively right away, so Brother Crow went on. 'Since we is all 'sembled right here together, and in regalia, how come we don't all form one big amalgamated, contaminated parade down to Sister Speckled-Hen's place and enjoy de consequences?'

"Dat sounded like a good idea to everybody, so dey agreed all at one time. Nobody was de first to agree, and nobody was de last. Brother Owl dusted hisself off and got ready. Brother Bull halted everything until he got his strutting hat set over one eye so it looked like it couldn't stay on, but was just too mean to fall off. He whirled his parading stick and told de professor of de band to turn it on.

"But Sister Buzzard raised a ruckus. Dey wasn't going to leave Cock Robin in front of *her* hotel, giving the place a bad name. Naw sir! Dey was going to take him up from dere and bury him.

"Feathers begin to crumple. Dey tried to make dis one and dat one do de burying, but everybody was otherwise engaged. 'Way after while Brother Owl told her, 'Oh, leave de white folks bury him! Dey always loves to take charge.'

"De band hit a hatful of notes at one lick, and Brother Bull led off. Sister Speckled-Hen sho done herself proud dat night. Lawd! I ain't never had dat much fun before nor since."

Uncle July looked kind of sheepish at Dooby. "Since I been saved, I forgot all about such doings. Never would have remembered it no more if dese white folks had of got de thing like it was sho 'nough."

"Humph!" A'nt Dooby snorted. "Old coon for cunning; young coon for running. Now tell me whut you done wid your wages. I know you been up to something. Tell me! You and your Muckty-Duckty Beetle-Bugs!"

Story
in Harlem
Slang*

Wait till I light up my coal-pot and I'll tell you about this Zigaboo called Jelly. Well, all right now. He was a sealskin brown and papa-tree-top-tall. Skinny in the hips and solid built for speed. He was born with this rough-dried hair, but when he laid on the grease and pressed it down overnight with his stocking-cap, it looked just like that righteous moss, and had so many waves you got seasick from looking. Solid, man, solid!

His mama named him Marvel, but after a month on Lenox Avenue, he changed all that to Jelly. How come? Well, he put it in the street that when it came to filling that long-felt need, sugar-curing the ladies' feelings, he was in a class by himself and nobody knew his name, so he had to tell 'em. "It must be Jelly, 'cause jam don't shake." Therefore, his name was Jelly. That was what was on his sign. The stuff was there and it was mellow. Whenever he was challenged by a hard-head or a frail eel on the right of his title he would eye-ball the idol-breaker with a slice of ice and put on his ugly-laugh, made up of scorn and pity, and say: "Youse just dumb to the fact, baby. If you don't know what you talking 'bout, you better ask Granny Grunt. I wouldn't mislead you, baby. I don't need to—not with the help I got."

*In her original manuscript, Hurston entitled this story "Now You Cookin' with Gas" (see page 233).

Then he would give the pimps'[1] sign, and percolate on down the Avenue. You can't go behind a fact like that.

So this day he was airing out on the Avenue. It had to be late afternoon, or he would not have been out of bed. All you did by rolling out early was to stir your stomach up. That made you hunt for more dishes to dirty. The longer you slept, the less you had to eat. But you can't collar nods all day. No matter how long you stay in bed, and how quiet you keep, sooner or later that big gut is going to reach over and grab that little one and start to gnaw. That's confidential right from the Bible. You got to get out on the beat and collar yourself a hot.

So Jelly got into his zoot suit with the reet pleats and got out to skivver around and do himself some good. At 132nd Street, he spied one of his colleagues on the opposite sidewalk, standing in front of a café. Jelly figured that if he bull-skated just right, he might confidence Sweet Back out of a thousand on a plate. Maybe a shot of scrap-iron or a reefer. Therefore, Jelly took a quick backward look at his shoe soles to see how his leather was holding out. The way he figured it after the peep was that he had plenty to get across and maybe do a little more cruising besides. So he stanched out into the street and made the crossing.

"Hi there, Sweet Back!" he exploded cheerfully. "Gimme some skin!"

"Lay de skin on me, pal!" Sweet Back grabbed Jelly's outstretched hand and shook hard. "Ain't seen you since the last time, Jelly. What's cookin'?"

"Oh, just like de bear—I ain't nowhere. Like de bear's brother, I ain't no further. Like de bear's daughter—ain't got a quarter."

Right away, he wished he had not been so honest. Sweet Back gave him a top-superior, cut-eye look. Looked at Jelly just like a showman looks at an ape. Just as far above Jelly as fried chicken is over branch water.

[1]In Harlemese, *pimp* has a different meaning than its ordinary definition as a procurer for immoral purposes. The Harlem pimp is a man whose amatory talents are for sale to any woman who will support him, either with a free meal or on a common law basis; in this sense, he is actually a male prostitute.

"Cold in hand, hunh?" He talked down to Jelly. "A red hot pimp like you *say* you is, ain't got no business in the barrel. Last night when I left you, you was beating up your gums and broadcasting about how hot you was. Just as hot as July-jam, you told me. What you doing cold in hand?"

"Aw, man, can't you take a joke? I was just beating up my gums when I said I was broke. How can I be broke when I got de best woman in Harlem? If I ask her for a dime, she'll give me a ten dollar bill: ask her for drink of likker, and she'll buy me a whiskey still. If I'm lying, I'm flying!"

"Gar, don't hang out dat dirty washing in my back yard! Didn't I see you last night with dat beat chick, scoffing a hot dog? Dat chick you had was beat to de heels. Boy, you ain't no good for what you live."

"If you ain't lying now, you flying. You ain't got de first thin. You ain't got nickel one."

Jelly threw back the long skirt of his coat and rammed his hand down into his pants pocket. "Put your money where your mouth is!" he challenged, as he mock-struggled to haul out a huge roll. "Back your crap with your money. I bet you five dollars!"

Sweet Back made the same gesture of hauling out non-existent money.

"I been raised in the church. I don't bet, but I'll doubt you. Five rocks!"

"I thought so!" Jelly crowed, and hurriedly pulled his empty hand out of his pocket. "I knowed you'd back up when I drawed my roll on you."

"You ain't drawed no roll on me, Jelly. You ain't drawed nothing but your pocket. You better stop dat boogerbooing. Next time I'm liable to make you do it." There was a splinter of regret in his voice. If Jelly really had had some money, he might have staked him, Sweet Back, to a hot. Good Southern cornbread with a piano on a platter. Oh, well! The right broad would, or might, come along.

"Who boogerbooing?" Jelly snorted. "Jig, I don't have to. Talking about *me* with a beat chick scoffing a hot dog! You must of not seen me, 'cause last night I was riding round in a Yellow Cab, with a yellow gal, drinking yellow likker and spending yellow money. Tell 'em 'bout me, tell 'em!''

"Git out of my face, Jelly! Dat broad I seen you with wasn't no pe-ola. She was one of them coal-scuttle blondes with hair just as close to her head as ninety-nine is to a hundred. She look-ted like she had seventy-five pounds of clear bosom, guts in her feet, and she look-ted like six months in front and nine months behind. Buy you a whiskey still! Dat broad couldn't make the down payment on a pair of sox.''

"Sweet Back, you fixing to talk out of place.'' Jelly stiffened.

"If you trying to jump salty, Jelly, that's your mammy.''

"Don't play in de family, Sweet Back. I don't play de dozens. I done told you.''

"Who playing de dozens? You trying to get your hips up on your shoulders 'cause I said you was with a beat broad. One of them lam blacks.''

"Who? Me? Long as you been knowing me, Sweet Back, you ain't never seen me with nothing but pe-olas. I can get any frail eel I wants to. How come I'm up here in New York? You don't know, do you? Since youse dumb to the fact, I reckon I'll have to make you hep. I had to leave from down south 'cause Miss Anne used to worry me so bad to go with me. Who, me? Man, I don't deal in no coal. Know what I tell 'em? If they's white, they's right! If they's yellow, they's mellow! If they's brown, they can stick around. But if they come black, they better git way back! Tell 'em bout me!''

"Aw, man, you trying to show your grandma how to milk ducks. Best you can do is to confidence some kitchen-mechanic out of a dime or two. Me, I knocks de pad with them cack-broads up on Sugar Hill, and fills 'em full of melody. Man, I'm quick death and easy judgment. Youse just a home-boy, Jelly. Don't try to follow me.''

"Me follow *you!* Man, I come on like the Gang Busters, and go off like The March of Time! If dat ain't so, God is gone to Jersey City and you know He wouldn't be messing 'round a place like that. Know what my woman done? We hauled off and went to church last Sunday, and when they passed 'round the plate for the *penny* collection, I throwed in a dollar. De man looked at me real hard for dat. Dat made my woman mad, so she called him back and throwed in a twenty dollar bill! Told him to take dat and go! Dat's what he got for looking at me 'cause I throwed in a dollar.''

"Jelly, de wind may blow and de door may slam; dat what you shooting ain't worth a damn!''

Jelly slammed his hand in his bosom as if to draw a gun. Sweet Back did the same.

"If you wants to fight, Sweet Back, the favor is in me.''

"I was deep-thinking then, Jelly. It's a good thing I ain't short-tempered. 'T'aint nothing to you, nohow. You ain't hit me yet.''

Both burst into a laugh and changed from fighting to lounging poses.

"Don't get too yaller on me, Jelly. You liable to get hurt some day.''

"You over-sports your hand your ownself. Too blamed astor-perious. I just don't pay you no mind. Lay de skin on me!''

They broke their handshake hurriedly, because both of them looked up the Avenue and saw the same thing. It was a girl and they both remembered that it was Wednesday afternoon. All of the domestics off for the afternoon with their pay in their pockets. Some of them bound to be hungry for love. That meant a dinner, a shot of scrap-iron, maybe room rent and a reefer or two. Both went into the pose and put on the look.

"Big stars falling!'' Jelly said out loud when she was in hearing distance. "It must be just before day!''

"Yeah, man!'' Sweet Back agreed. "Must be a recess in Heaven—pretty angel like that out on the ground.''

The girl drew abreast of them, reeling and rocking her hips.

"I'd walk clear to Diddy-Wah-Diddy to get a chance to speak to a pretty lil' ground-angel like that,'' Jelly went on.

"Aw, man, you ain't willing to go very far. Me, I'd go slap to Ginny-Gall, where they eat cow-rump, skin and all.''

The girl smiled, so Jelly set his hat and took the plunge.

"Baby," he crooned, "what's on de rail for de lizard?"

The girl halted and braced her hips with her hands. "A Zigaboo down in Georgy, where I come from, asked a woman that one time and the judge told him 'ninety days.' "

"Georgy!" Sweet Back pretended to be elated. "Where 'bouts in Georgy is you from? Delaware?"

"Delaware?" Jelly snorted. "My people! My people! Free schools and dumb jigs! Man, how you going to put Delaware in Georgy? You ought to know dat's in Maryland."

"Oh, don't try to make out youse no northerner, you! Youse from right down in 'Bam your ownself!" The girl turned on Jelly.

"Yeah, I'm *from* there and I aims to stay from there."

"One of them Russians, eh?" the girl retorted. "Rushcd up here to get away from a job of work."

That kind of talk was not leading towards the dinner table.

"But baby!" Jelly gasped. "Dat shape you got on you! I bet the Coca Cola Company is paying you good money for the patent!"

The girl smiled with pleasure at this, so Sweet Back jumped in.

"I know youse somebody swell to know. Youse real people. You grins like a regular fellow." He gave her his most killing look and let it simmer in. "These dickty jigs round here tries to smile. S'pose you and me go inside the café here and grab a hot?"

"You got any money?" the girl asked, and stiffened like a ram-rod. "Nobody ain't pimping on me. You dig me?"

"Aw, now, baby!"

"I seen you two mullet-heads before. I was uptown when Joe Brown had you all in the go-long last night. Dat cop sure hates a pimp! All he needs to see is the pimps' salute, and he'll out with his night-stick and whip your head to the red. Beat your head just as flat as a dime!" She went off into a great blow of laughter.

"Oh, let's us don't talk about the law. Let's talk about us," Sweet Back persisted. "You going inside with me to holler 'let one come flopping! One come grunting! Snatch one from de rear!' "

"Naw indeed!" the girl laughed harshly. "You skillets is trying to promote a meal on me. But it'll never happen, brother. You barking up the wrong tree. I wouldn't give you air if you was stopped up in a jug. I'm not putting out a thing. I'm just like the cemetery—I'm not putting out, I'm taking in! Dig?"

"I'll tell you like the farmer told the potato—plant you now and dig you later."

The girl made a movement to switch on off. Sweet Back had not dirtied a plate since the day before. He made a weak but desperate gesture.

"Trying to snatch my pocketbook, eh?" she blazed. Instead of running, she grabbed hold of Sweet Back's draping coat-tail and made a slashing gesture. "How much split you want back here? If your feets don't hurry up and take you 'way from here, you'll *ride* away. I'll spread my lungs all over New York and call the law. Go ahead. Bedbug! Touch me! And I'll holler like a pretty white woman!"

The boys were ready to flee, but she turned suddenly and rocked on off with her ear-rings snapping and her heels popping.

"My people! My people!" Sweet Back sighed.

"I know you feel chewed," Jelly said, in an effort to make it appear that he had had no part in the fiasco.

"Oh, let her go," Sweet Back said magnanimously. "When I see people without the periodical principles they's supposed to have, I just don't fool with 'em. What I want to steal her old pocketbook with all the money I got? I could buy a beat chick like her and give her away. I got money's mammy and Grandma change. One of my women, and not the best one I got neither, is buying me ten shag suits at one time."

He glanced sidewise at Jelly to see if he was convincing. But Jelly's thoughts were far away. He was remembering those full, hot meals he had left back in Alabama to seek wealth and splendor in Harlem without working. He had even forgotten to look cocky and rich.

GLOSSARY OF HARLEM SLANG

Air out leave, flee, stroll

Astorperious haughty, biggity

Aunt Hagar Negro race *(also Aunt Hagar's chillun)*

Bad hair Negro type hair

Balling having fun

'Bam, and *down in 'Bam* down South

Battle-hammed badly formed about the hips

Beating up your gums talking to no purpose

Beluthahatchie next station beyond Hell

Big boy stout fellow. But in the South, it means fool and is a prime insult.

Blowing your top getting very angry; occasionally used to mean, "He's doing fine!"

Boogie-woogie type of dancing and rhythm. For years, in the South, it meant secondary syphilis.

Brother-in-black Negro

Bull-skating Bragging

Butt sprung a suit or a skirt out of shape in the rear

Coal scuttle blonde black woman

Cold exceeding, well, etc., as in "He was cold on that trumpet!"

Collar a nod sleep

Collar a hot eat a meal

Color scale high yaller, yaller, high brown, vaseline brown, seal brown, low brown, dark black

Conk buster cheap liquor; also an intellectual Negro

Cruising parading down the Avenue. Variations: *oozing*, *percolating*, and *free-wheeling*. The latter implies more briskness.

Cut doing something well

Dark black a casually black person. Superlatives: *low black*, a blacker person; *lam black*, still blacker; and *damn black*, blackest man, of whom it is said: "Why, lightning bugs follow him at 12 o'clock in the day, thinking it's midnight."

Dat thing sex of either sex

Dat's your mammy same as, "So is your old man."

Diddy-Wah-Diddy a far place, a measure of distance. (2) another suburb of Hell, built since way before Hell wasn't no bigger than Baltimore. The folks in Hell go there for a big time.

Dig understand. "Dig me?" means, "Do you get me? Do you collar the jiver?"

Draped down dressed in the height of Harlem fashion; also *togged down*.

Dumb to the fact "You don't know what you're talking about."

Dusty butt cheap prostitute

Eight-rock very black person

Every postman on his beat kinky hair

First thing smoking a train. "I'm through with this town. I mean to grab the first thing smoking."

Frail eel pretty girl

Free schools a shortened expression of deprecation derived from "free schools and dumb Negroes," sometimes embellished with "free schools, pretty yellow teachers and dumb Negroes."

Function a small, unventilated dance, full of people too casually bathed

Gator-faced long, black face with big mouth

Getting on some stiff time really doing well with your racket

Get you to go power, physical or otherwise, to force the opponent to run

Ginny Gall a suburb of Hell, a long way off

Git up off of me quit talking about me, leave me alone

Go when the wagon comes another way of saying, "You may be acting biggity now, but you'll cool down when enough power gets behind you."

Good hair Caucasian-type hair

Granny Grunt a mythical character to whom most questions may be referred

Ground rations sex, also under rations

Gum beater a blowhard, a braggart, idle talker in general

Gut-bucket low dive, type of music, or expression from same

Gut-foot bad case of fallen arches

Handkerchief-head sycophant type of Negro; also an Uncle Tom

Hauling fleeing on foot. "Man! He cold hauled it!"

I don't deal in coal "I don't keep company with black women."

I'm cracking but I'm facking "I'm wisecracking, but I'm telling the truth."

Inky dink very black person

I shot him lightly and he died politely "I completely outdid him."

Jar head Negro man

Jelly sex

Jig Negro, a corrupted shortening of Zigaboo

Jook a pleasure house, in the class of gut-bucket; now common all over the South

Jooking playing the piano, guitar, or any musical instrument in the manner of the Jooks (pronounced like "took") (2) dancing and 'scronching,' ditto

Juice liquor

July jam something very hot

Jump salty get angry

Kitchen mechanic a domestic

Knock yourself out have a good time

Lightly, slightly and politely doing things perfectly

Little sister measure of hotness: "Hot as little sister!"

Liver-lip pendulous, thick purple lips

Made hair hair that has been straightened

Mammy a term of insult. Never used in any other way by Negroes.

Miss Anne a white woman

Mister Charlie a white man

Monkey chaser a West Indian

Mug Man small-time thug or gangster

My people! My people! Sad and satiric expression in the Negro language; sad when a Negro comments on the backwardness of some members of his race; at other times, used for satiric or comic effect.

Naps kinky hair

Nearer my God to Thee good hair

Nothing to the bear but his curly hair "I call your bluff," or "Don't be afraid of him; he won't fight."

Now you cookin' with gas now you're talking, in the groove, etc.

Ofay white person

Old cuffee Negro (genuine African word for the same thing)

Palmer House walking flat-footed, as from fallen arches

Pancake a humble type of Negro

Park ape an ugly, underprivileged Negro

Peckerwood poor and unloved class of Southern whites

Peeping through my likkers carrying on even though drunk

Pe-ola a very white Negro girl

Piano spare ribs (white rib-bones suggest piano keys)

Pig meat young girl

Pilch house or apartment; residence

Pink toes yellow girl

Playing the dozens low-rating the ancestors of your opponent

Red neck poor Southern white man

Reefer marijuana cigarette, also *a drag*

Righteous mass or grass good hair

Righteous rags the components of a Harlem-style suit

Rug-cutter originally a person frequenting house-rent parties, cutting up the rugs of the host with his feet; a person too cheap or poor to patronize regular dance halls; now means a good dancer.

Russian a Southern Negro up north. "Rushed up here," hence a Russian.

Scrap iron cheap liquor

Sell out run in fear

Sender he or she who can get you to go, i.e., has what it takes. Used often as a compliment: "He's a solid sender!"

Smoking, or *smoking over* looking someone over

Solid perfect

Sooner anything cheap and mongrel, now applied to cheap clothes, or a shabby person

Stanch, or *stanch out* to begin, commence, step out

Stomp low dance, "but hat man!"

Stormbuzzard shiftless, homeless character

Stroll doing something well

Sugar Hill northwest sector of Harlem, near Washington Heights, site of the newest apartment houses, mostly occupied by professional people. (The expression has been distorted in the South to mean a Negro red light district.)

The bear confession of poverty

The big apple, also *the big red apple* New York City

The man the law, or powerful boss

Thousand on a plate beans

Tight head one with kinky hair

Trucking strolling. (2) dance step from the strolling motif

V and X five-and-ten-cent store

West Hell another suburb of Hell, worse than the original

What's on the rail for the lizard? suggestion for moral turpitude

Whip it to the red beat your head until it is bloody

Woofing aimless talk, as a dog barks on a moonless night

Young suit ill-fitting, too small. Observers pretend to believe you're breaking in your little brother's suit for him.

Your likker told you misguided
  behavior
Zigaboo a Negro
Zoot suit with the reet
  pleat Harlem style suit, padded shoulders, 43-inch trousers at the knee with cuff so small it needs a zipper to get into, high waistline, fancy lapels, bushels of buttons, etc.

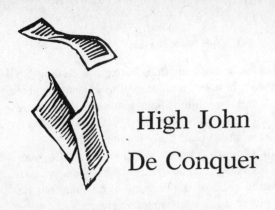

High John
De Conquer

Maybe, now, we used-to-be black African folks can be of some help to our brothers and sisters who have always been white. You will take another look at us and say that we are still black and, ethnologically speaking, you will be right. But nationally and culturally, we are as white as the next one. We have put our labor and our blood into the common causes for a long time. We have given the rest of the nation song and laughter. Maybe now, in this terrible struggle, we can give something else—the source and soul of our laughter and song. We offer you our hope-bringer, High John de Conquer.

High John de Conquer came to be a man, and a mighty man at that. But he was not a natural man in the beginning. First off, he was a whisper, a will to hope, a wish to find something worthy of laughter and song. Then the whisper put on flesh. His footsteps sounded across the world in a low but musical rhythm as if the world he walked on was a singing-drum. The black folks had an irresistible impulse to laugh. High John de Conquer was a man in full, and had come to live and work on the plantations, and all the slave folks knew him in the flesh.

The sign of this man was a laugh, and his singing-symbol was a drum-beat. No parading drum-shout like soldiers out for show. It did not call to the feet of those who were fixed to hear it. It was an inside thing to live by. It was sure to be heard when and where the work was the hardest, and the lot the most cruel. It helped the slaves endure. They knew that something better was coming. So they laughed in the face of things and sang, "I'm so glad! Trouble don't last always." And the white people who heard them were struck dumb that they could laugh. In an outside way, this was Old Massa's fun, so what was Old Cuffy laughing for?

Old Massa couldn't know, of course, but High John de Conquer was there walking his plantation like a natural man. He was treading the sweat-flavored clods of the plantation, crushing out his drum tunes, and giving out secret laughter. He walked on the winds and moved fast. Maybe he was in Texas when the lash fell on a slave in Alabama, but before the blood was dry on the back he was there. A faint pulsing of a drum like a goat-skin stretched over a heart, that came nearer and closer, then somebody in the saddened quarters would feel like laughing, and say, "Now, High John de Conquer, Old Massa couldn't get the best of *him*. That old John was a case!" Then everybody sat up and began to smile. Yes, yes, that was right. Old John, High John could beat the unbeatable. He was top-superior to the whole mess of sorrow. He could beat it all, and what made it so cool, finish it off with a laugh. So they pulled the covers up over their souls and kept them from all hurt, harm and danger and made them a laugh and a song. Night time was a joke, because daybreak was on the way. Distance and the impossible had no power over High John de Conquer.

He had come from Africa. He came walking on the waves of sound. Then he took on flesh after he got here. The sea captains of ships knew that they brought slaves in their ships. They knew about those black bodies huddled down there in the middle passage, being hauled across the waters to helplessness. John de Conquer was walking the very winds that filled the sails of the ships. He followed over them like the albatross.

It is no accident that High John de Conquer has evaded the ears of white people. They were not supposed to know. You can't know what folks won't tell you. If they, the white people, heard some scraps, they could not understand because they had nothing to hear things like that with. They were not looking for any hope in those days, and it was not much of a strain for them to find something to laugh over. Old John would have been out of place for them.

Old Massa met our hope-bringer all right, but when Old Massa met him, he was not going by his right name. He was traveling, and touristing around the plantations as the laugh-provoking Brer Rabbit. So Old Massa and Old Miss and their young ones laughed with and at Brer Rabbit and wished him well. And all the time, there was High John de Conquer playing his tricks of making a way out of no-way. Hitting a straight lick with a crooked stick. Winning the jack pot with no other stake but a laugh. Fighting a mighty battle without outside-showing force, and winning his war from within. Really winning in a permanent way, for he was winning with the soul of the black man whole and free. So he could use it afterwards. For what shall it profit a man if he gain the whole world, and lose his own soul? You would have nothing but a cruel, vengeful, grasping monster come to power. John de Conquer was a bottom-fish. He was deep. He had the wisdom tooth of the East in his head. Way over there, where the sun rises a day ahead of time, they say that Heaven arms with love and laughter those it does not wish to see destroyed. He who carries his heart in his sword must perish. So says the ultimate law. High John de Conquer knew a lot of things like that. He who wins from within is in the "Be" class. *Be* here when the ruthless man comes, and *be* here when he is gone.

Moreover, John knew that it is written where it cannot be erased, that nothing shall live on human flesh and prosper. Old Maker said that before He made any more sayings. Even a man-eating tiger and lion can teach a person that much. His flabby muscles and mangy hide can teach an emperor right from wrong. If the emperor would only listen.

II

There is no established picture of what sort of looking-man this John de Conquer was. To some, he was a big, physical-looking man like John Henry. To others, he was a little, hammered-down, low-built man like the Devil's doll-baby. Some said that they never heard what he looked like. Nobody told them, but he lived on the plantation where their old folks were slaves. He is not so well known to the present generation of colored people in the same way that he was in slavery time. Like King Arthur of England, he has served his people, and gone back into mystery again. And, like King Arthur, he is not dead. He waits to return when his people shall call again. Symbolic of English power, Arthur came out of the water, and with Excalibur, went back into the water again. High John de Conquer went back to Africa, but he left his power here, and placed his American dwelling in the root of a certain plant. Only possess that root, and he can be summoned at any time.

"Of course, High John de Conquer got plenty power!" Aunt Shady Anne Sutton bristled at me when I asked her about him. She took her pipe out of her mouth and stared at me out of her deeply wrinkled face. "I hope you ain't one of these here smart colored folks that done got so they don't believe nothing, and come here questionizing me so you can have something to poke fun at. Done got shamed of the things that brought us through. Make out 'tain't no such thing no more."

When I assured her that that was not the case, she went on.

"Sho John de Conquer means power. That's bound to be so. He come to teach and tell us. God don't leave nobody ignorant, you child. Don't care where He drops you down, He puts you on a notice. He don't want folks taken advantage of because they don't know. Now, back there in slavery time, us didn't have no power of protection, and God knowed it, and put us under watch-care. Rattlesnakes never bit no colored folks until four years after freedom was declared. That was to give us time to learn and to know. 'Course, I don't know nothing about slavery personal like. I wasn't born till two years after the Big Surrender. Then I wasn't nothing but a infant baby when I was born, so I couldn't know nothing but what they told me. My mama told me, and I know that she wouldn't mislead me, how High John de Conquer helped us out. He had done teached the black folks so they knowed a hundred years ahead of time that freedom was coming. Long before the white folks knowed anything about it at all.

"These young Negroes reads they books and talk about the war freeing the Negroes, but Aye, Lord! A heap sees, but a few knows. 'Course, the war was a lot of help, but how come the war took place? They think they knows, but they don't. John de Conquer had done put it into the white folks to give us our freedom, that's what. Old Massa fought against it, but us could have told him that it wasn't no use. Freedom just *had* to come. The time set aside for it was there. That war was just a sign and a symbol of the thing. That's the truth! If I tell the truth about everything as good as I do about that, I can go straight to Heaven without a prayer."

Aunt Shady Anne was giving the inside feeling and meaning to the outside laughs around John de Conquer. He romps, he clowns, and looks ridiculous, but if you will, you can read something deeper behind it all. He is loping on off from the Tar Baby with a laugh.

Take, for instance, those words he had with Old Massa about stealing pigs.

Old John was working in Old Massa's house that time, serving around the eating table. Old Massa loved roasted young pigs, and had them often for dinner. Old John loved them too, but Massa never allowed the slaves to eat any at all. Even put aside the left-over and ate it next time. John de Conquer got tired of that. He took to stopping by the pig pen when he had a strong taste for pig-meat, and getting himself one, and taking it on down to his cabin and cooking it.

Massa began to miss his pigs, and made up his mind to squat for who was taking them and give whoever it was a good hiding. So John kept on taking pigs, and one night Massa walked him down. He stood out there in the dark and saw John kill the pig and went on back to the "big house" and waited till he figured John had it dressed and cooking. Then he went on down to the quarters and knocked on John's door.

"Who dat?" John called out big and bold, because he never dreamed that it was Massa rapping.

"It's me, John," Massa told him. "I want to come in."

"What you want, Massa? I'm coming right out."

"You needn't to do that, John. I want to come in."

"Naw, naw, Massa. You don't want to come into no old slave cabin. Youse too fine a man for that. It would hurt my feelings to see you in a place like this here one."

"I tell you I want to come in, John!"

So John had to open the door and let Massa in. John had seasoned that pig *down*, and it was stinking pretty! John knowed Old Massa couldn't help but smell it. Massa talked on about the crops and hound dogs and one thing and another, and the pot with the pig in it was hanging over the fire in the chimney and kicking up. The smell got better and better.

Way after while, when that pig had done simbled down to a low gravy, Massa said, "John, what's that you cooking in that pot?"

"Nothing but a little old weasly possum, Massa. Sickliest little old possum I ever did see. But I thought I'd cook him anyhow."

"Get a plate and give me some of it, John. I'm hungry."

"Aw, naw, Massa, you ain't hongry."

"Now, John, I don't mean to argue with you another minute. You give me some of that in the pot, or I mean to have the hide off of your back tomorrow morning. Give it to me!"

So John got up and went and got a plate and a fork and went to the pot. He lifted the lid and looked at Massa and told him, "Well, Massa, I put this thing in here a possum, but if it comes out a pig, it ain't no fault of mine."

Old Massa didn't want to laugh, but he did before he caught himself. He took the plate of brownded-down pig and ate it up. He never said nothing, but he gave John and all the other house servants roast pig at the big house after that.

III

John had numerous scrapes and tight squeezes, but he usually came out like Brer Rabbit. Pretty occasionally, though, Old Massa won the hand. The curious thing about this is, that there are no bitter tragic tales at all. When Old Massa won, the thing ended up in a laugh just the same. Laughter at the expense of the slave, but

laughter right on. A sort of recognition that life is not one-sided.
A sense of humor that said, "We are just as ridiculous as anybody
else. We can be wrong, too."

There are many tales, and variants of each, of how the Negro
got his freedom through High John de Conquer. The best one
deals with a plantation where the work was hard, and Old Massa
mean. Even Old Miss used to pull her maids' ears with hot fire-
tongs when they got her riled. So, naturally, Old John de Conquer
was around that plantation a lot.

"What we need is a song," he told the people after he had
figured the whole thing out. "It ain't here, and it ain't no place I
knows of as yet. Us better go hunt around. This has got to be a
particular piece of singing."

But the slaves were scared to leave. They knew what Old Massa
did for any slave caught running off.

"Oh, Old Massa don't need to know you gone from here. How?
Just leave your old work-tired bodies around for him to look at,
and he'll never realize youse way off somewhere, going about
your business."

At first they wouldn't hear to John, that is, some of them. But,
finally, the weak gave in to the strong, and John told them to get
ready to go while he went off to get something for them to ride on.
They were all gathered up under a big hickory nut tree. It was
noon time and they were knocked off from chopping cotton to eat
their dinner. And then that tree was right where Old Massa and
Old Miss could see from the cool veranda of the big house. And
both of them were sitting out there to watch.

"Wait a minute, John. Where we going to get something to
wear off like that. We can't go nowhere like you talking about
dressed like we is."

"Oh, you got plenty things to wear. Just reach inside yourselves
and get out all those fine raiments you been toting around with
you for the last longest. They is in there, all right. I know. Get 'em
out, and put 'em on."

So the people began to dress. And then John hollered back for
them to get out their musical instruments so they could play music

on the way. They were right inside where they got their fine raiments from. So they began to get them out. Nobody remembered that Massa and Miss were setting up there on the veranda looking things over. So John went off for a minute. After that they all heard a big sing of wings. It was John come back, riding on a great black crow. The crow was so big that one wing rested on the morning, while the other dusted off the evening star.

John lighted down and helped them, so they all mounted on, and the bird took out straight across the deep blue sea. But it was a pearly blue, like ten squillion big pearl jewels dissolved in running gold. The shore around it was all grainy gold itself.

Like Jason in search of the golden fleece, John and his party went to many places, and had numerous adventures. They stopped off in Hell where John, under the name of Jack, married the Devil's youngest daughter and became a popular character. So much so, that when he and the Devil had some words because John turned the dampers down in old Original Hell and put some of the Devil's hogs to barbecue over the coals, John ran for High Chief Devil and won the election. The rest of his party was overjoyed at the possession of power and wanted to stay there. But John said no. He reminded them that they had come in search of a song. A song that would whip Old Massa's earlaps down. The song was not in Hell. They must go on.

The party escaped out of Hell behind the Devil's two fast horses. One of them was named Hallowed-Be-Thy-Name, and the other, Thy-Kingdom-Come. They made it to the mountain. Somebody told them that the Golden Stairs went up from there. John decided that since they were in the vicinity, they might as well visit Heaven.

They got there a little weary and timid. But the gates swung wide for them, and they went in. They were bathed, robed, and given new and shining instruments to play on. Guitars of gold, and drums, and cymbals and wind-singing instruments. They walked up Amen Avenue, and down Hallelujah Street, and found with delight that Amen Avenue was tuned to sing bass and alto. The west end was deep bass, and the east end alto. Hallelujah Street was tuned for tenor and soprano, and the two promenades met right in front of the throne and made harmony by themselves. You could make any tune you wanted to by the way you walked. John and his party had a very good time at that and other things. Finally, by the way they acted and did, Old Maker called them up before His great workbench, and made them a tune and put it in their mouths. It had no words. It was a tune that you could bend and shape in most any way you wanted to fit the words and feelings that you had. They learned it and began to sing.

Just about that time a loud rough voice hollered, "You Tunk! You July! You Aunt Diskie!" Then Heaven went black before their eyes and they couldn't see a thing until they saw the hickory nut tree over their heads again. There was everything just like they had left it, with Old Massa and Old Miss sitting on the veranda, and Massa was doing the hollering.

"You all are taking a mighty long time for dinner," Massa said. "Get up from there and get on back to the field. I mean for you to finish chopping that cotton today if it takes all night long. I got something else, harder than that, for you to do tomorrow. Get a move on you!"

They heard what Massa said, and they felt bad right off. But John de Conquer took and told them, saying, "Don't pay what he say no mind. You know where you got something finer than this plantation and anything it's got on it, put away. Ain't that funny? Us got all that, and he don't know nothing at all about it. Don't tell him nothing. Nobody don't have to know where us gets our pleasure from. Come on. Pick up your hoes and let's go."

They all began to laugh and grabbed up their hoes and started out.

"Ain't that funny?" Aunt Diskie laughed and hugged herself with secret laughter. "Us got all the advantage, and Old Massa think he got us tied!"

The crowd broke out singing as they went off to work. The day didn't seem hot like it had before. Their gift song came back into their memories in pieces, and they sang about glittering new robes and harps, and the work flew.

IV

So after a while, freedom came. Therefore High John de Conquer has not walked the winds of America for seventy-five years now. His people had their freedom, their laugh and their song. They have traded it to the other Americans for things they could use like education and property, and acceptance. High John knew that that was the way it would be, so he could retire with his secret smile into the soil of the South and wait.

The thousands upon thousands of humble people who still believe in him, that is, in the power of love and laughter to win by their subtle power, do John reverence by getting the root of the plant in which he has taken up his secret dwelling, and "dressing" it with perfume, and keeping it on their person, or in their houses in a secret place. It is there to help them overcome things they feel that they could not beat otherwise, and to bring them the laugh of the day. John will never forsake the weak and the helpless, nor fail to bring hope to the hopeless. That is what they believe, and so they do not worry. They go on and laugh and sing. Things are bound to come out right tomorrow. That is the secret of Negro song and laughter.

So the brother in black offers to these United States the source of courage that endures, and laughter. High John de Conquer. If the news from overseas reads bad, and the nation inside seems like it is stuck in the Tar Baby, listen hard, and you will hear John de Conquer treading on his singing-drum. You will know then, that no matter how bad things look now, it will be worse for those who seek to oppress us. Even if your hair comes yellow, and your eyes are blue, John de Conquer will be working for you just the same. From his secret place, he is working for all America now. We are all his kinfolks. Just be sure our cause is right, and then you can lean back and say, "John de Conquer would know what to do in a case like this, and then he would finish it off with a laugh."

White America, take a laugh out of our black mouths, and win! We give you High John de Conquer.

Hurricane*

Since Tea Cake and Janie had friended with the Bahaman workers in the 'Glades, they, the "Saws," had been gradually drawn into the American crowd. They quit hiding out to hold their dances when they found that their American friends didn't laugh at them as they feared. Many of the Americans learned to jump and liked it as much as the "Saws." So they began to hold dances night after night in the quarters, usually behind Tea Cake's house. Often now, Tea Cake and Janie stayed up so late at the fire dances that Tea Cake would not let her go with him to the field. He wanted her to get her rest.

So she was home by herself one afternoon when she saw a band of Seminoles passing by. The men walking in front and the laden, stolid women following them like burros. She had seen Indians several times in the 'Glades, in twos and threes, but this was a large party. They were headed towards the Palm Beach road and kept moving steadily. About an hour later another party appeared and went the same way. Then another just before sundown. This time she asked where they were all going and at last one of the men answered her.

"Going to high ground. Saw-grass bloom. Hurricane coming."

Everybody was talking about it that night. But nobody was worried. The fire dance kept up till nearly dawn. The next day,

*From *Their Eyes Were Watching God*

more Indians moved east, unhurried but steady. Still a blue sky and fair weather. Beans running fine and prices good, so the Indians could be, *must* be, wrong. You couldn't have a hurricane when you're making seven and eight dollars a day picking beans. Indians are dumb anyhow, always were. Another night of Stew Beef making dynamic subtleties with his drum and living, sculptural, grotesques in the dance. Next day, no Indians passed at all. It was hot and sultry and Janie left the field and went home.

Morning came without motion. The winds, to the tiniest, lisping baby breath had left the earth. Even before the sun gave light, dead day was creeping from bush to bush watching man.

Some rabbits scurried through the quarters going east. Some possums slunk by and their route was definite. One or two at a time, then more. By the time the people left the fields the procession was constant. Snakes, rattlesnakes began to cross the quarters. The men killed a few, but they could not be missed from the crawling horde. People stayed indoors until daylight. Several times during the night Janie heard the snort of big animals like deer. Once the muted voice of a panther. Going east and east. That night the palm and banana trees began that long distance talk with rain. Several people took fright and picked up and went in to Palm Beach anyway. A thousand buzzards held a flying meet and then went above the clouds and stayed.

One of the Bahaman boys stopped by Tea Cake's house in a car and hollered. Tea Cake came out throwin' laughter over his shoulder into the house.

"Hello Tea Cake."

"Hello 'Lias. You leavin', Ah see."

"Yeah man. You and Janie wanta go? Ah wouldn't give nobody else uh chawnce at uh seat till Ah found out if you all had any way tuh go."

"Thank yuh ever so much, 'Lias. But we 'bout decided tuh stay."

"De crow gahn up, man."

"Dat ain't nothin'. You ain't seen de bossman go up, is yuh? Well all right now. Man, de money's too good on de muck. It's liable tuh fair off by tuhmorrer. Ah wouldn't leave if Ah wuz you.''

"Mah uncle come for me. He say hurricane warning out in Palm Beach. Not so bad dere, but man, dis muck is too low and dat big lake is liable tuh bust.''

"Ah naw, man. Some boys in dere now talkin' 'bout it. Some of 'em been in de 'Glades fuh years. 'Tain't nothin' but uh lil blow. You'll lose de whole day tuhmorrer tryin' tuh git back out heah.''

"De Indians gahn east, man. It's dangerous.''

"Dey don't always know. Indians don't know much uh nothin', tuh tell de truth. Else dey'd own dis country still. De white folks ain't gone nowhere. Dey oughta know if it's dangerous. You better stay heah, man. Big jumpin' dance tuhnight right heah, when it fair off.''

'Lias hesitated and started to climb out, but his uncle wouldn't let him. "Dis time tuhmorrer you gointuh wish you follow crow,'' he snorted and drove off. 'Lias waved back to them gaily.

"If Ah never see you no mo' on earth, Ah'll meet you in Africa.''

Others hurried east like the Indians and rabbits and snakes and coons. But the majority sat around laughing and waiting for the sun to get friendly again.

Several men collected at Tea Cake's house and sat around stuffing courage into each other's ears. Janie baked a big pan of beans and something she called sweet biscuits and they all managed to be happy enough.

Most of the great flame-throwers were there and naturally, handling Big John de Conquer and his works. How he had done everything big on earth, then went up tuh heben without dying atall. Went up there picking a guitar and got all de angels doing the ring-shout round and round de throne. Then everybody but God and Old Peter flew off on a flying race to Jericho and back and John de Conquer won the race; went on down to hell, beat the old devil and passed out ice water to everybody down there. Somebody tried to say that it was a mouth organ harp that John was playing, but the rest of them would not hear that. Don't care how good anybody could play a harp, God would rather to hear a guitar. That brought them back to Tea Cake. How come he couldn't hit that box a lick or two? Well, all right now, make us know it.

When it got good to everybody, Muck-Boy woke up and began to chant with the rhythm and everybody bore down on the last word of the line:

> Yo' mama don't wear no Draws
> Ah seen her when she took 'em Off
> She soaked 'em in alcoHol
> She sold 'em tuh de Santy Claus
> He told her 'twas aginst de Law
> To wear dem dirty Draws

Then Muck-Boy went crazy through the feet and danced himself and everybody else crazy. When he finished he sat back down on the floor and went to sleep again. Then they got to playing Florida flip and coon-can. Then it was dice. Not for money. This was a show-off game. Everybody posing his fancy shots. As always it broiled down to Tea Cake and Motor Boat. Tea Cake with his shy grin and Motor Boat with his face like a little black cherubim just from a church tower doing amazing things with anybody's dice. The others forgot the work and the weather watching them throw. It was art. A thousand dollars a throw in Madison Square Garden wouldn't have gotten any more breathless suspense. It would have just been more people holding in.

After a while somebody looked out and said, "It ain't gitting no fairer out dere. B'lieve Ah'll git on over tuh mah shack." Motor Boat and Tea Cake were still playing so everybody left them at it.

Sometime that night the winds came back. Everything in the world had a strong rattle, sharp and short like Stew Beef vibrating the drum head near the edge with his fingers. By morning Gabriel was playing the deep tones in the center of the drum. So when Janie looked out of her door she saw the drifting mists gathered in the west—that cloud field of the sky—to arm themselves with thunders and march forth against the world. Louder and higher and lower and wider the sound and motion spread, mounting, sinking, darking.

It woke up old Okechobee and the monster began to roll in his bed. Began to roll and complain like a peevish world on a grumble. The folks in the quarters and the people in the big houses further around the shore heard the big lake and wondered. The people felt uncomfortable but safe because there were the seawalls to chain the senseless monster in his bed. The folks let the people do the thinking. If the castles thought themselves secure, the cabins needn't worry. Their decision was already made as always. Chink up your cracks, shiver in your wet beds and wait on the mercy of the Lord. The bossman might have the thing stopped before morning anyway. It is so easy to be hopeful in the day time when you can see the things you wish on. But it was night, it stayed night. Night was striding across nothingness with the whole round world in his hands.

A big burst of thunder and lightning that trampled over the roof of the house. So Tea Cake and Motor stopped playing. Motor looked up in his angel-looking way and said, "Big Massa draw him chair upstairs."

"Ah'm glad y'all stop dat crap-shootin' even if it wasn't for money," Janie said. "Ole Massa is doin' *His* work now. Us oughta keep quiet."

They huddled closer and stared at the door. They just didn't use another part of their bodies, and they didn't look at anything but the door. The time was past for asking the white folks what to look for through that door. Six eyes were questioning God.

Through the screaming wind they heard things crashing and things hurtling and dashing with unbelievable velocity. A baby rabbit, terror ridden, squirmed through a hole in the floor and squatted off there in the shadows against the wall, seeming to know that nobody wanted its flesh at such a time. And the lake got madder and madder with only its dikes between them and him.

In a little wind-lull, Tea Cake touched Janie and said, "Ah reckon you wish now you had of stayed in yo' big house 'way from such as dis, don't yuh?"

"Naw."

"Naw?"

"Yeah, naw. People don't die till dey time come nohow, don't keer where you at. Ah'm wid mah husband in uh storm, dat's all."

"Thanky, Ma'am. But 'sposing you wuz tuh die, now. You wouldn't git mad at me for draggin' yuh heah?"

"Naw. We been tuhgether round two years. If you kin see de light at daybreak, you don't keer if you die at dusk. It's so many people never seen de light at all. Ah wuz fumblin' round and God opened de door."

He dropped to the floor and put his head in her lap. "Well then, Janie, you meant whut you didn't say, 'cause Ah never *knowed* you wuz so satisfied wid me lak dat. Ah kinda thought—"

The wind came back with triple fury, and put out the light for the last time. They sat in company with the others in other shanties, their eyes straining against crude walls and their souls asking if He meant to measure their puny might against His. They seemed to be staring at the dark, but their eyes were watching God.

As soon as Tea Cake went out pushing wind in front of him, he saw that the wind and water had given life to lots of things that folks think of as dead and given death to so much that had been living things. Water everywhere. Stray fish swimming in the yard. Three inches more and the water would be in the house. Already in some. He decided to try to find a car to take them out of the 'Glades before worse things happened. He turned back to tell Janie about it so she could be ready to go.

"Git our insurance papers tuhgether, Janie. Ah'll tote mah box mahself and things lak dat."

"You got all de money out de dresser drawer, already?"

"Naw, git it quick and cut uh piece off de tablecloth tuh wrap it up in. Us liable tuh git wet tuh our necks. Cut uh piece uh dat oilcloth quick fuh our papers. We got tuh go, if it ain't too late. De dish can't bear it out no longer."

He snatched the oilcloth off the table and took out his knife. Janie held it straight while he slashed off a strip.

"But Tea Cake, it's too awful out dere. Maybe it's better tuh stay heah in de wet than it is tuh try tuh—"

He stunned the argument with half a word. "Fix," he said and fought his way outside. He had seen more than Janie had.

Janie took a big needle and ran up a longish sack. Found some newspaper and wrapped up the paper money and papers and thrust them in and whipped over the open end with her needle. Before she could get it thoroughly hidden in the pocket of her overalls, Tea Cake burst in again.

" 'Tain't no cars, Janie."

"Ah thought not! Whut we gointuh do now?"

"We got tuh walk."

"In all dis weather, Tea Cake? Ah don't b'lieve Ah could make it out de quarters."

"Oh yeah you kin. Me and you and Motor Boat kin all lock arms and hold one 'nother down. Eh, Motor?"

"He's sleep on de bed in yonder," Janie said. Tea Cake called without moving.

"Motor Boat! You better git up from dere! Hell done broke loose in Georgy. Dis minute! How kin you sleep at uh time lak dis? Water knee deep in de yard."

They stepped out in water almost to their buttocks and managed to turn east. Tea Cake had to throw his box away, and Janie saw how it hurt him. Dodging flying missiles, floating dangers, avoiding stepping in holes and warmed on the wind now at their backs until they gained comparatively dry land. They had to fight to keep from being pushed the wrong way and to hold together. They saw other people like themselves struggling along. A house down, here and there, frightened cattle. But above all the drive of the wind and the water. And the lake. Under its multiplied roar could be heard a mighty sound of grinding rock and timber and a wail. They looked back. Saw people trying to run in raging waters and screaming when they found they couldn't. A huge barrier of the makings of the dike to which the cabins had been added was rolling and tumbling forward. Ten feet higher and as far as they could see the muttering wall advanced before the braced-up waters like a road crusher on a cosmic scale. The monstropolous beast had left his bed. The two hundred miles an hour wind had loosed his chains. He seized hold of his dikes and ran forward until he met the quarters; uprooted them like grass and rushed on after his supposed-to-be conquerors, rolling the dikes, rolling the houses, rolling the people in the houses along with other timbers. The sea was walking the earth with a heavy heel.

"De lake is comin'!' " Tea Cake gasped.

"De lake!" In amazed horror from Motor Boat, "De lake!"

"It's comin' behind us!" Janie shuddered. "Us can't fly."

"But we still kin run," Tea Cake shouted and they ran. The gushing water ran faster. The great body was held back, but rivers spouted through fissures in the rolling wall and broke like day. The three fugitives ran past another line of shanties that topped a slight rise and gained a little. They cried out as best they could, "De lake is comin'!" and barred doors flew open and others joined them in flight crying the same as they went. "De lake is comin'!" and the pursuing waters growled and shouted ahead, "Yes, Ah'm comin'!" and those who could fled on.

They made it to a tall house on a hump of ground and Janie said, "Less stop heah. Ah can't make it no further. Ah'm done give out."

"All of us is done give out," Tea Cake corrected. "We'se goin' inside out dis weather, kill or cure." He knocked with the handle of his knife, while they leaned their faces and shoulders against the wall. He knocked once more then he and Motor Boat went round to the back and forced a door. Nobody there.

"Dese people had mo' sense than Ah did," Tea Cake said as they dropped to the floor and lay there panting. "Us oughta went on wid 'Lias lak he ast me."

"You didn't know," Janie contended. "And when yuh don't know, yuh just don't know. De storms might not of come sho nuff."

They went to sleep promptly but Janie woke up first. She heard the sound of rushing water and sat up.

"Tea Cake! Motor Boat! De lake is comin'!"

The lake was coming on. Slower and wider, but coming. It had trampled on most of its supporting wall and lowered its front by spreading. But it came muttering and grumbling onward like a tired mammoth just the same.

"Dis is uh high tall house. Maybe it won't reach heah at all," Janie counselled. "And if it do, maybe it won't reach tuh de upstairs part."

"Janie, Lake Okechobee is forty miles wide and sixty miles long. Dat's uh whole heap uh water. If dis wind is shovin' dat whole lake disa way, dis house ain't nothin' tuh swaller. Us better go. Motor Boat!"

"Whut you want, man?"

"De lake is comin'!"

"Aw, naw it 'tain't."

"Yes, it is so comin'! Listen! You kin hear it way off."

"It kin jus' come on. Ah'll wait right here."

"Aw, get up, Motor Boat! Less make it tuh de Palm Beach road. Dat's on uh fill. We'se pretty safe dere."

"Ah'm safe here, man. Go ahead if yuh wants to. Ah'm sleepy."

"What you gointuh do if de lake reach heah?"

"Go upstairs."

"S'posing it come up dere?"

"Swim, man. Dat's all."

"Well, uh, good bye, Motor Boat. Everything is pretty bad, yuh know. Us might git missed of one 'nother. You sho is a grand friend fuh uh man tuh have."

"Good bye, Tea Cake. Y'all oughta stay here and sleep, man. No use in goin' off and leavin' me lak dis."

"We don't wanta. Come on wid us. It might be night time when de water hem you up in heah. Dat's how come Ah won't stay. Come on, man."

"Tea Cake Ah got tuh have mah sleep. Definitely."

"Good bye, then, Motor. Ah wish you all de luck. Goin' over tuh Nassau fuh dat visit widja when all dis is over."

"Definitely, Tea Cake. Mah mama's house is yours."

Tea Cake and Janie were some distance from the house before they struck serious water. Then they had to swim a distance, and Janie could not hold up more than a few strokes at a time, so Tea

Cake bore her up till finally they hit a ridge that led on towards the fill. It seemed to him the wind was weakening a little so he kept looking for a place to rest and catch his breath. His wind was gone. Janie was tired and limping but she had not had to do that hard swimming in the turbulent waters, so Tea Cake was much worse off. But they couldn't stop. Gaining the fill was something but it was no guarantee. The lake was coming. They had to reach the six-mile bridge. It was high and safe perhaps.

Everybody was walking the fill. Hurrying, dragging, falling, crying, calling out names hopefully and hopelessly. Wind and rain beating on old folks and beating on babies. Tea Cake stumbled once or twice in his weariness and Janie held him up. So they reached the bridge at Six Mile Bend and thought to rest.

But it was crowded. White people had pre-empted that point of elevation and there was no more room. They could climb up one of its high sides and down the other, that was all. Miles further on, still no rest.

They passed a dead man in a sitting position on a hummock, entirely surrounded by wild animals and snakes. Common danger made common friends. Nothing sought a conquest over the other.

Another man clung to a cypress tree on a tiny island. A tin roof of a building hung from the branches by electric wires and the wind swung it back and forth like a mighty ax. The man dared not move a step to his right lest this crushing blade split him open. He dared not step left for a large rattlesnake was stretched full length with his head in the wind. There was a strip of water between the island and the fill, and the man clung to the tree and cried for help.

"De snake won't bite yuh," Tea Cake yelled to him. "He skeered tuh go intuh uh coil. Skeered he'll be blowed away. Step round dat side and swim off!"

Soon after that Tea Cake felt he couldn't walk anymore. Not right away. So he stretched long side of the road to rest. Janie spread herself between him and the wind and he closed his eyes and let the tiredness seep out of his limbs. On each side of the fill was a great expanse of water like lakes—water full of things living and dead. Things that didn't belong in water. As far as the eye

could reach, water and wind playing upon it in fury. A large piece
of tar-paper roofing sailed through the air and scudded along the
fill until it hung against a tree. Janie saw it with joy. That was the
very thing to cover Tea Cake with. She could lean against it and
hold it down. The wind wasn't quite so bad as it was anyway. The
very thing. Poor Tea Cake!

She crept on hands and knees to the piece of roofing and caught
hold of it by either side. Immediately the wind lifted both of them
and she saw herself sailing off the fill to the right, out and out over
the lashing water. She screamed terribly and released the roofing
which sailed away as she plunged downward into the water.

"Tea Cake!" He heard her and sprang up. Janie was trying to
swim but fighting water too hard. He saw a cow swimming slowly
towards the fill in an oblique line. A massive built dog was sitting
on her shoulders and shivering and growling. The cow was approaching Janie. A few strokes would bring her there.

"Make it tuh de cow and grab hold of her tail! Don't use yo'
feet. Jus' yo' hands is enough. Dat's right, come on!"

Janie achieved the tail of the cow and lifted her head up along
the cow's rump, as far as she could above water. The cow sunk a
little with the added load and thrashed a moment in terror.
Thought she was being pulled down by a gator. Then she continued on. The dog stood up and growled like a lion, stiff-standing
hackles, stiff muscles, teeth uncovered as he lashed up his fury for
the charge. Tea Cake split the water like an otter, opening his
knife as he dived. The dog raced down the back-bone of the cow
to the attack and Janie screamed and slipped far back on the tail
of the cow, just out of reach of the dog's angry jaws. He wanted
to plunge in after her but dreaded the water, somehow. Tea Cake
rose out of the water at the cow's rump and seized the dog by the
neck. But he was a powerful dog and Tea Cake was over-tired. So
he didn't kill the dog with one stroke as he had intended. But the
dog couldn't free himself either. They fought and somehow he
managed to bite Tea Cake high up on his cheek-bone once. Then
Tea Cake finished him and sent him to the bottom to stay there.
The cow relieved of a great weight was landing on the fill with

Janie before Tea Cake stroked in and crawled weakly upon the fill again.

Janie began to fuss around his face where the dog had bitten him but he said it didn't amount to anything. "He'd uh raised hell though if he had uh grabbed me uh inch higher and bit me in mah eye. Yuh can't buy eyes in de store, yuh know." He flopped to the edge of the fill as if the storm wasn't going on at all. "Lemme rest awhile, then us got tuh make it on intuh town somehow."

It was next day by the sun and the clock when they reached Palm Beach. It was years later by their bodies. Winters and winters of hardship and suffering. The wheel kept turning round and round. Hope, hopelessness and despair. But the storm blew itself out as they approached the city of refuge.

Havoc was there with her mouth wide open. Back in the Everglades the wind had romped among lakes and trees. In the city it had raged among houses and men. Tea Cake and Janie stood on the edge of things and looked over the desolation.

"How kin Ah find uh doctor fuh yo' face in all dis mess?" Janie wailed.

"Ain't got de damn doctor tuh study 'bout. Us needs uh place tuh rest."

A great deal of their money and perseverance and they found a place to sleep. It was just that. No place to live at all. Just sleep. Tea Cake looked all around and sat heavily on the side of the bed.

"Well," he said humbly, "reckon you never 'spected tuh come tuh dis when you took up wid me, didja?"

"Once upon uh time, Ah never 'spected nothin' Tea Cake but bein' dead from the standin' still and tryin' tuh laugh. But you come 'long and made somethin' outa me. So Ah'm thankful fuh anything we come through together."

"Thanky, Ma'am."

"You was twice noble tuh save me from dat dawg. Tea Cake, Ah don't speck you seen his eyes lak Ah did. He didn't aim fuh jus' bite me, Tea Cake. He aimed tuh kill me stone dead. Ah'm never tuh fuhgit dem eyes. He wuzn't nothin' all over but pure hate. Wonder where he come from?"

"Yeah, Ah did see 'im too. It wuz frightenin'. Ah didn't mean tuh take his hate neither. He had tuh die uh me one. Mah switch blade said it wuz him."

"Po' me, he'd tore me tuh pieces, if it wuzn't fuh you, honey."

"You don't have tuh say, if it wuzn't fuh me, baby, cause Ah'm *heah*, and then Ah want yuh tuh know it's uh man heah."

The
Conscience
of the Court

The clerk of the court took a good look at the tall brown-skinned woman with the head rag on. She sat on the third bench back with a husky officer beside her.

"The People versus Laura Lee Kimble!"

The policeman nudged the woman to get to her feet and led her up to the broad rail. She stood there, looking straight ahead. The hostility in the room reached her without her seeking to find it.

Unpleasant things were ahead of Laura Lee Kimble, but she was ready for this moment. It might be the electric chair or the rest of her life in some big lonesome jail house, or even torn to pieces by a mob, but she had passed three long weeks in jail. She had come to the place where she could turn her face to the wall and feel neither fear nor anguish. So this here so-called trial was nothing to her but a form and a fashion and an outside show to the world. She could stand apart and look on calmly. She stood erect and looked up at the judge.

"Charged with felonious and aggravated assault. Mayhem. Premeditated attempted murder on the person of one Clement Beasley. Obscene and abusive language. Laura Lee Kimble, how do you plead?"

Laura Lee was so fascinated by the long-named things that they were accusing her of that she stood there tasting over the words. *Lawdy me!* she mused inside herself. *Look like I done every crime excepting habeas corpus and stealing a mule.*

"Answer the clerk!" The officer nudged Laura Lee. "Tell him how you plead."

"Plead? Don't reckon I make out just what you all mean by that." She looked from face to face and at last up at the judge, with bewilderment in her eyes. She found him looking her over studiously.

The judge understood the look in her face, but he did not interfere so promptly as he ordinarily would have. This was the man-killing bear cat of a woman that he had heard so much about. Though spare of fat, she was built strongly enough, all right. An odd Negro type. Gray-green eyes, large and striking, looking out of a chestnut-brown face. A great abundance of almost straight hair only partially hidden by the high-knotted colored kerchief about her head. Somehow this woman did not look fierce to him at all. Yet she had beaten a man within an inch of his life. Here was a riddle to solve. With the proud, erect way she held herself, she might be some savage queen. The shabby housedress she had on detracted nothing from this impression. She was a challenge to him somehow or other.

"Perhaps you don't understand what the clerk means, Laura," the judge found himself saying to her in a gentle voice. "He wants you to say whether you are guilty of the charges or not."

"Oh, I didn't know. Didn't even know if he was talking to me or not. Much obliged to you, sir." Laura Lee sent His Honor a shy smile. " 'Deed I don't know if I'm guilty or not. I hit the man after he hit me, to be sure, Mister Judge, but if I'm guilty I don't know for sure. All them big words and all."

The clerk shook his head in exasperation and quickly wrote something down. Laura Lee turned her head and saw the man on the hospital cot swaddled all up in bandage rags. Yes, that was the very man who caused her to be here where she was.

"All right, Laura Lee," the judge said. "You can take your seat now until you are called on."

The prosecutor looked a question at the judge and said, "We can proceed." The judge nodded, then halted things as he looked down at Laura Lee.

"The defendant seems to have no lawyer to represent her." Now he leaned forward and spoke to Laura Lee directly. "If you have no money to hire yourself a lawyer to look out for your interests, the court will appoint one for you."

There was a pause, during which Laura Lee covered a lot of ground. Then she smiled faintly at the judge and answered him. "Naw sir, I thank you, Mister Judge. Not to turn you no short answer, but I don't reckon it would do me a bit of good. I'm mighty much obliged to you just the same."

The implications penetrated instantly and the judge flushed. This unlettered woman had called up something that he had not thought about for quite some time. The campus of the University of Virginia and himself as a very young man there, filled with a reverence for his profession amounting to an almost holy dedication. His fascination and awe as a professor traced the more than two thousand years of growth of the concepts of human rights and justice. That brought him to his greatest hero, John Marshall, and his inner resolve to follow in the great man's steps, and even add to interpretations of human rights if his abilities allowed. No, he had not thought about all this for quite some time. The judge flushed slowly and deeply.

Below him there, the prosecutor was moving swiftly, but somehow his brisk cynicism offended the judge. He heard twelve names called, and just like that the jury box was filled and sworn in.

Rapidly now, witnesses took the stand, and their testimony was all damaging to Laura Lee. The doctor who told how terribly Clement Beasley had been hurt. Left arm broken above the elbow, compound fracture of the forearm, two ribs cracked, concussion of the brain and various internal injuries. Two neighbors who had heard the commotion and arrived before the house in time to see Laura Lee fling the plaintiff over the gate into the street. The six arresting officers all got up and had their say, and it was very bad for Laura Lee. A two-legged she-devil no less.

Clement Beasley was borne from his cot to the witness stand, and he made things look a hundred times blacker. His very ap-

pearance aroused a bumble of pity, and anger against the defendant. The judge had to demand quiet repeatedly. Beasley's testimony blew strongly on the hot coals.

His story was that he had come in conflict with this defendant
by loaning a sizable sum of money to her employer. The money
was to be repaid at his office. When the date was long past due,
he had gone to the house near the river, just off Riverside Drive,
to inquire why Mrs. Clairborne had not paid him, nor even come
to see him and explain. Imagine his shock when he wormed it out
of the defendant that Mrs. Clairborne had left Jacksonville. Further, he detected evidence that the defendant was packing up the
things in the house. The loan had been made, six hundred dollars,
on the furnishings of the entire house. He had doubted that the
furnishings were worth enough for the amount loaned, but he had
wanted to be generous to a widow lady. Seeing the defendant
packing away the silver, he was naturally alarmed, and the next
morning went to the house with a moving van to seize the furniture and protect the loan. The defendant, surprised, attacked him
as soon as he appeared at the front door, injured him as he was,
and would have killed him if help had not arrived in time.

Laura Lee was no longer a spectator at her own trial. Now she
was in a flaming rage. She would have leaped to her feet as the
man pictured Miz' Celestine as a cheat and a crook, and again as
he sat up there and calmly lied about the worth of the furniture.
All of those wonderful antiques, this man making out that they did
not equal his minching six hundred dollars! That lie was a sin and
a shame! The People was a meddlesome and unfriendly passel and
had no use for the truth. It brought back to her in a taunting way
what her husband, Tom, had told her over and over again. This
world had no use for the love and friending that she was ever
trying to give.

It looked now that Tom could be right. Even Miz' Celestine had
turnt her back on her. She was here in this place, the house of The
People, all by herself. She had ever disbelieved Tom and had to get
to be forty-nine before she found out the truth. Well, just as the old
folks said, "It's never too long for a bull frog to wear a stiff-bosom

shirt. He's bound to get it dirtied some time or other.''

"You have testified,'' Laura Lee heard the judge talking, "that you came in contact with the defendant through a loan to Mrs. J. Stuart Clairborne, her employer, did you not?''

"Yes, Your Honor,'' Beasley answered promptly and glibly.

"That being true, the court cannot understand why that note was not offered in evidence.''

Beasley glanced quickly at the prosecutor and lowered his eyes. "I—I just didn't see why it was necessary, Your Honor. I have it, but——''

"It is not only pertinent, it is of the utmost importance to this case. I order it sent for immediately and placed in evidence.''

The tall, lean, black-haired prosecutor hurled a surprised and betrayed look at the bench, then, after a pause, said in a flat voice, "The State rests.''

What was in the atmosphere crawled all over Laura Lee like reptiles. The silence shouted that her goose was cooked. But even if the sentence was death, she didn't mind. Celestine Beaufort Clairborne had failed her. Her husband and all her folks had gone on before. What was there to be so happy to live for any more? She had writ that letter to Miz' Celestine the very first day that she had been placed in jail. Three weeks had gone by on their rusty ankles, and never one word from her Celestine. Laura Lee choked back a sob and gritted her teeth. You had to bear what was placed on your back for you to tote.

"Laura Lee Kimble,'' the judge was saying, "you are charged with serious felonies, and the law must take its course according to the evidence. You refused the lawyer that the court offered to provide for you, and that was a mistake on your part. However, you have a right to be sworn and tell the jury your side of the story. Tell them anything that might help you, so long as you tell the truth.''

Laura Lee made no move to get to her feet and nearly a minute passed. Then the judge leaned forward.

"Believe it or not, Laura Lee, this is a court of law. It is needful to hear both sides of every question before the court can reach a conclusion and know what to do. Now, you don't strike me as a person that is unobliging at all. I believe if you knew you would be helping me out a great deal by telling your side of the story, you would do it."

Involuntarily Laura Lee smiled. She stood up. "Yes, sir, Mister Judge. If I can be of some help to you, I sure will. And I thank you for asking me."

Being duly sworn, Laura Lee sat in the chair to face the jury as she had been told to do.

"You jury-gentlemens, they asked me if I was guilty or no, and I still don't know whether I is or not. I am a unlearnt woman and common-clad. It don't surprise me to find out I'm ignorant about a whole heap of things. I ain't never rubbed the hair off of my head against no college walls and schooled out nowhere at all. All I'm able to do is to tell you gentlemens how it was and then you can tell me if I'm guilty or no.

"I would not wish to set up here and lie and make out that I never hit this plaintive back. Gentlemens, I ain't had no malice in my heart against the plaintive. I seen him only one time before he come there and commenced that fracas with me. That was three months ago, the day after Tom, my husband, died. Miz' Celestine called up the funeral home and they come and got Tom to fix him up so we could take him back to Georgia to lay him to rest. That's where us all come from, Chatham County—Savannah, that is.

"Then now, Miz' Celestine done something I have never knowed her to do be-fore. She put on her things and went off from home without letting me know where she was bound for. She come back afterwhile with this plaintive, which I had never seen before in all my borned days. I glimpsed him good from the kitchen where I was at, walking all over the dining room and the living room with Miz' Celestine and looking at things, but they was talking sort of low like, and I couldn't make out a word what they was talking about. I figgered that Miz' Celestine must of been kind of beside herself, showing somebody look like this plaintive all her fine things like that. Her things is fine and very scarce old antiques, and I know that she have been offered vast sums of money for 'em, but she would never agree to part with none. Things that been handed down in both the Beaufort and the Clairborne families from way back. That little old minching six hundred dollars that the plaintive mentioned wouldn't even be worth one piece of her things, not to mention her silver. After a while they went off and when Miz' Celestine come back, she told me that everything had been taken care of and she had the tickets to Savannah in her purse.

"Bright and soon next morning we boarded the train for Savannah to bury Tom. Miz' Celestine done even more than she had promised Tom. She took him back like she had promised, so that he could be buried in our family lot, and he was covered with flowers, and his church and his lodges turned out with him, and he was put away like some big mogul of a king. Miz' Celestine was there sitting right along by my side all the time. Then me and Miz' Celestine come on back down here to Jacksonville by ourselves.

"And Mrs. Clairborne didn't run off to keep from paying nobody. She's a Clairborne, and before that, she was born a Beaufort. They don't owe nobody, and they don't run away. That ain't the kind of raising they gets. Miz' Clairborne's got money of her own, and lives off of the interest which she receives regular every six months. She went off down there to Miami Beach to sort of refresh herself and rest up her nerves. What with being off down here in Florida, away from all the folks she used to know, for three whole years, and cooped up there in her house, and remembering her dear husband being dead, and now Tom gone, and nobody left of the old family around excepting her and me, she was nervous and peaked like. It wasn't her, it was me that put her up to going off down there for a couple of months so maybe she would come back to herself. She never cheeped to me about borrowing no money from nobody, and I sure wasn't packing nothing up to move off when this plaintive come to the door. I was just gleaming up the silver to kill time whilst I was there by myself.

"And, gentlemens, I never tackled the plaintive just as soon as he mounted the porch like he said. The day before that, he had come there and asked-ed me if Miz' Clairborne was at home. I told him no, and then he asked-ed me just when I expected her back. I told him she was down at Miami Beach, and got the letter that she had sent me so he could get her right address. He thanked me and went off. Then the next morning, here he was back with a great big moving wagon, rapped on the door and didn't use a bit of manners and politeness this time. Without even a 'Good morning' he says for me to git out of his way because he come to haul off all the furniture and things in the house and he is short for time.

"You jury-gentlemens, I told him in the nicest way that I knowed how that he must of been crazy. Miz' Celestine was off from home and she had left me there as a kind of guardeen to look after her house and things, and I sure couldn't so handy leave nobody touch a thing in Mrs. Clairborne's house unlessen she was there and said so.

"He just looked at me like I was something that the buzzards laid and the sun hatched out, and told me to move out of his way so he could come on in and get his property. I propped myself and braced one arm across the doorway to bar him out, reckoning he would have manners enough to go on off. But, no! He flew just as hot as Tucker when the mule kicked his mammy and begun to cuss and double-cuss me, and call me all out of my name, something nobody had never done be-fore in all my borned days. I took it to keep from tearing up peace and agreement. Then he balled up his fistes and demanded me to move 'cause he was coming in.

" 'Aw, naw you ain't,' I told him. 'You might think that you's going to grow horns, but I'm here to tell you you'll die butt-headed.'

"His mouth slewed one-sided and he hauled off and hit me in my chest with his fist two times. Hollered that nothing in the drugstore would kill me no quicker than he would if I didn't git out of his way. I didn't, and then he upped and kicked me.

"I jumped as salty as the 'gator when the pond went dry. I stretched out my arm and he hit the floor on a prone. Then, that truck with the two men on it took off from there in a big hurry. All I did next was to grab him by his heels and frail the pillar of the porch with him a few times. I let him go, but he just laid there like a log.

" 'Don't you lay there, making out you's dead, sir!' I told him. 'Git up from there, even if you is dead, and git on off this place!'

"The contrary scamp laid right there, so I reached down and muscled him up on acrost my shoulder and toted him to the gate, and heaved him over the fence out into the street. None of my business what become of him and his dirty mouth after that.

"I figgered I done right not to leave him come in there and haul off Miz' Celestine's things which she had left there under my trust and care. But Tom, my husband, would have said I was wrong for taking too much on myself. Tom claimed that he ever loved me harder than the thunder could bump a stump, but I had one habit that he ever wished he could break me of. Claimed that I always placed other folks's cares in front of my own, and more expecially Miz' Celestine. Said that I made out of myself a wishbone shining in the sun. Just something for folks to come along and pick up and rub and pull and get their wishes and good luck on. Never looked out for nothing for my ownself.

"I never took a bit of stock in what Tom said like that until I come to be in this trouble. I felt right and good, looking out for Miz' Celestine's interest and standing true and strong, till they took me off to jail and I writ Miz' Celestine a letter to please come see 'bout me and help me out, and give it to the folks there at the jail to mail off for me."

A sob wrestled inside Laura Lee and she struck silence for a full minute before she could go on.

"Maybe it reached her, and then maybe again it didn't. Anyhow, I ain't had a single scratch from Miz' Celestine, and here I is. But I love her so hard, and I reckon I can't help myself. Look, gentlemens, Celestine was give to me when I was going on five—"

The prosecutor shot up like a striking trout and waved his long arm. "If the court please, this is not a street corner. This is a court of law. The witness cannot be allowed to ramble—"

The judge started as if he had been shaken out of a dream. He looked at the prosecutor and shook his head. "The object of a trial, I need not remind you, is to get at the whole truth of a case. The defendant is unlearned, as she has said. She has no counsel to guide her along the lines of procedure. It is important to find out why an act was committed, as you well know. Please humor the court by allowing the witness to tell her story in her own way." The judge looked at Laura Lee and told her to go ahead. A murmur of approval followed this from all over the room.

"I don't mean that her mama and papa throwed her away. You know how it used to be the style when a baby was born to place it under the special care of a older brother or sister, or somebody that had worked on the place for a long time and was apt to stay. That's what I mean by Celestine was give to me.

"Just going on five, I wasn't yet old enough to have no baby give to me, but that I didn't understand. All I did know that some way I loved babies. I had me a old rag doll-baby that my mama had made for me, and I loved it better'n anything I can mention.

"Never will forget the morning mama said she was going to take me upstairs to Miz' Beaufort's bedroom to lemme see the new baby. Mama was borned on the Beaufort place just like I was. She was the cook, and everything around the place was sort of under her care. Papa was the houseman and drove for the family when they went out anywhere.

"Well, I seen that tee-ninchy baby laying there in a pink crib all trimmed with a lot of ribbons. Gentlemens, it was the prettiest thing I had ever laid my eyes on. I thought that it was a big-size doll-baby laying there, and right away I wanted it. I carried on so till afterwhile Miz' Beaufort said that I could have it for mine if I wanted it. I was so took with it that I went plumb crazy with joy. I ask-ed her again, and she still said that she was giving it to me. My mama said so too. So, for fear they might change they minds, I said right off that I better take my baby home with me so that I could feed it my ownself and make it something to put on and do for it in general.

"I cried and carried on something terrible when they wouldn't leave me take it on out to the little house where we lived on the place. They pacified me by telling me I better leave it with Miz' Beaufort until it was weaned.

"That couldn't keep me from being around Celestine every chance I got. Later on I found out how they all took my carrying-on for jokes. Made out they was serious to my face, but laughing fit to kill behind my back. They wouldn't of done it if they had knowed how I felt inside. I lived just to see and touch Celestine— my baby, I thought. And she took to me right away.

"When Celestine was two, going on three, I found out that they had been funning with me, and that Celestine was not my child at all. I was too little to have a baby, and then again, how could a colored child be the mother of a white child? Celestine belonged to her papa and mama. It was all right for me to play with her all I wanted to, but forget the notion that she was mine.

"Jury-gentlemens, it was mighty hard, but as I growed on and understood more things I knowed what they was talking about. But Celestine wouldn't allow me to quit loving her. She ever leaned on me, and cried after me, and run to me first for every little thing.

"When I was going on sixteen, papa died and Tom Kimble, a young man, got the job that papa used to have. Right off he put in to court me, even though he was twelve years older than me. But lots of fellows around Savannah was pulling after me too. One wanted to marry me that I liked extra fine, but he was settling in Birmingham, and mama was against me marrying and settling way off somewhere. She ruthered for me to marry Tom. When Celestine begin to hang on me and beg and beg me not to leave her, I give in and said that I would have Tom, but for the sake of my feelings, I put the marriage off for a whole year. That was my first good chance to break off from Celestine, but I couldn't.

"General Beaufort, the old gentleman, was so proud for me to stay and pacify Celestine, that he built us a nice house on the place and made it over to us for life. Miz' Beaufort give me the finest wedding that any colored folks had ever seen around Savannah. We stood on the floor in the Beaufort parlor with all the trimmings.

"Celestine, the baby, was a young lady by then, and real pretty with reddish-gold hair and blue eyes. The young bloods was hanging after her in swarms. It was me that propped her up when she wanted to marry young J. Stuart Clairborne, a lawyer just out of school, with a heap of good looks, a smiling disposition, a fine family name and no money to mention. He did have some noble old family furniture and silver. So Celestine had her heart's desire, but little money. They was so happy together that it was like a play.

"Then things begin to change. Mama and Miz' Beaufort passed on in a year of each other. The old gentleman lingered around kind of lonesome, then one night he passed away in his sleep, leaving all he had to Celestine and her husband. Things went on fine for five years like that. He was building up a fine practice and things went lovely.

"Then, it seemed all of a sudden, he took to coughing, and soon he was too tired all the time to go to his office and do around like he used to. Celestine spent her money like water, sending her husband and taking him to different places from one end of the nation to the other, and keeping him under every kind of a doctor's care.

"Four years of trying and doing like that, and then even Celestine had to acknowledge that it never did a bit of good. Come a night when Clairborne laid his dark curly head in her lap like a trusting child and breathed his last.

"Inside our own house of nights, Tom would rear and pitch like a mule in a tin stable, trying to get me to consent to pull out with him and find us better-paying jobs elsewhere. I wouldn't hear to that kind of a talk at all. We had been there when times was extra good, and I didn't aim to tear out and leave Miz' Celestine by herself at low water. This was another time I passed up my chance to cut aloose.

"The third chance wasn't too long a-coming. A year after her husband died, Miz' Celestine come to me and told me that the big Beaufort place was too much for her to keep up with the money she had on hand now. She had been seeking around, and she had found a lovely smaller house down at Jacksonville, Florida. No big grounds to keep up and all. She choosed that instead of a smaller place around Savannah because she could not bear to sing small where she had always led off. An' now she had got hold of a family who was willing to buy the Beaufort estate at a very good price.

"Then she told me that she wanted me to move to Florida with her. She realized that she had no right to ask me no such a thing, but she just could not bear to go off down there with none of her family with her. Would I please consent to go? If I would not go with her, she would give Tom and me the worth of our property in cash money and we could do as we pleased. She had no call to ask us to go with her at all, excepting for old-time love and affection.

"Right then, jury-gentlemens, I knowed that I was going. But Tom had ever been a good husband to me, and I wanted him to feel that he was considered, so I told her that I must consult my pillow. Give her my word one way or another the next day.

"Tom pitched a acre of fits the moment that it was mentioned in his hearing. Hollered that we ought to grab the cash and, with what we had put away, buy us a nice home of our own. What was wrong with me nohow? Did I aim to be a wishbone all my days? Didn't I see that he was getting old? He craved to end his days among his old friends, his lodges and his churches. We had a fine cemetery lot, and there was where he aimed to rest.

"Miz' Celestine cried when he told her. Then she put in to meet all of Tom's complaints. Sure, we was all getting on in years, but that was the very reason why we ought not to part now. Cling together and share and lean and depend on one another. Then when Tom still helt out, she made a oath. If Tom died before she did, she would fetch him back and put him away right at her own expense. And if she died before either of us, we was to do the same for her. Anything she left was willed to me to do with as I saw fit.

"So we put in to pack up all the finest pieces, enough and plenty to furnish up our new home in Florida, and moved on down here to live. We passed three peaceful years like that, then Tom died."

Laura Lee paused, shifted so that she faced the jury more directly, then summed up.

"Maybe I is guilty sure enough. I could be wrong for staying all them years and making Miz' Celestine's cares my own. You gentlemens is got more book-learning than me, so you would know more than I do. So far as this fracas is concerned, yeah, I hurted this plaintive, but with him acting the way he was, it just couldn't be helped. And 'tain't nary one of you gentlemens but what wouldn't of done the same."

There was a minute of dead silence. Then the judge sent the prosecutor a cut-eye look and asked, "Care to cross-examine?"

"That's all!" the prosecutor mumbled, and waved Laura Lee to her seat.

"I have here," the judge began with great deliberation, "the note made by Mrs. J. Stuart Clairborne with the plaintiff. It specifies that the purpose of the loan was to finance the burial of Thomas Kimble." The judge paused and looked directly at Laura Lee to call her attention to this point. "The importance to this trial, however, is the due date, which is still more than three months away."

The court officers silenced the gasps and mumbles that followed this announcement.

"It is therefore obvious why the plaintiff has suppressed this valuable piece of evidence. It is equally clear to the court that the plaintiff knew that he had no justification whatsoever for being upon the premises of Mrs. Clairborne."

His Honor folded the paper and put it aside, and regarded the plaintiff with cold gray eyes.

"This is the most insulting instance in the memory of the court of an attempt to prostitute the very machinery of justice for an individual's own nefarious ends. The plaintiff first attempts burglary with forceful entry and violence and, when thoroughly beaten for his pains, brazenly calls upon the law to punish the faithful watch-dog who bit him while he was attempting his trespass. Further, it seems apparent that he has taken steps to prevent any word from the defendant reaching Mrs. Clairborne, who certainly would have moved heaven and earth in the defendant's behalf, and rightfully so."

The judge laced the fingers of his hands and rested them on the polished wood before him and went on.

The protection of women and children, he said, was inherent, implicit in Anglo-Saxon civilization, and here in these United States it had become a sacred trust. He reviewed the long, slow climb of humanity from the rule of the club and the stone hatchet to the Constitution of the United States. The English-speaking people had given the world its highest concepts of the rights of the individual, and they were not going to be made a mock of, and nullified by this court.

"The defendant did no more than resist the plaintiff's attempted burglary. Valuable assets of her employer were trusted in her care, and she placed her very life in jeopardy in defending that trust, setting an example which no decent citizen need blush to follow. The jury is directed to find for the defendant."

Laura Lee made her way diffidently to the judge and thanked him over and over again.

"That will do, Laura Lee. I am the one who should be thanking you."

Laura Lee could see no reason why, and wandered off, bewildered. She was instantly surrounded by smiling, congratulating strangers, many of whom made her ever so welcome if ever she needed a home. She was rubbed and polished to a high glow.

Back at the house, Laura Lee did not enter at once. Like a pilgrim before a shrine, she stood and bowed her head. "I ain't fitten to enter. For a time, I allowed myself to doubt my Celestine. But maybe nobody ain't as pure in heart as they aim to be. The cock crowed on Apostle Peter. Old Maker, please take my guilt away and cast it into the sea of forgetfulness where it won't never rise to accuse me in this world, nor condemn me in the next."

Laura Lee entered and opened all the windows with a ceremonial air. She was hungry, but before she would eat, she made a ritual of atonement by serving. She took a finely wrought silver platter from the massive old sideboard and gleamed it to perfection. So the platter, so she wanted her love to shine.

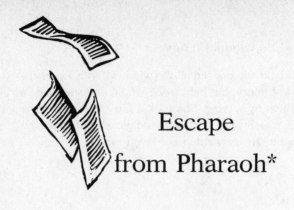

Escape
from Pharaoh*

Africa has her mouth on Moses . . .

Night came walking through Egypt swishing her black dress. The palace and the peasant slept. Pharaoh and the servants of Pharaoh had assured the Egyptians that the terrors of Moses were ended. He had said that Moses must cease and the word of Pharaoh was enough. So the nation slept its sleep untroubled.

In Goshen the blind-eyed goddess of night huddled close, and families stayed inside their houses and waited. A bloody bunch of hyssop had swished against every door in Goshen three times—once on the lintel overhead and once on the door facing at either side. Then the people had gone inside and sat behind the blood and waited as Moses had ordered. Their new god, who had chosen them through Moses, was going to fight Pharaoh for their sake. He had asked the sign of the three bloody marks on the door and the people had done their part. The rest was for Moses and God to do. So the dark stillness in Goshen was not sleeping darkness. It meant waiting. The lamb had been sacrificed and eaten in every house in the land and his signal blood guarded the doors. The night went on its way.

Darkness balanced up on midnight looking both ways for day. Then the great cry arose in Egypt. They cried and died in Egypt. It was the great cry that had issued first from the throat of Israel years before and spread to the rim bones of the world and come

*From *Moses: Man of the Mountain*

back again. And now it poured out through the mouth of the Egyptian nation. It was such a cry that there was none like it since the morning stars sang together, and never shall be another like it as long as heaven is happy. Egypt cried out at the death of the first-born. Every house in Egypt was bloody. Blood outside the door in Goshen, blood inside every other house in Egypt.

Pharaoh looked upon his first-born and wept. His son was dead and the son of his son was dead in his own blood. There were snorts and bellows from his stables from the smell of animal blood. So Pharaoh cried for his dead with all of his voice. Every house in Egypt strained its voice trying to express its bereavement. The noise of it struck the sky and came back to the Nile and ran with it to the sea, the Egyptian chorus of sorrow indoors.

Outside, the paths and pavements were full of soft, swift feet fleeing into Goshen with its listening ears. These were the sounds of the night, sounds without words.

With the sunrise, Princes and people said, "This is the hand, the right hand of Moses." They lifted their dead from beds and said in awe, "Moses and the God of the Israelites." They rolled their dead from straw mats and pallets and said, "Moses and his right hand." They crowded in and around the palace and shouted, "Get Moses and the Hebrews out of Egypt. If you don't, everybody in Egypt will be dead."

So Pharaoh sent for Moses to dismiss him, his God and his people from Egypt. He was no longer proud Pharaoh with the masklike face. He was a man whose son was dead. But Moses refused to go see Pharaoh all that day. Burials went on and burials went out from houses all day in long lines and solemn weeping, and all Egypt was in tears. Pharaoh sent messengers to Moses again telling him not that the Hebrews might go, but that they must go.

Moses heard the message sitting in his house but he didn't say a word right then. The news was too big to speak at once. He had to sit with his feelings for a while. Afterwards he called his leaders to him and told them, "Your slavery is over. Pharaoh is broken at last. We march out of Egypt with a free people. We march out with a high hand."

The people cried when Moses told them. He had expected wild clamor; the sound of cymbals and exultant singing and dancing. But the people wept out of their eyes. Goshen was very still. No songs and shouts.

"Free at last! Free at last! Thank God Almighty I'm free at last! No more toting sand and mixing mortar! No more taking rocks and building things for Pharaoh! No more whipping and bloody backs! No more slaving from can't see in the morning to can't see at night! Free! Free! So free till I'm foolish!" They just sat with centuries in their eyes and cried. A few could express themselves like that. But the majority just sat in the doors of their dwellings staring out at life.

But Moses put a stop to all of that. "You won't be free for long if you keep that up. Stop that shouting, and stop that sitting, people! Get everything you got together and let's go, and that quick."

"Why, Moses?" some of them asked. "We're free now and we can take our own time about everything."

"You people been around Pharaoh all this time and don't know him no better than that? He is scared today and so he says you can go. Tomorrow or next day he will realize what he's losing and send his army into Goshen to put you back to work. Grab up your things right now. Tonight we leave Egypt forever."

"Good gracious!" somebody grumbled, "I was figuring on going fishing tomorrow morning. I don't want to be bothered with no packing up today. It's too much like work and I just got free this morning."

"That's the heaven's truth, too," plenty of others chimed in. "Looks like we done swapped one bossman for another one. I don't want nobody giving me no orders no more."

"But it was Moses that got us free," Joshua told them. "If it hadn't been for him we would be hauling rocks right this minute."

"Oh, I don't know about that. This God that done chose us

would have got us free anyhow. I never did much care for this Moses like some of you all.''

''What's the matter with Moses? He got us free all right.''

''Oh, I have every confidence in the man, I just don't trust him.''

But Moses himself moved from place to place urging hurry and everybody, unwilling or not, did what he said. The women told Miriam's committee that they just couldn't get ready because it was baking day. ''We got dough set to rise and we can't disturb it or it won't be light.'' Miriam went back and told Moses what they said and he went to see about it himself. ''Mix your dough,'' Moses told them, ''but don't put your seasoning in it so it won't spoil, and while you are at it, mix enough for a week. And that is just part of what I want done. Everybody roast a lamb so that everybody in Goshen can eat a full meal with some greens to settle the stomach. We got a long, hard march in front of us tonight!''

Finally Moses got them ready in the spirit so everywhere in Goshen the people were saying, ''Tonight!''

Everybody said it according to their thought and their feelings. Some talked it with the edge of their lips. Some rolled it deep in their throats. Some throbbed it inside their hearts and let their bodies move with the rhythm. Some said it with their eyes, with a gleam, with future-searching gazes. Some said it with a question, ''Tonight?''

They fixed and they did around and got ready. Nothing was still. Children hunted the bitter herbs. Men slaughtered beasts and tied bundles. Women mixed dough and cooked. And all the time everybody thought back over the years and every now and then they breathed, ''Tonight!'' Moses had inspired them for the journey and they were going.

The God of the two horizons took flight beyond the western line and the frenzied hurry of the day took shape. Flocks and herds gathered and ready. Bundles tied. Every group had met its leader and been told.

''Now,'' Moses said to a group of men under Nun, ''go quickly to the tomb of Joseph and bring me the casket with his bones. He brought Israel into Egypt and Israel must take him out of a land that is no longer fit for his dust. Hurry!''

The gorgeous carved and painted casket of Joseph rested on a pedestal before the house of Moses, and its bearers were appointed. So Moses told everybody to eat in haste, leaving nothing to eat behind them when they were ready to go.

They sang a song. Now that they were ready to go and going, it was triumphant but it was sad. It was a long time since Israel had done any singing much and they had forgotten how to shout. Moses noticed that their glad notes broke on wails. Israel was used to wailing now. They had forgotten how to laud. His heart hurt for them. So he said to himself that they should see glory mountains and shiny valleys and they should learn to sing.

He led them out of Goshen with a high hand. Out and out the tread of the tribes behind him. A great horde of mixed-blooded people grabbed up their things and joined the hosts of Israel. ''Let us be free too,'' they begged and Moses said yes to them. His fighting men in front and behind with Joshua's volunteer boys in the center to give aid and assistance to women and children. Out and out he led. People cried and died and stayed where they fell. Aged ones hobbled and were partly carried, old ones, crippled by the generations behind them and blinded by the look ahead, grasped and clutched at young shoulders and gasped, ''Don't leave me behind.'' Babies borned themselves and joined the procession out. Out was such a big word in Egypt to the Hebrews.

''Which way, Moses?'' Aaron asked.

''By the wilderness of the Red Sea.''

''It's a whole heap shorter through the land of the Philistines.''

''I know, Aaron. But our people are leaving slavery. It takes free men for fighting. The Philistines might let us through without fighting but it's too much of a risk. If these people see an army right now they would turn right around and run back into Goshen. So let's head them for the Red Sea.''

The soft murmur of sandals and bare feet kept up in the night without a moon as Moses and his hosts moved on.

''On our way at last,'' Aaron said happily to Nun.

"After four hundred and thirty years to the day. It still seems like it ain't so to me, Aaron. Ain't but one thing I'm sorry about."

"What is that, Nun? I can't imagine any sorrows connected with the thing."

"I sure hate to miss seeing those Egyptians doing our work in all that hot sun."

"I hadn't thought of that, Nun, but it sure would be a lovely sight. I never want to even see a brick again—not even a brick house to live in."

"Me neither. Where we going now?"

"Out, Nun, out!"

"I don't mean that. I mean just exactly where we're going to live permanent when we get out?"

"Moses may know, but if he does he ain't told nobody yet."

"You reckon it's all right to ask him?"

"I guess so. You can ask him if you want to."

"Where is he now?"

"He was just ahead of us a few minutes ago."

The two men looked up and became conscious of a changed rhythm in the multitudes around them and behind them. It was a sort of spontaneous mass halt and they saw the reason right away. Ahead of them at a short distance was a column of fire. What it consumed was hard to understand for it towered up steady and solid as no flame they had ever seen. It was like an illumination that glowed but never flamed. It brightened the countryside, but never grew more nor less.

"What is that?" Nun asked in fear.

"It must be where Moses is. You think it is his right hand shining like that?"

"It could be. Is nothing impossible to Moses?"

"It don't look like it. Let's go ahead to see what it is."

The two leaders marching ahead of the host hurried nearer the fiery column and stopped. It was moving ahead as if it was borne but nothing was holding it up. Its many colored lights just moved along ahead of Moses like a vertical beam.

"Moses! Moses!" Aaron gasped. "What is that?"

"The pillar of fire that will always go in front of us at night. It is the sign of the Presence. In the daytime it will be a cloud. Go tell the people not to be afraid."

With the fiery sign the people marched all night and camped next day far from the city of Rameses at Pihahiroth on the shore of the sea to rest and eat. Moses gazed across the water and exulted.

Next morning Pharaoh woke up and looked out of the window on the city, new and fine, its towers, its parks and streets, which the Hebrews had built for his father and him. He had a strange feeling of newness as if he had not seen these sights for a long time. As if he had awakened among familiar surroundings after a long, horrid dream. Then he noticed something. No work was going on around the half-finished public building near the palace grounds. He called a servant right away and asked about it. The servant didn't know.

"Well, go find out," Pharaoh snapped and ordered his breakfast. After a while the servant came back and said that no Hebrews had been seen that morning by anybody except a very sick old Hebrew found by the road by some fishermen. No work had been done for two whole days.

"Two days! You must be wrong.

"Send to Goshen and find out what's the matter. Some more foolishness out of that Moses, I reckon. If it is, I'm through playing with that man. He dies today, him and all his magic. I don't see why I stood him as long as I did."

The word came back, "A great song was heard, then the whole host of the Israelites were seen marching out, driving their flocks and herds, two days ago. Nobody has heard from them since."

"Oh, that worship they were talking about. I did say that they could go. I was too worried about the funeral of the first-born to notice things. It is a terrible thing to lose a son." Then Pharaoh became alarmed. "Do you suppose those Hebrews have run away?"

"A lot of people are saying the same thing, and they want their work done and they aren't getting a bit done today."

Pharaoh thought a minute and his blood jumped salty. He was angry with himself. He could have killed Moses and saved himself this trouble. But he had yearned to humble the man first. To outwit him and shame him. Then would have come death for Moses. But the man had made a fool of him instead before the whole nation, and now he was gone with the Hebrews as he had threatened. Pharaoh was resolved on his death if he could lay hands on him now. He rose up with a great scowl on his face. "That's my trouble," he said, "I'm too good-natured."

"That's right, you certainly are," all the servants and courtiers agreed.

"I must have been out of my head to let those people go off and now we have nobody to work for us. That is, I mean that just because I was grieved down at the death of my son and my grandson and the first-born of all the other people and said things, this man Moses takes advantage of my good nature and runs off with our Hebrews."

"And why should we let them stop working for us and go off like that?" one of the courtiers asked. "It's a sin and a shame when you come to think about it. Them Hebrews off doing nothing and our work going undone."

"It's worse than that," one of the others agreed. "And they could be stopped, you know. They couldn't be very far by now, and them on foot, too."

"Get me my war chariots!" Pharaoh shouted. "Six hundred fighting chariots and men to fill them and have them ready in half an hour. I'm going after those Hebrews and I'm going to bring 'em back. And so far as that Moses is concerned I mean to kill him with my own hands. That rascal has been imposing on me for thirty-odd years. Always some trick up his sleeve. Get me my fighting chariots and do it now!"

People scurried in every direction and Pharaoh began to dress himself for war.

"My finest sword and javelin! I am a man of war today and it is the happiest day of my life. I have been tricked and tricked and made a fool of by that Moses ever since he was weaned from his nurse. He is facing me today for the last time. Where are my chariots and men?''

With a kill-mad cry, the six hundred chariots with Pharaoh in the lead thundered out of the city before a cloud of road dust, and raced down the road to way off.

It was late afternoon of the second day when Moses came down to the sea. He ordered rest overnight and plenty cooking and eating to keep up the strength of the hosts. Some people grumbled about sore feet and some missed their beds and houses. Moses let the Elders take care of that. He went down to look at the sea. He studied the wind and sky and looked at the sea and beyond.

That was the way things were when Joshua came running and shouting, ''Pharaoh! The Egyptians! They are coming down behind us. Chariots!''

Moses hurried back to the Israelites. By now the thunder of hoofs and the growl of chariot wheels were easy to hear.

Women screamed in open-mouthed terror and whimpered in fear. Men cursed, cried out and milled about in great whorls. Some tried to run away to the woods to hide, others just stood or squatted on the ground in dumb fear. When they saw Moses come among them they crowded about him. Some clung to him while others screamed at him. He shook them off roughly and kept marching towards the rear.

''I always told my husband not to bother with this mess,'' one woman sobbed. ''I tried to tell him we was getting along all right under the Egyptians. But he was so hard-headed he had to go and get mixed up in it.''

Voices broke out everywhere and all were sprung with fear. The war chariots of Pharaoh were in plain view now though distant on the plain. Moses could hear many things as he shoved through the camp.

''Couldn't that man find graves enough in Egypt to bury us all without dragging us out here in the wilderness to die?''

''Didn't I say all along that this Moses was some fake prophet? That god he made up out of his own head—''

"Didn't I always tell you all that them Egyptians was nice peo-ple to work for? You couldn't find better bossmen nowhere."

"The idea of coming and fooling people off from home and leaving 'em with no protection. I mean to tell Pharaoh just how it was."

"Didn't I always say we was better off in slavery than we would be wandering all over the wilderness following after some stray man that nobody don't know nothing about? Tell the truth, didn't I always say that?"

"I told you all a long time ago that we had enough gods in Egypt without messing with some fool religion that nobody don't know nothing about but Moses. You all just let him make a fool out of you. I always knowed it was some trick in it. That man is a pure Egyptian and Pharaoh is his brother. He just told us off so his brother could butcher us in the wilderness. I told you all so."

"You heard me at the meeting distinctly tell that man to leave us alone and let us serve our Egyptian masters in peace, didn't you? We was getting along fine—plenty to eat and a place to sleep and everything. We wouldn't be in the fix we're in right now if that Moses had of let us alone."

"Who asked him to butt in nohow? Our business didn't concern him, did it? It was our backs they was beating. It wasn't none of his and if we was satisfied he ought to been tickled to death. Now Pharaoh is going to kill us all."

"Great Ra! Great Horus! Great Thoth! Great Isis and the forty-two gods of the double justice! Save us."

Slowed down by the weight of the chariots over the rough ground, the horses were coming in a walk. Moses reached the rear of his great huddle of trembling humanity and took his stand, between danger and his charges. Again, he was one against all Egypt. Listening and thinking back, it was hard to keep his feel-ings from flying to his head. He had but to step aside and leave them to Pharaoh and his servants. But Pharaoh himself was driv-ing the first chariot as the cavalcade approached, and he wanted to face him and beat him one last time. He laughed to himself as he thought, "Pharaoh thinks he's pursuing me, but it's the other way around. I been on his trail for thirty years, and now I got the old coon at last, as Jericho would say. Let me fuddle him all up for a night and then I will raise my hand. First and last, I'm showing him my ugly laugh.''

As the chariots drew near the panic grew in Israel. They committed every kind of folly and showed their inside weakness. Then Moses showed his power again. He turned his back on the Egyptian horde and spoke to his people. Spoke to them in their own dialect as one of them.

''Stand still!'' he commanded in a sterner voice than they had ever heard before. ''Stand still, every last one of you and stop that screaming and yelling. You haven't got a thing to be scared of. That ain't nobody but Pharaoh and his army and we done beat them too many times before. Don't get so excited about nothing! The Lord is going to fight for you just as He's been doing all along. Stand still and see the salvation of the Lord which He is going to show you today. See those Egyptians there? Take a good look at 'em, because those Egyptians that you are looking at today, you're never going to see *them* no more as long as you live. And nobody else won't be seeing them either. Stand still and keep quiet is all I ask you to do.''

Moses didn't lift his hand while he talked but the command in his voice was calming. Suddenly everybody felt secure and brave.

Moses just stood and looked and the pillar of cloud that went before the host moved around from the sea and spread itself like a great plumey curtain between the Israelites and Pharaoh and hid each camp from the other. The Israelites felt shut in and safe. The Egyptians felt shut out and puzzled. They were afraid to attack until they could know what went on behind that cloud screen, so Pharaoh ordered his forces to camp until next day and then to attack with vigor.

''They can't get away from us so we might as well get some sleep. Our horses need freshening too,'' Pharaoh ordered. ''We got them in a trap—between us and the sea. We'll close the trap in the morning.'' So they turned in and rested so they could have plenty of vim to butcher Hebrews in the morning.

But Moses never slept. The signal pillar of fire glowed behind the cloud screen and lighted the camp of Israel. Moses himself went back to the sea and stood. When the hour came he called up the east wind and stretched out his hand. They broke the head of the eastern drum and marched out on the sea. The retreating tidal waters did not creep on as was their habit; they fell back from the strait on either side like two mighty armies in retreat. Both sides shrank away from the uplifted hand like lambs before a lion. The waters fled back and back and back and stood in a solid wall on either side and waited on the powers to close them up again.

Then Moses ordered the march. In the same order in which they had come down to the sea, Moses told his hosts to cross over. Flocks first, then women and children followed by the six hundred thousand men of fighting age armed with whatever Moses could find in Egypt to put in their hands—clubs, spears, javelins, old swords, sticks and anything that could wound and tear.

The bones of Joseph crossed over after the women and children. Then Moses challenged Pharaoh. The smoky cloud screen lifted. The fiery pillar again went before the hosts and the sentries of the Egyptian army saw that the children of Israel were escaping across the sea and ran to wake up the camp. "Wake up! The Hebrews have broke camp and are gone."

The camp woke up by degrees. Nobody could believe the sentry at first. They had to get to their feet and get their heads clear of dreams first, and then the peeping dawn did the rest. It was hard to believe, but the sea was really divided and the Hebrews were tramping across on dry land.

"Well, I'll be—" Pharaoh began, then sprang to action. "Get up and harness the horses! Don't let 'em get away! A palace and high houses to the man who overtakes Moses and hands him over to me alive! Get up and get after our slaves."

In a few minutes the camp was furiously alive. Leaping into chariots, shouts, cries, plunging and neighing of horses, clash of arms on shields, posing Pharaoh's chariot with its three Arabian horses in front of the forces and the furious charge to the sea crossing while the last ranks of the Hebrews were still in sight.

Moses heard the commotion in the Egyptian camp and knew that his movements had been seen as he intended them to be. He hurried across after the last man and waited. He saw the mad charge down the beach. He saw them hesitate there to debate the wisdom of trying the unusual crossing. Then he deliberately showed himself to Pharaoh and the frenzied pursuit was on. The six hundred chariots dashed down into the sea ten and twenty abreast. The Egyptians shouted in triumph as they viewed the cowering Israelites on the opposite shore.

Then when the Egyptians had thoroughly committed themselves to the sea bed and wagered their lives and their vengeance on it, Moses stood on the opposite shore and looked hard at his pursuers. He could distinguish the royal chariot with its fiery Arabians well in the lead. Those were fine horses, Moses recognized, and a splendid chariot. But Ta-Phar had always thought too well of chariots. He could not see his uncle's face at that distance and read its expression, but he could feel it, the hatred, the bafflement and the lust for vengeance. Behind him the Israelites were already over their joy at the miraculous crossing and were beginning to cry out in fear.

"Moses! The Egyptians are coming after us! Ain't no more seas for us to cross."

"I see them. Don't worry."

What he knew must come, happened. Away from the smooth sand of the shore, the horses and the heavy chariots struck rough going. Horses began to flounder and fall as they stepped into holes and soft clay. Chariots swerved, overturned, and control was lost. Chariots coming after plunged into the tangle and were themselves overturned. Then Moses lifted his hand.

The gripping east wind loosed its mighty fingers and the sea water came rushing back to its bed. It was a moving time. There was the outspoken voice of the wind going east; the mad grumble and shout of the waves as they raced back to embrace each other over the clamor of men in fright, the scream of drowning horses, the last mad struggle of the chariots. That all made a boiling place in the sea for a space. Then there was just the heaving Red Sea with its two shores. Egypt on one side and Moses and his mission on the other. Moses stood and looked on the sea. It was a long time before he thought to change his rod from his right hand to his left and let the wind and the sea subside.

Behind him he heard the people exulting. "Didn't we outdo old Pharaoh, though?" Miriam was asking everybody. "It was a great victory for our God," Aaron was saying. "The Lord is a man of war. The Lord is His name." "Old Pharaoh thought he knew who to fool with and who to let alone." "We showed him something. Yeah, he's dead out there in the ocean and there ain't no help for it. That's one old Pharaoh won't have no great big old tombstone over him."

"Well, he's got the great big sea over him, and I reckon that's big enough to suit anybody."

They made a song on that and danced it off. A man with a good voice got out in the center of the ring and sang.

"Old Pharaoh's dead!"

And the chorus answered, "How did he die?"

And the solo man went to dancing and said: "Well, he died like this!" and he danced that off. Then he sang another part and everybody went on dancing and shouting.

> Oh, he died in his chariot and he died in the sea
> And he wouldn't have died at all if he let us be.

They sang that over and over and danced on it until they got tired. Then Miriam took the cymbal and some more women went behind her and they went all over the camp singing:

> Oh, Miriam played the cymbal over the Red Sea
> Miriam played the cymbal over the Red Sea
> Miriam played the cymbal over the Red Sea.
> Oh, Miriam played the cymbal right over.

And they clapped time on that with their hands and danced and double clapped it off like they did the other song because everybody was happy and felt like clapping and dancing. Then Moses told them to make camp for the night.

Moses strolled down the beach a little way and sat down on the same boulder that he had sat down on after the first crossing so many years ago. It was another morning and another crossing and so he thought thoughts again. This time he had crossed over safely with a nation behind him and no weapon worth talking about but his right hand. Well, the present was an egg laid by the past that had the future inside its shell. So Moses sat on the rock and said, "You, Voice, you told me to lead out, and by the hardest, I did it. So I'm down here by the Red Sea with these people. You know more about 'em than I do, Lord. What must I do with them now?"

A little tee-nincy voice raised up in the back of his mind and said: "Old Rameses is dead. Ta-Phar is dead. The set who bucked against you and hated you are dead. You know one time you were the idol of Egypt. The army still thinks you are the biggest man they ever made. Moses, you can go back to Egypt and be King. You can do even better than that. You can control the army which controls the King. The Voice told you to lead out and you have led out with a high hand. You have done your duty. The Israelites are out of Egypt and they are free. If they fall into slavery again somewhere else that's none of your business. You set them free. Moses, there is Egypt right over there and the King is dead in the sea."

Moses sat on the rock and thought back. He had sat on this rock when he fled from Pharaoh the first time and something had shown him clearly the futility of a life of war. Right on this rock he had forsworn the sword and glory. He got to his feet and looked earnestly at the camp for a while, then he said, "Which way, Lord, which way must I lead Your people?"

The
Tablets of
the Law*

Moses lifted the freshly chiseled tablets of stone in his hands and gazed down the mountain to where Israel waited in the valley. He knew a great exultation. Now men could be free because they could govern themselves. They had something of the essence of divinity expressed in order. They had the chart and compass of behavior. They need not stumble into blind ways and injure themselves. This was bigger than Israel itself. It comprehended the world. Israel could be a heaven for all men forever, by these sacred stones.

With flakes of light still clinging to his face, Moses turned down the mountain with the tablets of testimony in his hands. He heard nothing earthly nor sensed anything about him until he descended to where Joshua waited for him. With his eyes turned inward, he sat down on a stone opposite Joshua to rest.

"Joshua, I have laws. Israel is going to know peace and justice."

Moses indicated the sacred stones on his lap.

Then from far off a sound, a noise made up of many sounds, came up to Moses and he listened. And his ears accepted what his soul refused. It was a wild and savage shout of voices and drums that Moses heard, but his spirit rejected it, because it injured his vision of destiny for Israel. It clashed with his exalted forty days.

*From *Moses: Man of the Mountain*

It soiled what had passed between him and God. So for a long time Moses sat silent and listened, hoping that he dreamed. Finally he asked Joshua, "Do I hear shouting and singing, Joshua, or is it just a ringing in my ears?"

"It's shouting and singing, Moses."

Moses sat sodden and sad for a long while and then a new hope crept into his voice.

"Do *you* hear anything that sounds like singing and cymbals, Joshua, or does it just sound like that to me because I'm tired and sort of frazzled out?"

Joshua looked at the face of Moses and pitied him.

"I hear a mighty loud noise down below," Joshua evaded.

Moses looked down at the stones in his lap and passed his hand over the carved figures reverently and then he looked back up the mountain as if he would retreat up there. Then he brought his attention back to the tumult below.

"Does it sound like the voice of the people shouting for victory, Joshua? Maybe the Amalekites have come up against Israel while we've been up here with God."

"No, Moses, it's not the voice of mastery that I hear. It's the voice of Israel, but they are not shouting for conquering anybody."

Moses sat and listened for a while longer, shutting his heart against what he feared.

"Well, Joshua," he said haltingly, "do they sound to you like they are crying out for help? They could be overcome, you know, by some nation that might attack, with both of us away."

Joshua listened carefully for a moment. "No, it's not the voice of them that cry for being overcome."

"What do you reckon could have happened to Israel, Joshua?" Moses tried to persevere in his hopes.

"Oh, that's singing and dancing that I hear. Sounds like the dance songs to Apis, the Bull-god, to me. Listen at those drums!"

Moses snatched his face away from Joshua and the last glimmer of light that had clung to his face from God died to ashes.

"Oh, no, Joshua, they couldn't do a thing like that. Not after all

we have been through from Egypt on! Not after they cried to God
to deliver them from Egypt and its sorrows! Not after the God of
the mountain sent me to save them from all harm and danger, and
brought them here to the mountain to give them laws and pledges!
No, Joshua, they wouldn't be back in unforgetfulness and ingratitude here at the foot of Sinai. They couldn't be howling in idolatry
in the very ears of God."

"It certainly is the sound of drumming and chanting to Apis that
I hear."

Moses stood up and closed his eyes with the tablets clasped
tightly to his breast. Then he started slowly up the mountainside
again. "I better go back and talk to God again about Israel. He'd
know better what to do than I would." He left Joshua behind him
and struggled on back toward God.

But he didn't get far. At first he thought it was the wind scuffling
around in the brush. Then he knew it was the Voice that spoke
and halted him.

"Moses," it said like a strong breeze in the pine tops, "don't
come up here to Me. Hurry down!"

"Lord," Moses sobbed, "have they betrayed You?"

"They have betrayed Me. They have betrayed you, and most of
all they have dirtied their souls by betraying themselves. Go down,
Moses, and halt them in their headlong flight. The people that you
have brought out of Egypt have soiled themselves and tempted Me
to destroy them. They are worshiping a calf of gold and giving it
the credit for bringing them out of the land of Egypt, and out of
the house of bondage. Go stop them before I get too tired of their
ingratitude and kill them."

The Voice was gone and the light was gone and Moses turned
cold and heavy and went down the mountain like God descending
into Eden. First it was the mountain top and then the high shoulder and then the heavy hips of the mountain and then the crumbling ankles of the mountain and then the plain where Israel
waited for a sign from God.

So Moses stood before the altar of the golden calf with the tables
of stone in his hands. Drunken shouts filled his ears; bodies drunk

on the liquor of feeling rocked and reeled and contorted about him with eyes glazed and covered. Aaron with his bearded chin stuck out in front of him was presiding at the altar. His two oldest sons, Abihu and Nadab, chief acolytes in the dance and revel, were shouting and leaping, and thumping their naked bodies and urging the people on.

"Aaron!" Moses cried at him with a stern voice. "Aaron, do you hear me?" Moses had to call three times before Aaron really saw him standing before the altar with the law from Sinai in his hands. Aaron took one long comprehending look and sunk behind the altar on his knees. The eyes of Moses had gutted him. Aaron hid himself behind the pagan altar while Moses towered tall and grim before it with the tablets of God in his hands. All around the spot the tumult boiled, for few had seen with their eyes or heard.

The calf and all its meaning and all the thoughts it collected glimmered and winked at Moses from its altar and suddenly Moses raised one of the tablets with its fine writings and hurled it at the graven image and saw the golden calf topple over on its side. The force of the impact shattered the sacred stone and crumbled it in pieces. Moses lifted the other stone and hurled it, and the calf broke in pieces and the pieces scattered around the altar. But in breaking the calf, the tablets of testimony had been broken to crumbling stone. Moses stood in his wrath and considered. The law from Sinai had broken the idol of Egypt, but the sacred tablets had themselves been destroyed in the clash. Egypt against Sinai. It was going to be a hard struggle.

The crash of stone on metal had attracted attention. Drums faltered and stopped. Dancers paused and looked and saw Moses destroying Apis and froze to sculpture in poses, which broke into flight. Some ran heedless. Some crept off slowly with dazed faces to hiding places. Before Apis and Aaron they were clothed in joy and license. Before Moses and Sinai they were naked to their souls. They slunk into places of concealment as best they could. Moses strode over the huge vacant square of celebration with Joshua at his heels, looking, looking and seeing. Looking inside of people by their outward appearance and sickening at what he saw. He circled and circled and came back to the naked altar and stopped.

Moses found Aaron squatting down behind the altar trying to hide himself. Moses kicked over the altar and snatched Aaron to his feet and looked him dead in the eye. He looked at the man and saw him as he was, stripped of the imitation of dignity that he affected lately; saw him naked of the imitation of himself that he wore as best he might.

"Aaron," he said, "what on earth did these people do to you to make you bring such a sin on everybody like you did?"

Aaron tried to back off but Moses had him by his whiskers and he wouldn't let him go. So Aaron cringed and fawned and said, "Lord, Moses, you're my bossman, and I know it. I wouldn't think of putting myself on an equal with you. You're a great big high cockadoo and I ain't nothing. So you oughtn't to be wasting your time getting mad with me. You done been round these people long enough to know 'em. You know they ain't nothing and if you and God fool with 'em you won't be nothing neither."

"Aaron, you haven't said a thing yet to excuse yourself for what you have done. Tell me and tell me quick why you have betrayed God and the people in the way you have done."

Aaron lifted his hand as if to break Moses' grip on his beard, but the eye of Moses forbade him. He winced and said, "You oughtn't to hold my whiskers like that, Moses, the people are looking at us, and me being a leader—"

"The people are looking at you naked and capering around like an old goat, too. Let's forget about that while you answer me."

Moses did not miss the look of hatred born of hurt vanity in Aaron's eyes as he sought to placate Moses by dissembling.

"Now, Moses, you know these people is always up for something that ain't no good. They don't mean nobody no good including theirselves. Know what they did? When you didn't come back right away they was going round behind your back running you down and scandalizing your name and making out you was dead or done run on off and they took and brought me all them ornaments, just because they knowed I used to work in gold, and they told me, we don't know what become of that man Moses. Make us some gods to march in front of us instead of that cloud. And they shoved all them earrings and things in my hands and naturally I didn't want to be bothered with the things, so just to get 'em out of my hands I took and threw 'em in the fire and what you reckon, boss? All I did was to fling them earrings into the fire, and out come that calf.''

"Aaron, you haven't said a thing yet and that is because you haven't thought a thing yet, nor felt anything except your own importance. Your whole body is nothing but a big bag to tote your littleness in.''

Moses thrust Aaron from him so roughly that he all but fell. Then Moses strode away, noting as he went how many people who had taken no part in the ceremony to the bull. There was open disgust on the faces of many and that made Moses think. Some were here because of Sinai and all that it meant and some were just here. A divided people, and that would never do, not at this point in their history. So Moses made a decision. He straightened his shoulders and marched to the gate of the camp and lifted both hands in the air.

People saw Moses standing like a crucifix and came. Moses still stood and they kept coming and questioning each other and coming. When a great multitude stood before him, Moses began to speak and cried out, "Who is on the Lord's side? Who is on the Lord's side?" Moses kept crying until the words became a chant. "Who is on the Lord's side?" Israel's ears were wrung. "Who is on the Lord's side?" It woke up fear in the guilty. Israel was stung. "Who is on the Lord's side?" It freshened hope in the hearts of the just. Israel was called. "Who is on the Lord's side?" And some young Levites were the first to come closer and say, "We are, Moses, we are for the Lord of Sinai." Then others joined until thousands upon thousands stood by Moses. Then he said, "You who are on the Lord's side, take your swords in your hands and come to me." The surging multitudes of young men gathered around Moses with ready swords. So Aaron saw one of his sons, Eleazar, and all the other Levites go to Moses with swords and he was afraid to stay away. He came to Moses also with his sword and his censer in his hand and stood.

Moses said, "You all know what a foul thing has happened in Israel today. You know better than I do who the leaders and the agitators were. If this is to be a great nation, it must be purged of such evildoers, or all Israel must perish. You have your eager weapons, men. Spare not a soul who is guilty." Their swords leaped out of their scabbards like day out of dawn.

The struggle began. Drunken people in hidden places roused from a stupor with their eyes wide open in judgment. Aaron saw two of his sons dragged forth and cut down before his eyes. He dropped his sword and swung his censer in wide arcs to call to the minds of the avengers that he was a priest. He stood between the living and the dead with his censer in his hand, weeping and quaking and cursing. He was afraid to fight, afraid to run and ashamed to cry out loud.

For hours there was fleeing and screaming and hiding and bloody swords. Then there was quiet again in the camp. It only remained to bury the dead. Aaron came creeping and looked down into the faces of Nadab and Abihu, his two dead sons, and wept. The men buried his sons with the other thousand leaders of the revolt slain by the sons of Levi. Aaron started a little song in his heart that went like this: "It's your time now, be mine after while. Oh, it's your time now, but be mine after while, oh, it's your time now, but it'll be mine after while." And from that minute on till the hour he died Aaron kept his eyes on Moses in secret and waited his chance. All he needed was the strength to seize his hour for vengeance. His hate was strong but his heart was weak. From then on for forty years the underhand struggle went on. Sometimes he made an open attack upon Moses when Aaron thought he could succeed, but always the secret struggle went on to destroy him and have Aaron in the saddle. And always the strength of Moses trampled down the weak cunning of Aaron.

Moses was hard on Israel, after that. He felt that only discipline would save what he had begun and so he chastened the people severely. They suffered epidemics of ailments and many discomforts. It was then that he established the House of God. It was called the Tabernacle of the Congregation and Moses set it apart from all other tents, even his own. He pitched it far outside the camp. And when Moses went out to the tabernacle everybody saw him go and everybody was afraid. Would he lift his rod against them? Would he raise that right hand? As Moses went the people stood in their tent doors and watched him pass. And every eye in Israel followed him in fear.

They watched him go inside the door of the new tabernacle and they saw the shimmering cloudy pillar descend and they saw it stand at the door of the tabernacle and in awe they rose as one man and worshiped the God who had chosen to live among them. They heard the Lord talking to Moses from the cloud like two friends talking face to face. They heard Moses tell the Lord, "If you don't go with us, don't send me by myself, Lord. Other people will make a fool out of us."

So the Lord told him, "I'll always be there, Moses, because I love you and I know you by your name."

"Thank you, Lord. One favor more I want to ask you while I am still on pleading terms with mercy."

"What is it, Moses?"

"Lord, I done seen your pillar of fire and your pillar of cloud and heard your voice in rumbling thunder. I done seen the cloudy cloak that hides your glory, but I ain't never seen your glory itself. Lord, be so pleased in your tender mercy as to show me your glory."

The Lord answered Moses and told him, "Moses, I will make all My goodness pass before you. And I will proclaim the name of the Lord before you and I will be gracious to whom I will be gracious, and show mercy unto whom I will show mercy, but, Moses, you just can't see My face, for no man can see My face and live. But, Moses, since it is you that ask me, look, see there is a place by Me and you go and stand upon that certain rock and when My Glory passes by, I'll take you and put you in a crack in the rock, and I will cover you with My hand while I pass by, then I will move My hand and you shall see the back parts of My Glory, but My face you shall never see."

So Moses thanked the Lord for letting him see that much and God told him, "Moses, get you two more nice smooth pieces of stone and bring it up to the top of the mountain so I can put those same laws that you broke upon that golden calf down again. These people need laws and rules to go by."

Moses got up early next morning and took the stones and went up to the top of the mountain and kept company with God again. And when he came down with the law in his hands, the skin of his face was iridescent and shining, but Moses didn't know it himself, that is, until the people gazed at him in awe and talked about his shining face. So they knew that God had covered Moses with His hand in the cleft of the rock and passed His Glory by Moses.

And Moses took the tables of testimony into the tabernacle and the pillar of cloud went in behind Moses and rested on the altar. So that was the first time that God had come inside the house to live with people.

Black Death

The Negroes in Eatonville know a number of things that the hustling, bustling white man never dreams of. He is a materialist with little ears for overtones.

For instance, if a white person were halted on the streets of Orlando and told that Old Man Morgan, the excessively black Negro hoodoo man, can kill any person indicated and paid for, without ever leaving his house or even seeing his victim, he'd laugh in your face and walk away, wondering how long the Negro will continue to wallow in ignorance and superstition. But no black person in a radius of twenty miles will smile, not much. They *know*.

His achievements are far too numerous to mention singly. Besides many of his curses or "conjures" are kept secret. But everybody knows that he put the loveless curse on Della Lewis. She has been married seven times but none of her husbands have ever remained with her longer than the twenty-eight days that Morgan had prescribed as the limit.

Hiram Lester's left track was brought to him with five dollars and when the new moon came again, Lester was stricken with paralysis while working in his orange grove.

There was the bloody-flux that he put on Lucy Potts; he caused Emma Taylor's teeth to drop out; he put the shed skin of a black snake in Horace Brown's shoes and made him as the Wandering

Jew; he put a sprig of Lena Merchant's hair in a bottle, corked it and threw it into a running stream with the neck pointing up stream, and she went crazy; he buried Lillie Wilcox's finger-nails with lizard's feet and dried up her blood.

All of these things and more can easily be proved by the testimony of the villagers. They ought to know.

He lives alone in a two-room hut down by Lake Blue Sink, the bottomless. His eyes are reddish and the large gold hoop ear-rings jangling on either side of his shrunken black face make the children shrink in terror whenever they meet him on the street or in the woods where he goes to dig roots for his medicines.

But the doctor does not spend his time merely making folks ill. He has sold himself to the devil over the powerful black cat's bone that alone will float upstream, and many do what he wills. Life and death are in his hands—he sometimes kills.

He sent Old Lady Grooms to her death in the Lake. She was a rival hoodoo doctor and laid claims to equal power. She came to her death one night. That very morning Morgan had told several that he was tired of her pretenses—he would put an end to it and prove his powers.

That very afternoon near sundown, she went down to the lake to fish, telling her daughter, however, that she did not wish to go, but something seemed to be forcing her. About dusk someone heard her scream and rushed to the Lake. She had fallen in and drowned. The white coroner from Orlando said she met her death by falling into the water during an epileptic fit. But the villagers *knew*. White folks are very stupid about some things. They can think mightily but cannot *feel*.

But the undoing of Beau Diddely is his masterpiece. He had come to Eatonville from up North somewhere. He was a waiter at the Park House Hotel over in Maitland where Docia Boger was a chamber-maid. She had a very pretty brown body and face, sang alto in the Methodist Choir and played the blues on her guitar. Soon Beau Diddely was with her every moment he could spare from his work. He was stuck on her all right, for a time.

They would linger in the shrubbery about Park Lane or go for long walks in the woods on Sunday afternoon to pick violets. They are abundant in the Florida woods in winter.

The Park House always closed in April and Beau was planning to go North with the white tourists. It was then Docia's mother discovered that Beau should have married her daughter weeks before.

"Mist' Diddely," said Mrs. Boger, "Ah'm a widder 'oman an' Deshy's all Ah got, an' Ah know youse gointer do what you orter." She hesitated a moment and studied his face. " 'Thout no trouble. Ah doan wanta make no talk 'round town."

In a split second the vivacious, smiling Beau had vanished. A very hard vitriolic stranger occupied his chair.

"Looka heah, Mis' Boger. I'm a man that's travelled a lot— been most everywhere. Don't try to come that stuff over me— What I got to marry Docia for?"

" 'Cause—'Cause"—the surprise of his answer threw the old woman into a panic. "Youse the cause of her condition, aintcher?"

Docia, embarrassed, mortified, began to cry.

"Oh, I see the little plot now!" He glanced maliciously toward the girl and back again to her mother. "But I'm none of your down-South-country-suckers. Go try that on some of these clod-hoppers. Don't try to lie on *me*—I got money to fight."

"Beau," Docia sobbed, "you ain't callin' me a liah, is you?" And in her misery she started toward the man who through four months' constant association and assurance she had learned to love and trust.

"Yes! You're lying—you sneaking little—oh you're not even good sawdust! Me marry you! Why I could pick up a better woman out of the gutter than you! I'm a married man anyway, so you might as well forget your little scheme!"

Docia fell back stunned.

"But, but Beau, you said you wasn't," Docia wailed.

"Oh," Beau replied with a gesture of dismissal of the whole affair. "What difference does it make? A man will say anything at times. There are certain kinds of women that men always lie to.''

In her mind's eye Docia saw things for the first time without her tinted glasses and real terror seized her. She fell upon her knees and clasped the nattily clad legs of her seducer.

"Oh Beau,'' she went, struggling to hold him, as he, fearing for the creases in his trousers, struggled to free himself—"You made—you—you promised"—

"Oh, well, you ought not to have believed me—you ought to have known I didn't mean it. Anyway I'm not going to marry you, so what're you going to do? Do whatever you feel big enough to try—my shoulders are broad.''

He left the house hating the two women bitterly, as we only hate those we have injured.

At the hotel, omitting mention of his shows of affection, his pleas, his solemn promises to Docia, he told the other waiters how that piece of earth's refuse had tried to inveigle, to coerce him into a marriage. He enlarged upon his theme and told them all, in strict confidence, how she had been pursuing him all winter; how she had waited in a bush time and again and dragged him down by the Lake, and well, he was only human. It couldn't have happened with the *right* kind of girl, and he thought too much of himself to marry any other than the country's best.

So the next day Eatonville knew; and the scourge of tongues was added to Docia's woes.

Mrs. Boger and her daughter kept strictly indoors, suffering, weeping, growing bitter.

"Mommer, if he jus' hadn't tried to make me out a bad girl, I could look over the rest in time, Mommer, but—but he tried to make out—ah—''

She broke down weeping again.

Drip, drip, drip, went her daughter's tears on the old woman's heart, each drop calcifying a little the fibers till at the end of four days the petrifying process was complete. Where once had been warm, pulsing flesh was now cold heavy stone, that pulled down pressing out normal life and bowing the head of her. The woman died, and in that heavy cold stone a tiger, a female tiger—was born.

She was ready to answer the questions Beau had flung so scornfully at her old head: "Well, what are you going to do?"

Docia slept, huddled on the bed. A hot salt tear rose to Mrs. Boger's eyes and rolled heavily down the quivering nose. Must Docia awake always to that awful desolation? Robbed of *everything,* even faith. She knew then that the world's greatest crime is not murder—its most terrible punishment is meted to her of too much faith—too great a love.

She turned down the light and stepped into the street.

It was near midnight and the village slept. But she knew of one house where there would be light; one pair of eyes still awake.

As she approached Blue Sink she all but turned back. It was a dark night but the Lake shimmered and glowed like phosphorous near the shore. It seemed that figures moved about on the quiet surface. She remembered that folks said Blue Sink the bottomless, was Morgan's graveyard and all Africa awoke in her blood.

A cold prickly feeling stole over her and stood her hair on end. Her feet grew heavy and her tongue dry and stiff.

In the swamp at the head of the Lake, she saw Jack-O-Lanteren darting here and there and three hundred years of America passed like the mist of morning. Africa reached out its dark hand and claimed its own. Drums, tom, tom, tom, tom, tom, beat her ears. Strange demons seized her. Witch doctors danced before her, laid hands upon her alternately freezing and burning her flesh, until she found herself within the house of Morgan.

She was not permitted to tell her story. She opened her mouth but the old man chewed a camphor leaf or two, spat into a small pail of sand and askcd:

"How do yuh wants kill 'im? By water, by sharp edge, or a bullet?"

The old woman almost fell off the chair in amazement that he knew her mind. He merely chuckled a bit and handed her a drinking gourd.

"Dip up a teeny bit of water an' po' hit on de flo',—by dat time you'll know."

She dipped the water out of a wooden pail and poured it upon the rough floor.

"Ah wanta shoot him, but how kin ah' 'thout . . . ?"—

"Looka heah." Morgan directed and pointed to a huge mirror scarred and dusty. He dusted its face carefully. "Look in dis glass 'thout turnin' yo' head an' when he comes, you shoot tuh kill. Take a good aim!"

Both faced about and gazed hard into the mirror that reached from floor to ceiling. Morgan turned once to spit into the pail of sand. The mirror grew misty, darker, near the center, then Mrs. Boger saw Beau walk to the center of the mirror and stand looking at her, glaring and sneering. She all but fainted in superstitious terror.

Morgan thrust the gun into her hand. She saw the expression on Beau Diddely's face change from scorn to fear and she laughed.

"Take good aim," Morgan cautioned. "You cain't shoot but once."

She leveled the gun at the heart of the apparition in the glass and fired. It collapsed; the mirror grew misty again, then cleared.

In horror she flung her money at the old man who seized it greedily, and fled into the darkness, dreading nothing, thinking only of putting distance between her and the house of Morgan.

The next day Eatonville was treated to another thrill.

It seemed that Beau Diddely, the darling of the ladies, was in the hotel yard making love to another chamber-maid. In order that she might fully appreciate what a great victory was here, he was reciting the Conquest of Docia, how she loved him, pursued him, knelt down and kissed his feet, begging him to marry her,—when suddenly he stood up very straight, clasped his hand over his heart, grew rigid, and fell dead.

The coroner's verdict was death from natural causes—heart failure. But they were mystified by what looked like a powder burn directly over the heart.

But the Negroes knew instantly when they saw that mark, but everyone agreed that he got justice. Mrs. Boger and Docia moved to Jacksonville where she married well.

And the white folks never knew and would have laughed had anyone told them,—so why mention it?

The
Bone of
Contention

Eatonville, Florida is a colored town and has its colored interests. It has not now, nor ever has had anything to rank Brazzle's yellow mule. His Yaller Highness was always mentioned before the weather, the misery of the back or leg, or the hard times.

The mule was old, rawbony and mean. He was so rawbony that he creaked as he ambled about the village street with his meanness shining out through every chink and cranny in his rattling anatomy. He worked little, ate heartily, fought every inch of the way before the plow and even disputed with Brazzle when he approached to feed him. Sale, exchange or barter was out of the question, for everybody in the county knew him.

But one day he died. Everybody was glad, including Brazzle. His death was one of those pleasant surprises that people hope for, but never expect to happen.

The city had no refuse plant so H.Y.H. went the way of all other domestic beasts who died among us. Brazzle borrowed Watson's two grey plugs and dragged the remains out to the edge of the cypress swamp, three miles beyond the city limits and abandoned them to the natural scavengers. The town attended the dragging out to a man. The fallen gladiator was borne from the arena on his sharp back, his feet stiffly raised as if in a parting gesture of defiance. We left him to the village. Satisfied that the only piece of unadulterated meanness that the Lord had ever made was gone from among us forever.

* * *

Three years passed and his bones were clean and white. They were scattered along the swamp edge. The children still found them sufficiently interesting to tramp out to gaze upon them on Sunday afternoons. The elders neglected his bones, but the mule remained with them in song and story as a simile, as a metaphor, to point a moral or adorn a tale. But as the mean old trouble-making cuss, they considered him gone for good.

II

It was early night in the village. Joe Clarke's store porch was full of chewing men. Some chewed tobacco, some chewed cane, some chewed straws, for the villager is a ruminant in his leisure. They sat thus every evening ostensibly waiting for the mail from Number 38, the south-bound express. It was seldom that any of them got any but it gave them a good excuse to gather. They all talked a great deal, and every man jack of them talked about himself. Heroes all, they were, of one thing or another.

Ike Pearson had killed a six-foot rattler in a mighty battle that grew mightier every time Ike told about it; Walter Thomas had chinned the bar twenty times without stopping; Elijah Moseley had licked a "cracker"; Brazzle had captured a live catamount; Hiram Lester had killed a bear; Sykes Jones had won the soda-cracker eating contest; AND JOE CLARKE HAD STARTED THE TOWN!

Reverend Simms, the Methodist preacher, a resident of less than a year, had done nothing to boast of, but it was generally known that he aspired to the seat of Joe Clarke. He wanted to be the mayor. He had observed to some of his members that it wasnt no sense in one man staying in office all the time.

"Looka heah," Clarke cut across whoever it was that was talking at the time, "when Ah started dis town, Ah walked right up to de white folks an' laid down TWO HUN'DED DOLLAHS WID DIS RIGHT HAND YOU SEE BEFO' YOU AN' GOT MAH PAPERS AN' PUT DIS TOWN ON DE MAP! It takes uh powerful lot uh sense an' grit tuh start uh town, yessirree!"

"Whut map did you put it on, Joe?" Lindsay disrespectfully asked. "Ah aint seed it on no map."

Seeing Clarke gored to his liver, Rev. Simms let out a gloating snicker and tossed a cane knot to Tippy, the Lewis' dejected dog frame hovering about the group hoping for something more tempting to a dog's palate than cane chews and peanut shells might drop. He tossed the knot and waited for Clarke to answer. His Honor ignored the thrust as being too low for him to stoop, and talked on. Was he not mayor, postmaster, storekeeper and Pooh Bah general? Insults must come to him from at least the county seat.

"Nother thing," Clarke continued, giving Simms a meaning look, "there's a heap goin' on 'round heah under the cover dat Ahm gointer put a stop to. Jim Weston done proaged through mah hen house enough. Last Sat'day Ah missed three uh mah bes' layin' hens, an' Ah been tol' he buried feathers in his backyard the very next day. Cose Ah caint prove nothin', but de minute he crooks his little finger, he goes 'way from mah town. He aint de onliest one Ah got mah eye on neither."

Simms accepted the challenge thrown at him.

"Fact is, the town aint run lak it might be. We oughta stop dat foolishness of runnin' folks outa town. We oughta jail 'em. They's got jails in all de other towns, an' we oughta bring ours up to date."

"Ah'll be henfired! Simms, you tries to know mo' 'bout runnin' de town than me! Dont you reckon a man thats got sense enough to start uh town, knows how tuh run it. Dont you reckon if de place had uh needed uh jailhouse Ah would have got one built long befo' you come heah?"

"We do so need a jail," Lindsay contended. "Jus' cause you stahted the town, dat dont make yo' mouf no prayer book nor neither yo' lips no Bible. They dont flap lak none tuh *me.*"

Lindsay was a little shriveled up man with grey hair and bow-legs. He was the smallest man in the village, who nevertheless did the most talk of fighting. That was because the others felt he was too small for them to hit. He was harmless, but known to be the nastiest threatener in the county.

Clarke merely snorted contemptuously at his sally and remarked dryly that the road was right there for all those who were not satisfied with the way he was running the town.

"Meaning to insult me?" Lindsay asked belligerently.

"Ah dont keer HOW yuh take it. Jus' take yo' rawbony cow an' gwan tuh de woods, fuh all I keer," Clarke answered.

Lindsay leaped from the porch and struck his fighting pose. "Jus' hit de ground an' Ah'll strow yuh all over Orange County! Aw, come on! Come on! Youse a big seegar, but Ah kin smoke yuh!"

Clarke looked at the little man, old, and less than half his size and laughed. Walter Thomas and 'Lige Moseley rushed to Lindsay and pretended to restrain him.

"That's right," Lindsay panted, "you better hold me offen him. Cause if I lay de weight uh dis right hand on him, he wont forget it long as he live."

"Aw, shet up, Lin'say, an' set down. If you could fight as good as you kin threaten, you'd be world's champeen'stead uh Jack Dempsey. Some uh dese days when youse hollerin' tuh be let loose, somebody's gointer take you at yo' word, then it will be jus' too bad about yuh," Lester admonished.

"Who?—"

The war was about to begin all over on another front when Dave Carter, the local Nimrod, walked, almost ran up the steps of the porch. He was bareheaded, excited and even in the poor light that seeped to the porch from the oil lamps within, it was seen that he was bruised and otherwise unusually mussed up.

"Mist' Clarke, Ah wants tuh see yuh," he said. "Come on inside."

"Sholy, Dave, sholy." The mayor responded and followed the young man into the store and the corner reserved for City Administration. The crowd from the porch followed to a man.

Dave wiped a bruise spot on his head. "Mist' Clarke, Ah wants uh warrant took out fuh Jim Weston. Ahm gointer law him outa dis town. He caint lam me over mah head wid no mule bone and steal mah turkey and go braggin' about it!''

Under the encouraging quiz of the mayor, Dave told his story. He was a hunter and fisherman, as everybody knew. He had discovered a drove of wild turkeys roosting in the trees along the edge of the cypress swamp near the spot where Brazzle's old mule had been left. He had watched them for weeks, had seen the huge gobbler that headed the flock and resolved to get him.

"Yes," agreed Clarke, "you said something to me about it yesterday when you bought some shells.''

"Yes, and thats how Jim knowed Ah was goin' turkey huntin'. He was settin' on de store porch and heard me talkin' to you. Today when Ah started out, jes 'bout sundown—dats de bes' time tuh get turkeys, when they goes tuh roost—he ups and says he's goin' long. Ah didnt keer 'bout dat, but when them birds goes tuh roost, he aint even loaded, so Ah had shot dat gobbler befo' he took aim. When he see dat great big gobbler fallin' he fires off his gun and tries tuh grab him. But Ah helt on. We got tuh pushin' and shovin' and tusslin' 'till we got to fightin'. Jim's a bully, but Ah wuz beatin' his socks offa him till he retched down and picked up de hock-bone of Brazzle's ol' mule and lammed me ovah mah head wid it and knocked me out. When Ah come to, he had done took mah turkey and gone. Ah wants uh warrant, Mist' Clarke. Ahm gointer law him outa dis town.''

"An' you sho gointer get, Dave. He oughter be run out. Comes from bad stock. Every last one of his brothers been run out as fast as they grow up. Daddy hung for murder.''

Clarke busied himself with the papers. The crowd looking on and commenting.

"See whut you Meth'dis' niggahs will do?'' asked Brazzle, a true Baptist. "Goin' round lammin' folks ovah the head an' stealin they turkeys.''

"Cose everybody knows dem Westons is a set uh bullies, but you Baptists aint such a much,'' Elijah Moseley retorted.

"Yas, but Ah know yuh know,'' put in Lindsay. "No Baptis' aint never done nothin' bad as dat. Joe Clarke is right. Jail is too good fuh 'em. The last one uh these heah half-washed christians oughta be run 'way from heah.''

"When it comes tuh dat, theres jus' as many no count Baptists as anybody else. Jus' aint caught 'em,'' Thomas said, joining the fray.

"Yas,'' Lindsay retorted, "but we done kotched yo' Meth'dis' niggah. Kotched him knockin' people ovah de head wid mule bones an' stealin' they turkeys, an' wese gointer run him slap outa town sure as gun's iron. The dirty onion!''

"We dont know whether you will or no, Joe Lindsay. You Baptists aint runnin' this town exactly.''

"Trial set for three oclock tomorrow at de Baptis' church, that being the largest meetin' place in town,'' Clarke announced with a satisfied smile and persuaded the men to go back to the porch to argue.

Clarke himself was a Methodist, but in this case, his interests lay with the other side. If he could get Jim to taste the air of another town, chicken mortality of the sudden and unexplained variety would drop considerably, he was certain. He was equally certain that the ambitious Simms would champion Jim's cause and losing the fight, lose prestige. Besides, Jim was a troublesome character. A constant disturber of the village peace.

III

It was evident to the simplest person in the village long before three oclock that this was to be a religious and political fight. The assault and the gobbler were unimportant. Dave was a Baptist, Jim a Methodist, only two churches in the town and the respective congregations had lined up solidly.

At three the house was full. The defendant had been led in and seated in the amen corner to the left of the pulpit. Rev. Simms had taken his place beside the prisoner in the role of defense counsel. The plaintiff, with Elder Long, shepherd of the Baptist flock in the capacity of prosecution, was seated at the right. The respective congregations were lined up behind their leaders.

Mutual glances of despisement and gloating are exchanged

across the aisle. Not a few verbal sorties were made during this waiting period as if they were getting up steam for the real struggle.

Wize Anderson (Meth.) Look at ole Dave tryin' to make out how Jim hurt his head! Yuh couldnt hurt a Baptist head wid a hammer—they're that hard.

Brother Poke (Bapt.) Well, anyhow we dont lie an' steal an' git run outa town lak de softhead Meth'dis' niggahs.

Some Baptist wag looked over at Jim and crowed like a rooster, the others took it up immediately and the place was full of hencackling and barnyard sounds. The implication was obvious. Jim stood up and said, "If I had dat mule bone heah, Ahd teach a few mo' uh you mud-turtles something." Enter His Honor at this moment. Lum Boger pompously conducted him to his place, the pulpit, which was doing duty as the bench for the occasion. The assembly unconsciously moderated its tone. But from the outside could still be heard the voices of the children engaged in fisticuffy trials of the case.

The mayor began rapping for order at once. "Cote is set. Cote is set! Looka heah, DIS COTE IS DONE SET! Ah wants you folks tuh dry up."

The courtroom grew perfectly still. The mayor prepared to read the charge to the prisoner, when Brother Stringer (Meth.) entered, hot and perspiring with coat over his arm. He found a seat near the middle of the house against the wall. To reach it, he must climb over the knees of a bench length of people. Before seating himself, he hung his coat upon an empty lamp bracket above his head.

Sister Lewis of the Baptist persuasion arose at once, her hands akimbo, her eyes flashing.

"Brothah Stringah, you take yo' lousy coat down off dese sacred walls! Aint you Meth'dis' got no gumption in the house uh washup?"

Stringer did not answer her, but he cast over a glance that said as plain as day, "Just try and make me do it!"

Della Lewis snorted, but Stringer took his seat complacently.

He took his seat, but rose up again as if he had sat on a hot needle point. The reason for this was that Brother Hambo on the Baptist side, a nasty scrapper, rose and rolled his eyes to the fighting angle, looking at Stringer. Stringer caught the look, and hurriedly pawed that coat down off that wall.

Sister Taylor (M.) took up the gauntlet dropped like a hot potato by Stringer. "Some folks," she said with a meaning look, "is a whole lot moh puhtic'lar bout a louse in they church than they is in they house." A very personal look at Sister Lewis.

"Well," said that lady, "mah house mought not be exactly clean. But nobody caint say *dat*"—indicating an infinitesimal amount on the end of her finger—"about my chaRACter! They didn't hafta git de sheriff to make Sam marry ME!"

Mrs. Taylor leaped to her feet and struggled to cross the aisle to her traducer but was restrained by three or four men. "Yas, they did git de sheriff tuh make Sam marry me!" She shouted as she panted and struggled, "And Gawd knows you sho oughter git him agin and make *some* of these men marry yo' Ada."

Mrs. Lewis now had to be restrained. She gave voice and hard, bone-breaking words flew back and forth across the aisle. Each was aided and abetted by her side of the house. His Honor was all the time beating the pulpit with his gavel and shouting for order. At last he threatened to descend in person upon the belligerents.

"Heah! You moufy wimmen! Shet up. Aint Ah done said cote was set? Lum Boger, do yo' duty. Make them wimmen dry up or put 'em outa heah."

Marshall Boger who wore his star for the occasion was full of the importance of his office for nineteen is a prideful age; he hurried over to Mrs. Taylor. She rose to meet him. "You better gwan 'way from me, Lum Boger. Ah jes' wish you would lay de weight of yo' han' on me! Ahd kick yo' cloes up round yo' neck lak a horse collar. You impident limb you."

Lum retreated before the awful prospect of wearing his suit about his neck like a horse collar. He crossed the aisle to the fiery Della and frowned upon her. She was already standing and ready to commence hostilities. One look was enough. He said nothing, but her threats followed him down the aisle as he retreated to the vestibule to shoo the noisy children away. The women subsided and the Mayor began.

"We come heah on very important business," he said. "Stan' up dere, Jim Weston. You is charged wid 'ssaultin' Dave Carter here wid a mule bone, and robbin' him uh his wild turkey. Is you guilty or not guilty?"

Jim arose, looked insolently around the room and answered the charge: "Yas, Ah hit him and took de turkey cause it wuz mine. Ah hit him and Ahll hit him agin, but it wasnt no crime this time."

His Honor's jaw dropped. There was surprise on the faces of all the Baptist section, surprise and perplexity. Gloating and laughter from the Methodists. Simms pulled Jim's coattail.

"Set down Jim," he cooed, "youse one of mah lambs. Set down. Yo' shepherd will show them that walks in de darkness wid sinners and republicans de light."

Jim sat down and the pastor got to his feet.

"Looka heah, Jim, this aint for no foolishness. Do you realize dat if youse found guilty, youse gonna be run outa town?"

"Yeah," Jim answered without rising. "But Ah aint gonna be found no guilty. You caint find me." There was a pleasurable stir on his side of the house. The Baptists were still in the coma which Jim's first statement had brought on.

"Ah say too, he aint guilty," began Rev. Simms with great unction in his tones. "Ah done been to de cot-house at Orlando an' set under de voice of dem lawyers an' heard 'em law from mornin' tell night. They says you got tuh have a weepon befo' you kin commit uh 'ssault. Ah done read dis heah Bible fum lid tuh lid" (he made a gesture to indicate the thoroughness of his search) "and it aint in no Bible dat no mule bone is a weepon, an' it aint in no white folks law neither. Therefo' Brother Mayor, Ah ast you tuh let Jim go. You gotta turn 'im loose, cause nobody kin run 'im outa town when he aint done no crime."

A deep purple gloom settled down upon the Mayor and his followers. Over against this the wild joy of the Methodists. Simms already felt the reins of power in his hands. Over the protest of the

Mayor he raised a song and he and his followers sang it with great gusto.

> *Oh Mary dont you weep, dont you mourn*
> *Oh Mary, dont you weep dont you mourn*
> *Pharaoh's army got drownded,*
> *O-O-oh Mary, dont you weep*

The troubled expression on the face of the Baptist leader, Rev. Long, suddenly lifted. He arose while yet the triumphant defense is singing its hallelujah. Mayor Clarke quieted the tumult with difficulty. Simms saw him rise but far from being worried, he sank back upon the seat, his eyes half closed, hands folded fatly across his fat stomach. He smirked. Let them rave! He had built his arguments on solid rock, and the gates of Baptist logic could not prevail against it!

When at last he got the attention of the assembly, he commanded Dave to stand.

"Ah jus want you all tuh take a look at his head. Anybody kin see dat big knot dat Jim put on dere." Jim, the Rev. Simms and all his communicants laughed loudly at this, but Long went on calmly. "Ah been tuh de cote-house tuh Orlando an' heard de white folks law as much as any body heah. And dey dont ast whether de thing dat a person gits hurt wid is uh weepon or not. All dey wants tuh fin' out is, 'did it hurt?' Now you all kin see dat mule bone did hurt Dave's head. So it must be a weepon cause it hurt him.—"

Rev. Simms had his eyes wide open now. He jumped to his feet.

"Never mind bout dem white folks laws at O'landa, Brother Long. Dis is a colored town. Nohow we oughter run by de laws uh de Bible. Dem white folks laws dont go befo' whuts in dis sacred book."

"Jes' hold yo' hot potater, Brother Simms, Ahm comin' tuh dat part right now. Jes lemme take yo' Bible a minute."

"Naw indeed. You oughter brought one of yo' own if you got one. Furthemo' Brother Mayor, we got work tuh do—Wese workin' people. Dont keep us in heah too long. Dis case is through wid.''

''Oh, naw it aint,'' the Mayor disagreed, ''you done talked yo' side, now you got tuh let Brother Long talk his. So fur as de work is concerned, it kin wait. One thing at a time. Come on up heah in yo' pulpit an' read yo' own Bible, Brother Long. Dont mind me being up heah.''

Long ascended the pulpit and began to turn the leaves of the large Bible. The entire assembly slid forward to the edges of the seat.

''Ah done proved by de white folks law dat Jim oughter be run outa town an' now Ahm gointer show by de Bible—''

Simms was on his feet again. ''But Brother Mayor—''

''Set down Simms'' was all the answer he got. ''Youse *entirely* outa order.''

''It says heah in Judges 15:16 dat Samson slewed a thousand Philistines wid de jaw-bone of a ass,'' Long drawled.

''Yas, but this wasnt no ass, this was a mule,'' Simms objected.

''And now dat bring us to de main claw uh dis subjick. It sho want no ass, but everybody knows dat a donkey is de father of every mule what ever wuz born. Even little chillen knows dat. Everybody knows dat little as a donkey is, dat if he is dangerous, his great big mule son is mo' so. Everybody knows dat de further back on a mule you goes, de mo' dangerous he gits. Now if de jawbone is as dangerous as it says heah, in de Bible, by de time you gits clear back tuh his hocks hes rank pizen.''

''AMEN!! Specially Brazzle's ol' mule,'' put in Hambo.

''An' dat makes it double 'ssault an' batt'ry,'' Long continued. ''Therefo' Brother Mayor, Ah ast dat Jim be run outa town fuh 'ssaultin Dave wid a deadly weepon an' stealin' his turkey while de boy wuz unconscious.''

It was now the turn of the Baptists to go wild. The faint protests of Simms were drowned in the general uproar.

''I'll be henfired if he aint right!'' the Mayor exclaimed when he could make himself heard. ''This case is just as plain as day.''

Simms tried once more. ''But Brother Mayor—''

"Aw be quiet, Simms. You done talked yo'self all outa joint already." His Honor cut him short. "Jim Weston, you git right outa *mah* town befo sundown an' dont lemme ketch you back heah under two yeahs, neither. You folks dats so rearin' tuh fight, gwan outside an' fight all you wants tuh. But dont use no guns, no razors nor no mule-bones. Cote's dismissed."

A general murmur of approval swept over the house. Clarke went on; unofficially, as it were. "By ziggity, dat ol' mule been dead three years an' still kickin'! An' he done kicked more'n one person outa whack today." And he gave Simms one of his most personal looks.

Book
of Harlem

1. A pestilence visiteth the land of Hokum, and the people cry out.
4. Toothsome, a son of Georgia returns from Babylon, and stirreth up the Hamites. 10. Mandolin heareth him and resolveth to see Babylon. 11. He convinceth his father and departs for Babylon. 21. A red-cap toteth his bag, and uttereth blasphemy against Mandolin. 26. He lodgeth with Toothsome, and trieth to make the females of Harlem, but is scorned by them. 28. One frail biddeth him sit upon a tack. 29. He taketh council with Toothsome and is comforted. 33. He goeth to an hall of dancing, and meeting a damsel there, shaketh vehemently with her. 42. He discloseth himself to her and she telleth him what to read. 49. He becometh Panic. 50. The Book of Harlem.

1. And in those days when King Volstead sat upon the throne in Hokum, then came a mighty drought upon the land, many cried out in agony thereof.

2. Then did the throat parch and the tongue was thrust into the cheek of many voters.

3. And men grew restless and went up and down in the land saying, "We are verily the dry-bones of which the prophet Ezekiel prophesied."

4. Then returned one called Toothsome unto his town of Standard Bottom, which is in the province of Georgia. And he was of the tribe of Ham.

5. And his raiment was very glad, for he had sojourned in the

city of Babylon, which is ruled by the tribe of Tammany. And his garments putteth out the street lamps, and the vaseline upon his head, yea verily the slickness thereof did outshine the sun at noonday.

6. And the maidens looked upon him and were glad, but the men gnasheth together their bridgework at sight of him. But they drew near unto him and listened to his accounts of the doings of Babylon, for they all yearned unto that city.

7. And the mouth of Toothsome flapped loudly and fluently in the marketplace, and the envy of his hearers increased an hundredfold.

8. Then stood one youth before him, and his name was called Mandolin. And he questioned Toothsome eagerly, asking "how come" and "wherefore" many times.

9. And Toothsome answered him according to his wit. Moreover he said unto the youth, "Come thou also to the city as unto the ant, and consider her ways and be wise."

10. And the heart of Mandolin was inflamed, and he stood before his father and said, "I beseech thee now, papa, to give unto me now my portion that I may go hence to great Babylon and see life."

11. But his father's heart yearned towards him, and he said, "Nay, my son, for Babylon is full of wickedness, and thou art but a youth."

12. But Mandolin answered him saying, "I crave to gaze upon its sins. What do you think I go to see, a prayer-meeting?"

13. But his father strove with him and said, "Why dost thou crave Babylon when Gussie Smith, the daughter of our neighbor, will make thee a good wife? Tarry now and take her to wife, for verily she is a mighty biscuit cooker before the Lord."

14. Then snorted Mandolin with scorn and he said, "What care I for biscuit-cookers when there be Shebas of high voltage on every street in Harlem? For verily man liveth not by bread alone, but by every drop of banana oil that drippeth from the tongue of the lovely."

15. Then strove they together all night. But at daybreak did

Mandolin touch the old man upon the hip, yea verily upon the pocket-bearing joint, and triumphed.

16. So the father gave him his blessing, and he departed out of Standard Bottom on his journey to Babylon.

17. And he carried with him of dreams forty-and-four thousands, and of wishes ten thousands, and of hopes ten thousands.

18. But of tears or sorrows carried he none out of all that land. Neither bore he any fears away with him.

19. And journeyed he many days upon the caravan of steel, and came at last unto the city of Babylon, and got him down within the place.

20. Then rushed there many upon him who wore scarlet caps upon the head, saying "Porter? Shall I tote thy bags for thee?"

21. And he marvelled greatly within himself, saying, "How charitable are the Babylons, seeing they permit no stranger to tote his own bag! With what great kindness am I met!"

22. And he suffered one to prevail and tote his bag for him. Moreover he questioned him concerning the way to Harlem which is a city of Ham in Babylonia.

23. And when he of the scarlet cap had conducted Mandolin unto a bus, then did Mandolin shake hands with him and thank him greatly for his kindness, and stepped upon the chariot as it rolled away, and took his way unto Harlem.

24. Then did the bag-toter blaspheme greatly, saying, "Oh, the cock-eyed son of a wood louse! Oh, the hawg! Oh, the sea-buzzard! Oh, the splay-footed son of a doodle bug and cockroach! What does he take me for? The mule's daddy! The clod-hopper! If only I might lay my hands upon him, verily would I smite him, yea, until he smelt like onions!"

25. But Mandolin journeyed on to Harlem, knowing none of these things.

26. And when he had come unto the place, he lodged himself with Toothsome, and was glad.

27. And each evening stood he before the Lafayette theatre and a-hemmed at the knees that passed, but none took notice of him.

28. Moreover one frail of exceeding sassiness bade him go to

and cook a radish, and seat himself upon a tack, which being interpreted is slander.

29. Then went he unto his roommate and saith, "How now doth the damsel think me? Have I not a smiling countenance, and coin in my jeans? My heart is heavy for I have sojourned in Harlem for many weeks, but as yet I have spoken to no female."

30. Then spoke Toothsome, and answered him saying, "Seek not swell Shebas in mail-order britches. Go thou into the market-place and get thee Oxford bags and jacket thyself likewise. Procure thee shoes and socks. Yea, anoint thy head with oil until it runneth over so that thou dare not hurl thyself into bed unless thou wear weed chains upon the head, lest thou skid out again."

31. "Moreover lubricate thy tongue with banana oil, for from the oily lips proceedeth the breath of love."

32. And Mandolin hastened to do all that his counsellor bade him.

33. Then hied him to the hall of dancing where many leaped with the cymbal, and shook with the drums.

34. And his belly was moved, for he saw young men seize upon damsels and they stood upon the floor and "messed around" meanly. Moreover many "bumped" them vehemently. Yea, there were those among them who shook with many shakings.

35. And when he saw all these things, Mandolin yearned within his heart to do likewise, but as yet he had spoken to no maiden.

36. But one damsel of scarlet lips smiled broadly upon him, and encouraged him with her eyes, and the water of his knees turned to bone, and he drew nigh unto her.

37. And his mouth flew open and he said, "See now how the others do dance with the cymbal and harp, yea, even the saxophone? Come thou and let us do likewise."

38. And he drew her and they stood upon the floor. Now this maiden was a mighty dancer before the Lord; yea, of the mightiest of all the tribe of Ham. And the shakings of the others were as one stricken with paralysis beside a bowl of gelatine. And the heart of the youth leaped for joy.

39. And he was emboldened, and his mouth flew open and the

banana oil did drip from his lips, yea even down to the floor, and the maiden was moved.

40. And he said, "Thou sure art propaganda! Yea, verily thou shakest a wicked ankle."

41. And she being pleased, answered him, "Thou art some sheik thyself. I do shoot a little pizen to de ankle if I do say so myself. Where has thou been all my life that I have not seen thee?"

42. Then did his mouth fly open, and he told her everything of Standard Bottom, Georgia, and of Babylon, and of all those things which touched him.

43. And her heart yearned towards him, and she resolved to take him unto herself and to make him wise.

44. And she said unto him, "Go thou and buy the books and writings of certain scribes and Pharisees which I shall name unto you, and thou shalt learn everything of good and of evil. Yea, thou shalt know as much as the Chief of the Niggerati, who is called Carl Van Vechten."

45. And Mandolin diligently sought all these books and writings that he was bidden, and read them.

46. Then was he sought for all feasts, and stomps, and shakings, and none was complete without him. Both on 139th Street and on Lenox Avenue was he sought, and his fame was great.

47. And his name became Panic, for they asked one of the other, "Is he not a riot in all that he doeth?"

48. Then did he devise poetry, and played it upon the piano, saying:

> *Skirt by skirt on every flirt*
> *They're getting higher and higher*
> *Day by day in every way*
> *There's more to admire*
> *Sock by sock and knee by knee*
> *The more they show, the more we see*
> *The skirts run up, the socks run down*
> *Jingling bells run round and round*

Oh week by week, and day by day
Let's hope that things keep on this way
Let's kneel right down and pray.

49. And the women all sought him, and damsels and the matrons and the grandmothers and all those who wear the skirt, and with them his name was continually Panic.

50. Of his doings and success after that, is it not written in The Book of Harlem?

Harlem
Slanguage*

Sugar Hill, the northwest corner of Harlem near Washington Heights where most of the newest-occupied large apartment houses for Negroes are. Mostly occupied by professional Negroes. Walter White and others of his financial standing live at 409 Edgecombe. NOTE: It is interesting to note that many expressions that come from the South, as this one does, have been distorted. In numerous southern towns, the Negro red-light district is called "Sugar Hill." The term was probably overheard without understanding its original meaning.

Pilch, house or apartment, residence

Scooter-pooker, a professional at sex

Scooter-pooking, practising, or the act of sex

Jelly, sex

Jelly bean, a man who lives by sex, a pimp

P.I., a pimp

Sweet-back, a pimp

Bull-diker, a flatter, a Lesbian

Flatter, Lesbian

Scrap iron, cheap likker

Conk buster, cheap likker

Reefer, marijuana cigarette

Drag, a reefer

Monkey chaser, a West Indian

Miss Anne, a white woman

Mister Charlie, white man

Ofay, white person

A Pan-cake, humble type of Negro

Handkerchief-head, sycophant type of Negro

Uncle Tom, same as above

Jar Head, Negro man

Zigaboo, Negro

---

*"Harlem Slanguage" is Hurston's unedited glossary as it appears in her original manuscript. In addition to the terms being alphabetized and condensed, many of the explicitly sexual definitions were eliminated before the list was published as the "Glossary of Harlem Slang" at the end of "Story in Harlem Slang."

Jig, Negro, a corrupted shortening of zigaboo

Aunt Hagar, Negro race

Aunt Hagar's Chillun, Negro race

Old cuffee, Negro (genuine African word for the same thing)

Smoking, or *Smoking over*, looking someone over

Gut-bucket, low dive, type of music or expression from same

Solid, perfect

Cut, doing something well

Stroll, doing something well

Cold, exceeding well, etc. "Yeah man! He was cold strolling on that trumpet!"

Palmer House, walking flat-footed as from fallen arches

Boogie-woogie, type of dancing and rhythm. For years in the South it meant secondary syphilis.

Park ape, an ugly under-privileged Negro

Can, rump

Stuff, sex, or excretion, according to how used

Butt sprung, a suit or a skirt out of shape in the rear

Battle-hammed, badly formed about the hips

Gator-faced, long black face with big mouth

Gut-foot, bad case of fallen arches

Liver-lip, pendulous, thick, purple lips

The Wagon, police patrol

The Man, the law, or powerful boss

Get you to go, power, physical or otherwise to force the opponent to run

Sell out, run in fear

Go when the wagon comes, another way of saying "You may be talking or acting biggity now, but you will cool down when enough power gets behind you. They all go when the wagon comes."

Sender, he or she who can get you to go, i.e. got what it takes. It is used often as a compliment. "Solid sender!!"

Jook, a pleasure house in the class of gut-bucket. The houses originated in the lumber, turpentine and railroad camps of Florida. Now common all over the South, even in the towns. They are the cradle of the Blues, and most of the dance steps that finally migrate north.

Jooking, playing the piano, guitar, or any musical instrument in the manner of the Jooks (pronounced like "took"). 2. Dancing and "schronching" in the manner. A player may be "getting low-down" at the piano and his listeners may yell out in admiration, "Jook it, papa! Jook!"

Sooner, anything cheap and mongrel. Once applied to mongrel dog who would eat anything, even excretion. "He'd sooner eat stuff as pork chops." Now it applies to cheap clothes, shabby man or woman, etc.

Dark black, a casually black person

Low black, a blacker person

Lam black, still blacker person

Damn black, blackest. "Why, lightning bugs follows him at twelve o'clock in the day, thinking it's midnight."

Balling, having fun

July jam, something very hot. "Hot as July jam."

Little sister, measure of hotness. "Hot as little sister!"

Peeping through my likkers, carrying on even though drunk

Your likker told you, misguided behavior, Dutch courage

Ginny Gall, a suburb of Hell, long way off. "Way off in Ginny Gall, where you have to eat cow cunt, skin and all."

West Hell, another suburb of Hell, worse than the original

Beluthahatchie, next station beyond Hell

Diddy-wah-diddy, a far place, measure of distance. 2. Another suburb of Hell, built on since way before Hell wasn't no bigger than Baltimore. Where the folks in Hell go for a big time. All the good jooking, barbecues, fish-frys, etc. are held.

Free schools, a shortened expression of deprecation. When something particularly stupid is done, a sad shake of the head, "Free schools, and dumb Negroes." Sometimes it is embellished with "Free schools, pretty yellow teachers, and dumb Negroes."

I'm cracking but I'm facking, "I am wise-cracking (supposedly joking) but I'm telling the truth."

Nothing to the bear but his curly hair, "I call your bluff." Or "Don't be afraid of him. He won't fight."

Dumb to the fact, "You don't know what you're talking about."

Lightly, slightly, and politely, doing things perfectly

I shot him lightly and he died politely, "I completely out-did him."

Georgia jumping-root, male sex organ

I don't deal in coal, "I don't keep company with black women. I prefer the mulatto kind."

Juice, another name for likker

My people! My people!, the saddest and the funniest expression in the Negro language. It is a sad sign when a progressive Negro observes the backwardness of some members, and realizes that there is nothing that he or she can do about it. For instance, seeing and hearing some loud-mouthed Negroes making themselves thoroughly disgusting in places common to both white and black. At other times it is used with hilarious effect. One story built around it goes like this:

A monkey was sitting in the middle of the highway playing with his tail and toes, when a Cadillac full of white people came along. Seeing the happy little monkey, they carefully drove off on the shoulder of the road to pass him without disturbing him. The monkey kept on playing. A Buick full of some more white folks came by and did the same. The monkey kept on playing. Then a T Model Ford came rattling down the road full of Negroes. Instead of trying not to disturb the monkey, they tried to run over him, and almost succeeded. The monkey leaped to the side of the road just in time to save his life. He watched the Ford rattling off with the driver cursing at him, and shook his head sadly and sighed, "My people! My people!!!" Some say that the monkey has stopped saying "my people, my people!" They say that he is now saying, "Those people! Those people!!"

Big Boy, stout fellow. But in the South it means fool and is a prime insult. Here again, it took up in the North without being understood. It is a fighting word in the South. If you call a Negro Big Boy, he will tell you something like this: "Don't you call me no Big Boy. Elephant is bigger than me, and he got a name. Taint no more Big Boy. (There are no more fools.) They kilt Big Boy shooting at Fat Sam."

Zoot suit with the reet pleat, Harlem style suit, padded shoulders, 43-inch trousers at the knee with cuff so small it needs a zipper to get into, high waist line, fancy lapels, bushels of buttons, etc.

Drapes, same thing as Zoot

Shags, same as above

Draped down, dressed in the height of Harlem mood

Togged down, same as above

Righteous rags, shags, zoots, drapes, etc.

Young suit, ill fitting, too small. You are supposed to be breaking in your little brother's suit for him. That is what the observers pretend to believe on seeing it.

Cabbage, female sex organ. "Oh, she cooks good cabbage."

Bread, female sex. "Good bread!"

Dat thing, sex of either sex

Ground rations, sex

Under rations, sex

Poontang, boody

Boody, female sex organ. "I hold my dress up to my knees, and I give my poontang to who I please. I hold my dress up in the back and I give my boody to white and black. Oh Poooooontang!!"

Rug-cutter, person who frequents house-rent parties, cutting up the rugs of the host with his feet. Now means a good dancer. Originally meant a person too cheap or too poor to patronize regular dance halls.

Stanch, or Stanch out, to begin, commence, step out

Air out, leave, flee, stroll

Russian, a southern Negro up North. "Rushed up here from Georgy," hence a rushian.

The bear, confession of poverty:
Just like de bear,
I ain't nowhere (broke).
Like de bear's brother,
I ain't no further.
Like de bear's daughter,
ain't got a quarter.

Function, from funk, a small unventilated dance full of people too casually bathed

Peckerwood, poor, and unloved class of southern whites

First thing smoking, a train. "Yeah man! I'm through with this town. I mean to grab the first thing smoking."

Hauling, fleeing on foot. "Man! He cold hauled it!"

Kitchen mechanic, domestic

Broad, girl or woman

Frail eel, pretty girl

Red neck, poor southern white man

Mack, a P.I., a jelly bean

Percolating, parading down the Avenue

Cruising, same as above

Oozing, same as above

Free-wheeling, same as above but more briskness is implied

Git up off of me!, quit talking about me, leave me alone

Now you cookin' with gas!, now you're talking, in the groove, etc.

Getting on some stiff time, really laying your racket

Spreading your jenk, same as above

Jump salty, get angry

Knock yourself out, have a good time

Dig, understand. "Dig me?" means do you get me? Do you collar the jive?

Collar a nod, sleep

I'll do like a farmer, plant you now and dig you later

Collar a hot, eat a meal

Gum beater, a blow-hard, a braggart, idle talker in general

Beating up your gums, talking to no purpose

Trucking, strolling; (2) dance step from the strolling motif

Dusty butt, cheap whore

Storm buzzard, shiftless, homeless character

V and X, Ten-Cent store

Good hair, Caucasian-type hair

Bad hair, Negro-type hair

Righteous moss or grass, good hair

Nearer my God to thee, good hair

Naps, kinky hair

Made hair, hair that has been straightened

Tight head, one with kinky hair

Every postman on his beat, kinky hair

Coal-scuttle blonde, black woman

Pink toes, yellow girl

Pig meat, young girl

Color scale:
    a. High yaller
    b. Yaller
    c. High brown
    d. Vaseline brown
    e. Seal brown
    f. Low brown
    g. Dark black (see blacks)

Knocking the pad, committing sex

Granny Grunt, a mythical character to whom moot questions may be referred

Baby, how is the drawbridge? Any boats passing? Suggestions for moral turpitude

What's on the rail for the lizard, same as above

Brother in black, Negro

Hambone, male sex organ

Getting my hambone boiled, committing sex

Stomp, low dance, but hot, man!

8-rock, very black person

Inky dink, same as above

The Big Apple, the Big Red Apple, New York City

Bam, Down in Bam, down South

Whip it to the red, beat your head until it is bloody

Playing the dozens, low-rating the ancestors of your opponent. Most unsafe game unless you are well armed.

Dat's your mammy, playing the dozens, same as "So is your old man"

Mammy, a term of insult. Never used by Negroes in any other way.

Girls as commented on in Harlemese:
    If she is white,
    she's all right.
    If she is yellow,
    she's mellow.
    If she is brown,
    she can stick around.
    If she's black,
    she better get 'way back!

Now You
Cookin'
with Gas*

Wait till I light up my coal-pot, and I'll tell you about this Zigaboo called Jelly.

Well, all right now. He was a seal-skin brown and papa-tree-top-tall. Skinny in the hips and solid built for speed. He was born with this rough-dried hair, but when he laid on the grease and pressed it down over night with his stocking-cap, it looked just like that righteous moss, and had so many waves till you got seasick from looking. Solid, man, solid!

His mama named him Marvel, but after a month on Lennox Avenue, he changed all that to Jelly. How come? Well, he put it in the street that when it came to filling that long-felt need, sugar-curing the ladies' feelings, pimping, sweet-backing, he was in a class by himself and nobody knew his name, so he had to tell 'em. "It must be Jelly, 'cause jam dont shake." Therefore, his name was Jelly. He was a Scooter-pooker from way back. That was what was on his sign. The stuff was there, and it was mellow. Whenever he was challenged by a hard-head or a frail eel on the right of his title, he would eye-ball idol-breaker with a slice of ice, and put on his ugly-laugh, made up out of scorn and pity and say, "Youse just dumb to the fact, baby. If you dont know what you

---

*"Now You Cookin' with Gas" is Hurston's unedited version of the story that appeared as "Story in Harlem Slang" in 1942 in *The American Mercury* (see page 127). This original version includes numerous sections that were edited out of the published version, including a reference to the killing of a white police officer.

talking 'bout, you better ask Granny Grunt. I wouldnt mislead you, baby. I don't need to,—not with the help I got." Then he would give the pimps' sign, and percolate on down the avenue. You can't go behind a fact like that.

So this day he was airing out on the Avenue. It had to be late afternoon, or he would not have been out of bed. All you did by rolling out early was to stir your stomach up. That made you hunt for more dishes to dirty. The longer you slept, the less you had to eat. But you cant collar nods all day. No matter how long you stayed in bed, and how quiet you kept, sooner or later that big gut is going to reach over and grab that little one and start to gnaw. Thats confidential right from the Bible. You got to get out on the beat and collar yourself a hot.

So Jelly got into his zoot suit with the reet pleats and got out to skivver around and do himself some good. At 132nd Street, he spied one of his colleagues across the street, standing in front of a cafe. Jelly figured that if he bull-skated just right, he might confidence Sweet-Back out of a thousand on a plate. Maybe a shot of scrap-iron or a reefer. Therefore, Jelly took a quick backwards look at his shoesoles to see how his leather was holding out. The way he figured it after the peep was that he had plenty to get across and maybe do a little more cruising besides. So he stanched out into the street and made the crossing.

"Hi there, Sweet Back!" he exploded cheerfully, "Gimme some skin!"

"Lay de skin on me, pal!" Sweet Back grabbed Jelly's out-stretched hand and shook hard. "Aint seen you since the last time, Jelly. Whats cookin'?"

"Oh, just like de bear—I aint nowhere. Like de bear's brother,—I aint no further. Like de bear's daughter—aint got a quarter."

Right away, he wished he had not been so honest. Sweet Back gave him a top-superior cut-eye look. Looked at Jelly just like a showman looks at an ape. Just as far above Jelly as fried chicken is over branch water.

"Cold in hand, hunh?" He talked down to Jelly. "A red hot

pimp like you say you is, aint got no business in the barrel. Last night when I left you, you was beating up your gums and broadcasting about how hot you was. Just as hot as July-jam, you told me. What you doing cold in hand?''

"Aw, man, cant you take a joke? I was just beating up my gums when I said I was broke. How can I be broke when I got de best woman in Harlem? If I ask her for a dime, she'll give me a ten dollar bill; ask her for a drink of likker, and she'll buy me a whiskey still. If I'm lying, I'm flying!''

"Gar, dont hang out dat dirty washing in my back yard! Didnt I see you last night with dat beat chick scoffing a hot dog? Dat chick you had was bet to de heels. Boy, you aint no good for what you live.''

"If you aint lying now, you flying. You aint got de first thin. You aint got nickel one.''

Jelly threw back the long skirt of his coat and rammed his hand down into his pants pocket.

"Put your money where your mouth is!'' he challenged as he mock-struggled to haul out a huge roll. "Back your crap with your money. I bet you five dollars!''

Sweet Back made the same gesture of hauling out non-existent money.

"I been raised in the church. I dont bet, but I'll doubt you. Five rocks!''

"I thought so!'' Jelly crowed and hurriedly pulled his empty hand out of his pocket." I knowed you'd back up when I drawed my roll on you.''

"You ain't drawed no roll on me, Jelly. You aint drawed nothing but your pocket. You better stop dat boogerbooing. Next time I'm liable to make you do it.'' There was a splinter of regret in his voice. If Jelly really had had some money, he might have staked him, Sweet Back to a hot. Good southern cornbread with a piano on a platter. Oh, well! The right browd would, or might come along.

"Who boogerbooing?'' Jelly snorted. "Jig, I dont have to. Talking about *me* with a beat chick scoffing a hot dog! Heh, heh! You must of not seen me, 'cause last night I was riding round in a Yellow Cab, with a yellow gal, drinking yellow likker and spending yellow money. Humph! Tell 'em 'bout me!"

"Git out of my face with that crap, Jelly! Dat broad I seen you with wasnt no pe-ola. She was one of them coal-scuttle blondes with hair just as close to her head as ninety-nine is to a hundred. She look-ted like she had seventy-five pounds of clear bosom, guts in her feet, and she look-ted like six months in front and nine months behind. Buy you a whiskey still! Humph! Dat broad couldnt make the down payment on a pair of sox."

"Sweet Back, you fixing to talk out of place." Jelly stiffened.

"If you trying to jump salt, Jelly, thats your mammy."

"Dont play in de family, Sweet Back. I dont play de dozens. I done told you."

"Who playing de dozens? You trying to get your hips up on your shoulders cause I said you was with a beat broad. One of them lam blacks."

"Who? Me? Long as you been knowing me, Sweet Back, you aint never seen me with nothing but pe-olas. I can get any frail eel I wants to. I can lay it! How come I'm up here in New York? You dont know, do you? Since youse dumb to the fact, I reckon I'll have to make you hep. I had to leave from down south cause Miss Anne used to worry me so bad to go with me. Who, Me? Man, I don't deal in no coal. Know what I tell 'em? If they's white, they's right! If they's yellow, they's mellow! If they's brown, they can stick around. But if they come black, they better git way back! Tell 'em bout me!"

"Aw, man, you trying to show your grandma how to milk ducks. Best you can do is to confidence some kitchen-mechanic out of a dime or two. Me, I knocks de pad with them cack-broads up on Sugar Hill, and fills 'em full of melody. Man, I'm quick death and easy judgment. Youse just a home-boy, Jelly. Dont try to follow me."

"Me follow *you!* Man, I come on like the Gang-Busters, and go off the MARCH OF TIME! If dat aint so, God is gone to Jersey City, and you know He wouldnt be messing round a place like that. Know what my woman done? We hauled off and went to church last Sunday, and when they passed round the plate for the *penny* collection, I throwed in a dollar. De man looked at me real hard for dat. Dat made my woman mad, so she called him back and throwed in a twenty dollar bill! Told him to take dat and go! Dats what he got for looking at me cause I throwed in a dollar."

"Jelly, de wind may blow and de door may slam; dat what you shooting aint worth a damn!"

Jelly slammed his hand in his bosom as if to draw a gun. Sweet Back did the same.

"If you wants to fight, Sweet Back, the favor is in me."

"I was deep-thinking then, Jelly. Its a good thing I aint short-tempered. Taint nothing to you. You aint hit me yet."

"Oh, I flies hot quick" Jelly said "But I'm mighty easy cooled if de man I'm salty with is bigger than me."

Both burst into a hearty laugh and changed from fighting to lounging poses.

"Dont get too yaller on me, Jelly. You liable to get hurt some day."

"You over-sports your hand your ownself. I just dont pay you no mind. I know taint nothing to de bear but his curly hair. Lay de skin on me!"

They broke their hand-shake hurriedly because both of them looked up the Avenue and saw the same thing. It was a girl, and they both remembered that it was Wednesday afternoon. All of the domestics off for the afternoon with their pay in their pockets. Some of them bound to be hungry for love. That meant a dinner, a shot of scrap-iron, maybe room-rent and a reefer or two. Well, it did happen sometimes, so that gave vapor to hope that some women would buy them forty zoot suits, a Packard, and plenty of money to flash. This one looked prosperous. Both of the Scooter-Pookers hoped that the other one had other fish to fry, but neither retired. Both went into the pose, set lapels and put on the look.

"Big stars falling!" Jelly said out loud when she was in hearing distance. "It must be just before day!" He put all the awe and admiration he could in his voice.

"Yeah Man!" Sweet Back agreed. "Must be a recess in Heaven—pretty angel like that out on the ground."

The girl drew abreast of them, long ear-rings swinging, reeling and rocking in her hips.

"I'd walk clear to Diddy-Wah-Diddy to get a chance to speak to a pretty lil' ground-angel like that." Jelly went on.

"Aw, man, you aint willing to go very far. Me, I'd go slap to Ginny-Gall, where they eat cow-rump, skin and all."

The girl smiled, so Jelly set his hat like it was hanging on one louse-leg and just too mean to fall off, and took the plunge.

"Baby," he crooned, "Whats on de rail for de lizard?"

The girl halted and braced her hips with her hands. "A Zigaboo down in Georgy where I come from asked a woman that one time, and the judge told him 'ninety days' ".

"Georgy!" Sweet Back pretended to be elated. "Where 'bouts in Georgy is you from? Delaware?"

"Delaware?" Jelly snorted. "My people! My people!! Free schools and dumb jigs! Man, how you going to put Delaware in Georgy? You ought to know dats in Maryland. Hah! Hah! Hah!"

"I never heard nothing about no Delaware—not in the part of Georgy I come from."

"We dont care nothing bout no Delaware. Lets me and you go back down there in Georgy and settle down." Sweet Back cooed.

"Go down in Georgy!" Jelly snorted. "You crazy in the head? Christ walked de water to go *around* Georgy. What you want to go in it for?"

"Oh dont try to make out youse no northerner, you! Youse from right down in Bam your ownself!" The girl turned on Jelly.

"Yeah, I'm *from* there, and I aims to stay from there.

"One of them Russians, eh?" The girl retorted. "Rushed up here to get away from a job of work."

"De work didnt worry me. Mister Charlie down there plays too rough to suit me. I aint none of them cowards like them shines down in Bam. I'm *mean!* I got Indian blood in *me*. Them pecker-woods down there liable to make me hurt some of 'em. So I just come on off to keep from killing somebody."

"I know its de truth!" The girl snorted and laughed.

But that kind of talk was not leading towards the dinner table.

"But Baby!" Jelly gasped. "Dat shape you got on you!" He dragged his eyes from her head to her feet." I bet the CocaCola Company is paying you good money for the patent!"

Their girl smiled with pleasure at this, so Sweet Back jumped in.

"I know youse somebody swell to know. Youse real people. You grins like a regular fellow." He gave her his most killing look and let it simmer in. "These dickty jigs round here tries to smile. Spose you and me go inside the cafe here and grab a hot?"

"You got any money?" The girl asked and stiffened like a ramrod. Nobody aint pimping on me. You dig me?"

"Aw, now, Baby!"

"I seen you two mullet-heads before. I was uptown when Joe Brown had you all in the go-long last night. Ha! Ha! Dat cop sure hates a pimp! All he needs to see is the pimps' salute, and he will out with his night-stick and whip your head to the red. Beat your head just as flat as a dime!" She went off into a great blow of laughter.

"Aw, I wasnt scared of him" Sweet Back tried to be casual. "I just know de fool is crazy. De way he carries on. You would think I been fooling with some of his wives. He never hit *me*. He just hit where I was."

"You all really did turn on the fan!" The gile kept on laughing, and both of the men jumped salty. But nothing they said showed it.

"Oh, seeing that he is one of my color, I let him go and call him lucky." Sweet Back went on. "A cracker cop down in Georgy got in my face one time and I shot him lightly and he died politely."

"I know its de truth!" The girl smiled salty like. "I bet you come away from there so fast till your hip pockets was dipping sand."

"Oh, lets us dont talk about the law. Lets talk about us." Sweet Back persisted. "You going inside with me to holler 'let one come flopping! One come grunting! Snatch one from de rear!"

"Naw indeed!" The girl laughed harshly. "You skillets is trying to promote a meal on me. But it will never happen, brother. You barking up the wrong tree. I wouldn't give you air if you was stopped up in a jug. I'm not putting out a thing. I'm just like the cemetery—I'm not putting out, I'm taking in!'' She reared back and regarded the two with scorn. ''Dig?''

''I'll tell you like the farmer told the potato—plant you now and dig you later.''

The girl made a movement to switch on off. Sweet Back had not dirtied a plate since the day before. He made a weak but significant gesture.

''Trying to snatch my pocket-book, eh?'' She blazed. Instead of running, she grabbed hold of Sweet Back's draping coat-tail and made a slashing gesture. ''How much split you want back here? If your feets dont hurry up and take you way from here you'll *ride* away. I'll spread my lungs all over New York and call the law. Go ahead, Bedbug! Touch me and I'll holler like a pretty white woman!''

The boys were ready to flee, but she turned suddenly and rocked on off with her ear-rings snapping and her heels popping.

''My people! My people!!'' Sweet Back sighed when he was calm enough to speak.

''I know you feel chewed,'' Jelly said in an effort to make it appear that he had had no part in the fiasco.

''Oh, let her go.'' Sweet Back said magnanimously. ''When I see people without the periodical principles they's supposed to have, I just dont fool with 'em. What I want to steal her old pocket-book with all the money I got? I could buy a beat chick like her and give her away. I got money's mammy and Grandma's change. One of my women, and not the best one I got neither, is buying me ten shag suits at one time. All I got to do is to go round to the tailor shop and try 'em on.''

He glanced sidewise at Jelly to see if he was convincing. But Jelly's thoughts were far away. He was remembering those full, hot meals he had left back in Alabama to seek wealth and splendor in Harlem without working. He had even forgotten to look cocky and rich. He was thinking corroding thoughts about the white folks in this man's town—so cold and finicky about jobs. So mean about folks being on time and things had to be done just so. They would call you 'Mister' all right, just like he had been told that they would. But they kept their old clothes and wore them themselves. You better not never ask them about a loan before pay-day. Then too, these Harlem landladies! They didnt want a thing out of you but your rent. One thing had been over-rated. These lady-people wasnt as lonesome for love as somebody had told him. His hunger brought him back to the present. He decided he had better mooch on around to a certain hair-dressing parlor. The woman who ran it usually gave him a dime or two if he ran errands for her, which was more work than he wanted to do, but which he did when the hunting was poor.

"Well, I better get on down town and see if them folks at de car place got my Packard ready for me. My woman just would buy it. Told her I didnt want to be bothered with no car." Jelly said this casually as if it bored him to death.

"Same here," Sweet Back came back snappily. "Okay, Jelly. See you in the funny papers. If I dont see you no more in this world, I'll meet you in Africa."

"Abyssinia," Jelly said. "Dont get into no more scrapes like you done just now."

"Oh, well, Jelly, if you dont bite, you dont taste."

Both of them stiffened their arms at their sides, pointed their first fingers rigidly at the ground in the pimps' salute and went their separate ways.

The Seventh Veil

The commanding officer emerged from the great gate of the Roman fort at Lyons. He was accompanied by a subordinate officer who had arrived only the day before—sent out with two additional legions to beef up the staff of this important post. He was being taken for a stroll around the Fort.

"But look," he indicated to the left of the road, a short distance from the entrance. "What wretchedness! Ignorance and poverty show there plainly on that old couple. Yet they have a neat cottage and a handsome though small orchard."

"And that confirms the deceptive nature of appearances." The commander answered quickly that the old man dressed in the clothing of a peasant is Antipas, prince of Judea, son of Herod the Great, and once possessed of one of the greatest fortunes in the empire, highly educated in Rome by the most eminent of our scholars and accustomed to the most luxurious living that Romans stationed in Asia took it as a high honor to be invited to be his guest in his white marble palace on the Lake of Galilee.

"By the fortune of Caesar! What brought a man like that to such a state?"

"The well known greed and corruption of Caligula and a bit of desert patriotism on the part of the prince. There was a slavish boot-licking brother of the wife of the prince—she is called Herodias, after her celebrated grandfather—who betrayed the patriotism of Antipas, who had once been imprisoned for his lack of morals by Tibernius, who was set free by Caligula who was of the same patterns and made king in the place of Antipas but fortunately did not live long to enjoy his evil-gotten gains."

"Good. But Caligula has been dead many years. Why has the prince not sued for the return of his fortune and his power?"

"Many have asked that and urged it upon Antipas, but he no longer desires it, it appears. He is content to sit there waiting for a religious prophet which he calls John the Baptist, who he is convinced will appear in Gaul one day."

"You certain it is not this Jesus Christ show followers are causing such disturbance in Rome at present?"

"No, John the Baptist is the name he states. And as decayed as that man and woman appear now, he was a robust figure of handsome face once, and this Herodias was rated as one of the most beautiful and elegantly dressed women who ever appeared in Rome and moved among the Patricians and Royal circles."

"Oh, how tragic! I am moved to go over and make them a present of money."

"No, you will only offend them. They desire nothing but the simplest things, and besides it is whispered that there are chests of gold and silver in that small cottage. Caligula did not completely succeed in his purpose. Those two want no more of luxuries. The money is for John the Baptist to distribute to the poor when he appears, or to found a mutual help for his followers."

"That is dedication. I should like to talk with them sometime."

"There is something more. Rumor has it that those two have lived a romantic life that may well be one of the great love affairs of the inhabitable world. Someday minstrels may sing of their love, who knows?"

"And now, Gallentins," the young officer nodded, "I remember seeing the old woman down at the Wharf when our ships docked on the Rhone peering eagerly at the faces of the passengers as they disembarked, then turning away at last in disappointment. Perhaps she was seeking this John the Baptist."

"Certainly they do that for every ship that comes up either of the two streams the Rhone and the Saone. And they watch the roads which come here from every part of Gaul the same way. It is truly remarkable.''

Herodias was seated in a rude chair whose seat was covered by a goat skin with the hair still on it, beside Antipas in an identical chair, before their simple cottage of four rooms. There were flowers blooming in the yard. A vineyard began at the rear of the house and extended for a hundred yards and off to the left of the house in front a vegetable garden where a man worked. To the right an animal enclosure with goats, sheep, fowls and in a separate enclosure, a magnificent Arabian stallion.

She was aware that they were the subject of discussion of the Roman officers. But they attracted attention at the Fort often. There were men there who had known them in their prime and even a few oldsters who had known of Herod the Great. Being an object of curiosity did not disturb her. The drowsing Antipas was not even aware of the men on the opposite side of the great highway.

Antipas had selected and bought this small homestead with great care. Just a short way north of the main entrance to the Roman fort. Nobody could enter nor leave it without his observation if he cared to watch. The fort of Lyons was the most important outside of Italy itself. It was just across the mountains and roads to every other point in Gaul ran from there. This arrangement had been made by Agrippa, 43 B.C. Augustus Caesar had built the ample aqueducts and other improvements and Lyons became the center of things beyond the Alps. Caligula had exiled Antipas to Lyons, believing he would be carefully watched there and not allowed to flee back to Asia and seize his former power. It was not because Antipas was so carefully watched, for few were sympathetic with Caligula, but that Antipas had no wish to return to power.

But the years went by and no John the Baptist appeared in Gaul, but Antipas would not give up hope and Herodias would not give up Antipas.

With her once luxuriant head of hair thinned and discolored by age and the contour of her face drooping and dripping down under her chin, she sat there in the afternoon sunlight beside Antipas, indifferent to stares and comment. Often she spent time retracing her steps to where she had come, this small but clean and comfortable cottage at the confluence of the Rhone and the Saone in Gaul. Passion, passion for a man, had brought her here, but she had no regrets. She still possessed Antipas, son of Herod the Great, and that was all she had ever *really* wanted in her turbulent life.

She remembered clearly how it all had begun. Her grandfather, Herod the Great, was on his death bed and his sons who were in school in Rome had been summoned back to Jerusalem.

From the chatter of hopeful mothers, Herodias heard the names of the returners but shut in the women's apartment she did not even glimpse them immediately. It was in the late afternoon of that day when a tall figure emerged from the door of the King's apartment into the huge enclosed rectangle that held some rose trees, shrubbery, two fountains and the houses of Herod's beloved doves.

This was a magnificent figure of a young man, beautiful of hair and face who bore himself with great confidence. He visited the dove houses, then glanced about the shrubbery lovingly, then precise he, headed towards the entrance of the women's apartment.

By that time, the little Herodias, aged 12, was in love. She wanted to rush to the door and fling herself into the arms of this Antipas. She knew it was he because his mother the very gentle Malthrace, the Samaritan, cried out, "It is Antipas my son who comes to see his mother!" The woman ran to the door, flung it open and herself into a tight embrace with the handsome young man. He was very tender with his mother and when the embrace was over presented her with a magnificent brooch and a chain for her neck of very fine gold and cunning workmanship, and another kiss on the cheek.

"Oh what a loving, tender, splendid and thoughtful son God has given me!" Malthrace buried her face again on the shoulder of Antipas. "But where is my first born?"

"Ah, after going in to our father Archelaus hurried off into the city to renew the acquaintance of his old association, Mother. I am certain that he will come in to see you presently."

And now Antipas saluted each of the wives of Herod respectfully by name, and the children in a group, which was a vast disappointment to the palpitating Herodias who had hoped to be greeted in the same emotion that she felt for her handsome young uncle. Then Antipas left by the same door by which he had entered, recrossed the garden and returned to the bedside of the King.

He left the women's apartment in a turmoil, for every mother there with a son had hopes for her offspring, and each hated the other for her hopes. Rumors flew thick and fast. It was known that Salome, the sister of Herod and his most trusted advisor, was with him constantly and that the King was writing his will.

Herodias saw Antipas again the following afternoon when every member of the royal house was summoned to appear in the King's private apartment to hear the reading of the will.

Salome made it known immediately that Herod favored Antipas as his successor because of his generous spirit and tender heart. He would be kind and considerate to the people, but since Jewish custom demanded the succession of the first born, he was naming Archelaus. It was explained why this prince or that one was passed over. Then it came to the disposition of every member of the family and who was to be mated with whom and the amount of money settled upon each.

Herodias was aflame with hope that she would be given to the handsome and kindly Antipas, but he was mated with the daughter of the King of Arabia Petra, as Herod wished to bind the two nations together.

The old woman seated before the little house in distant Gaul felt a tremor over her whole body and her toes grip at the soles of her sandals at the memory. She had the impulse to leap to her feet and cry out in protest to the King propped up by many pillows in his enormous bed. But a glimpse at the face of Salome warned her. It reminded her that she was the daughter of Aristobulus who was the second son of Miriamne of the power-greedy Asamoneans, who had plotted with his brother Alexander to murder their father Herod to obtain the government. And while the King was tenderness itself with his grandchildren made fatherless by the execution of the two conspirators, the inhabitants of the women's apartment did not spare them. She was accustomed to frequent slighting remarks intended to wound which were made about murderers so vile that they would treacherously slay their own father, so what could you look forward to in the offspring of such foul ingrates? The overflowing kindness in the face of Antipas on his short visit to the women's apartment and the fact that he did not look at her nor others of the children of the conspirators any different than the other children endeared him further and made her want to take refuge in him, until by this hour Antipas seemed necessary to her very existence.

But the inexorable voice of the King went on, "Herod son of Miriamne, the daughter of Simon the high priest, and Herodias, daughter of Aristobulus, son of Miriamne, of the Asamoneans will please come to me and join hands in marriage and may the blessing of God be upon you and go with you."

And Herodias managed to follow the command without fainting. She glanced at Antipas seeking dissatisfaction in his face, but there was none. He appeared utterly indifferent to the undeveloped girl who was being pledged to his half brother, who was several years his senior. This Herod, son of the famous Alexandrian beauty who had captured the heart of Herod after the execution of that first Miriamne, was handsome enough but weak of face and somewhat lacking in personality. At one time he had been considered as the successor of the King, but his mother was found to be in a conspiracy against the King and excluded from the throne. As in each case the amount of money settled upon each was announced.

Herodias was grateful that her marriage was near the end of the list so that she could flee the room now hateful to her. She was given to uninteresting Herod and Antipas did not even care! Oh but he would! When she was grown, he would repent his indifference of this hour. She would make him love her.

The old woman turned her head and gazed at the old man sitting beside her with great satisfaction. "And I made him love me. That I did. Few women of the world have been so loved."

In retrospect Herodias skipped over those years during which she and Herod dwelt in Rome and lived in luxury as members of the Patrician society and received at the palace. Herodias was looked upon as among the reigning beauties and distinctive dressers of Rome. Herod was the rich husband of Herodias. She bore him a daughter in her sixteenth year, a beautiful, sprightly auburn-haired little being which Herod ignored more or less because it was not a son. And seeing the child with so much personality as well as beautiful, Herodias thought it fitting to name her after her own grandmother Salome, who was the sister of the late King, Herod the Great.

Little Salome was in her second year and walking well, when Antipas Tetrarch of Galilee came to Rome on business, and on the urging of his brother made their home his own during his stay in Rome.

Six years had passed since the elaborate funeral of Herod the Great and when she had last seen Antipas. And she now considered that God had granted her the opportunity she had prayed for. And she had no intention of wasting it. She dressed for him and acted to catch his attention and to please him. She now had a matured body to fight with, and she made the most of it. It so happened that they both were fond of the theatre and Herod was not, so they attended together. Antipas was particularly devoted to the dance and they took in all that Rome was offering at the time, attracting much attention and admiration by the splendid appearance that they made as a couple.

Then Herodias found that fate had provided her with another weapon. Antipas, like his father, was very fond of children and his marriage with the daughter of Aretas had provided him with none so he began to shower great affection upon the little Salome. Herodias continually threw them together when they did not go out. Both she and Antipas had keen senses of humor and shared lots of jokes which went right over the head of her husband. Antipas had an abundance of old friends in Rome and Herodias encouraged him to entertain them in her home as if it were his own and no function was too elaborate for her to prepare for him for his friends.

Then when she deemed that the time was ripe, one day when Antipas reclined on a long seat in the little garden with Salome cuddled in his arms, she put matters to a test.

"You hurt me terribly on one occasion, O Antipas."

"It was certainly not intentional, O beauteous Herodias. Tell me how and when it happened."

"On the occasion when the King was mating us all up. I yearned desperately to be given to you, but the King gave me to Herod. I looked at your face to see if you were as displeased and disappointed as I was, but you appeared utterly indifferent and it broke my heart."

"But you were nothing but a child at the time, O Herodias. You can be certain that I am no longer indifferent to such a great treasure. By the fortune of Caesar, I now desire you more than any other woman of the world, and want you to be my wife."

"More than your Arabian princess?"

"I said more than any woman of the inhabitable earth, and if it is pleasing to you, I will divorce her and marry you and be a faithful and devoted husband to you and a kind loving father to your child."

Herodias ran across to the bench and flung herself in his arms and covered his face with kisses.

"You have my answer, Beloved, and I will quickly divorce Herod. The King did what was expedient. None of our feelings were taken into account. I do not believe that Herod ever loved me anymore than I do him. There is a certain Roman matron to whom I feel he is devoted. So let it be."

"Very well, when I have finished my business with the palace, I will return to Galilee and divorce my wife, and you must follow me and share my fortunes what ever they may be."

Their right hands clasped tightly.

"Whatever happens to you, my beloved, happens to me, till death do us part. That I swear, Antipas," and once more Herodias fell to kissing and embracing the man on the marble bench.

Just at that moment, Herod emerged upon the portico, but Herodias did not spring away from her embrace.

"How fortunate that you have appeared at this moment, Herod. I am desperately in love with Antipas, and am now asking you to divorce me so that I can marry him."

At that moment Herod's chariot drew up at the door.

"As you will," Herod said in a flat tone of voice. "And you can take with you all the money which the King gave her, any of the household furnishings that she desires she can take."

"Oh no, brother," Antipas interjected. "I have planned a new and splendid city on the shores of Lake Galilee which I shall name after the emperor Tiberius, and there I shall build a palace for myself sparing no expenses to make it truly magnificent. It will be furnished exactly as Herodias wishes—to the last detail. She will require nothing from you."

"As you will," said Herod with indifference, and stepping into his chariot was driven away swiftly.

The Tetrarch of Galilee was not so fortunate with his Arabian princess. He kept his new alliance secret or so he thought; until he could return her to her father with all formality and dignity, but some how she got wind of it and fled to Petra Arabia and told her story. Therefore, shortly after Herodias joined Antipas in Galilee, Aretas marched against Antipas with a great army.

Here Antipas was confronted with a matter of conscience. He was a man deeply in love and had no intention of abandoning Herodias, but he had a feeling of guilt as regarding Aretas and of violating the plan made by his father. What to do? As a matter of diplomatic appeasement, he summoned few troops, fought faintly and so Aretas could boast of a victory over him and march back to Arabia consoled. So far as Herodias was concerned, he lost nothing. He did not give her up, and fought a battle for her. She was exalted and felt herself deeply loved.

In time, the white marble palace was duly completed. It had a land and a water entrance. The long eastern portico had steps which dipped down into the waters of Lake Galilee, so that the boats of Antipas could discharge and take on passengers there. He was extremely fond of boating and boats. He had a very luxurious seafaring vessel which he kept at Caesarea. It was a pleasure to Herodias to stretch herself on a couch on this eastern portico and listen to the little waves slapping at the stone steps and watch the movement of fishing and pleasure boats out on the lake.

Then came this John the Baptist. He was a barrel-chested, heavily bearded man of about her own age from among the River bathers from a spot known as the Desert of Quietude on the eastern shore of the Jordan just before it entered the Dead Sea. They belonged to the sect of the Essenes.

Herodias never knew what moved this man to come northward to Galilee and denounce her marriage to Antipas, unless the fact that Herod the Great had a sort of affiliation with the Essenes. They walked in and out of his palace at will, ate, and took what they wanted and scolded the King as if he were no more than a common workman if they saw fit. Herod's submission to the Essenes was so complete that the Pharisees complained that "Herod treated the Essenes with a greater reverence than their mortal nature requires."

So the young Essene erupted into Galilee, to reprove the Tetrarch for his divorce and remarriage to his former sister-in-law, feeling, no doubt, that the public scolding would be accepted by the son of Herod the Great in the spirit it was given.

The reports of the denunciation of her great happiness were brought to her by many.

"I am not at all distressed by this man," Herodias assured her maid. "For the Tetrarch will punish his vile insolence with instant death. Did he not fight a war with the King of Arabia on my account?"

"But that is just the difficulty, O beautiful Herodias. The Tetrarch appears not to be offended by this religious fanatic, but accepts the charge as no more than the scoldings of a father to a son. He consorts with him and listens humbly."

"Consorts with him—listens humbly."

These words burned like tongues of flames across the brain of Herodias. And a great fear arose in her soul. Could this hairy monster from the Desert of Quietude exert a power that was greater than all others even her own over the Tetrarch? Antipas was a worshiper and imitator of his father who was known to be a subject of the River Bretheren. How far had Antipas committed himself to their doctrines? Could he be persuaded to put her away? She had not defense if he decided to do so.

Herodias was sipping some fresh pressed grapes from Italy when Antipas appeared about two agonizing hours later. And pretending to be calm and unconcerned, when she broached the matter.

"Of course you will order this monster slain for the insults that he has offered to you as the ruler of Galilee and to your wife."

"Oh no, my beloved Herodias. I cannot lay violent hands upon such a holy man."

"Holy man!" Herodias leaped to her feet. "What sacrilege! Do you no longer love me, my beloved?"

"More than anybody or anything else on earth, Herodias. But I revere him. I am not certain that these Essenes are just mortal men. Maybe they are reflections of spirits in Heaven. I fear to touch that man. Let him scold away. I will never put you away. You can be sure of that, but I will never slay this prophet either."

"Then I will!" Herodias screamed. "This beast who would deprive me of the only happiness I have ever known. I will kill him like any other raving beast! I will shed his blood with my own hands!"

"That I cannot permit, Herodias. But do not distress yourself further. He cannot turn me from you."

Antipas would not discuss the matter further, and the next day he disappeared and did not return until the third day. What troubled Herodias was that John the Baptist vanished from Galilee at the same time and none could tell what had become of him. She sent out spies, but none could find a trace of the Essene, and

Antipas refused to answer any of her questions concerning the man.

"But Beloved," Herodias protested, "when did you become so pious? I have never noted it in you previously."

"There was no occasion for it. This is a very serious matter, song of my soul. Think of being privileged to meet a deity in the flesh."

"Pooh! deity indeed! Nothing more than a hairy rustic from that waste place, the Desert of Quietude where nothing lives but an abundance of little owls and Essenes, I am told. In fact this John the Baptist has a pet, one which rides about on his shoulder and sleeps in his thick matted hairs. Deity indeed! Just let me get my hands upon him and I will show you how mortal he is!"

"It is my responsibility to see to it that he does not come into your hands, Beloved. What a sacrilege you contemplate! And what a tremendous honor you would deprive me of—the earthly arm of a new and true religion. Forget your petty spite and look carefully after the instruction of our daughter. How does she do with the Seven Veils?"

"If anything better than her celebrated teacher. The child is a genius at the dance. I am quite proud of her."

"I am eager to see her performance, but have not the time at present, but oh, how I love her. She's the jewel of my life."

"Very strange to hear you say that my dear, when you allow this John the Baptist to destroy the very foundations of her life."

"You willfully misinterpret the facts, my beautiful Herodias. Because I will not lay violent hands upon a deity that does not mean that I no longer love my family."

Herodias sought to pull him down upon the many-cushioned couch with embraces, but Antipas prevented her.

"I must hasten away, song of my soul. Many important things to be attended to if Asia is ever to cast off the yoke of Rome. Under the rule of my noble father, Rome was the friend of southwest Asia, so it must be weakness on my part if this Pilate can play the vicious and obscene tricks on Judea and Samaria. He has even molested Galileans, who were placed under my special care and protection by my father. He flashed his sword in protection of Galilee and always loved it best of all. He exacted a solemn oath from me that I would protect the Galileans well, and I gave my solemn word.''

"But you are ruler of Galilee only, not of Judea and Samaria.''

"Every Jew in the inhabitable world can claim my sympathy and protection, Herodias, and as you know, my mother is a Samaritan. Mt. Zion and Mount Gerizzim are one in my heart. Pilate's outrages against both has my blood boiling. But just words mean nothing if you are powerless to strike. We have at present the arms and equipment for 70,000 men; when we can field 100,000 I shall make a strong protest to Tibernius and if we are not treated with respect, we shall fight. Nor have I concealed my rage at the shameful abuse of my people from Pilate. He fears that I shall place the matter before Tibernius, but I will not until I am prepared to fight. I leave you again today Beloved to confer with other potent men of Asia who share my views.''

"And where will you meet, object of my soul?''

"That I am not permitted to reveal.'' Antipas turned sharply on his heel. "I must hasten away. Do not expect my return under seven days, Beloved.''

Herodias went to the west portico to wave him good-bye as usual and in less than an hour he thundered off without looking in on Salome's dancing instructions, which was strange indeed.

Herodias returned to the eastern portico to watch the activity on the lake. But fear had grown in her until it all but choked her. And fear is the mother of hatred. The more she feared for her security with Antipas the more she hated John the Baptist. She said to herself, "All right, he has put me away, now what is my life?" But she could not conjure up any compensating benefits, spiritual nor material. Oh, she would not be poor. There untouched were the two chests of money inherited from her grandfather, but what benefit to her derived from spending it, separated from Antipas. He was her life, her very breath and blood. This was love in its purest form. She could not be deprived of Antipas without giving up her very existence. And she was prepared to fight to the death for him. But let her get her hands on this John the Baptist and he would not disturb the happiness of any other woman. That hairy beast and his owl! Oh how she hated!

She heard a chariot make a furious stop at the western portico and was on her feet in an instant and running through the great hall of reception. She was deflated when she saw that it was her brother Agrippa, who had been staying with them for several months now. He was a tall, handsome ne'er-do-well who would spend his last coin to entertain someone like the kin of royalty—make an impression and leave nothing to support his wife and children who were at present in Ituraea being cared for by her family, while Agrippa, who was to be known later as King Agrippa, lived with Herodias and Antipas.

"Oh, it is only you," Herodias said flatly. "I thought that my husband might have turned back for some reason."

"No chance of that, my proud and arrogant sister. He has important matters to attend to. I am his trusted assistant in the matter. A new shipment of arms from the east is coming across the lake this night. I was left behind to see them safely across the lake and stored in the palace."

"It is time you did something to justify the enormous expenses of your extravagances, Agrippa. You will impoverish my generous husband."

"Nonsense! With what his father willed to him and his enormous revenues coming from his office as Tetrarch, his is one of the biggest fortunes in the empire."

"Which a sycophant of a waster like you envy him."

"Frankly I wish I had even a half of it." Agrippa was possessed of great charm of manner and he knew it. Now he illuminated his features and continued, "I would be extremely grateful for a mere talent of seven right now and the loan of the pale pair of arabian horses and the chariot of white and gold. I promised some friends to meet them at an inn in Caesarea the day after tomorrow."

"I am very glad that it is I and not my open-handed husband that you approach, my wastrel of a brother, for I can and do refuse you with a firm voice. I was lamenting that Antipas did not tell me where he was going, so now, not knowing, I cannot tell you where to find him.''

''That I already know. I know that he left here to meet others at the Fort of Macherus: that he hides there also John the Baptist with whom he converses at every opportunity and feasts every evening.''

Herodias could not quite suppress a gasp of surprise and pleasure, then covered her failure by flipping.

''Oh, that I know of—I mean the presence of the prophet at Macherus. A good place for him to be confined too.''

''You knew no such thing, insolent sister. You think I have not heard of your frantic efforts to find this John the Baptist and lay hands upon him. I told you because I thought you might give me some of the generous sums you promise others to locate him, even though I betray Antipas by letting it slip.''

''Very well, Agrippa, 100 shekels of silver from my own purse, but not the horses and chariot of my husband.''

''Why not? He would never know. I would be back long before he finishes with the conspirators at Macherus.''

''Are you insane, Agrippa? You are only my brother, and that by an accident of nature, but Antipas, greatly beloved, is my husband, and I will allow none to exploit him. I am his wife.''

''Very well. I will accept the mira and hire a rig and be off to the coast. You are indeed a husband-worshipping female if ever one existed.''

''That is my glorious privilege to worship at the feet of Antipas. What created woman could wish for more? I would prefer death to the loss of him.''

''Antipas talks that kind of drivel concerning you, but I thought you were more sensible.''

''Thank God, I am not. Now, go away and let me enjoy my thoughts of my husband while my maid rubs me down with that youth preserving ointment that Antipas bought for me in Alexandria. How thoughtful, kind and indulgent is Antipas! He built and furnished this palace to my wishes and specifications, my clothes and ornaments leave nothing to be desired to say nothing of what he lavishes upon my daughter—the expensive dancing teacher, the bands of musicians to accompany her movements, her costumes, and ornaments. And would I sit like a dolt and allow some hairy prophet with the one the Romans call a bubo riding him around like a charioteer, and no doubt this owl is the source of his divine instruction part no one from another under the name of righteousness, when in fact pure love like ours is the highest virtue? I will not allow it. No! Nothing but death shall part me from my Antipas.''

"I am willing to go, my sister, but where is the talent of silver that you promised me?''

"One moment, and you shall have it." She turned to her maid. "Fetch me my purse from my apartment, Iris, and make haste, so this wastrel and drunkard may be on his way to the coast. The very presence of this eternal beggar offends me.''

She all but flung the heavy purse in her brother's face and turned on her face for two reasons. The obvious one being to allow the maid to massage her back, but the real one that the triumph in her face might not be observed. Aha! Antipas was check-mated. She had come upon his secret, now this John the Baptist would be brought to justice and dealt with according to his deserts. This would-be Wrecker of perfect love blotted from the earth.

But to get hold of him and get him in her power? Herodias dwelt upon these questions until around sundown when she summoned Salome to the east portico with its 20 Corinthian columns, its couches piled high with silk cushions and potted plants, and told her, "My beautiful daughter, light of my life, do you want to please your father very much?''

"Oh yes, Mother, you know that I do. My love for him consumes me.''

"Good! Then have your most elaborate dance costumes packed and we shall take your musicians and set out to where he is and you shall dance for him and his eminent guests.''

Salome flung her slender arms around Herodias and embraced her warmly.

"Oh, Mother! Nothing would please me more. I love to dance

at any rate, and if I were not the daughter of a Tetrarch and a princess I would make it my profession. And Antipas is such a connoisseur of the dance, and when I please him, I am most exalted. I shall exert myself to satisfy him and his guests, you can be assured. Oh, Mother!''

"That is what I desire and expect of you, my beautiful. It is of the greatest importance that your performance please Antipas completely, who has expended such extravagant sums upon your instruction. I might persuade him to allow you to perform publicly.''

"I'd love that more than anything in the world, adored mother. And I am certain that I can please him now my instructor has repeatedly declared that she has nothing more to teach me.''

"Well, make ready to depart before dawn of tomorrow, my precious love.''

"Oh, glorious!'' the girl exclaimed, executed a perfect whirl and vanished.

At sunrise the party was rounding the southern end of the lake to cross the Jordan entrance at Gadara. There they would wing southward by the road that paralleled the river along its eastern shore as the captain of the guard considered they would be less likely to encounter bandits there than on the road which ran along the Jordan to the west. They were traveling through what was known as the Decapolis—the Ten Greek cities. They were in the deep, hot, narrow valley of the Jordan, the result of some violent upheaval of nature which dropped this gulch many hundred feet below sea-level and ended in what is known as the Dead Sea. On the urgings of Herodias, the cavalcade moved at a smart pace, so that in the early afternoon, it passed through the Desert of Quietude and ahead of the community of the River Bretheren, the one to which John the Baptist belonged. A cultivated spot of green in otherwise grayness.

"I suggest we make camp here briefly for rest and refreshment,'' the captain said as he dropped back and rode beside Herodias.

"No! I want nothing to do with religious fanatics and owls.''

"It is not necessary to enter the community, but it is safest in this vicinity."

To this Herodias agreed. The party halted, had bread, meat and wine and set out again with the hope of reaching the mountainous area that fronted three ways: Midia, Arabia and Judea. Herod the Great had created an impregnable fortress called Macherus on this strategic spot.

And now they entered the dirty gray salt deposits of fantastic hills and hummocks rising from the shores of the Jordan before it gave up its life and everything living in the Dead Sea. They knew that Fort Macherus was near and could be reached before darkness fell.

Now the way was upward and their mounts labored as they climbed. Suddenly the scowling ramparts of Macherus appeared above them, and Herodias was surprised to find that those in the fort were not surprised but had had her party under observation for nearly an hour. So well was this fort planned and constructed. The Tetrarch was merely astonished to find his wife and daughter there.

"How did you know where to find me, Beloved of my soul?" Antipas inquired as he embraced Herodias warmly, "and why have you come to this terrible place?"

"Oh, the intuition bred of love, my beloved husband, and I yearned so for the sight of you, and Salome came to dance for you and to entertain your distinguished guests. She thought it might please you and so persuaded me to undertake the journey."

Antipas expressed great pleasure at this and said that at the end of the feast in the banquet hall of the fort, he would be delighted to have Salome perform for his guests and himself.

Herodias and Salome were promptly installed in the quarters of the commanding officer, and Antipas left them and went about his official affairs.

The strange sight in a grim fort was Herodias and Salome, arrayed in the elegance that would have befitted the royal palace in Rome, waiting around in their suite for the fateful hour, which seemed a very long time coming for both Herodias and Salome,

Herodias for her vengeance and the slim Salome for her triumph. She already saw herself a public performer and the toast of Rome, Alexandria and Corinth. Her ever tender and indulgent father would not refuse her when she pled after a marvelous performance of the Seven Veils. That was his favorite ballet because of the tender beauty of the themes.

The Woman
in Gaul*

Herodias, wife of Antipas, who was Tetrarch of Galilee, reclined her beautiful body on a rich couch on the portico of the white marble palace at Tiberias, the magnificent city which her husband had built on the shores of the body of water that originally was called the Lake of Gennesareth, then the Sea of Galilee, and now Lake of Tiberias, after the Roman Emperor, Tiberius, with whom Antipas was in great favor.

This portico was both deep and long, and decorated by Corinthian columns. It was the water gate to the white marble palace. It was appropriately furnished with marble benches, elegant chairs, and this rich couch on which Herodias spent frequent hours when the weather was warm. It jutted out into the lake, for Antipas was a boating enthusiast, and this portico was his landing.

Now, on this afternoon, Herodias lounged on the couch with a serving maid of her body sitting crossed-legged on the stone floor tinting her her toe-nails with henna in the Egyptian fashion. This Egyptian maid worked gently on the feet of Herodias while she

*The manuscript of this unpublished story was partially burned in the fire that destroyed some of Hurston's manuscripts shortly after her death. The edges of five pages of the original manuscript, now housed in the department of Rare Books and Manuscripts of the University of Florida Library, are badly charred. In this edition, the missing words have been represented by brackets, with the space in between the brackets corresponding to the amount of text that has been lost. As with all of the previously unpublished material, Hurston's own misspellings, typos, and textual errors have been left uncorrected.

read, or pretended to read from an elegantly produced scroll, a play by Euripides. It was not that Herodias experienced any difficulty with reading the script, for all members of the family of Herod the Great were educated to a degree, Herod the Great having that passion for learning, and Greek learning in particular. Herodias was very proficient.

It was very difficult for the wife of the Tetrarch to concentrate this day. She now impatiently waited for the return of a trusted steward of her house named Callimander, whom she had sent on a confidential mission many days before, and was suffering tortures now because she had had no word from him as yet.

Now the skilled maid, finished with the tinting of the nails of Herodias, began to massage her feet and legs with a fragrant lotion obtainable only at Alexandria, Egypt. Herodias had recently acquired this one and another from Egypt to attend her body, because Egypt had the reputation of producing women and men who the most skilled in creating and preserving beauty than any nation in the then known world. Herodias had felt the necessity for such expert care only in the last year, for she was nearer forty than she cared to think about, and besides, things had occurred during that time to cause her to fear that she might lose her trememndous hold over the heart of the Tetrarch.

From the apartment of Salome, her beautiful teen-aged daughter, came the strain of the plaintive tune which accompanied the temple dance of the Seven Veils. So she knew that Salome was at her dancing lessons. The music produced by wood-wind and strings, came from an orchestra of six men whom Antipas had gathered in Canetha, one of the cities of the Decapolis—the ten Greek cities east of the Jordan—where there was a famous theater. There also Antipas had found the celebrated dancer whom he had immediately engaged to instruct his step-daughter. The sounds lightened the spirits of Herodias, for it called to her mind how her husband had exhibited no decrease in his fondness and indulgence of her daughter. And how delighted he was in Salome's rapid progress in the dance, and particularly in her mastery of the dance of the Seven Veils. This was a pantomime, and acting out the story of the love of the goddess Ashtar for her husband, Adonis. So profound was her passion that when Adonis died, she set out to pass the seven barriers down into Hades to obtain some of the water of life that would restore him to life. It was a tense, but beautiful drama when skillfully performed. Antipas was already declaring that his daughter already showed greater skill and talent than her famous teacher. So Herodias smiled wanly. Antipas was such a doting father that anybody would think that Salome was his child, instead of the child of his half-brother.

"Replace my sandals," she now ordered the maid, "and go to the apartment of my daughter and say to her that her mother thinks that she gives too many hours to her dancing lessons. And say that I wish her to come here and keep me company."

In a few minutes, Salome appeared, but with a protesting face. She sat down petulantly on a carved stool, but said nothing.

"My beloved daughter," Herodias began after a long silence, "you do not appear grateful that I attempt to prevent you from wearing your beauty away at these dancing lessons. The Tetrarch says you are already perfect. Why continue?"

"But I am not so perfect as he makes me out to be. He is a loving and indulgent father to me, and so he sees perfection before it is accomplished."

Herodias smiled with satisfaction.

"Yes, having no child of his own, he has proved himself a most affectionate father to you. Much better than that society-mad Philip who begot you. He was a cold and indifferent man indeed. So long as he was immersed in the social life of the Roman patricians, and a guest at all their affairs, he was fulfilled. His horses, his clubs, and the dancing girls of the taverns were his life. Antipas is fond of his family as his royal father was." Herodias halted and studied the face of Salome. "I thought you might care to rest from your studies for a while by going for a sail on the lake with me."

"It would be pleasant if I were not so eager to work on my movements at the last barrier some more. Where I make the prayer for the water of life to the King of Hades. Now—"

At that moment, the young man who always stood at the front entrance to the palace entered, genuflected and when Herodias gave him permission to speak, announced that Callimander was returned and was most urgent to speak to Herodias.

"Then return to your lessons, since you are so eager, my beloved daughter," Herodias told her hastily. "You seem never to want to go on the lake unless Antipas manages the small boat. Since he is not here, perhaps I will not go either. Go, my child."

Callimander really had news for Herodias. She could detect it in his eyes as he stepped out upon the portico and cut through all formality to save time.

"You have found where that monster hides who would part me from my beloved husband?"

"Yes, noble-born Herodias. John the Baptist does not really hide himself, but is hidden by Antipas."

"Where?" Herodias shouted in wild triumph.

"In the strong fort of Macherus, there on the border of Moab, and from its great elevation, that over-looks the mountains of Arabia. The place made so strong as not to be taken by your grandfather, Herod the Great."

"You do not deceive me and raise my hopes in vain?"

"I would not so betray your confidence in me, nor yet would I dare to be found deceiving you."

"It would be very dangerous to you to do so, Callimander. But tell me all that you have learned. You may seat yourself."

"He is imprisoned by Antipas at Macherus but it is not for his punishment, but his safety from you. Antipas has shown him every kindness and sworn to protect him. He is furnished with every delicacy of diet—the fat tails of sheep, every sort of fruits and vegetables, wines, and an abundance of bread and cakes. However, he consumes little of the rich foods, being very austere in his diet, and only used to rough foods. But it has been provided by your husband anyway, to show his admiration of the man. And, for his greater satisfaction, and that his imprisonment may not weigh heavily upon this John the Baptist, has sent to his associates in that dismal spot, the Desert of Quietude along the lower Jordan and brought three of these men to bear him company."

"What?" Herodias almost screamed. "This barbarous creature has indeed bewitched the mind of my husband! Antipas will be persuaded at last to do anything which this John advises. Oh, what will become of me and my daughter? How many days will pass before he resolves to put me away from him? Herod the Great, his father and my grandfather, indeed had a great reverence for these river bretheren all his life, and Antipas imitates his father as far as he can in all things. But never did the King allow those fanatics to interfere in his home. That is, if they ever tried, which I never heard of. However, the King was often persuaded by them in matters of government."

A sick silence prevailed for a time, then Herodias reflected in a bitter voice.

"So that is where my husband has been for the eight days that he has been absent from me, taking delight in the rude discourses of that hairy monster. I will have the head of that beast and in no long time. Somehow, I will find a way."

"You are mistaken, O noble Herodias. He has been there for only the last three days. He was somewhere east of the Jordan before, I [ ] told. The guard at the entrance of the fort—who was grateful for the present of money that I made him, told me that. Antipas was going about summoning potent men to be guests at his birthday celebration three days from this day."

"That is true, Callimander. He spoke to me of that. This year he will not observe the feast here at his palace as formerly. I had forgotten, but I had assumed that he would celebrate his birthday at his palace at Jerusalem."

Herodias was not truthful when she said this. Except in the case of John the Baptist, Antipas confided everything to her. Therefore she was only too aware that her husband was to meet certain rulers in that part of Asia and other influential friends at Macherus on his birthnight. The meeting was to further the plans of Antipas to attack and slay Pontius Pilate, and if possible, to deliver Palestine from Roman rule. The son of Herod the Great was grim and determined on this.

The reason for his rage was that the cruelly sadistic Pilate had manufactured occasions for butchering hundreds of Jews, Samaritans and Galileans. His father had tenderly left the care of Galilee, his favored province to Antipas, and charging him earnestly to take the best possible care of the people there. His mother, Malthrace, had been a Samaritan, and Pilate had rejoiced in slaughtering hundreds of them at Mount Gerizzim needlessly. Recalling that his father had offered to fight Sosius, the Roman general who aided Herod in the war against Antigonus, last of the Asamonean claimants to the throne of Judea, which Rome had conferred on Herod, if Sosius allowed his Roman soldiers to enter the temple, plunder Jerusalem, or to touch even one Jewish woman, Antipas was convinced that he would be despicable if he did not avenge Galilee and Samaria. He was implementing his rage by secretly collecting arms. Already, he had secured enough to arm 50,000 men, and planned to attack when he had 100,000 under arms. Most of these weapons had been bought beyond the Euphrates, and arriving under the cover of night on the eastern shore of the lake, were brought across by Galilean fishermen while it was still night to the landing of the palace, and stored by them in a great storaged beneath the palace before dawn. Herodias knew all of this, and was [   ] and encouraging. She knew also that her husband was now securing others to aid him in the plot, but she had not the slightest intention of confiding in Callimander, a Greek out of Corinth, in the matter. After a few minutes of cold rage, she said, you have done well, Callimander.''

"I am overcome with pleasure at your words, O daughter of a noble house."

"I shall have pulled down that small house which you now occupy and have built one more suited to you faithfulness and abilities. The moment that my husband returns, it shall be done."

With Callimander thus bound to secrecy, Herodias gave him permission to leave her and fell into deep thought as how to bring about the death of the man who so threatened her way of life.

There was no denying that this hairy meddler, John the Baptist, has some mysterious power to so affect the mind of her husband. This [   ] who had valued her to the extent of wresting her from his half-bro[ther] Philip, divorcing the Arabian princess for her sake, and fightin[g   ] war with Aretas, her father, for sending his daughter, humiliate[d   ] being discarded, back to Petra, the rose-red capital of Arabia. [   ] is, Antipas had refused to change his plans nor apologize to Areta[s   ] sending his daughter back and stood up to him in battle. He had made her daughter his own, and had, all these years, been the most affect[ionate] and indulgent husband in the known world.

For example, her weaving women were never required to weave for her body, nor that of her daughter. Antipas provided an abundance of the finest linen from Egypt, and rare, expensive silk from the island of Cos for them. Nor was there any shortage of purple for dying, and other colors. Their ornaments were of unusual design because Antipas had stewards to be present when great caravans from the east passed along the ancient highway, and likewise those moving north from Egypt, or south from India and Persia, and to bring for her inspection what they thought she might like. No rare perfumes nor ointments were too costly for him to indulge her in. Therefore this influence of the preacher from the river bottoms was something most formidable. Yes, this man must die. When months before she had come to realize that Antipas, rather than resenting his criticism of their marriage, had taken it as a son being corrected by his father, she had sensed the danger she was in. It was then that she had sworn to her husband to destroy the man, and she meant it. She was a hundred-fold more determined now that Antipas had deceived her and prevented the man from being punished for meddlesome audacity by concealing him from her just indignation. John the Baptist was going to lose his head.

The how of it came to Herodias almost immediately. The triumphant burst of music that went with the movements of the last barrier of the story and signified that Ashtar had gained the flask of the water of life came to her ears.

That was it! The pleasure of Antipas in the performance of his daughter would do excellently for a weapon. She would surprise him by being a guest at his birth-day banquet.

By noon the next day, Herodias and her party, which included Salome and the orchestra, were far along the highway that ran along the Jordan but east of that river. What with the military escort, the wagons of provisions to refresh them along the way, her servitors and all, the entourage was over three hundred.

Herodius [ ]ed that Salome was no longer sullen. She was enjoying the trip since she had her musicians along and could rehearse while she was there. More than that, Herodius stimulated her daughter by telling her how pleased Antipas would be that she had come this distance to dance for him at his banquet. Mother and daughter rode along in high spirits, but for different reasons. Salome, because she was going to give great pleasure to the man who had been an affectionate and indulgent father to her, and allowed her artistic inclinations scope. Herodias, because she was going to outwit that same man. With his head separated from his body, no more would that foul mouth utter words that could destroy her utterly. Shortly, she would procure his death. Dead men do not meddle.

So the dismal streth south of Jericho did not depress her spirits, but rather held a fascination for her. Down here below sea-level the heat was oppressive, and the great cubes of dirty salt where no vegetation existed was awful in implication. Great hills of dirty-gray salt rose up from the shallow water on either side; great cubes of it, and she did not wonder at the title the river bretheren had given it was understandable. It could not avoid being a "Desert of Quietude" being what it was. Who or what, except fanatical preachers could find any reason for being there?

On the morning of the birthday, the caravan began to climb the frowning ramparts of the Fort, situated so high up in the mountains, passed the hot springs of Callahorhe, and in mid-afternoon, was at the entrance of the impregnable fort.

To say that Antipas was surprised when he, seated down in the dungeon conversing with John the Baptist was told that his wife was there would be a vast understatement. He came up to receive them, and have installed in the royal apartment that his father had built into the fort. These rooms were luxurious and large. Preparations were going on in the great banquet hall for the celebration. Herodias, knowing that women could not be present by custom, went on into the other part and went to bed to rest her body.

The celebration had been going on for a full hour before she sent for Salome and directed her to prepare for her dance. Then she sent word to Antipas to let him know that Salome was going to dance for him. Soon the musicians were stationed and the dance began.

At the end, Antipas was transported as were his guests. It was then that he told his daughter the she could have anything, ANYTHING, that she might demand.

The innocent girl, having everything that she had ever wished for, did not know what to say. She therefore ran down the corridor to the room where Herodias reclined, and smiling happily, asked her mother what to demand. This was the moment that Herodias had hoped and longed for. This was her hour of triumph.

"Demand the head of John the Baptist."

Flushed with victory, the unthinking girl, now with a robe about her, raced back to the banqueting hall and like a child asking for a toy, smilingly asked for what her mother had told her. Only when the dead silence enveloped the room did she begin to realize that something dreadful had happened. The look of horror on the face of Antipas, succeeded by deep gloom, began to penetrate her exhiliration. And only when the horrid gift on the salver was in her hands, did the full realization reach her. Overwhelmed by horror and disgust, Salome fled down the corridor and thrust the grisley object into her mother's willing hands and ran weeping to her own room.

Herodias sat triumphant in spite of her daughter with the great silver platter resting heavily upon her lap and gazed in triumphant hatred into the dead face of John the Baptist. But her victory was brief. She had only time to spit upon the head of the man she had so hated and feared and slap the cheeks spitefully twice when she heard the tread of several feet marching down the corridor and approaching her door. There was a repeated rap, and when she demanded to know who knocked, the voice of an officer answered her.

"Antipas, Tetrarch of Galilee, governor of Perea sends us for the head of the prophet John the Baptist, so that it may be joined again to his body and receive decent burial."

This formal demand struck cold fear into the heart of Herodias. Her husband had not come himself to speak with her about the matter. He had sent a dozen soldiers, led by a captain to get it. Had she lost entirely by her victory?

The armed men tramped away with the head and Herodias shook with fright for an hour before she could even muster enough composure to send for her daughter. The servant returned to say that Salome could not come because she was in bed with an illness of her head.

Herodias suffered for an hour more, then got up and went into the room of Salome. She found her daughter with swollen eyes, stretched on the bed, with her serving maid rubbing her face with a liquid made from the balm of the trees that were native to the Jericho area.

"O you stupid little prig, you! Self-righteous little upstart. You lie there in judgment of your own mother. Because you are familiar with Meander and Euripides, the poets and the dance like the hetairai of the coastal cities that you know everything that is to be known of life. But wait until you find yourself lonely and neglected, even secretly despised as I was after my father had been strangled for conspiring to murder his father. Many to fawn upon you openly, but despise you secretly, then to find one who truly and warmly loves you as did Antipas, and see if you will allow yourself to be separated from him lightly. O you—"

"Please be quiet, Mother," the slender girl on the bed, begged. "I have no wish to, nor do I sit in judgment upon your actions. As for myself, I shall never dance again. You and Antipas have made a betrothal between Philip, governor of Batania and Trachopitis, and half-brother to Antipas. But yesterday I felt I could wait a year to consummate my marriage because I loved the dance. Now, I beg of you to marry me to him as quickly as possible. Please, dear mother."

The plea was a crushing stone against the temple of Herodias. This daughter upon whom she had rained so much love and affection was afraid of her as if she were some murderous monster with the blood of God and man upon her hands. Involuntarily, she lifted and examined her hands for blood, then becoming conscious of the act, lowered them guiltily. With tremendous effort she regained composure and spoke with dignity.

"Yes, I understand. Philip is called the beneficent and the just, and you wish to flee to him. As you know, your dowrey and the household goods required in marriage have been ready for nearly a year. You can complete your marriage as soon as we can return to Tiderias. I will go and tell the Tetrarch of your wishes at once."

Herodias almost raced along the corridor. Her feet were hastened by another consideration. What was her status with the Tetrarch now? Was it divorce, banishment of a place in the dungeon which John the Baptist had just vacated? She must know. The suspense was worse than death.

She found the banquet hall not only deserted, but utterly dark. Dark and abominally still. A nothingness that affrighted the soul. She fled back to her chamber which was lighted by eight clusters of candles and found it a haven of delight.

Summoning a guard, she ordered him to go and say to the Tetrarch that she wished to speak to him at once on a matter of importance.

The expression on the face of the man told her that he took cruel pleasure in telling her: "does not the noble-born wife of the Tetrarch know that he is no longer in the fort? Dressed in humble clothing, he departed the fort immediately after the head of the River Brother was returned. He went with the two live bretheren and twelve men of his guard up the Jordan to buy a sepulcre and give this John the Baptist a proper burial. He appeared most grieved at the death of this man."

When Herodias regained her composure, she said, "I dismiss you for the present."

Herodias and Salome had been back at the palace in Tiberias for ten full days when Antipas returned. They had been ten days of terror and agony for Antipas. Even if her husband had the intention of ordering her execution, which he had the power to do, she would noy have cared so long as the agonising suspense was ended. Antipas returned by a fisherman's boat well after midnight, and was dressed in the clothing of a workman.

Herodias was awakened by a cheerful greeting as he entered her bedchamber. She leaped from her bed and prostrated herself before and began to beg his pardon.

"But you are mistaken, flower of my heart," Antipas raised her tenderly. "Whatever you might have intended, you did not bring about the death of John the Baptist, my Beloved, for he is not dead."

"He is not dead? But that is impossible. I saw and touched—"

"Ah, yes, but John the Baptist is not a mere man. We shall see him again and in good health. Think no more of the matter, Beloved Herodias. Through your action, you have brought me an experience with divinity. Prepare your tenderest carresses for me. I am going into the bath and return to you very shortly."

The Tetrarch hurried to his own apartment, leaving Herodias dazed with puzzlement and trembling with fright.

"What deceit is this that my husband practices on me? He holds something terrible in his heart as a punishment for me. What does he intend?"

But Antipas soon returned and embraced her warmly. And never did he bring up that night at Macherus to her. His silence tortured her like the point of a javelin into the arm-pit.

So a great change came over the white marble palace on the lake. Where once Antipas had humored Herodias like a baby and bowed to her every wish, she now humbled herself and behaved with the insecurity of a concubine. She was jealous in seeking ways and opportunity to please him and bind him closer to her.

Herodias suffered terribly in silence the night during the Passover when the guards brought Jesus Christ to their palace in Jerusalem from Pilate for Antipas to pass on His guilt.

"I have heard much of this man in Galilee," Antipas said, leaping from his bed to interview him. "It is my opinion that he is none other than John the Baptist. I am most eager to talk with him, and question him concerning the miracles that he performs."

No sooner did Antipas cross the doorsill of the room and head for his Audience Hall, than Herodias creep from bed, throw on a loose robe and follow to near enough where she could overhear what was said.

"Are you not John the Baptist?" she heard Antipas ask eagerly. But this bound and beaten man said nothing. During the entire interview this Jesus gave no information that Antipas could use to defend him. So he soon ended the audience, and returned to his bed a disappointed man.

"That man is not John the Baptist, Beloved, though there is a slight resemblance. Had it been John, I would have freed him even if I had to use my Galilean troops to achieve it. But I believe that he knows where John is hiding. Oh, well. He will reappear when he wills."

"Will I never be quit of this John the Baptist and feel secure with my husband again?" Herodias conversed inwardly with her self.

And so she became more zealous in binding Antipas to her through gratitude, and her zeal brought on the final catastrophe in Galilee.

Tiberius, step-son of Augustus Caesar, that tough old veteran of the wars in Gaul, had passed away. He had been a suspicious, puritanical ruler, and had imprisoned the gay, gambling and drinking Agrippa for saying to his equally dissolute nephew, Caligula, that he wished that Tiberius would hurry and die so that his more accommodating friend, this Caligula could become emperor. By malevolent chance, now, Caligula had succeeded Tiberius, and immediately freed Agrippa, brother of Herodias, and made him King of Judea.

Herodias was enraged when the news reached her. A drinking, gambling, squanderer of a snob and sychophant like Agrippa ruling over the territory which had been so ably governed by her gifted grandfather Herod the Great? And when her noble and able husband, and one who had a better claim to the dignity was over-looked? It was simply not to be borne.

Partly to place Antipas in her debt, but also because she really considered the appointment an outrage, Herodias began to goad her easy-going husband to sail for Rome and protest to Caligula. Go there and demand that he himself be made king instead of Agrippa. It did no good for Antipas to insist that he was satisfied where he was, and moreover that when and if his secret plan matured, the Romans would no longer be in position to shove their favorites, however callous and inept, over Palestine. Herodias kept right on needling him until Antipas reluctantly agreed with her.

But Agrippa, hearing of the resolve of Antipas, and realizing that his uncle-brother-in-law did have a more valid claim, hastened off a long letter to his [b n] companion in which among other charges he made against Antipas, tattled what he knew about the secret accumulation of arms, the purpose of them, and where they were concealed.

So when Antipas berthed his luxurious yacht at Brundisium and raced behind his four fine horses to Rome, Caligula was ready for him. In the audience chamber of the Caesars, Antipas was accused as an enemy of Rome, harshly questioned, and finally sentenced to be stripped of his wealth and banished to Lugdunum (Lyons, France now) in Gaul. Caligula then ordered him to be led from the room.

Although Caius Caesar, called Caligula, was yet a young man, he was already notorious for his seductions of married women. All the time that he was examining Antipas, he was stealing glances at Herodias and assessing her good points, and Herodias was in possession of some most excellent good points. She was one of those rare, late developing women like her maternal grandmother, Salome, who seem to lie fallow during her maiden years, only to develop into a woman truly disturbing to men in middle age.

So now Caius Caligula looked hard at her and said, "Since you are the sister of my beloved friend, Agrippa, I grant you pardon for all charges, Herodias. Nor are you required to accompany your seditious husband, Antipas into banishment. Caius Caesar, Imperator, grants you permission to remain here at Rome where you have relatives and friends, Further, you are granted permission to retain the considerable sum of money which Herod the Great, your noble grandfather willed to you."

A dramatic hush fell upon the chamber at this surprising announcement. Romans being a highly materialistic nation of people, few in the room expected Herodias to reject such generous terms. A short pause found Herodias on her feet and standing very erect. Then she opened her mouth.

"I am most grateful for your generosity, O noble Caesar, but since I have had the good fortune to be the companion of Antipas, son of the Great Herod during his years of enormous wealth and power, I will not desert him now that he has been reduced to poverty and exile. In fact, I look upon it as an honorable privilege to accompany him.

The hall was saturated with applause, but the ominous glare of Caius Caligula prevented it from expression with the hands.

"Then you also, Herodias, shall be stripped of your money."

"So be it, O Caligula," Herodias uttered proudly, and with head erect, she marched out to join here husband. By midnight, Herodias was the heroine of a great love story all over Rome.

The truth is, however, that they were not to face the grim poverty that Caligula and Agrippa intended. Antipas was more capable of devious tricks than either of them, and so he embarked for Lugdunum with 20 talents in coined gold and a great part of their expensive ornaments and wearing apparel aboard. That was because the palms of Roman officials eternally itched for graft. In addition, the cold, coarse dissolute Caligula's reign of two years had caused him to be thoroughly hated by all except his close associates. His assassination which came about two years later was already predicted.

Lugdunum, now known as Lyins, France, struck admiration

from both Herodias and her husband. "What a magnificent site to build a great city!", Antipas exclaimed. He gazed and gazed upon the great rock fully two miles in width at the confluence of the two rivers, the Rhone and the Saone. The Saone made a great circle, or half circle about this elevation then joined the Rhone which flowed down the western side of the rock, joined it briefly, then parted again as both the streams ran south for a long stretch towards the Mediterranean.

Their ship had ascended the Rhone, and immediately on the arrival at the warf, they were conducted to the governor of this important military post within the fort which was upon the rocky eminence, about 500 feet above the shores of the two rivers. From there, they could look out over the country for miles in every direction.

Agrippa, the military commander-in-chief of Augustus, had chosen this location as the first Roman post in Gual. From Lugdunum, fanned out the four great highways that touched all of Gallia Cometa, the sixty cities in Gaul under Roman rule. Augustus Caesar had built the city, the great acqueducts, one coming 52 miles, and pouring 11,000,000 gallons of excellent water a day into the city. He built also temples and a theatre, gave it a senate, and made it the seat of an annual assembly of deputies from all over Gaul. It gained great importance and grew rapidly. Looking about them now, Herodias and Antipas agreed that banishment to this spot was no severe punishment.

The governor received them, registered them, and when Antipas had tactfully made him the present of money always expected by Roman officials in the provinces, assigned them a comfortable and attractive villa on the banks of the Rhône where most of his officers lived. A short time later, he permitted Antipas to buy a piece of ground on the elevated section, a little north of the fort, out of consideration that the communities along the river banks were sometimes inundated by the spring rains, and because Antipas had earned the reputation of generosity. Nor were Herodias and Antipater here unknown as they thought they would be. Few there were among the officers and men of means who had not heard the name of Herod the Great, close friend and associate of both Augustus Caesar and Agrippa. Numerous of the men had known Antipater himself when he was a student at Rome, or had met him on his numerous visits to Rome later, and his unmatched stable of fine horses were celebrated as the first in the empire. And being banished by Caligula hurt his prestige not at all. Numerous men of high character and family had been banished. To an extent, it was a testimony of honor.

"But this is troublesome to me," Antipater complained to Herodias. "When my real plan is to build a small in there at the divergence of the four great roads where I have bought the land."

"Inn?" screamed Herodias. "Small inn? What does the son of a great king do with an inn?"

"Await there the coming of John the Baptist. Somehow, I feel that someday he will come along this road that branches out to all parts of Europe. You know that this sect of Christians are being persecuted in Rome, and some are fleeing to all parts of the known world from there. Some have already penetrated into Gual. What, then, is more natural than that John the Baptist to come on a journey of proselyting? I will build an inn just where the four highways begin and wait for him there."

Herodias groaned internally. Even here, that disturber of her life threatened her. He was more tenacious dead than alive. Death concealed his human traits and permitted him to become a god. And there was nothing that she could do against a bodyless being. But perhaps, being a political prisoner in a way, the governor would not permit Antipas to build an inn.

But her hopes were immediately dashed. The governor rather urged him on, saying that a good, roomy inn which served good food and wines was just what had been lacking so far. It was impossible to furnish accomodations now that Rome had so extended itself in Gaul, for all the parties of important officials who came to Lugdunum now, let alone those who stopped there on their way to distant points in Gaul. And who had better taste in living, and more concepts in building than Antipas? He was just the man. And as governor, he could assist in the matter by cutting the cost of building by sending all offenders among the common soldiers to do the rough work of construction, such as digging foundations and mixing mortar and lifting stones.

So the inn was built, though not the small, plain thing that Antipas had contemplated. The nature of Antipas also got the better of him, and when finished, the inn had a small garden with flowering things and a fountain playing. There were extensive stables, servant quarters, and a well-stocked wine cellar and pantry. Rare delicacies from all parts of the world could be found there.

Herodias felt content that the expectation of the Fore-Runner would be driven from the mind of Antipas now, but she was shocked to find that in addition to the twenty spacious apartments for lodging that entourages of the mighty, there was a small room eternally reserved for John the Baptist. No matter how crowded the inn might become, that room was never rented. Her chagrin was great.

The inn was an instant success. It became the meeting place at night of all the high officials of the city and fort, the men of commerce as well as those passing through. After expensive meals, they lounged and discussed the news of the day or indulged in philosophical discussions in which Antipas could hold his own with the best. In fact, the host lent luster to the place. He had so entrenched himself with the powerful, that when the news came of the assassination of Caligula, some urged him to appeal to Caligula's successor for reinstatement as Tetrarch of Galilee, while others cried that he could not be spared where he was. When shortly after, the report came of the sudden death of Kibg Agrippa, he was urged again to vindicate himself, but Herodius was surprised to find that neither herself nor Antipas wanted to go. Instead, they decided to send to Arabia for six choice young palomino mares and a stallion and breed Arabian horses to satisfy the demands of numerous wealthy officials there, and the love of horses of Antipas himself. That was the only lack with them.

Then, one morning, Herodias noticed that the movements of her husband had become slow and uneven. Antipas was old. And while she was fifteen years younger than he, her metal mirror told her that she was old herself. The tracks of time were all over her face and body.

The thought of being deprived of the company of her husband in her old age was too devastating. She became more tender, and urged Antipas to take better care of himself.

"But I can hardly do less, Beloved." Antipas pointed out. "My steward looks after all the business, you know, and hands over the earnings of the inn on the first day of every month. But the dignateries who patronize the place expect to see me there. As you know, I am the great attraction to the inn. And now I fear that I must exert myself for a time, for the Emperor Nero is reported to be coming into gaul about three months from now, when the snow has completely vanished from the roads. We shall require at least double the lodging space that we have now. Another dining pavillion will be necessary also, for we are always over taxed for space there as it is."

Herodias did not like this, but there was nothing she could do, what with the governor urging and depending upon Antipas. She knew that his passion for building, she knew that she could not constrain him from the planning and over-seeing the work.

And out of his fertile imagination, something entrancing emerged. He did not extend the building at the back, as was taken for granted, nor add the conventional wings. Out of his ancestry he produced a large circular structure on either side that resembled the tents of black goat hair of Arabia reproduced in stone with glass windows. From Parthia he had brought rich rugs of excellent design that were hung between the windows and covered the floors deeply. These rooms were furnished with pillows instead of chairs. Long, thick pillows for reclining to eat, and round ones for sitting. These cushions were rich and very comfortable. For the food, tables of fine wood that rose no more than two feet from the floor. Elegant silk hangings supplemented the rugs hung on the walls.

No detail was neglected. From his background, Antipas knew how to command and get things done. A vast amount of oysters arrived from Britain. Thousands of live quail from southern Palestine, peacocks from Greece and Italy. The wines of Gaul being admired as [   ] superior of all on earth, they were brought in in great quantity [   ] north and south of the Rhine. Geese, ducks, and fat [   ] goats were also available in Gaul and they were on hand [   ] a great quantity of sausages from the Germans north of the [   ] entertainment, he hired dancing girls and strolling makers [   ] with their instruments to be handy.

Nero had summoned the governors of the sixty cities in Gaul, they arrived before the Emperor, and were on hand to give him a g[   ] reception. He was swept off his feet as soon as he beheld the inn [   ] Antipas and with the most important men present, lodged there. He declared all to be more than perfect there and gorged himself continuously on the fare. On his third night of residence, as he reclined on a long cushion, one of the strolling singers accompanied himself on a lyre as he presented a song in praise of Nero which he had composed. At the finish of it, Nero sprang up, took the lyre and for a half hour sang songs of his own composition. His face was flushed with pleasure when he ended.

"Antipater, son of Herod the Great shows himself to be a [   ] of numerous talents. Some years ago, this man was falsely accused of being an enemy of Rome. I, Nero, Imperator, declare this to be a lie. He is in spirit a Roman, and a patrician Roman. I will [   ] be Tetrarch of Galilee, or even King of all the territories which his noble father governed, at any time thaat he desires. But [   ] he would prefer not to further involve himself with that [   ] naation of religious fanatics who show themselves the enemies of mankind. They are creating disturbances in Rome at this moment [   ] in the Empire.

Antipater thanked him, but declined on the [   ] of his age. He said that he no longer desired to be annoyed with [   ] of government. And neither had he a son to succeed him.

Nero then paid Antipas other compliments. The inn [   ] dwelling of Antipas were the only structures in Lugdunum fit to look at or to live in. The others were not fit for anything but swine.

Two days before the departure of Nero for Rome, the city

[   ] on fire as if by accident, and burned to the ground. The inn and [   ] home of Antipas were north of the city, and so were not injured. Nero ordered Lugdunum rebuilt in a much improved manner, and left for Rome.

Herodias was very happy to see Nero go, and deeply regretted that he had ever come, though the inn prospered at the rate of more than a talent a day for the two weeks that he had been there, for she accused him of driving Antipas to his death-bed. Utterly exhausted, he was forced to take to his bed.

Herodias hovered about him with tears in her eyes, and refu[sed] to allow her servants to do anything for him, continually waited on him herself. Antipas lay there following her every movement while he was awake.

"Come to me, perfume of my soul," Antipas murmured to her on the fourth day in bed. "Come sit beside me on the bed."

Herodias sat so that she could cradle his head in her lap and sat there gently stroking it and looking down into his face.

"Perhaps I shall never leave this bed, beloved—"

"And John the Baptist has not arrived," she finished for him.

"No, but I no longer expect him. I am convinced he is dead."

"Dead, Antipas?"

"Yes, for if he were alive, as diligently as I have searched [   ] some trace of him. I was attracted to him first [   ] at Jerusalem had become so cold and cynical [   ] required something more. I yearned for a revival of goodness. [   ] attracted for the same reason that my father revered the Essenes. [   ] that at one time I considering abandoning my gov[   ] and becoming one of them. But there was a barrier to that."

"What barrier, my love?"

"You. Their way of life bars the association with women as an expression of daily love, and—well, you remember my disappearance on that night at Macherus?"

"Can I ever forget it?"

"Overwhelmed by his death, I resolved to abandon everything and to join them. Almost instantly I felt the hunger for your love and beseeched them to allow you to join me. That they refused.

Do you recall that I returned in the dress of a workman?"

"Yes, I remember everything."

"That was the dress I would have to wear as a disciple. But when I was certain that they would not admit you, I left them and returned to you."

"You never considered divorcing me, then?"

"Never. I so told John the Baptist months before his death. He knew that I would not. We talked earnestly of starting another sect where people lived simply and pure, but where women also were included."

With this information sinking in, Herodias sat numb and silent. The doing away with John the Baptist, and all that had followed in its train to bring her to Gaul and this bed-side—all through not knowing.

"The world, especially public life," Antipas continued, "seemed so full of evil that I longed for escape to simplicity, but my love for you was so strong that I could not face it. Torn between love and a wish to escape, I have suffered as few men have. But no matter what, love was ever the stronger. The two have only been reconciled since I have been here. And strangely enough, I became more and more bound to you as we grew older. You grow more beautiful all the time."

The thinned, pale eyelids closed weakly and wearily, and Herodias sat hovering and contemplated. Her husband's skull was now asserting itself. In fact, his whole, tall frame outlined beneath the sheets appeared to be dismissing the flesh as something temporary taking its leave. But then, the flesh of her body was no longer firm either. But involved as she was, the infirmity of the body of her husband was somehow mingled up with his youthful years and all the beauty of [ ] In spite of all the years of fear and doubt and warmth and glory and misery, she knew that she would choose this man again if she had the opportunity again. She had really known love.

But what was love? It surely was not happiness. She thought and thought as Antipas breathed in a way that indicated sleep.

"He suffered; I suffered; he accepted all things, including my slaying of a man and causing him to lose a kingdom and banishment to be with me. I suffered to keep him." Herodias sighed deeply and bent to gently press her lips upon his, and sighed again.

Perhaps love is a compelling necessity imposed on man by God that has something to do with suffering."

Afterword

ZORA NEALE HURSTON: "A NEGRO WAY OF SAYING"

The Reverend Harry Middleton Hyatt, an Episcopal priest whose five-volume classic collection, *Hoodoo, Conjuration, Witchcraft, and Rootwork*, more than amply returned an investment of forty years' research, once asked me during an interview in 1977 what had become of another eccentric collector whom he admired. "I met her in the field in the thirties. I think," he reflected for a few seconds, "that her first name was Zora." It was an innocent question, made reasonable by the body of confused and often contradictory rumors that make Zora Neale Hurston's own legend as richly curious and as dense as are the black myths she did so much to preserve in her classic anthropological works, *Mules and Men* and *Tell My Horse*, and in her fiction.

A graduate of Barnard College, where she studied under Franz Boas, Zora Neale Hurston published seven books—four novels, two books of folklore, and an autobiography—and more than fifty shorter works between the middle years of the Harlem Renaissance and the end of the Korean War, when she was the dominant black woman writer in the United States. The dark obscurity into which her career then lapsed reflects her staunchly independent political stances rather than any deficiency of craft or vision. Virtually ignored after the early 1950s, even by the Black Arts movement in the 1960s, an otherwise noisy and intense spell of black image- and myth-making that rescued so many black writers from remaindered oblivion, Hurston embodied a more or less harmonious but nevertheless problematic unity of opposites. It is this complexity that refuses to lend itself to the glibness of categories such as "radical" or "conservative," "black" or "Negro," "revolutionary" or "Uncle Tom"—categories of little use in literary criticism. It is this same complexity, embodied in her fiction, that, until Alice Walker published her important essay ("In Search of Zora Neale Hurston") in *Ms.* magazine in 1975, had made Hurston's place in black literary history an ambiguous one at best.

The rediscovery of African-American writers has usually turned on larger political criteria, of which the writer's work is supposedly a mere reflection. The deeply satisfying aspect of the rediscovery of Zora Neale Hurston is that black women generated it primarily to establish a maternal literary ancestry. Alice Walker's moving essay recounts her attempts to find Hurston's unmarked grave in the Garden of Heavenly Rest, a segregated cemetery in Fort Pierce, Florida. Hurston became a metaphor for the black woman writer's search for tradition. The craft of Alice Walker, Gayl Jones, Gloria Naylor, and Toni Cade Bambara bears, in markedly different ways, strong affinities with Hurston's. Their attention to Hurston signifies a novel sophistication in black literature: They read Hurston not only for spiritual kinship inherent in such relations but because she used black vernacular speech and rituals, in ways subtle and various, to chart the coming to consciousness of black women, so glaringly absent in other black fiction. This use of the vernacular became the fundamental framework for all but one of Hurston's novels and is particularly effective in her classic work *Their Eyes Were Watching God*, published in 1937, which is more closely related to Henry James's *The Portrait of a Lady* and Jean Toomer's *Cane* than to Langston Hughes's and Richard Wright's proletarian literature, so popular in the Depression.

The charting of Janie Crawford's fulfillment as an autonomous imagination, *Their Eyes* is a lyrical novel that correlates the need of her first two husbands for ownership of progressively larger physical space (and the gaudy accoutrements of upward mobility) with the suppression of self-awareness in their wife. Only with her third and last lover, a roustabout called Tea Cake whose unstructured frolics center around and about the Florida swamps, does Janie at last bloom, as does the large pear tree that stands beside her grandmother's tiny log cabin:

> She saw a dust bearing bee sink into the sanctum of a bloom; the thousand sister calyxes arch to meet the love embrace and the ecstatic shiver of the tree from root to tiniest branch creaming in every blossom and frothing with delight. So this was a marriage!

To plot Janie's journey from object to subject, the narrative of the novel shifts from third to a blend of first and third person (known as "free indirect discourse"), signifying this awareness of self in Janie. *Their Eyes* is a bold feminist novel, the first to be explicitly so in the African-American tradition. Yet in its concern with the project of finding a voice, with language as an instrument of injury and salvation, of selfhood and empowerment, it suggests many of the themes that inspirit Hurston's oeuvre as a whole.

One of the most moving passages in American literature is Zora Neale Hurston's account of her last encounter with her dying mother, found in a chapter entitled "Wandering" in her autobiography, *Dust Tracks on a Road* (1942):

> As I crowded in, they lifted up the bed and turned it around so that Mama's eyes would face the east. I thought that she looked to me as the head of the bed reversed. Her mouth was slightly open, but her breathing took up so much of her strength that she could not talk. But she looked at me, or so I felt, to speak for her. She depended on me for a voice.

We can begin to understand the rhetorical distance that separated Hurston from her contemporaries if we compare this passage with a similar scene published just three years later in *Black Boy* by Richard Wright, Hurston's dominant black male contemporary and rival: "Once, in the night, my mother called me to her bed and told me that she could not endure the pain, and she wanted to die. I held her hand and begged her to be quiet. That

night I ceased to react to my mother; my feelings were frozen.''
If Hurston represents her final moments with her mother in terms
of the search for voice, then Wright attributes to a similar experience a certain "somberness of spirit that I was never to lose,"
which "grew into a symbol in my mind, gathering to itself . . . the
poverty, the ignorance, the helplessness. . . .'' Few authors in the
black tradition have less in common than Zora Neale Hurston and
Richard Wright. And whereas Wright would reign through the
1940s as our predominant author, Hurston's fame reached its
zenith in 1943 with a *Saturday Review* cover story honoring the
success of *Dust Tracks*. Seven years later, she would be serving as
a maid in Rivo Alto, Florida; ten years after that she would die in
the County Welfare Home in Fort Pierce, Florida.

How could the recipient of two Guggenheims and the author of
four novels, a dozen short stories, two musicals, two books on
black mythology, dozens of essays, and a prizewinning autobiography virtually "disappear" from her readership for three full
decades? There are no easy answers to this quandary, despite the
concerted attempts of scholars to resolve it. It is clear, however,
that the loving, diverse, and enthusiastic responses that Hurston's
work engenders today were not shared by several of her influential black male contemporaries. The reasons for this are complex
and stem largely from what we might think of as their "radical
ideologies.''

Part of Hurston's received heritage—and perhaps the para-
mount received notion that links the novel of manners in the
Harlem Renaissance, the social realism of the 1930s, and the
cultural nationalism of the Black Arts movement—was the idea
that racism had reduced the black people to mere ciphers, to
beings who only react to an omnipresent racial oppression, whose
culture is "deprived" where different, and whose psyches are in
the main "pathological.'' Albert Murray, the writer and social
critic, calls this "the Social Science Fiction Monster.'' Socialists,
separatists, and the civil rights advocates alike have been de-
voured by this beast.

Hurston thought this idea degrading, its propagation a trap, and railed against it. It was, she said, upheld by "the sobbing school of Negrohood who hold that nature somehow has given them a dirty deal." Unlike Hughes and Wright, Hurston chose deliberately to ignore this "false picture that distorted. . . ." Freedom, she wrote in *Moses, Man of the Mountain*, "was something internal. . . . The man himself must make his own emancipation." And she declared her first novel a manifesto against the "arrogance" of whites assuming that "black lives are only defensive reactions to white actions." Her strategy was not calculated to please.

What we might think of as Hurston's mythic realism, lush and dense within a lyrical black idiom, seemed politically retrograde to the proponents of a social or critical realism. If Wright, Ellison, Brown, and Hurston were engaged in a battle over ideal fictional modes with which to represent the Negro, clearly Hurston lost the battle.

But not the war.

After Hurston and her choice of style for the black novel were silenced for nearly three decades, what we have witnessed since is clearly a marvelous instance of the return of the repressed. For Zora Neale Hurston has been "rediscovered" in a manner unprecedented in the black tradition: Several black women writers, among whom are some of the most accomplished writers in America today, have openly turned to her works as sources of narrative strategies, to be repeated, imitated, and revised, in acts of textual bonding. Responding to Wright's critique, Hurston claimed that she had wanted at long last to write a black novel, and "not a treatise on sociology." It is this urge that resonates in Toni Morrison's *Song of Solomon* and *Beloved*, and in Alice Walker's depiction of Hurston as our prime symbol of "racial health—a sense of black people as complete, complex, *undiminished* human beings, a sense that is lacking in so much black writing and literature." In a tradition in which male authors have ardently denied black literary paternity, this is a major development, one that heralds the refinement of our notion of tradition: Zora and her daughters are a tradition-within-the-tradition, a black woman's voice.

*   *   *

Rereading Hurston, I am always struck by the density of intimate experiences she cloaked in richly elaborated imagery. It is this concern for the figurative capacity of black language, for what a character in *Mules and Men* calls "a hidden meaning, jus' like de Bible . . . de inside meanin' of words," that unites Hurston's anthropological studies with her fiction. For the folklore Hurston collected so meticulously as Franz Boas's student at Barnard became metaphors, allegories, and performances in her novels, the traditional recurring canonical metaphors of black culture. Always reading more like novels than social science, even Hurston's academic collections center on the quality of imagination that makes these lives whole and splendid. But it is in the novel that Hurston's use of the black idiom realizes its fullest effect. In *Jonah's Gourd Vine*, her first novel, for instance, the errant preacher, John, as described by her biographer Robert Hemenway, "is a poet who graces his world with language but cannot find the words to secure his own personal grace." This concern for language and for the "natural" poets who "bring barbaric splendor of word and song into the very camp of the mockers" not only connects her two disciplines but also makes of "the suspended linguistic moment" a thing to behold indeed. Invariably, Hurston's writing depends for its strength on the text, not the context, as does John's climactic sermon, a tour de force of black image and metaphor. Image and metaphor define John's world; his failure to interpret himself leads finally to his self-destruction. As Hemenway concludes, "Such passages eventually add up to a theory of language and behavior."

Using "the spy-glass of Anthropology," her work celebrates rather than moralizes; it shows rather than tells, such that "both behavior and art become self-evident as the tale texts and hoodoo rituals accrete during the reading." As author she functions as "a midwife participating in the birth of a body of folklore, . . . the first wondering contacts with natural law." The myths she describes so accurately are in fact "alternative modes for perceiving reality," and never just condescending depictions of the quaint. Hurston

sees "the Dozens," for example, the age-old black ritual of grace-
ful insult as, among other things, a verbal defense of the sanctity
of the family, conjured through ingenious plays on words. Though
attacked by Wright and virtually ignored by his literary heirs,
Hurston's ideas about language and craft undergird many of the
most successful contributions to African-American literature that
followed.

We can understand Hurston's complex and contradictory legacy
more fully if we examine *Dust Tracks on a Road*, her own contro-
versial account of her life. Hurston did make significant parts of
herself up, like a masquerader putting on a disguise for the ball,
like a character in her own fictions. In this way, Hurston *wrote*
herself, and sought in her works to rewrite the "self" of "the
race" in its several private and public guises, largely for ideologi-
cal reasons. That which she chooses to reveal is the life of her
imagination, as it sought to mold and interpret her environment.
That which she silences or deletes, similarly, is all that her readership would draw upon to delimit or pigeonhole her life as a synec-
doche of "the race problem," an exceptional part standing for the
debased whole.

Hurston's achievement in *Dust Tracks* is twofold. First, she
gives us a *writer's* life, rather than an account, as she says, of "the
Negro problem." So many events in this text are figured in terms
of Hurston's growing awareness and mastery of books and language, language and linguistic rituals as spoken and written both
by masters of the Western tradition and by ordinary members of
the black community. These two "speech communities," as it
were, are Hurston's great source of inspiration not only in her
novels but also in her autobiography.

The representation of her sources of language seems to be her
principal concern, as she shifts back and forth between her "liter-
ate" narrator's voice and a highly idiomatic black voice found in
wonderful passages of free indirect discourse. Hurston moves in
and out of these distinct voices effortlessly, seamlessly, just as she
does in *Their Eyes* to chart Janie's coming to consciousness. It is

this usage of a *divided* voice, a double voice unreconciled, that strikes me as her great achievement, a verbal analogue of her double experiences as a woman in a male-dominated world and as a black person in a nonblack world, a woman writer's revision of W.E.B. Du Bois's metaphor of "double consciousness" for the hyphenated African-American.

Her language, variegated by the twin voices that intertwine throughout the text, retains the power to unsettle:

> There is something about poverty that smells like death. Dead dreams dropping off the heart like leaves in a dry season and rotting around the feet; impulses smothered too long in the fetid air of underground caves. The soul lives in a sickly air. People can be slave-ships in shoes.

Elsewhere she analyzes black "idioms" used by a culture "raised on smile and invective. They know how to call names," she concludes, then lists some, such as "gator-mouthed, box-ankled, puzzle-gutted, shovel-footed: Eyes looking like skint-ginny nuts, and mouth looking like a dishpan full of broke-up crockery!"

Immediately following the passage about her mother's death, she writes:

> The Master-Maker in His making had made Old Death. Made him with big, soft feet and square toes. Made him with a face that reflects the face of all things, but neither changes itself, nor is mirrored anywhere. Made the body of death out of infinite hunger. Made a weapon of his hand to satisfy his needs. This was the morning of the day of the beginning of things.

Language, in these passages, is not merely "adornment," as Hurston described a key black linguistic practice; rather, manner and meaning are perfectly in tune: She says the thing in the most meaningful manner. Nor is she being "cute," or pandering to a condescending white readership. She is "naming" emotions, as she says, in a language both deeply personal and culturally specific.

The second reason that *Dust Tracks* succeeds as literature arises from the first: Hurston's unresolved tension between her double voice signifies her full understanding of modernism. Hurston uses the two voices in her text to celebrate the psychological fragmentation both of modernity and of the black American. As Barbara Johnson has written, hers is a rhetoric of division, rather than a fiction of psychological or cultural unity. Zora Neale Hurston, the "real" Zora Neale Hurston that we long to locate in this text, dwells in the silence that separates these two voices: she is both, and neither; bilingual, and mute. This strategy helps to explain her attraction to so many contemporary critics and writers, who can turn to her works again and again only to be startled at her remarkable artistry.

But the life that Hurston could write was not the life she could live. In fact, Hurston's life, so much more readily than does the standard sociological rendering, reveals how economic limits determine our choices even more than does violence or love. Put simply, Hurston wrote well when she was comfortable, wrote poorly when she was not. Financial problems—book sales, grants and fellowships too few and too paltry, ignorant editors and a smothering patron—produced the sort of dependence that affects, if not determines, her style, a relation she explored somewhat ironically in "What White Publishers Won't Print." We cannot oversimplify the relation between Hurston's art and her life; nor can we reduce the complexity of her postwar politics, which, rooted in her distaste for the pathological image of blacks, were markedly conservative and Republican.

Nor can we sentimentalize her disastrous final decade, when she found herself working as a maid on the very day the *Saturday Evening Post* published her short story "The Conscience of the Court" and often found herself without money, surviving after 1957 on unemployment benefits, substitute teaching, and welfare checks. "In her last days," Hemenway concludes dispassionately, "Zora lived a difficult life—alone, proud, ill, obsessed with a book she could not finish."

The excavation of her buried life helped a new generation read

Hurston again. But ultimately we must find Hurston's legacy in her art, where she "ploughed up some literacy and laid by some alphabets." Her importance rests with the legacy of fiction and lore she constructed so cannily. As Hurston herself noted, "Roll your eyes in ecstasy and ape his every move, but until we have placed something upon his street corner that is our own, we are right back where we were when they filed our iron collar off." If, as a friend eulogized, "She didn't come to you empty," then she does not leave black literature empty. If her earlier obscurity and neglect today seem inconceivable, perhaps now, as she wrote of Moses, she has "crossed over."

Henry Louis Gates, Jr.

Bibliography

Abbott, Dorothy. "Recovering Zora Neale Hurston's Work." *Frontiers: A Journal of Women Studies* (1991): 174–81.

Abel, Elizabeth. "Black Writing, White Reading: Race and the Politics of Feminist Interpretation." *Critical Inquiry* (Spring 1993): 470(29).

Academic Conference of the Zora Neale Hurston Festival of the Arts (1990, Eatonville, Florida). *All About Zora: Views and Reviews by Colleagues and Scholars,* (ed. by Alice Morgan Grant. Four-G: Winter Park FL, 1991).

Alps, Sandra. "Concepts of Selfhood in *Their Eyes Were Watching God* and *The Color Purple.*" *Pacific Review* (Spring 1986): 106–112.

Awkward, Michael. " 'The inaudible voice of it all': Silence, Voice, and Action in *Their Eyes Were Watching God.*" In Weixlmann, Joe and Houston A. Baker, Jr., eds., *Black Feminist Criticism and Critical Theory* (Penkevill: Greenwood, FL, 1988): 57–109.

———. *Inspiring Influences: Tradition, Revision, and Afro-American Women's Novels.* Columbia University Press: New York, 1991.

———, ed., *New Essays on Their Eyes Were Watching God.* (Cambridge University Press: Cambridge, 1990): 29–49.

Batker, Carol J. *Ethnic Women's Literature and Politics: The Cultural Construction of Gender in Early Twentieth-Century America.* 1993.

Bauer, Margaret D. "The Sterile New South: An Intertextual Reading of *Their Eyes Were Watching God* and *Absalom, Absalom!*" CLA Journal (June 1993): 384(22).

Behar, Ruth. "Dare We Say 'I?' Bringing the Personal into Scholarship." *Chronicle of Higher Education* (June 1994): B1(2).

Benesch, Klaus. "Oral Narrative and Literary Text: Afro-American Folklore in *Their Eyes Were Watching God.*" *Callaloo* (Summer 1988): 627–35.

Bethel, Lorraine. " 'This Infinity of Conscious Pain': Zora Neale Hurston and the Black Female Literary Tradition." In Hull, Gloria and Barbara Smith, eds. and introds.; Patricia Bell Scott, ed.; Mary Berry (foreword), *All the Women Are White, All the Blacks Are Men, but Some of Us Are Brave: Black Women's Studies* (Feminist Press: Old Westbury, NY, 1982): 176–188.

Bigsby, Chris. "A Rage in Harlem: Black American Culture Has Built on Foundations Laid in the Jazz Age." *New Statesman & Society* (July 1991): 28(2).

Bloom, Harold, ed. *Zora Neale Hurston.* Chelsea: New York, 1986.

———, ed. *Zora Neale Hurston's Their Eyes Were Watching God.* Chelsea: New York, 1987.

Boi, Paola. "Moses, Man of Power, Man of Knowledge: A 'Signifying' Reading of Zora Neale Hurston (Between a Laugh and a Song)." In Diedrich, Maria and Dorothea Fischer-Hornung, eds., *Women and War: The Changing Status of American Women from the 1930's to the 1950's.* (Berg: New York, 1990): 107–26.

Bone, Robert. *The Negro Novel in America.* Yale University Press: New Haven, 1958.

Borders, Florence Edwards. "Zora Neale Hurston: Hidden Woman." *Callaloo* (May 1979): 89–92.

Bray, Rosemary. "Now Our Eyes Are Watching Her." *The New York Times Book Review* (Feb. 25, 1990): 11.

Brock, Sabine and Anne Koenen. "Alice Walker in Search of Zora Neale Hurston: Rediscovering a Black Female Tradition." In Lenz, Gunter H., ed., *History and Tradition in Afro-American Culture* (Campus: Frankfurt, 1984): 167–80.

Brown, Elizabeth Abigail. *A Porch of Her Own: The Politics of Domestic Space in Chopin, Hurston and McCullers.* 1991.

Brown, Lloyd W. "Zora Neale Hurston and the Nature of the Female Perceptions." *Obsidian* (1978): 39–45.

Burke, Virginia M. "Zora Neale Hurston and Fannie Hurst as They Saw Each Other." *CLA Journal* (June 1977): 435–47.

Bus, Heiner. "The Establishment of Community in Zora Neale Hurston's *The Eatonville Anthology* (1926) and Rolando Hinojosa's *Estampas del Valle* (1973)." In Febre, Genevieve, ed., *European Perspectives on Hispanic Literature of the United States* (Arte Publico: Houston, 1988): 66–81.

Bush, Trudy Bloser. "Transforming Vision: Alice Walker and Zora Neale Hurston." *The Christian Century* (Nov. 16, 1988): 1035–40.

Byrd, James W. "Zora Neale Hurston: A Negro Folklorist." *Tennessee Folklore Society Bulletin.* (June 1955): 37–41.

Byrd, James W. "Black Collectors of Black Folklore: An Update on Zora Neale Hurston and J. Mason Brewer." *Louisiana Folklore Miscellany* (1986–87): 1–7.

Byrd, Rudolph P. "Shared Orientation and Narrative Acts in *Cane, Their Eyes Were Watching God*, and *Meridian*." *Melus* (Winter 1991): 41(16).

Callahan, John F. " 'Mah Tongue Is in Mah Friend's Mouf': The Rhetoric of Intimacy and Immensity in *Their Eyes Were Watching God*." In Bloom, Harold, ed., *Zora Neale Hurston's Their Eyes Were Watching God* (Chelsea: New York, 1987): 87–113.

Cantrow, Ellen. "Sex, Race and Criticism: Thoughts of a White Feminist and Kate Chopin and Zora Neale Hurston." *Radical Teacher* (Sept. 1978): 30–33.

Caputi, Jane. " 'Specifying Fannie Hurst: Langston Hughes's *Limitations of Life*, Zora Neale Hurston's *Their Eyes Were Watching God*, and Toni Morrison's *The Bluest Eye* as Answers to Hurst's 'Imitation of Life.' " *Black American Literature Forum* (Winter 1990): 697(20).

Carby, Hazel V. "The Politics of Fiction, Anthropology, and the Folk: Zora Neale Hurston." In Awkward, Michael, ed., *New Essays on Their Eyes Were Watching God* (Cambridge University Press: Cambridge, 1990): 71–93.

Carr, Glynis. "Storytelling as Building in Zora Neale Hurston's *Their Eyes Were Watching God*." *CLA Journal* (Dec. 1987): 189–200.

Cassidy, Thomas. "Janie's Rage: The Dog and the Storm in *Their Eyes Were Watching God*." *CLA Journal* (March 1993): 260(10).

Christian, Barbara. *Black Women Novelists: The Development of a Tradition 1892–1976*. Greenwood Press: Westport CT, 1980.

Coleman, Ancilla. "Mythological Structure and Psychological Significance in Hurston's 'Seraph on the Suwanee.' " *Publications of the Mississippi Philological Association* (1988): 21–27.

Crabtree, Claire. "The Confluence of Folklore, Feminism, and Black Self-Determination in Zora Neale Hurston's *Their Eyes Were Watching God*." *Southern Literary Journal* (Spring 1985): 54–66.

Dalgarno, Emily. "Words Walking Without Masters: Ethnography and Creative Process in *Their Eyes Were Watching God*." *American Literature* (Sept. 1992): 519(23).

Dance, Daryl C.. "Zora Neale Hurston." In Duke, Maurice; Jackson R. Bryer, and M. Thomas Inge, eds., *American Women Writers: Bibliographical Essays* (Greenwood: Westport CT, 1983): 321–51.

Davies, Kathleen. "Zora Neale Hurston's Poetics of Embalmment: Articulating the Rage of Black Women and Narrative Self-Defense." *African American Review* (Spring 1992): 147(13).

Davis, Jane. *"The Color Purple:* A Spiritual Descendant of Hurston's *Their Eyes Were Watching God." Griot* (Summer 1987): 79–96.

Deck, Alice. "Zora Neale Hurston, Noni Jabavu, and Cross-Disciplinary Discourse." *Black American Literature Forum* (Summer 1990): 237–57.

Dickerson, Vanessa D. " 'It Takes Its Shape from de Shore It Meets': The Metamorphic God in Hurston's *Their Eyes Were Watching God." Lit: Literature Interpretation Theory* (1991): 221–30.

Dolby-Stahl, Sandra. "Literary Objectives: Hurston's Use of Personal Narrative in *Mules and Men." Western Folklore* (Jan. 1992): 51(13).

duCille, Ann. "The Intricate Fabric of Feeling: Romance and Resistance in *Their Eyes Were Watching God." The Zora Neale Hurston Forum* (Spring 1990): 1–16.

DuPlessis, Rachel Blau. "Power, Judgment, and Narrative in a Work of Zora Neale Hurston: Feminist Cultural Studies." In Awkward, Michael, ed., *New Essays on Their Eyes Were Watching God* (Cambridge University Press: Cambridge, 1990): 95–123.

Dutton, Wendy. "The Problem of Invisibility: Voodoo and Zora Neale Hurston." *Frontiers* (Summer 1992): 131(22).

Fannin, Alice. "A Sense of Wonder: The Pattern for Psychic Survival in *Their Eyes Were Watching God* and *The Color Purple." The Zora Neale Hurston Forum* (Fall 1986): 1–11.

Faulkner, Howard J. "Mules and Men: Fiction as Folklore." *CLA Journal* (March 1991): 331–40.

Ferguson, SallyAnn. "Folkloric Men and Female Growth in *Their Eyes Were Watching God." Black American Literature Forum* (Spring-Summer 1987): 185–97.

Flores, Toni. "Claiming and Making: Ethnicity, Gender, and the Common Sense in Leslie Marmon Silko's *Ceremony* and Zora Neale Hurston's *Their Eyes Were Watching God." (Frontiers:* 1989): 52–58.

Foreman, Gabrielle. "Looking Back from Zora, or Talking Out Both Sides My Mouth for Those Who Have Two Ears." *Black American Literature Forum* (Winter 1990): 649–67.

Fox-Genovese, Elizabeth. "To Write My Self: The Autobiographies of Afro-American Women." In Benstock, Shari, ed., and Catharine R. Stimpson, introd., *Feminist Issues in Literary Scholarship* (Indiana University Press: Bloomington, 1987): 161–80.

————. "My Statue, My Self: Autobiographical Writings of Afro-American Women." In Benstock, Shari, ed., *The Private Self: Theory and Practice of Women's Autobiographical Writings* (University of North Carolina Press: Chapel Hill, 1988): 63–89.

————. "Myth and History: Discourse of Origins in Zora Neale Hurston and Maya Angelou." *Black American Literature Forum* (Summer 1990): 221–36.

Freeman, Alma S. "Zora Neale Hurston and Alice Walker: A Spiritual Kinship." *SAGE* (Spring 1985): 37–40.

Gates, Henry Louis, Jr. "Why the *Mule Bone* Debate Goes On." *New York Times* (Feb. 10, 1991): II, 5:1.

Giovanni, Nikki. "Sisters, Too; Great Women in African-American History." *The Black Collegian* (Jan.–Feb. 1992): 60–64.

Glassman, Steve and Kathryn Lee Seidel, eds., *Zora in Florida*. University of Central Florida Press: Orlando; University Presses of Gainesville, Florida, 1991.

Grant, Alice Morgan. *Jump at the Sun: Zora Neale Hurston and Her Eatonville Roots: A Guide for Teachers*. Association to Preserve Eatonville Community: Eatonville, FL, 1991.

Hale, David G. "Hurston's 'Spunk' and Hamlet." (Summer 1993): 397(2).

Hattenhauer, Darryl. "Hurston's *Their Eyes Were Watching God.*" *The Explicator* (Winter 1992): 111(2).

Hemenway, Robert. *The Harlem Renaissance Remembered*. ("Zora Neale Hurston and the Eatonville Anthropology") ed. by Arna Bontemps. Dodd, Mead and Co., New York, 1972.

————. "Folklore Field Notes From Zora Neale Hurston." *Black Scholar* (1976): 39–46.

————. *Zora Neale Hurston: A Literary Biography*. University of Illinois Press: Chicago, 1977.

————. *Dust Tracks on a Road: An Autobiography*, 2nd ed. University of Illinois Press: Urbana, 1984.

————. "The Personal Dimension in *Their Eyes Were Watching God.*" In Awkward, Michael, ed., *New Essays on Their Eyes Were Watching God* (Cambridge University Press: Cambridge, 1990): 29–49.

Hite, Molly. "Romance, Marginality, Matrilineage: Alice Walker's *The Color Purple* and Zora Neale Hurston's *Their Eyes Were Watching God.*" *Novel* (Spring 1989): 257–73.

Holloway, Karla F.C. *The Character of the Word: The Texts of Zora Neale Hurston*. Greenwood Press: New York, 1987.

hooks, bell. "Zora Neale Hurston: A Subversive Reading." *Matatu* (1989): 5–23.

Howard, Lillie P., ed. *Alice Walker and Zora Neale Hurston: The Common Bond.* Westport, Conn.: Greenwood Press, 1993.

———. "Marriage: Zora Neale Hurston's System of Values." *CLA Journal* (Dec. 1977): 256–68.

———. *Zora Neale Hurston.* Twayne Publishers: Boston, 1980.

Hubbard, Dolan. " '. . . Ah said Ah'd save de text for you': Recontextualizing the Sermon to Tell (Her) Story in Zora Neale Hurston's *Their Eyes Were Watching God.*" *African American Review* (Summer 1993): 167(12).

Hudson, Gossie Harold. "Zora Neale Hurston and Alternative History." *MAWA Review* (Summer-Fall 1982): 60–64.

Hughes, Carl Milton. *The Negro Novelist.* (Citadel Press: New York, 1953): 172–78.

Hurst, Fannie. "Zora Neale Hurston: A Personality Sketch." *Yale University Library Gazette* (1960): 17–22.

Hurston, Zora Neale. "Self-Help—Hoodoo Style: How to Ward Off Enemies and Make Love Charms." Excerpted from *Journal of American Folklore* (1931), 174. Published in: *Utne Reader* (May–June 1990): 121(2).

Isaacs, D.S. "Zora Neale Hurston: Critical Perspectives Past and Present." *Choice* (Jan 1994): 785(1).

Johnson, Barbara. "Metaphor, Metonymy, and Voice in *Their Eyes Were Watching God.*" In Gates, Henry Louis, Jr., ed., *Black Literature and Literary Theory* (Methuen, New York, 1984): 205–19.

Johnson, Lonnell E. "The Defiant Black Heroine: Ollie Miss and Janie Mae—Two Portraits from the 30's." *The Zora Neale Hurston Forum* (Spring 1990): 41–46.

Jones, Evora W. "The Pastoral and the Picaresque in Zora Neale Hurston's 'The Gilded Six-Bits.' " *CLA Journal* (March 1992): 316(9).

Jones, Kirkland C. "Folk Humor as Comic Relief in Hurston's *Jonah's Gourd Vine.*" *The Zora Neale Hurston Forum* (Fall 1986): 26–31.

Jordan, Jennifer. "Feminist Fantasies: Zora Neale Hurston's *Their Eyes Were Watching God.*" *Tulsa Studies in Women's Literature* (Spring 1988): 105–17.

Jordan, June. "On Richard Wright and Zora Neale Hurston: Notes Toward a Balance of Love and Hatred." *Black World* (Aug 1974): 4–8.

Kalb, John D. "The Anthropological Narrator of Hurston's *Their Eyes Were Watching God.*" *Studies in American Fiction* (Fall 1988): 169–80.

Kim, Myung Ja. "Zora Neale Hurston's Search for Self: *Their Eyes Were Watching God.*" *The Journal of English Language and Literature* (Fall 1990): 491–513.

King, Sigrid. "Naming and Power in Zora Neale Hurston's *Their Eyes Were Watching God." Black American Literature Forum* (Winter 1990): 683–97.

Kitch, Sally L. "Gender and Language: Dialect, Silence, and the Disruption of Discourse." *Women's Studies* (1987): 66–78.

Krasner, James. "The Life of Women: Zora Neale Hurston and Female Autobiography." *Black American Literature Forum* (Spring 1989): 113–27.

Kubitschek, Missy Dehn. " 'Tuh de Horizon and Back': The Female Quest in *Their Eyes Were Watching God." Black American Literature Forum* (Fall 1983): 109–15.

Lenz, Gunter H. "Southern Exposure: The Urban Experience and the Re-Construction of Black Folk Culture and Community in the Works of Richard Wright and Zora Neale Hurston." *New York Folklore* (Summer 1981): 3–39.

LeSeur, Geta. "Janie as Sisyphus: Existential Heroism in *Their Eyes Were Watching God." The Zora Neale Hurston Forum* (Spring 1990): 33–40.

Lewis, Vashti Crutcher. "The Declining Significance of the Mulatto Female as Major Character in the Novels of Zora Neale Hurston." *CLA Journal* (Dec. 1984): 127–49.

Lindberg-Seyersted, Brita. "The Color Black: Skin Color as Social, Ethical, and Esthetic Sign in Writings by Black American Women." *English Studies* (Feb. 1992): 51(1-7).

Lindroth, James R. "Generating the Vocabulary of Hoodoo: Zora Neale Hurston and Ishmael Reed." *The Zora Neale Hurston Forum* (Fall 1987): 27–34.

Love, Theresa R. "Zora Neale Hurston's America." *Papers on Language and Literature* (Fall 1976): 422–37.

Lowe, John. "Hurston, Humor, and the Harlem Renaissance." In Kramer, Victor A., ed., *The Harlem Renaissance Re-Examined* (AMS: New York, 1987): 283–313.

———. *Jump at the Sun: Zora Neale Hurston's Cosmic Comedy.* University of Illinois Press, Urbana, 1995.

Lupton, Mary Jane. "Zora Neale Hurston and the Survival of the Female." *Southern Literary Journal* (Fall 1982): 45–54.

———. "Black Women and Survival in Comedy: American Style and *Their Eyes Were Watching God." The Zora Neale Hurston Forum* (Fall 1986): 38–44.

MacKethan, Lucinda H. "Mother Wit: Humor in Afro-American Women's Autobiography." *Studies in American Humor* (Spring-Summer 1985): 51–61.

Marks, Donald R. "Sex, Violence and Organic Consciousness in Zora Neale Hurston's *Their Eyes Were Watching God*." *Black American Literature Forum* (Winter 1985): 152–57.

Matza, Diane. "Zora Neale Hurston's *Their Eyes Were Watching God* and Toni Morrison's *Sula*: A Comparison." *MELUS* (Fall 1985): 43–54.

McCredie, Wendy J. "Authority and Authorization in *Their Eyes Were Watching God*." *Black American Literature Forum* (Spring 1982): 25–28.

McKay, Nellie. " 'Crayon Enlargements of Life': Zora Neale Hurston's *Their Eyes Were Watching God* as Autobiography." In Awkward, Michael, ed., *New Essays on Their Eyes Were Watching God* (Cambridge University Press: Cambridge, 1990): 51–70.

Mikell, Gwendoly. "When Horses Talk: Reflections on Zora Neale Hurston's Haitian Anthropology." *Phylon* (Sept 1982): 218–30.

Nathiri, N. Y. *Zora! Zora Neale Hurston, a Woman and Her Community*. Sentinel Communications Co.: Orlando, 1991.

Naylor, Carolyn A. "Cross-Gender Significance of the Journey Motif in Selected Afro-American Fiction." *Colby Library Quarterly* (March 1982): 26–38.

Neal, Carry. "Eatonville's Zora Neale Hurston: A Profile." In *Black Review* Vol. 2. William Morrow Publishers: New York, 1972.

Newson, Adele S. " 'The Fiery Chariot': A One-Act Play by Zora Neale Hurston." *The Zora Neale Hurston Forum* (Fall 1986): 32–37.

———. *Zora Neale Hurston: A Reference Guide*. G. K. Hall: Boston MA, 1987.

Olaniyan, Tejumola. "God's Weeping Eyes: Hurston and the Anti-Patriarchal Form." *Obsidian II* (Summer 1990): 30–45.

Paquet, Sandra Pouchet. "The Ancestor as Foundation in *Their Eyes Were Watching God* and *Tar Baby*." *Callaloo* (Summer 1990): 499–515.

Peterson, Dale E. "Response and Call: The African American Dialogue with Bakhtin." *American Literature* (Dec. 1993): 761(15).

Plant, Deborah G. "The Folk Preacher and Folk Sermon Form in Zora Neale Hurston's *Dust Tracks on a Road*." *Folklore Forum* (1988): 3–19.

Pondrom, Cyrena N. "The Role of Myth in Hurston's *Their Eyes Were Watching God*." *American Literature* (May 1986): 181–202.

Raynaud, Claudine. "Autobiography as a 'Lying' Session: Zora Neale Hurston's *Dust Tracks on a Road*." In Weixlmann, Joe and Houston

A. Baker, Jr., eds., *Black Feminist Criticism and Critical Theory* (Penkevill, Greenwood, FL, 1988): 111–38.

Rayson, Ann L. "The Novels of Zora Neale Hurston." *Studies in Black Literature* (Winter 1974): 1–11.

Reich, Alice. "Phoeby's Hungry Listening." *Women's Studies* (1986): 163–69.

Robey, Judith. "Generic Strategies in Zora Neale Hurston's *Dust Tracks on a Road.*" Black American Literature Forum (Winter 1990): 667–83.

Robinson, Wilhelmena. *Historical Negro Biographies.* (Publisher's Co.: New York, 1967): 208–10.

Roemer, Jule. "Celebrating the Black Female Self: Zora Neale Hurston's American Classic *(Their Eyes Were Watching God).*" *English Journal* (Nov. 1989): 70–73.

Rosenblatt, Jean. "Charred Manuscripts Tell Zora Neale Hurston's Poignant and Powerful Story." *The Chronicle of Higher Education* (June 5, 1991): B4.

Ryan, Bonnie Crarey. "Zora Neale Hurston—A Checklist of Secondary Sources." *Bulletin of Bibliography* (March 1988): 33–39.

Sadoff, Dianne F. "Black Matrilineage: The Case of Alice Walker and Zora Neale Hurston." *Signs* (Fall 1985): 4–26.

Saunders, James Robert. "Womanism as the Key to Understanding Zora Neale Hurston's *Their Eyes Were Watching God* and Alice Walker's *The Color Purple.*" *The Hollins Critic* (Oct. 1988): 1–11.

Schmidt, Rita T. "The Fiction of Zora Neale Hurston: An Assertion of Black Womanhood." *Ilha do Desterro* (1985): 53–70.

Schwalbenberg, Peter. "Time as Point of View in Zora Neale Hurston's *Their Eyes Were Watching God.*" *Negro American Literature Forum* (Fall 1976): 104–108.

Setterberg, Fred. "Zora Neale Hurston in the Land of 1,000 Dances." *The Georgia Review* (Winter 1992): 627(17).

Sheffey, Ruthe T. "Zora Neale Hurston's *Moses, Man of the Mountain:* A Fictionalized Manifesto on the Imperatives of Black Leadership." *CLA Journal* (Dec. 1985): 206–20.

Sheppard, David M. "Living by Comparisons: Janie and Her Discontents." *English Language Notes* (Dec. 1992): 63(13).

Smith-Wright, Geraldine. "Revision as Collaboration: Zora Neale Hurston's *Their Eyes Were Watching God* as Source for Alice Walker's *The Color Purple.*" *SAGE* (Fall 1987): 20–25.

Sollors, Werner. "Of Mules and Mares in a Land of Difference; or, Quadrupeds All?" *American Quarterly* (June 1990): 167–91.

Speisman, Barbara. "A Tea with Zora and Marjorie: A Series of Vignettes Based on the Unique Friendship of Zora Neale Hurston and Marjorie Kinnan Rawlings." *Rawlings Journal* (1988): 67–100.

St. Clair, Janet. "The Courageous Undertow of Zora Neale Hurston's 'Seraph on the Suwanee.'" *Modern Language Quarterly* (March 1989): 38–57.

Stadler, Quandra Prettyman. "Visibility and Difference: Black Women in History and Literature: Pieces of a Paper and Some Ruminations." In Eisenstein, Hester, ed. and introd.; Alice Jardine, ed. and pref., *The Future of Difference* (Hall, Boston, 1980): 239–46.

Stetson, Erlene. "*Their Eyes Were Watching God:* A Woman's Story." *Regionalism and the Female Imagination* (1979): 30–36.

Story, Ralph D. "Gender and Ambition: Zora Neale Hurston in the Harlem Renaissance." *The Black Scholar* (May–July 1989): 25(7).

———. "Patronage and the Harlem Renaissance: You Get What You Pay For." *CLA Journal* (March 1989): 284–95.

Sundquist, Eric J. *The Hammers of Creation: Folk Culture in Modern African-American Fiction.* University of Georgia Press: Athens, 1992.

Thomas, Marion A. "Reflections on the Sanctified Church as Portrayed by Zora Neale Hurston." *Black American Literature Forum* (Spring 1991): 35–42.

Thornton, Jerome E. " 'Goin' on de Muck': The Paradoxical Journey of the Black American Hero" (notes) *CLA Journal* (March 1988): 261–80.

Turner, Darwin. *Minor Chord: Three Afro-American Writers and Their Search for Identity.* Southern Illinois University Press: Carbondale, 1971.

Urgo, Joseph R. "The Tune is the Unity of the Thing: Power and Vulnerability in Zora Hurston's *Their Eyes Were Watching God.*" *The Southern Literary Journal* (Spring, 1991): 40–55.

Wald, Priscilla. "Becoming 'Colored': The Self-Authorized Language of Difference in Zora Neale Hurston." *American Literary History* (Spring 1990): 79–100.

Walker, Alice. "In Search of Zora Neale Hurston." *Ms* (March 1975): 74–82.

———, and Mary Helen Washington, *I Love Myself When I Am Laughing . . . and Then Again When I Am Looking Mean and Impressive: A Zora Neale Hurston Reader.* Feminist Press: New York, 1979.

———. "Looking for Zora." In Ascher, Carol; Louise DeSalvo, and Sara Ruddick, eds., *Between Women: Biographers, Novelists, Critics,*

Teachers, and Artists Write about Their Work on Women (Beacon Press: Boston, 1984): 431–47.

Walker, S. Jay. "Zora Neale Hurston and *Their Eyes Were Watching God:* Black Novel of Sexism." *Modern Fiction Studies* (Winter 1975): 519–27.

Wall, Cheryl A. "Mules and Men and Women: Zora Neale Hurston's Strategies of Narration and Visions of Female Empowerment." *Black American Literature Forum* (Winter 1989): 661–80.

Welsh-Asante, Dariamu. "Dance as Metaphor in Zora Neale Hurston's *Their Eyes Were Watching God."* *The Zora Neale Hurston Forum* (Spring 1990): 18–31.

Wilentz, Gay. "White Patron, and Black Artist: The Correspondence of Fannie Hurst and Zora Neale Hurston." *Library Chronicle of the University of Texas* (1986): 20–43.

———. "Defeating the False God: Janie's Self-Determination in Zora Neale Hurston's *Their Eyes Were Watching God."* In Kessler-Harris, Alice and William McBrien, eds., *Faith of a (Woman) Writer* (Greenwood: Westport CT, 1988): 28.

Williams, Delores S. "Black Women's Literature and the Task of Feminist Theory." In Atkinson, Clarissa W. and Constance H. Buchanan, eds. and prefs.; Margaret R. Miles, ed., pref., and intro., *Immaculate and Powerful: The Female in Sacred Image and Social Reality* (Beacon Press: Boston, 1985): 88–110.

Williams, Donna M. "Our Love/Hate Relationship with Zora Neale Hurston." *The Black Collegian* (Jan–Feb 1994): 86(3).

Williams, Sherley Ann, Ruby Dee, and Jerry Pinkney, *Their Eyes Were Watching God.* University of Illinois Press: Urbana, 1991.

Willis, Miriam DeCosta. "Folklore and the Creative Artist: Lydia Cabrera and Zora Neale Hurston." *CLA Journal* (Sept. 1983): 81–90.

About the author

About the book

Read on

Insights,
Interviews
& More . . .

"In Search of Zora Neale Hurston"

by Alice Walker

The work of Zora Neale Hurston was relatively unknown in 1975, when Alice Walker, beloved author of The Color Purple, *wrote her groundbreaking essay "In Search of Zora Neale Hurston" (*Ms. *magazine, March 1975). In this seminal piece, reprinted here in its entirety, Walker illuminates her idol's life and work.*

"ON JANUARY 16, 1959, Zora Neale Hurston, suffering from the effects of a stroke and writing painfully in longhand, composed a letter to the 'editorial department' of Harper & Brothers inquiring if they would be interested in seeing 'the book I am laboring upon at the present—a life of Herod the Great.' One year and twelve days later, Zora Neale Hurston died without funds to provide for her burial, a resident of the St. Lucie County, Florida, Welfare Home. She lies today in an unmarked grave in a segregated cemetery in Fort Pierce, Florida, a resting place generally symbolic of the black writer's fate in America.

"Zora Neale Hurston is one of the most significant unread authors in America, the author of two minor classics and four other major books."

—*Robert Hemenway, "Zora Hurston and the Eatonville Anthropology," from* The Harlem Renaissance Remembered, *edited by Arna Bontemps (Dodd, 1972)*

Courtesy of the Estate of Carl Van Vechten, Joseph Solomon, Executor

On August 15, 1973, I wake up just as the plane is lowering over Sanford, Florida, which means I am also looking down on Eatonville, Zora Neale Hurston's birthplace. I recognize it from Zora's description in *Mules and Men*: "the city of five lakes, three croquet courts, three hundred brown skins, three hundred good swimmers, plenty guavas, two schools, and no jailhouse." Of course I cannot see the guavas, but the five lakes are still there, and it is the lakes I count as the plane prepares to land in Orlando.

From the air, Florida looks completely flat, and as we near the ground this impression does not change. This is the first time I have seen the interior of the state, which Zora wrote about so well, but there are the acres of orange groves, the sand, mangrove trees, and scrub pine that I know from her books. Getting off the plane I walk through the hot moist air of midday into the tacky but air-conditioned airport. I search for Charlotte Hunt, my companion on the Zora Hurston expedition. She lives in Winter Park, Florida, very near Eatonville, and is writing her graduate dissertation on Zora. I see her waving—a large pleasant-faced white woman in dark glasses. We have written to each other for several weeks, swapping our latest finds (mostly hers) on Zora, and trying to make sense out of the mass of information obtained (often erroneous or simply confusing) from Zora herself—through her stories and autobiography—and from people who wrote about her.

Eatonville has lived for such a long time in my imagination that I can hardly believe it will be found existing in its own right. But after twenty minutes on the expressway, Charlotte turns off and I see a small settlement of ▶

houses and stores set with no particular pattern in the sandy soil off the road. We stop in front of a neat gray building that has two fascinating signs: EATONVILLE POST OFFICE and EATONVILLE CITY HALL.

Inside the Eatonville City Hall half of the building, a slender, dark, brown-skin woman sits looking through letters on a desk. When she hears we are searching for anyone who might have known Zora Neale Hurston, she leans back in thought. Because I don't wish to inspire foot-dragging in people who might know something about Zora they're not sure they should tell, I have decided on a simple, but I feel profoundly *useful*, lie.

"I am Miss Hurston's niece," I prompt the young woman, who brings her head down with a smile.

"I think Mrs. Moseley is about the only one still living who might remember her," she says.

"Do you mean *Mathilda* Moseley, the woman who tells those 'woman-is-smarter-than-man' lies in Zora's book?"

"Yes," says the young woman. "Mrs. Moseley is real old now, of course. But this time of day, she should be at home."

I stand at the counter looking down on her, the first Eatonville resident I have spoken to. Because of Zora's books, I feel I know something about her; at least I know what the town she grew up in was like years before she was born.

"Tell me something," I say, "do the schools teach Zora's books here?"

"No," she says, "they don't. I don't think most people know anything about Zora Neale

Hurston, or knew about any of the great things she did. She was a fine lady. I've read all of her books myself, but I don't think many other folks in Eatonville have."

"Many of the church people around here, as I understand it," says Charlotte in a murmured aside, "thought Zora was pretty loose. I don't think they appreciated her writing about them."

"Well," I say to the young woman, "thank you for your help." She clarifies her directions to Mrs. Moseley's house and smiles as Charlotte and I turn to go.

"The letter to Harper's does not expose a publisher's rejection of an unknown masterpiece, but it does reveal how the bright promise of the Harlem Renaissance deteriorated for many of the writers who shared in its exuberance. It also indicates the personal tragedy of Zora Neale Hurston: Barnard graduate, author of four novels, two books of folklore, one volume of autobiography, the most important collector of Afro-American folklore in America, reduced by poverty and circumstance to seek a publisher by unsolicited mail."
—*Robert Hemenway*

"Zora Neale Hurston was born in 1901, 1902, or 1903—depending on how old she felt herself to be at the time someone asked."
—*Librarian, Beinecke Library, Yale University*

THE MOSELEY HOUSE is small and white and snug, its tiny yard nearly swallowed up by oleanders and hibiscus bushes. Charlotte and I knock on the door. I call out. But there is no ▶

answer. This strikes us as peculiar. We have had time to figure out an age for Mrs. Moseley—not dates or a number, just old. I am thinking of a quivery, bedridden invalid when we hear the car. We look behind us to see an old black-and-white Buick—paint peeling and grillwork rusty—pulling into the drive. A neat old lady in a purple dress and white hair is straining at the wheel. She is frowning because Charlotte's car is in the way.

Mrs. Moseley looks at us suspiciously. "Yes, I knew Zora Neale," she says, unsmilingly and with a rather cold stare at Charlotte (who I imagine feels very *white* at that moment), "but that was a long time ago, and I don't want to talk about it."

"Yes ma'am," I murmur, bringing all my sympathy to bear on the situation.

"Not only that," Mrs. Moseley continues, "I've been sick. Been in the hospital for an operation. Ruptured artery. The doctors didn't believe I was going to live, but you see me alive, don't you?"

"Looking well, too," I comment.

Mrs. Moseley is out of her car. A thin, sprightly woman with nice gold-studded false teeth, uppers and lowers. I like her because she stands there *straight* beside her car, with a hand on her hip and her straw pocketbook on her arm. She wears white T-strap shoes with heels that show off her well-shaped legs.

"I'm eighty-two years old, you know," she says. "And I just can't remember things the way I used to. Anyhow, Zora Neale left here to go to school and she never really came back to live. She'd come here for material for her books, but that was all. She spent most of her time down in South Florida."

"You know, Mrs. Moseley, I saw your name in one of Zora's books."

"You did?" She looks at me with only slightly more interest. "I read some of her books a long time ago, but then people got to borrowing and borrowing and they borrowed them all away."

"I could send you a copy of everything that's been reprinted." I offer. "Would you like me to do that?"

"No," says Mrs. Moseley promptly. "I don't read much any more. Besides, all of that was *so* long ago. . . ."

Charlotte and I settle back against the car in the sun. Mrs. Moseley tells us at length and with exact recall every step in her recent operation, ending with: "What those doctors didn't know—when they were expecting me to die (and they didn't even think I'd live long enough for them to have to take out my stitches!)—is that Jesus is the best doctor, and if *He* says for you to get well, that's all that counts."

With this philosophy, Charlotte and I murmur quick assent: being Southerners and church bred, we have heard that belief before. But what we learn from Mrs. Moseley is that she does not remember much beyond the year 1938. She shows us a picture of her father and mother and says that her father was Joe Clarke's brother. Joe Clarke, as every Zora Hurston reader knows, was the first mayor of Eatonville; his fictional counterpart is Jody Starks of *Their Eyes Were Watching God*. We also get directions to where Joe Clarke's store *was*—where Club ▶

"In Search of Zora Neale Hurston" *(continued)*

Eaton is now. Club Eaton, a long orange-beige nightspot we had seen on the main road, is apparently famous for the good times in it regularly had by all. It is, perhaps, the modern equivalent of the store porch, where all the men of Zora's childhood came to tell "lies," that is, black folktales, that were "made and used on the spot," to take a line from Zora. As for Zora's exact birthplace, Mrs. Moseley has no idea.

After I have commented on the healthy growth of her hibiscus bushes, she becomes more talkative. She mentions how much she *loved* to dance, when she was a young woman, and talks about how good her husband was. When he was alive, she says, she was completely happy because he allowed her to be completely free. "I was so free I had to pinch myself sometimes to tell if I was a married woman."

Relaxed now, she tells us about going to school with Zora. "Zora and I went to the same school. It's called Hungerford High now. It *was* only to the eighth-grade. But our teachers were so good that by the time you left you knew college subjects. When I went to Morris Brown in Atlanta, the teachers there were just teaching me the same things I had already learned right in Eatonville. I wrote Mama and told her I was going to come home and help her with her babies. I wasn't learning anything new."

"Tell me something, Mrs. Moseley," I ask, "why do you suppose Zora was against integration? I read somewhere that she was against school desegregation because she felt it was an insult to black teachers."

"Oh, one of them [white people] came

around asking me about integration. One day I was doing my shopping. I heard 'em over there talking about it in the store, about the schools. And I got on out of the way because I knew if they asked me, they wouldn't like what I was going to tell 'em. But they came up and asked me anyhow. 'What do you think about this integration?' one of them said. I acted like I thought I had heard wrong. 'You're asking *me* what *I* think about integration?' I said. 'Well, as you can see I'm just an old colored woman'—I was seventy-five or seventy-six then—'and this is the first time anybody ever asked me about integration. And nobody asked my grandmother what she thought, either, but her daddy was one of you all.'" Mrs. Moseley seems satisfied with this memory of her rejoinder. She looks at Charlotte. "I have the blood of three races in my veins," she says belligerently, "white, black, and Indian, and nobody asked me *anything* before."

"Do you think living in Eatonville made integration less appealing to you?"

"Well, I can tell you this: I have lived in Eatonville all my life and I've been in the governing of this town. I've been everything but Mayor and I've been *assistant* Mayor. Eatonville was and is an all-black town. We have our own police department, post office, and town hall. Our own school and good teachers. Do I need integration?

"They took over Goldsboro, because the black people who lived there never incorporated like we did. And now I don't even know if any black folks live there. They built big houses up there around the lakes. But we didn't let that happen in Eatonville, ▶

and we don't sell land to just anybody. And you see, we're still here."

When we leave, Mrs. Moseley is standing by her car, waving. I think of the letter Roy Wilkins wrote to a black newspaper blasting Zora Neale for her lack of enthusiasm about the integration of schools. I wonder if he knew the experience of Eatonville she was coming from. Not many black people in America have come from a self-contained, all-black community where loyalty and unity are taken for granted. A place where black pride is nothing new.

There is, however, one thing Mrs. Moseley said that bothered me.

"Tell me, Mrs. Moseley," I had asked, "Why is it that thirteen years after Zora's death, no marker has been put on her grave?"

And Mrs. Moseley answered: "The reason she doesn't have a stone is because she wasn't buried here. She was buried down in South Florida somewhere. I don't think anybody really knew where she was."

"Only to reach a wider audience, need she ever write books—because she is a perfect book of entertainment in herself. In her youth she was always getting scholarships and things from wealthy white people, some of whom simply paid her just to sit around and represent the Negro race for them, she did it in such a racy fashion. She was full of sidesplitting anecdotes, humorous tales, and tragicomic stories, remembered out of her life in the South as a daughter of a traveling minister of God. She could make you laugh one minute and cry the next. To many of her white friends, no doubt, she was a perfect 'darkie,' in the nice meaning they give the term—that is, a naïve, childlike, sweet, humorous, and highly colored Negro.

"But Miss Hurston was clever, too—a student who didn't let college give her a broad 'a' and who had great scorn for all pretentions, academic or otherwise. That is why she was such a fine folklore collector, able to go among the people and never act as if she had been to school at all. Almost nobody else could stop the average Harlemite on Lenox Avenue and measure his head with a strange-looking, anthropological device and not get bawled out for the attempt, except Zora, who used to stop anyone whose head looked interesting, and measure it."

—*Langston Hughes,* The Big Sea *(Knopf)*

"What does it matter what white folks must have thought about her?"

—*Student, Black Women Writers Class,*
Wellesley College

MRS. SARAH PEEK PATTERSON is a handsome, red-haired woman in her late forties, wearing orange slacks and gold earrings. She is the director of Lee-Peek Mortuary in Fort Pierce, the establishment that handled Zora's burial. Unlike most black funeral homes in Southern towns that sit like palaces among the general poverty, Lee-Peek has a run-down, *small* look. Perhaps this is because it is painted purple and white, as are its Cadillac chariots. These colors do not age well. The rooms are cluttered and grimy, and the bathroom is a tiny, stale-smelling prison, with a bottle of black hair dye (apparently used to touch up the hair of the corpses) dripping into the face bowl. Two pine burial boxes are resting in the bathtub.

Mrs. Patterson herself is pleasant and helpful.

"As I told you over the phone, Mrs. Patterson," I begin, shaking her hand and looking into her penny-brown eyes, "I am Zora Neale Hurston's niece, and I would like to have a marker put on her grave. You said, when I called you last week, that you could tell me where the grave is."

By this time I am, of course, completely into being Zora's niece, and the lie comes with perfect naturalness to my lips. Besides, as far as I'm concerned, she *is* my aunt—and that of all black people as well.

"She was buried in 1960," exclaims Mrs. Patterson. "That was when my father was running this funeral home. He's sick now or I'd let you talk to him. But I know where she's buried. She's in the old cemetery, the Garden of the Heavenly Rest, on Seventeenth Street. Just when you go in the gate there's a circle, and she's buried right in the middle of it. Hers is the only grave in that circle—because people don't bury in that cemetery any more."

She turns to a stocky, black-skinned woman in her thirties, wearing a green polo shirt and white jeans cut off at the knee. "This lady will show you where it is," she says.

"I can't tell you how much I appreciate this," I say to Mrs. Patterson, as I rise to go. "And could you tell me something else? You see, I never met my aunt. When she died I was still a junior in high school. But could you tell me what she died of, and what kind of funeral she had?"

"I don't know exactly what she died of," Mrs. Patterson says, "I know she didn't have any money. Folks took up a collection to bury her. . . . I believe she died of malnutrition."

"*Malnutrition?*"

Outside, in the blistering sun, I lean my head against Charlotte's even more blistering cartop. The sting of the hot metal only intensifies my anger. "*Malnutrition?*" I manage to mutter. "Hell, our condition hasn't changed *any* since Phillis Wheatley's time. *She* died of malnutrition!"

"Really?" says Charlotte, "I didn't know that."

"One cannot overemphasize the extent of her commitment. It was so great that her marriage in the spring of 1927 to Herbert Sheen was short-lived. Although divorce did not come officially until 1931, the two separated amicably after only a few months, Hurston to continue her collecting, Sheen to attend Medical School. Hurston never married again."

—*Robert Hemenway*

"WHAT IS YOUR NAME?" I ask the woman who has climbed into the back seat.

"Rosalee," she says. She has a rough, pleasant voice, as if she is a singer who also smokes a lot. She is homely, and has an air of ready indifference.

"Another woman came by here wanting to see the grave," she says, lighting up a cigarette. "She was a little short, dumpy white lady from one of these Florida schools. Orlando or Daytona. But let me tell you something before we get started. All I know is where the ▶

cemetery is. I don't know one thing about that grave. You better go back in and ask her to draw you a map."

A few moments later, with Mrs. Patterson's diagram of where the grave is, we head for the cemetery.

We drive past blocks of small, pastel-colored houses and turn right onto Seventeenth Street. At the very end, we reach a tall curving gate, with the words "Garden of Heavenly Rest" fading into the stone. I expected, from Mrs. Patterson's small drawing, to find a small circle—which would have placed Zora's grave five or ten paces from the road. But the "circle" is over an acre large and looks more like an abandoned field. Tall weeds choke the dirt road and scrape against the sides of the car. It doesn't help either that I step out into an active anthill.

"I don't know about y'all," I say, "but I don't even believe this." I am used to the haphazard cemetery-keeping that is traditional in most Southern black communities, but this neglect is staggering. As far as I can see there is nothing but bushes and weeds, some as tall as my waist. One grave is near the road, and Charlotte elects to investigate it. It is fairly clean, and belongs to someone who died in 1963.

Rosalee and I plunge into the weeds; I pull my long dress up to my hips. The weeds scratch my knees, and the insects have a feast. Looking back, I see Charlotte standing resolutely near the road.

"Aren't you coming?" I call.

"No," she calls back. "I'm from these parts and I know what's out there." She means snakes.

"Shit," I say, my whole life and the people I love flashing melodramatically before my eyes. Rosalee is a few yards to my right.

"How're you going to find anything out here?" she asks. And I stand still a few seconds, looking at the weeds. Some of them are quite pretty, with tiny yellow flowers. They are thick and healthy, but dead weeds under them have formed a thick gray carpet on the ground. A snake could be lying six inches from my big toe and I wouldn't see it. We move slowly, very slowly, our eyes alert, our legs trembly. It is hard to tell where the center of the circle is since the circle is not really round, but more like half of something round. There are things crackling and hissing in the grass. Sandspurs are sticking to the inside of my skirt. Sand and ants cover my feet. I look toward the road and notice that there are, indeed, *two* large curving stones, making an entrance and exit to the cemetery. I take my bearings from them and try to navigate to exact center. But the center of anything can be very large, and a grave is not a pinpoint. Finding the grave seems positively hopeless. There is only one thing to do:

"Zora!" I yell as loud as I can (causing Rosalee to jump), "are you out here?"

"If she is, I sho hope she don't answer you. If she do, I'm gone."

"Zora!" I call again, "I'm here. Are you?"

"If she is," grumbles Rosalee, "I hope she'll keep it to herself."

"Zora!" Then I start fussing with her. "I hope you don't think I'm going to stand out here all day, with these snakes watching me and these ants having a field day. In fact, I'm going to ▶

call you just one or two more times." On a clump of dried grass, near a small busy tree, my eye falls on one of the largest bugs I have ever seen. It is on its back, and is as large as three of my fingers. I walk toward it, and yell "Zo-ra!" and my foot sinks into a hole. I look down. I am standing in a sunken rectangle that is about six feet long and about three or four feet wide. I look up to see where the two gates are.

"Well," I say, "this is the center, or approximately anyhow. It's also the only sunken spot we've found. Doesn't this look like a grave to you?"

"For the sake of not going no farther through these bushes," Rosalee growls, "yes, it do."

"Wait a minute," I say, "I have to look around some more to be sure this is the only spot that resembles a grave. But you don't have to come."

Rosalee smiles—a grin, really—beautiful and tough.

"Naw," she says, "I feels sorry for you. If one of these snakes got a hold of you out here by yourself I'd feel *real* bad." She laughs. "I done come this far, I'll go on with you."

"Thank you, Rosalee," I say. "Zora thanks you too."

"Just as long as she don't try to tell me in person," she says, and together we walk down the field.

"The gusto and flavor of Zora Neal[e] Hurston's storytelling, for example, long before the yarns were published in *Mules and Men* and other books, became a local legend which might . . . have spread further under different conditions. A tiny shift in the center of gravity could have made them best-sellers."

—*Arna Bontemps,* Personals *(Paul Bremen, Ltd., London; 1963)*

"Bitter over the rejection of her folklore's value, especially in the black community, frustrated by what she felt was her failure to convert the Afro-American world view into the forms of prose fiction, Hurston finally gave up."

—*Robert Hemenway*

WHEN CHARLOTTE AND I drive up to the Merritt Monument Company, I immediately see the headstone I want.

"How much is this one?" I ask the young woman in charge, pointing to a tall black stone. It looks as majestic as Zora herself must have been when she was learning voodoo from those root doctors down in New Orleans.

"Oh, *that* one," she says, "that's our finest. That's Ebony Mist."

"Well, how much is it?"

"I don't know. But wait," she says, looking around in relief, "here comes somebody who'll know."

A small, sunburned man with squinty green eyes come sup. He must be the engraver, I think, because his eyes are contracted into slits as if he has been keeping stone dust out of them for years.

"That's Ebony Mist," he says. "That's our best."

"How much is it?" I ask, beginning to realize I probably *can't* afford it. ▶

He gives me a price that would feed a dozen Sahelian drought victims for three years. I realize I must honor the dead, but between the dead great and the living starving, there is no choice.

"I have a lot of letters to be engraved," I say, standing by the plain gray marker I have chosen. It is pale and ordinary, not at all like Zora, and makes me momentarily angry that I am not rich.

We got into his office and I hand him a sheet of paper that has:

ZORA NEALE HURSTON
"A GENIUS OF THE SOUTH"
NOVELIST   FOLKLORIST
ANTHROPOLOGIST
1960

"A genius of the South" is from one of Jean Toomer's poems.

"Where is this grave?" the monument man asks. "If it's in a new cemetery, the stone has to be flat."

"Well, it's not a new cemetery and Zora—my aunt—doesn't need anything flat because with the weeds out there, you'd never be able to see it. You'll have to go out there with me."

He grunts.

"And take a long pole and 'sound' the spot," I add. "Because there's no way of telling it's a grave, except that it's sunken."

"Well," he says, after taking my money and writing up a receipt, in the full awareness that he's the only monument dealer for miles, "you take this flag" (he hands me a four-foot-long pole with a red-metal marker on top) "and take it out to the cemetery and put it where you think the grave is. It'll take us about three weeks to get the stone out there."

I wonder if he knows he is sending me to another confrontation with the snakes. He probably does. Charlotte has told me she will cut my leg and suck out the blood, if I am bit.

"At least send me a photograph when it's done, won't you?"

He says he will.

"Hurston's return to her folklore-collecting in December of 1927 was made possible by Mrs. R. Osgood Mason, an elderly white patron of the arts, who at various times also helped Langston Hughes, Alain Locke, Richmond Barthe, and Miguel Covarrubias. Hurston apparently came to her attention through the intercession of Locke, who frequently served as a kind of liaison between the young black talent and Mrs. Mason. The entire relationship between this woman and the Harlem Renaissance deserves extended study, for it represents much of the ambiguity involved in white patronage of black artists. All her artists were instructed to call her 'Godmother'; there was a decided emphasis on the 'primitive' aspects of black culture, apparently a holdover from Mrs. Mason's interest in the Plains Indians. In Hurston's case there were special restrictions imposed by her patron: although she was to be paid a handsome salary for her folklore collecting, she was to limit her correspondence and publish nothing of her research without prior approval."

—*Robert Hemenway* ▶

"In Search of Zora Neale Hurston" *(continued)*

"You have to read the chapters Zora *left out* of her autobiography."
—*Student, Special Collections Room*
Beinecke Library, Yale University

DR. BENTON, a friend of Zora's and a practicing M.D. in Fort Pierce, is one of those old, good-looking men whom I always have trouble not liking. (It no longer bothers me that I may be constantly searching for father figures; by this time, I have found several and dearly enjoyed knowing them all.) He is shrewd, with steady brown eyes under hair that is almost white. He is probably in his seventies, but doesn't look it. He carries himself with dignity, and has cause to be proud of the new clinic where he now practices medicine. His nurse looks at us with suspicion, but Dr. Benton's eyes have the penetration of a scalpel cutting through skin. I guess right away that if he knows anything at all about Zora Hurston, he will not believe I am her niece. "Eatonville?" Dr. Benton says, leaning forward in his chair, looking first at me, then at Charlotte. "Yes, I know Eatonville, I grew up not far from there. I knew the whole bunch of Zora's family." (He looks at the shape of my cheekbones, the size of my eyes, and the nappiness of my hair.) "I knew her daddy. The old man. He was a hardworking, Christian man. Did the best he could for his family. He was the mayor of Eatonville for a while, you know.

"My father was the mayor of Goldsboro. You probably never heard of it. It never incorporated like Eatonville did, and has just about disappeared. But Eatonville is still all-black."

He pauses and looks at me. "And you're Zora's niece," he says wonderingly.

"Well," I say with shy dignity, yet with some tinge, I hope, of a nineteenth-century blush, "I'm illegitimate. That's why I never knew Aunt Zora."

I love him for the way he comes to my rescue. "You're *not* illegitimate!" he cries, his eyes resting on me fondly. "All of us are God's children! Don't you even *think* such a thing!"

And I hate myself for lying to him. Still I ask myself, would I have gotten this far toward getting the headstone and finding out about Zora Hurston's last days without telling my lie? Actually I probably would have. But I don't like taking chances that could get me stranded in Central Florida.

"Zora didn't get along with her family. I don't know why. Did you read her autobiography, *Dust Tracks on a Road*?"

"Yes, I did," I say. "It pained me to see Zora pretending to be naïve and grateful about the old white 'Godmother' who helped finance her research, but I loved the part where she ran off from home after falling out with her brother's wife.

Dr. Benton nodded. "When she got sick, I tried to get her to go back to her family, but she refused. There wasn't any real hatred; they just never had gotten along and Zora wouldn't go to them. She didn't want to go to the country home, either, but she had to, because she couldn't do a thing for herself."

"I was surprised to learn she died of malnutrition."

Dr. Benton seems startled. "Zora *didn't* die of malnutrition," he says indignantly. ▶

"Where did you get that story from? She had a stroke and she died in the welfare home." He seems particularly upset, distressed, but sits back reflectively in his chair: "She was an incredible woman," he muses. "Sometimes when I closed my office, I'd go by her house and just talk to her for an hour or two. She was a well-read, well-traveled woman and always had her own ideas about what was going on . . ."

"I never knew her, you know. Only some of Carl Van Vechten's photographs and some newspaper photographs. . . . What did she look like?"

"When I knew her, in the fifties, she was a big woman, *erect*. Not quite as light as I am [Dr. Benton is dark beige], and about five foot, seven inches, and she weighed about two hundred pounds. Probably more. She . . . "

"What! Zora was *fat!* She wasn't in Van Vechten's pictures!"

"Zora loved to eat," Dr. Benton says complacently. "She could sit down with a mound of ice cream and just eat and talk till it was all gone."

While Dr. Benton is talking, I recall that the Van Vechten pictures were taken when Zora was still a young woman. In them she appears tall, tan, and healthy. In later newspaper photographs—when she was in her forties—I remembered that she seemed heavier and several shades lighter. I reasoned that the earlier photographs were taken while she was busy collecting folklore materials in the hot Florida sun.

"She had high blood pressure. Her health

wasn't good. . . . She used to live in one of my houses—on School Court Street. It's a block house . . . I don't recall the number. But my wife and I used to invite her over to the house for dinner. *She always ate well,*" he says emphatically.

"That's comforting to know," I say, wondering where Zora ate when she wasn't with the Bentons.

"Sometimes she would run out of groceries—after she got sick—and she'd call me. 'Come over here and see 'bout me,' she'd say. And I'd take her shopping and buy her groceries.

"She was always studying. Her mind— before the stroke—just worked all the time. She was always going somewhere, too. She once went to Honduras to study something. And when she died, she was working on that book about Herod the Great. She was so intelligent!

And really had perfect expressions. Her English was beautiful." (I suspect that is a clever way to let me know Zora herself didn't speak in the "black English" her characters used.)

"I used to read all of her books," Dr. Benton continues, "but it was a long time ago. I remember one about . . . it was called, I think, 'The Children of God' [*Their Eyes Were Watching God*], and I remember Janie and Teapot [Teacake] and the mad dog riding on the cow in that hurricane and bit old Teapot on the cheek. . . ."

I am delighted that he remembers even this much of the story, even if the names are wrong, but seeing his affection for Zora I ▶

feel I must ask him about her burial. "Did she *really* have a pauper's funeral?"

"She *didn't* have a pauper's funeral!" he says with great heat. "Everybody around here *loved* Zora."

"We just came back from ordering a headstone," I say quietly, because he *is* an old man and the color is coming and going on his face, "but to tell the truth, I can't be positive what I found is the grave. All I know is the spot I found was the only grave-size hole in the area."

"I remember it wasn't near the road," says Dr. Benton, more calmly. "Some other lady came by here and we went out looking for the grave and I took a long iron stick and poked all over that part of the cemetery but we didn't find anything. She took some pictures of the general area. Do the weeds still come up to your knees?"

"And beyond," I murmur. This time there isn't any doubt. Dr. Benton feels ashamed.

As he walks us to our car, he continues to talk about Zora. "She couldn't really write much near the end. She had the stroke and it left her weak; her mind was affected. She couldn't think about anything for long.

"She came here from Daytona, I think. She owned a houseboat over there. When she came here, she sold it. She lived on that money, then she worked as a maid—for an article on maids she was writing—and she worked for the *Chronicle* writing the horoscope column.

"I think black people here in Florida got mad at her because she was for some politician they were against. She said this politician *built* schools for blacks while the one they wanted just talked about it. And although Zora wasn't egotistical, what she thought, she thought; and generally what she thought, she said."

When we leave Dr. Benton's office, I realize I have missed my plane back home to Jackson, Mississippi. That being so, Charlotte and I decide to find the house Zora lived in before she was taken to the country welfare home to die. From among her many notes, Charlotte locates a letter of Zora's she has copied that carries the address: 1734 School Court Street. We ask several people for directions. Finally, two old gentlemen in a dusty gray Plymouth offer to lead us there. School Court Street is not paved, and the road is full of mud puddles. It is dismal and squalid, redeemed only by the brightness of the late afternoon sun. Now I can understand what a "block" house is. It is a house shaped like a block, for one thing, surrounded by others just like it. Some houses are blue and some are green or yellow. Zora's is light green. They are tiny— about fifty by fifty feet, squatty with flat roofs. The house Zora lived in looks worse than the others, but that is its only distinction. It also has three ragged and dirty children sitting on the steps.

"Is this where y'all live?" I ask, aiming my camera.

"No, ma'am" they say in unison, looking at me earnestly. "We live over yonder. This Miss So-and-So's house; but she in the hospital."

We chatter inconsequentially while I take more pictures. A car drives up with a young ▶

black couple in it. They scowl fiercely at Charlotte and don't look at me with friendliness, either. They get out and stand in their doorway across the street. I go up to them to explain. "Did you know Zora Hurston used to live right across from you?" I ask.

"Who?" They stare at me blankly, then become curiously attentive, as if they think I made the name up. They are both Afro-ed and he is somberly dashiki-ed.

I suddenly feel frail and exhausted. "It's too long a story," I say, "but tell me something, is there anybody on this street who's lived here for more than thirteen years?"

"That old man down there," the young man says, pointing. Sure enough, there is a man sitting on his steps three houses down. He has graying hair and is very neat, but there is a weakness about him. He reminds me of Mrs. Turner's husband in *Their Eyes Were Watching God*. He's rather "vanishing"-looking, as if his features have been sanded down. In the old days, before black was beautiful, he was probably considered attractive, because he has wavy hair and light-brown skin; but now, well, light skin has ceased to be its own reward.

After the preliminaries, there is only one thing I want to know: "Tell me something," I begin, looking down at Zora's house, "did Zora like flowers?"

He looks at me queerly. "As a matter of fact," he says, looking regretfully at the bare, rough yard that surrounds her former house, "she was crazy about them. And she was a great gardener. She loved azaleas, and that running and blooming vine [morning glories], and she really loved that night-smelling flower [gardenia]. She kept a vegetable garden year-round, too. She raised collards and tomatoes and things like that.

"Everyone in this community thought well of Miss Hurston. When she died, people all up and down this street took up a collection for her burial. We put her away nice."

"Why didn't somebody put up a headstone?"

"Well, you know, one was never requested. Her and her family didn't get along. They didn't even come to the funeral."

"And did she live there by herself?"

"Yes, until they took her away. She lived with—just her and her companion, Sport."

My ears perk up. "Who?"

"Sport, you know, her dog. He was her only companion. He was a big brown-and-white dog."

When I walk back to the car, Charlotte is talking to the young couple on their porch. They are relaxed and smiling.

"I told them about the famous lady who used to live across the street from them," says Charlotte as we drive off. "Of course they had no idea Zora ever lived, let alone that she lived across the street. I think I'll send some of her books to them."

"That's real kind of you," I say.

"I am not tragically colored. There is no great sorrow dammed up in my soul, nor lurking behind my eyes. I do not mind at all. I do not belong to the sobbing school of Negrohood who hold that nature somehow has given them a lowdown dirty deal and whose feelings ▶

are all hurt about it. . . . No, I do not weep at the world—I am too busy sharpening my oyster knife."

—*Zora Neale Hurston, "How It Feels to Be Colored Me,"* World Tomorrow, *1928*

THERE ARE TIMES—and finding Zora Hurston's grave was one of them—when normal responses of grief, horror, and so on, do not make sense because they bear no real relation to the depth of the emotion one feels. It was impossible for me to cry when I saw the field full of weeds where Zora is. Partly this is because I have come to know Zora through her books and she was not a teary sort of person herself; but partly, too, it is because there is a point at which even grief feels absurd. And at this point laughter gushes up to retrieve sanity.

It is only later, when the pain is not so direct a threat to one's own existence that what was learned in that moment of comical lunacy is understood. Such moments rob us of both youth and vanity. But perhaps they are also times when greater disciplines are born. ᑫ

Alice Walker is the author of Revolutionary Petunias and Other Poems *(Harcourt), which was nominated for a National Book Award, and* In Love & Trouble: Stories of Black Women (Harcourt), *which received the Rosenthal Foundation Award from the National Institute of Arts and Letters.*

Rescued from the Flames

Typescript of "The Woman in Gaul"

AFTER ZORA NEALE HURSTON died on January 28, 1960, in a Fort Pierce, Florida, hospital, her papers were ordered to be burned. A law officer and friend, Patrick DuVal, passing by the house where she had lived, stopped and put out the fire, thus saving an invaluable collection of literary documents for posterity. The original manuscript of "The Woman in Gaul," an unpublished story, was partially burned in the fire. Following are two charred pages from the manuscript, now preserved in the Department of Special and Area Studies Collections at the University of Florida.

Courtesy of the Estate of Zora Neale Hurston

Zora drumming on her trip to Haiti, where she penned *Their Eyes Were Watching God* and collected information on Vodou for her nonfiction work *Tell My Horse*.

29

THE   WOMAN   IN   GAUL

Am I to be disposed of like a dishonest servant - I,the grand-
of Herod the Great, and with the royal blood of the Asamoneans
ursing in my veins?" Herodias, wife of Antipas, Tetrarch of Galilee
reclined on an elaborately draped couch on the East Portico of the white
marble palace beside the Lake of Tiberias. " It is not to be borne!"
In her left hand was an exquisetely worked scroll of a drama by Euripides
which she now flung to the marble floor of the portico. " If Antipas
thinks that he can discard me as he did the daughter of Aretas of Arabia,
he deceives himself. Am I to be exorcised from his bed and house like
an evil spirit by that desert-dwelling, hairy monster, John the Baptist? It is not to be borne! Does Antipas forget that I have made a vow
to destroy that monster? I have made a vow to God to behead that John
the Baptist if and when he is found. And that I will do, in spite of my
weak-hearted husband."

Sitting on a tasselled cushion near the lapping water of the
lake was Asenath, the Egyptian ladies-maid of Herodias. She sat with
her legs crossed under her like a scribe. She had lifted her eyes for
the tenth part of a second when Herodias began her outburst, the dropped
them and fixed her gaze as if in deep contemplation of the wide expanse of the lake. Now she moved her head quickly towards her mistress
as if she had only that moment become aware that Herodias had spoken,
leaped to her feet, and ran to kneel beside the couch which stood against
the house wall. She struck a convincing pose of guilt and contrition
and spoke.

" The reprimand which you gave me is just and merciful,
born Herodias. I do not forget that you paid a most magni
at Alexandria to obtain my services, and that you are
generous to me.

Page 1, typescript of "The Woman in Gaul"

But I, wretch that I am, sat here being fed on the beauty of the lake and the movement of the boats of fishermen far out there, when I should have been ministering to your comfort. Chastize me as you will."

For a minute, Herodias was struck dumb. Her outburst had indeed been involuntary - forced out by the termendous emotional pressure from ▮thin - and she had expected that it could not escape being overheard ▮r maid. Now, she breathed deeply in relief that Asenath had not

But Herodias was mistaken. Egypt of her time had the reputation ▮▮▮re secrets for cultivating and preserving beauty than any ▮▮▮▮▮▮▮known world, and the college of beauty at Alexan-
▮▮▮▮▮▮▮▮▮▮▮▮▮▮▮▮▮▮▮▮▮. The graduates were eagerly seized
around the ▮▮▮▮▮▮▮▮▮▮▮▮▮▮▮st and most powerful ladies
cosmetics, massage ▮▮▮▮▮▮▮▮▮▮▮▮▮▮▮▮▮▮▮▮ of ointments,
knowledge of the affairs ▮▮▮▮▮▮▮▮▮▮▮▮▮▮▮▮▮▮▮▮▮▮▮▮
Asenath had merely reacted to her in▮▮▮▮▮▮▮▮▮▮▮▮▮▮▮us.
heard and seen nothing, which in this insta▮▮▮▮▮▮▮▮▮
complished acting.

" I grant you my pardon this time," Herodias ne▮▮▮▮▮▮▮er▮ said indulgently. " As you know, I myself spend many hours on this por▮ tico when the weather is pleasant, gazing upon the lake. It steals the entire attention."

" I am thankful for your kind understanding, O beaute ous mistress. What was it that you were commanding me to do for you?"

" To do something, O skilled Egyptian maiden, to increase my beauty. Call upon the most valued and potent secrets in your knowledge and work your great skill upon me." Asenath could see th▮ building up in Herodias again. " I am nearer forty th▮ think about. I have a daughter well past her nubil▮ that I am no longer very young. I was reminding ▮ very negligent of me today."

Less than an hour before, Asenath had fini▮ ment which was supposed to preserve - indeed re▮

Page 2, typescript of "The Woman in Gaul"

Have You Read?
More by
Zora Neale Hurston

JONAH'S GOURD VINE

Zora Neale Hurston's first novel tells the story of John Buddy Pearson, a young minister who loves too many women for his own good even though he is married to Lucy, his one true love. In this sympathetic portrait of a man and his community, Hurston shows that faith and tolerance and good intentions cannot resolve the tension between the spiritual and the physical.

MULES AND MEN

The fruit of Hurston's labors as a folklorist and anthropologist, this celebrated treasury of black American folklore includes stories, "big old lies," songs, Vodou customs, superstitions—all the humor and wisdom that is the matchless heritage of American blacks.

TELL MY HORSE

This firsthand account of the mysteries of Vodou is based on Hurston's personal experiences in Haiti and Jamaica, where she participated as an initiate and not just an observer of Vodou practices in the 1930s. Of great cultural interest, her travelogue paints a vividly authentic picture of ceremonies, customs, and superstitions.

MOSES, MAN OF THE MOUNTAIN

Based on the familiar story of the Exodus, Hurston blends the Moses of the Old Testament with the Moses of black folklore and song to create a compelling allegory of power, redemption, and faith.

DUST TRACKS ON A ROAD

First published in 1942 at the crest of her popularity as a writer, this is Hurston's imaginative and exuberant account of her rise from childhood poverty in the rural South to a prominent place among the leading artists and intellectuals of the Harlem Renaissance. It is a book full of the wit and wisdom of a proud and spirited woman who started off low and climbed high.

SERAPH ON THE SUWANEE

Hurston's novel of turn-of-the-century white Florida "crackers"marks a daring departure for the author famous for her complex accounts of black culture and heritage.Hurston explores the evolution of a marriage full of love but very little communication and the desires of a young woman in search of herself and her place in the world.

EVERY TONGUE GOT TO CONFESS

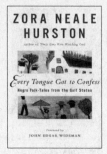

African American folklore was Zora Neale Hurston's first love. Collected in the late 1920s, these hilarious, bittersweet, often saucy folk-tales—some of which date back to the Civil War—provide a fascinating, verdant slice of African American life in the rural South at the turn of the twentieth century. Arranged according to subject—from God Tales, Preacher Tales, and Devil Tales to Heaven Tales, White-Folk Tales, and Mistaken Identity Tales—they reveal attitudes about slavery, faith, race relations, family, and romance that have been passed on for generations. They capture the heart and soul of the vital, independent, and creative community that so inspired Zora Neale Hurston.

ALSO BY
ZORA NEALE HURSTON

THE COMPLETE STORIES
Introduction by Henry Louis Gates, Jr., and Sieglinde Lemke
978-0-06-135018-4 (paperback)
This gathering of Hurston's short fiction—most of which appeared only in literary magazines during her lifetime—spans the years 1921-1955 and includes such works as "John Redding Goes to Sea," "Cock Robin Beale Street," "Hurricane," and "Book of Harlem."

DUST TRACKS ON A ROAD: REVISED
An Autobiography
Foreword by Maya Angelou
978-0-06-085408-9 (paperback)
First published in 1942, this is Zora Neale Hurston's exuberant account of her rise from childhood poverty in the rural South to a prominent place among the leading artists and intellectuals of the Harlem Renaissance.
"Warm, witty, imaginative, and down-to-earth by turns, this is a rich and winning book by one of our genuine, Grade A folk writers." —*The New Yorker*

EVERY TONGUE GOT TO CONFESS
Negro Folk-tales from the Gulf States
Foreword by John Edgar Wideman
Edited and with an Introduction by Carla Kaplan
978-0-06-093454-5 (paperback) • 978-0-694-52645-1 (unabridged cassette)
A collection of African American folklore compiled from Hurston's anthropological travels through the American South in the 1920s. These 500 tales reflect the sorrows and joys of African American heritage with wit, wisdom, compassion, and style.

JONAH'S GOURD VINE
Foreword by Rita Dove
978-0-06-091651-0 (paperback) • 978-0-06-135019-1 (paperback)
Hurston's first novel tells the story of John Buddy Pearson, "a living exultation" of a young man who loves too many women for his—and their—own good.
"A bold and beautiful book . . . priceless and unforgettable."—Carl Sandburg

MOSES, MAN OF THE MOUNTAIN
Foreword by Deborah McDowell
978-0-06-091994-8 (paperback)
Taking off from the familiar story of the Exodus, Hurston blends the Moses of the Old Testament with the Moses of black folklore to create a powerful novel of the persecution of slavery and the dream of freedom.
"A narrative of great power." —*New York Times*

MULE BONE
A Comedy of Negro Life in Three Acts
978-0-06-096885-4 (paperback)
This three-act play is the only collaboration between the brightest lights of the Harlem Renaissance—Zora Neale Hurston and Langston Hughes. This volume contains the play, the Hurston short story on which it was based, and a detailed account of the literary dispute between Hurston and Hughes which delayed the introduction of this revolutionary piece of African American drama to readers.

MULES AND MEN
A Treasure of Black American Folklore
Foreword by Arnold Rampersad
978-0-06-135017-7 (paperback)
"A classic in style and form. . . . Introduces the reader to the whole world of jook joints, lying contests, and tall-tale sessions that make up the drama of the folk life of black people in the rural South." —Mary Helen Washington

SERAPH ON THE SUWANEE
Foreword by Hazel V. Carby
978-0-06-097359-9 (paperback)
A departure for Hurston, *Seraph on the Suwanee* is the story of two turn-of-the-century white "Florida Crackers" at once deeply in love, and deeply at odds.
"A simple, colorfully written, and moving novel." —*Saturday Review of Literature*

TELL MY HORSE
Voodoo and Life in Haiti and Jamaica
Foreword by Ishmael Reed
978-0-06-091649-7 (paperback)
Based on Hurston's visits to Haiti and Jamaica in the 1930s, this travelogue paints an authentic picture of ceremonies and customs of great cultural interest.
"Strikingly dramatic, yet simple and unrestrained . . . unusual and intensely interesting."
—*New York Times Book Review*

THEIR EYES WERE WATCHING GOD
978-0-06-083867-6 (paperback) • 978-0-06-112006-0 (deluxe paperback)
978-0-06-147037-0 (large print) • 978-0-06-077653-4 (unabridged CD)
978-1-559-94500-4 (abridged cassette)
In this American classic, Hurston tells with haunting sympathy and piercing immediacy the story of one black woman's evolving selfhood through three marriages.
"There is no book more important to me than this one." —Alice Walker

HARPER ● PERENNIAL

Available wherever books are sold, or call 1-800-331-3761 to order.